PRAISE FOR TAHOE CHASE

"I CAN GUARANTEE THAT THE OLD MAN WILL HAVE YOU CHEERING OUT LOUD BEFORE THE END OF THE BOOK"
- Cathy Cole, Kittling: Books

"BE WARNED (THIS BOOK) MIGHT BE ADDICTING"
- Gloria Sinibaldi, Tahoe Daily Tribune

"ANOTHER THRILLING ADVENTURE"
- Harvee Lau, Book Dilettante

PRAISE FOR TAHOE TRAP

"AN OPEN-THROTTLE RIDE"
- Wendy Schultz, Placerville Mountain Democrat

"A CONSTANTLY SURPRISING SERIES OF EVENTS INVOLVING MURDER...and the final motivation of the killer comes as a major surprise. (I love when that happens.)"
- Yvette, In So Many Words

"I LOVE TODD BORG'S BOOKS... There is the usual great twist ending in Tahoe Trap that I never would have guessed"
- JBronder Book Reviews

"ANOTHER MUST READ FOR MYSTERY LOVERS"
- Taylor Flynn, Tahoe Mountain News

"THE PLOTS ARE HIGH OCTANE AND THE ACTION IS FASTER THAN A CHEETAH ON SPEED"
- Cathy Cole, Kittling: Books

"YOU WILL FALL IN LOVE with the almost-silent, unemotional Paco"
- Elizabeth, Silver's Reviews

"TAHOE TRAP OFFERS A CHILLING THRILLER"
- Caleb Cage, The Nevada Review

"THE CHASE FOR THE BOY IS FRIGHTENINGLY FAST-PACED. In desperation, McKenna sets a trap, with Paco as the bait. And it almost works. The impending catastrophe takes a sudden twist"
- Bookin' With Sunny

"A FASCINATING STORY WITH FIRST CLASS WRITING and, of course, my favorite character, Spot, a Great Dane that steals most of the scenes."   *- Mary Ligno, Feathered Quill Book Reviews*

"SUPER CLEVER... More twists in the plot toward the end of the book turn the mystery into an even more suspenseful thriller."
-Harvee Lau, Book Dilettante

"AN EXCITING MURDER MYSTERY... I watch for the ongoing developments of Jack Reacher, Joanna Brady, Dismas Hardy, Peter and Rina Decker, and Alex Cross to name a few. But these days I look forward most to the next installment of Owen McKenna."
- China Gorman blog

PRAISE FOR TAHOE HIJACK

"BEGINNING TO READ TAHOE HIJACK IS LIKE FLOOR-BOARDING A RACE CAR... RATING: A+"
- Cathy Cole, Kittling Books

"A THRILLING READ... any reader will find the pages of his thrillers impossible to stop turning"
- Caleb Cage, The Nevada Review

"NOW I'M HOOKED...Borg not only offers a good mystery, but does a terrific job with some fascinating California history that is both enlightening and gripping"
- Sunny Solomon, Bookin' with Sunny

"THE BOOK CLIMAXES WITH A TWIST THE READER DOESN'T SEE COMING, WORTHY OF MICHAEL CONNELLY"
- Heather Gould, Tahoe Mountain News

"I HAD TO HOLD MY BREATH DURING THE LAST PART OF THIS FAST-PACED THRILLER"
- Harvee Lau, Book Dilettante

PRAISE FOR TAHOE HEAT

"IN TAHOE HEAT, BORG MASTERFULLY WRITES A SEQUENCE OF EVENTS SO INTENSE THAT IT BELONGS IN AN EARLY TOM CLANCY NOVEL"

Titles by Todd Borg:

TAHOE DEATHFALL

TAHOE BLOWUP

TAHOE ICE GRAVE

TAHOE KILLSHOT

TAHOE SILENCE

TAHOE AVALANCHE

TAHOE NIGHT

TAHOE HEAT

TAHOE HIJACK

TAHOE TRAP

TAHOE CHASE

For Kit

ACKNOWLEDGMENTS

Many people helped me with this story.

Special thanks go to Lieutenant Warren Smith, ret., El Dorado County Sheriff's Office. Warren gave me insight into how cops work and think and how local law enforcement functions. His expert guidance was invaluable, and I'm grateful for the big picture as well as the little snapshots... like the line about combat Tupperware! Warren deserves credit for anything I got right, while any mistakes are mine alone.

Many thanks to my agent Barbara Braun who, along with John Baker, gave me much guidance. As before, she helped me sort out how to tell this story.

Thanks to Gary Bell for answering my questions about the equipment and the sport of mountain biking. As one of the original mountain bike pioneers in the '70s, he knows it all.

Jenny Ross turned her alert radar on my story, found many glitches and helped make it much better. Many thanks for her help.

Thanks to Marvin Weitzenhoffer for answering questions about Karmann Ghias.

Thanks once again to Liz Johnston for great editing. The quantity of my mistakes is impressive, and I'm very lucky that Liz maintains enthusiasm for tackling such a big project.

I'm especially fortunate that Keith Carlson produced another spectacular cover. Along with the great interior map, I'm in good hands indeed.

While other writers could only dream of the perfect writer's companion, I've got my dream girl. Not only is Kit the ideal story editor, BS detector, and character judge, she is my Muse. I can't thank her enough.

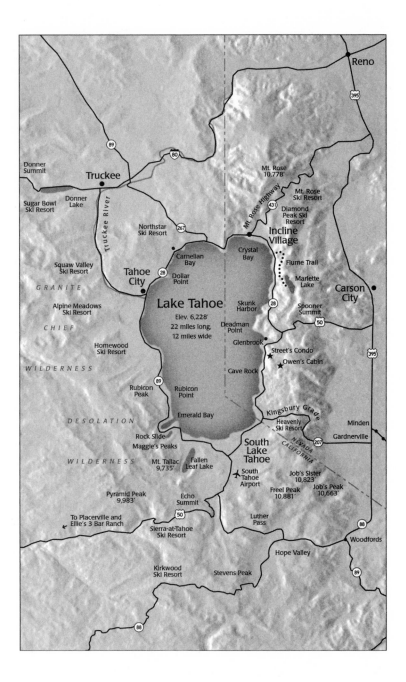

PROLOGUE

The shooter lay hidden under the thick low boughs of a red fir, twenty feet from the Flume Trail. He had a clear sight line to the path that once held a flume, a wooden aqueduct that floated logs. The flume was now gone, and the narrow ledge, 1600 feet above the east shore of Lake Tahoe, was used as a mountain bike trail.

The shooter held a small custom crossbow, constructed to fire stones. Like a short-barreled handgun, the crossbow was not accurate at any distance. But at close range it was devastating. Unlike a gun, it was silent and left no bullets or shell casings to trace.

Three miles south, two mountain bikers labored up the canyon that runs north from Spooner Lake near Highway 50. In front was the pop star Glory, in Tahoe to perform two shows on Friday night, two more on Saturday.

Following so close behind that his front tire almost brushed her rear tire was Tyrone Handkins, Glory's bodyguard and trainer and reputed lover. Although she was in front, he set the pace.

"Downshift one gear, girl," he called out. "Pick up your cadence. A little faster. Perfect! Hold that pace. Remember, deep breaths. Nice and easy."

Glory shifted and pedaled faster, her latte legs blurring into a circle beneath tight turquoise bicycling shorts. The air rushed around her gold wrap-around sunglasses. Her black ponytail stretched out behind her golden helmet.

"In twenty yards, the trail gets steeper. Just after the curve to the left," Tyrone said as he raced behind, his taut skin flashing ebony in the morning sunlight. "I want you to lean into the turn, then grab a gear and bring your cadence back up where it was before. Your body is a machine. Your legs are pistons. Okay, here it comes. Ready. Heads up. Go."

Glory leaned hard to the left as the trail arced around a house-sized boulder. She shifted again, legs churning. She drew deep breaths in a smooth rhythm, the intense Bay Area training paying off now that she was at high altitude.

Tyrone timed his pedaling to Glory's. He matched every nuance of her climb up the mountain. Their feet moved up and down in unison, their breathing at the same rate, their tires just inches apart.

The sniper lay on a ridge at 7900 feet of elevation. Behind him was Marlette Lake, tucked up high in a wrinkle of the Carson Range and sparkling through the pine and fir. In front stretched the vast blue of Lake Tahoe.

The man had been watching Tahoe for wind patterns. At dawn, the 22 mile-long lake was smooth as a mirror. Two hours later, barely a ripple marred the surface. The conditions were a sniper's dream. The sun was hot, but the typical thermals of August hadn't begun to kick up. The air was so still that the cries of seagulls could be heard all the way up from Sand Harbor.

The crossbow was loaded and cocked. Fired at the victim's face or neck, the stone would deliver a deadly blow. Perfect for a bike rider on a cliff trail. The stone had been handled with gloves, and the crossbow was designed to leave the projectile clean.

The crossbow would be disposed of in the lake. There would be no murder weapon, no clues to trace.

The shooter lay waiting, silent, hyper-alert.

Glory and Tyrone came to the crest of the trail and stopped, side by side, to take in the view.

"God, it's beautiful," Glory said, gazing down at Marlette Lake and Tahoe beyond. "I wish I could camp up here on the mountain. Sleep in a tent like normal people." She had a contralto voice, radiant and warm.

"Normal people don't win Grammys and have major label recording contracts and fill showrooms with fans."

Glory turned to Tyrone. "But it's like prison. Do you know I've never slept in a tent? I could wake up to this view. Instead, I pace in hotel rooms, scared to death that I'll screw up my next performance. I want out."

"Listen, kid. The gift of your pipes comes with a responsibility to share it with the world." He moved his elbow out to give her a gentle bump on her arm. "Besides, we need the money. We've got serious overhead to cover. You don't want to go back to waiting tables in Oakland."

"It's not something to joke about, Ty. I've thought about this. I don't want to continue. I like to sing, but not where I throw up every time before I walk through that curtain."

"It's just nerves, girl. You'll rock the crowd as always. Now focus on this route. Exercise always makes you feel better." Tyrone pointed down the mountain. "The trail goes down to Marlette Lake and follows it around to the far side. There's a little dam where the mountain drops away. From that point on is the Flume Trail. I don't want to scare you, but it's narrow and you can't afford any mistakes. Don't think about singing or anything else."

"I know, I know," Glory said. "Concentrate on where I'm going."

"Exactly. I'll be right behind as always."

"Okay, I'm off." Glory pedaled away and flew down the trail.

The shooter heard the sound of voices first, then the soft grinding hum of knobby mountain bike tires on gravel and rock.

Glory was in the lead as they carved through a curve in the trail, their legs pumping at high speed, perfectly synchronized. The trail was a ledge, only three feet wide in some places. On one side the mountain rose up above. On the other side, thin air.

The shooter lifted the crossbow and took aim. He took a breath, let it out, and was squeezing the trigger when screaming chatter erupted from a red squirrel on a branch four feet above. The man jerked with surprise as his crossbow fired.

The stone struck Glory on the shoulder and spun her sideways. It wasn't a deadly blow. But the cliff was high, and there was nothing below but rocks. The angry red squirrel ran out across the path as the woman and her bike shot off the cliff and into the air.

ONE

I'd been rearranging the art in my office on Kingsbury Grade when the phone rang. The Hopper was retired to the corner and my new favorite painting went opposite the window wall. It was a print of an oil by Turner, a maelstrom of wind and snow and a boat being tossed about by huge waves under ferocious storm clouds. I leaned back in my desk chair, looked at the Turner and answered the phone.

"McKenna Investigations."

"Hello, my name is Faith Runyon," the woman on the phone said. Her voice was shrill and tense. "I'm frightened, Mr. McKenna." She sounded desperate. "I've heard of you. I don't know who else to call."

"What are you frightened of?"

"I think I'm in danger. I overheard something about Glory's death."

"The singer who died yesterday. I thought it was an accident."

"No, it wasn't. Can we meet? I need to talk to you." She was speaking fast.

"What did you say your name was?"

"Faith Runyon. I live in Squaw Valley, only I can't meet you here. I'm calling on a borrowed cell phone because I think my phone is monitored."

"Why don't you drive down to the South Shore? We can talk at my office."

"No, I can't drive to meet you. Someone could follow me. I'm being watched. The only place I can be alone and away from prying eyes is out on the water. Do you have a boat? We could meet on the lake."

"Faith, I'm sure we don't need to go to that length. Can't you just tell me about it on the phone?"

"No."

"You can call me from a pay phone if you'd like."

"No. If they saw me using a pay phone then they'd know for sure that I was telling someone."

"Who is 'they'?"

"I can't say!" She sounded frantic. "Someone could be listening."

"What kind of business are you in?"

"I do personal consulting. Don't worry about your fee. I can afford it."

"Faith, you should tell me about it now."

"No."

"At least give me your phone number."

"I can't! If you had it and they traced…"

The woman was making no sense. "Faith, listen to me. You need to…"

"What I need," she interrupted, "is to tell you in person! I have something you need to see!"

She sounded like she was going to crack if I didn't agree to her request.

"Okay," I said. "I'll get a boat. When do you want to meet?"

"This afternoon? I'm running out of time."

"I can't get a boat that fast. Maybe tomorrow."

She sighed with frustration. "Tomorrow noon?"

"Okay," I said.

"We'll meet out in the middle of the lake away from other boats so I can see if anyone comes close to us. What kind of boat will you have?"

I thought of Jennifer Salazar's speedboat. "It's a big powerboat, I don't know the make. It has an open cockpit, no cabin. White with blue striping."

"Mine is a thirty-three foot cruiser. A Bertram," she said. "It's white with a red design on the side, kind of like a couple of Nike swooshes. Where is a good place?"

"Why don't we meet off Glenbrook?" I said. "About a mile straight out? We can each wave a flag or something."

"I know where that is." She took a couple of deep breaths. "Mr. McKenna?"

"Yeah?"

"I just want you to know that things are... It's just that I was finally getting control of my life. Believe me, it's been a long road. And now, everything is at stake again, but this time I have something to lose. Please don't stand me up."

"I'll be there, Faith."

After we hung up I sat and wondered about Faith Runyon and her distress and my lack of work and Turner's snowstorm.

It had a long title:

"Snowstorm – steamboat off a harbour's mouth making signals in shallow water and going by lead."

I'd had the print framed in a simple wood moulding with a wide double mat, off-white over off-white. The frame shop woman said it was a subtle approach, words that sounded just right to a six-foot, six-inch ex-cop with a 170-pound Harlequin Great Dane. I could use subtle wherever I could get it.

"What do you think, your largeness? Maybe I should move it down a couple inches so it doesn't look like I tried to line up the top of the frame with the top of the door? More artistic, huh?"

Spot was lying in front of the door, his front legs splayed, neck and jaw stretched out on the carpet. He rolled his eyes up toward me for a moment, then shut them and appeared to go to sleep.

I took that for approval. I got my hammer back out of the bottom drawer, lifted the painting off the wall and moved the hook down a bit. What a sophisticate.

I dialed Jennifer Salazar, thinking she would still be on summer break from Harvard. The caretaker answered, said she wasn't in and offered to put me through to her voice mail. So I left a message asking if I could borrow her powerboat.

Next, I called Street Casey at her insect lab. Her machine answered, so I tried her condo.

"Hello?" Only one word, but still her voice gave my heart rate a boost.

"Street, my sweet, I'm about to head home and fire up the barbecue."

"Owen, hon, I..."

"I was thinking of something simple like garlic bread, T-bone steaks, new potatoes, corn on the cob. However, if you were to join me I'd open a Berenger Private Reserve."

"You know I'd love to, but I've got another three or four hours of work to do on my latest bark beetle report for the Forest Service."

"Well," I said, "if you can't join me, we could just have phone sex and I'll still open the Private Reserve."

"Aren't you getting a little old for that?"

"With a voice like yours?"

"Owen..."

"Aced out by bugs again, am I?"

"Sorry."

I told Street about Faith Runyon's phone call and asked if she'd like to join me for a boat ride at noon the next day. She said she was going to be at the Forest Service at the same hour. We spoke some more, traded I-love-yous and hung up.

TWO

Jennifer called back early the next morning while I was still on my first cup of coffee and trying to decide how much time it would take to get down to the Zephyr Cove Marina and rent a boat.

"Sorry I didn't get back to you right after you called, but I'm in India and it was the middle of the night here when you left your message."

"India?"

"Yeah, and Owen, India is so cool! I'm doing a research internship studying elephants."

"Is that part of the animal intelligence thing you were working on last year?"

"Yes. Elephants are fantastic! Did you know that they... Oh, here I go, flapping off at the mouth. You said you wanted to use the boat? Of course. You are always welcome."

"Is Alicia living at the house?"

"No, mom got a place of her own. She couldn't stand the idea of living in the family manor. So I'll let the caretaker know you're coming."

"Thanks, Jen. You are great. How are the elephants, anyway?"

She spoke with great excitement, telling me how they communicate at long distance by using low-frequency sound and how their social structure is complex and matriarchal. Then she interrupted herself, saying, "Anyway, I'm coming home for a few days at the end of the month. Maybe I could get together with you and Street?"

"We'd love to," I said. "Give a call."

When I'd finished another couple cups of coffee, I leaned out the deck door.

Spot was standing guard on one corner of the deck. A Steller's jay landed on the deck rail four feet away and screamed at Spot. He barked. The bird flew away. Goes to show how effective a watch dog can be.

"Wanna go for a boat ride?" I called out.

Spot turned and wagged so hard his entire body moved. Then he did the little bounce thing on his front feet. Maybe jays aren't that exciting.

We headed south down the East Shore with the windows open and Spot hanging his head out. I pulled in at the grand gated entrance to the Salazar residence and pushed the button on the call box. The caretaker answered and the gate opened inward. We followed the long curving drive under towering Jeffrey pines, passed the caretaker's house, came around a curve and parked in front of the forty-room French Renaissance palace. A cool breeze off the lake wafted across the expansive lawn.

The caretaker had the boathouse unlocked and the boat ready to go. When I let Spot into the boathouse, he immediately ran past the little runabout and jumped into the powerboat. I turned on the bilge pump, then hit the button to raise the door. There were life jackets hanging on the wall. I tossed a few into the boat. After a minute, I started the engine and slowly backed out into the lake.

The water had a medium chop and sparkled deep blue. When I'd turned the boat around and gotten 500 feet from shore, I throttled up. The engine roared and the boat jumped up onto plane. I brought her around in a big sweeping turn to the north and came to the east shore community of Glenbrook a few minutes later. I turned the wheel, made another fast turn to the west and headed straight out into the lake. I slowed after half a minute and the boat settled down into the water, rocking fore and aft as the wake smoothed out.

There were no boats nearby. I looked at my watch. It was five minutes before noon. I wasn't a mile out yet, so I kept the boat headed west at low throttle. I'd forgotten my cell phone in the Jeep, but I couldn't have called Faith anyway because she'd refused to give me her number.

I'd gone several hundred yards farther when I spotted a boat a mile or more to the north. It started as a white speck and soon grew into a cruiser coming toward me. I got the binoculars out of the locker. Through the glasses I saw a woman up on the flying bridge, standing behind the wheel, leaning into the wind. She had long black hair, streaming back in the wind, snapping like a flag.

As she drew closer, I spotted the custom red paint job she'd described. I raised a hand towel I'd brought and waved it above my head. She saw me waving. She slowed until her boat dropped out of plane and plowed forward, nose high and trailing a large wake. When she was fifty yards away I looked again through the binoculars. She was wearing white shorts and a white sleeveless blouse. She had striking looks, a thin, willowy body and a face that was beautiful in spite of an intense frown. Even at that distance I could see the blue of her eyes, a cobalt color that glowed under her black hair.

"Mr. McKenna!" she called out, cupping her hands around her mouth. "Just stay there. I'll pull alongside of your boat."

She put her boat into a big curve that was designed to bring her parallel to my boat. I popped the lens covers onto the binoculars and stowed them back in the locker. She slowed to idle as she coasted closer.

Her boat was twenty yards away when it blew up.

THREE

The boat lifted in the water. Flames shot out from the boat's sides. The entire boat blew into splinters. A huge fireball ballooned into the sky.

I turned to throw myself over Spot, but the shock wave swatted us off our feet and into the water.

The water was like ice. I jerked around toward our boat. The explosion had blown it up on edge. It loomed above us, dark and massive, balancing for a moment. I thrashed around and saw Spot behind me. I kicked and pulled with my arms. Grabbed his head. Pushed him under as our boat crashed down on us.

I held onto the skin of Spot's neck and pulled him with me as I swam sideways to get out from under the boat. He got the idea and swam hard. We aimed for the bright, wavy surface to the side of the boat. We cleared the boat and surfaced, gasping.

Pieces of flaming wreckage fell from the sky. They hissed when they hit the water. Little bits of green paper flickered in the air like confetti. An angry cloud of smoke and ash blocked the sun. I spun around and saw our boat upside down. The stern was low in the water, the bow higher.

Even in August, Lake Tahoe is so cold that it sometimes gives swimmers heart attacks. I didn't know what the temperature was or how long it would be before Spot and I would succumb to hypothermia. For a moment I regretted that I hadn't worn a life vest and strapped one around Spot as well. But as I had tossed them into the boat, I'd remembered the joke that Tahoe is so cold that hypothermia will kill you anyway. All a life vest does is help people find the body.

I swam over to the stern of the overturned boat. One of the life vests was floating in the water. I grabbed it, stuck my arms through the shoulder holes and pulled it on. The strap of another vest was protruding from under the edge of the boat. I pulled it out.

"Spot! Over here!" I shouted the words, but heard nothing over the ringing in my ears. Spot shook his head. I realized that he was deafened as well. I yelled again. He paddled over.

I grabbed his front legs and put them through the shoulder straps of the vest. Spot floated at an awkward angle, more vertical than is comfortable for a dog. But if he got too cold to swim, it would help keep his head above water.

I turned back to the upside-down boat and tried to figure out a way up onto the smooth boat hull. My swim strokes were weakened by the cold. I swam around to the stern where the prop poked out of the water. It was stationary. The engine had stopped. I grabbed onto the prop with my right hand, put my left on the boat hull and boosted myself up.

The stern sunk another foot down into the water. I got my foot on the front edge of the prop and pushed up onto the hull. Air burped out from under the boat. The stern sunk farther.

I straddled the deep-V of the hull, my knees bent like a jockey on a very wide horse. One of the tourist sternwheelers was far to the south, making its way across to Emerald Bay. I knew they could never get to us in time. But I hoped that one of the tourists had binoculars trained this way when Faith's boat blew up. The sheriff's patrol boat or the Coast Guard could already be on their way. I scanned the rest of the lake. There was the usual assortment of boats scattered here and there, but none were closer than a couple of miles. And none were coming our way.

Spot swam to the stern of the boat. He got one of his front paws up on the slippery boat bottom. He had a strange look in his eyes. If swimming is supposed to be fun, how come we are freezing? Why couldn't we hear anything but a shrill ringing? His jaw vibrated and his teeth chattered. I had to get him out fast.

I inched my way up the hull toward the bow. The V of the hull got more pronounced as I moved forward. Spot could never get up at the front of the boat. The slope was too steep, too high and too slippery. But pulling him up on the stern would release the remaining air that kept the boat afloat. I turned back toward Spot. He'd taken his paw off the stern. Dogs don't tread water. He was swimming in circles. I dove in.

I'd only been out of the water a minute, yet the cold was as shocking as before. I submerged and propelled myself under the boat.

My head was in the air pocket of the boat's cockpit. It was too dark to see. I swept my arms across the water's surface. My hand hit a life jacket. I clenched its straps. Then I hit a seat cushion. Boat cushions are designed to float. Most of the seat cushions were still attached to the seats. I found the Velcro patches and tugged them free.

There were cleats on the corners of the stern where the rear of the boat was under water. I submerged with a cushion, dragging it underwater, and wrapped the Velcro loop around the cleat. It took a couple minutes to get all the cushions and the other life vests attached. When I was done I'd added several hundred pounds of buoyancy to the stern of the boat.

Spot was still swimming in circles when I emerged from under the boat back into the blinding daylight. He was moving slowly, a dull confusion on his face.

"C'mon, your largeness," I said. My enunciation was slurred with cold.

He didn't hear me. I gestured. He swam toward the stern which was floating higher than before.

"Up on the boat, boy," I said as he drew close. He put a paw up on the slippery hull. I grabbed onto the prop. "You gotta push off, Spot. Use my legs."

Spot didn't respond. I reached down and caught one of his rear legs. I pulled it up across my thighs. I got an arm under his abdomen and heaved up. Spot slapped his other front paw up onto the hull. He dug his claws into the slippery surface. He kept his chest to the hull as he clawed and slipped his way forward a foot, just to the left of the prop. He was wracked with shivers. I knew he could slip at any moment and slide back into the lake. He had all four legs spread out, claws trying to grip the algae-slick hull.

"Okay, boy, up a little and shift to the right." He was about to slide off to the left. I was unable to push him farther up the hull. I lowered back down into the water and went around to the right side of the prop. If I got my weight to the right side of the hull, maybe I'd cancel out Spot being on the left.

I kicked and raised myself up a bit. But I was too weak with cold and could do nothing more than hang there. Most of me was still in the water. We clung to the boat, shivering violently. The sun was hot, but it wasn't slowing our descent into hypothermic shock.

Air bubbled up on the sides of the boat. It rode lower in the water and listed to the left. My thinking was dulled by cold. More air came out. Each time the cockpit burped, the boat sank farther. Soon, the prop was low enough that it was under water. As was all of me from the neck down. We were going to sink, and there was nothing I could do.

FOUR

Words came from behind me. I strained to make them out through the ringing in my ears.

"Easy, now, Tam," a voice shouted. "I'll hold course straight into the wind. We should have just enough momentum to come up next to the boat's stern. She'll be on our port side. Get ready with the boat hook."

"What do you want me to grab? The guy?"

"No, the prop. Can you see it? Under the water, next to him? Shit, we're going too fast. Okay, ready? Grab it, Tam! Grab it!"

I turned to see a large sailboat drawing up alongside, its sails luffing in the breeze. A woman was leaning out, hanging onto the headstay with one hand. Her other hand held a boat hook. She aimed in my direction and missed. The sailboat was coasting upwind, right on past our boat.

The woman ran down the side of their boat, trying to keep even with ours. She reached the boat hook out over the water again.

I grabbed the end of the boat hook with one hand while I held the prop of our boat with the other. The sailboat's momentum brought me around through the water until I was strung tight between the two boats.

"Hold on, Tam!" the man shouted. He jumped up from the tiller and grabbed onto the boat hook. The two of them held tight while my shoulders threatened to dislocate. I concentrated on making my hands grip. The sailboat stopped moving and the two boats drew back together.

"Tam, can you release the halyard and drop the mainsail? Then the jib? I'll shift to the stern. We'll let Bessie drift around, bow downwind. The overturned powerboat will act like a sea anchor. Then we can get this man and his dog aboard."

The man tossed me a line which I fumbled around the prop. I couldn't manage a knot, so I wrapped it around several times. The man pulled the boats stern-to-stern and lashed them together. I got my arms around Spot and helped him slide down the hull to where the two boats met.

The sailboat had a platform at water level to make it easy for swimmers to climb aboard. I helped Spot step onto it. From there he put his front feet on the transom and climbed over it into the cockpit of the sailboat. I was next. It took both the man and the woman to get me out of the water and into the boat. The woman put a jacket around my shoulders, then handed me a towel and helped me dry off.

"Michael Lemas," the man said, putting his hand out. His voice sounded like it came through a string and tin can.

"Owen McKenna. Thank you." I lifted my numb hand and we shook. His hand was like fire on my frozen fingers.

"I'm just glad you're alive. Your dog, too. Tamara and I were coming out from Glenbrook when we saw a fireball. A huge boom came a few seconds later. Frankly, I'm surprised your boat is still floating, even if it is upside down. All the fire damage is top side?"

"No, it was another boat that exploded. Someone I was meeting."

Michael's face went pale. He turned to Tamara. She put her hand on his arm. "The other person is..."

"I don't think she felt a thing."

"Oh, my God." He sat down on the cockpit chair. Tamara leaned against him, horror in her eyes.

Pointing downwind, the sailboat was much less stable than Jennifer's powerboat had been. Spot stood with his legs spread wide, trying to balance, lethargic with cold, still shivering.

"Should I get something for your dog?" Tamara finally said. "Poor thing is freezing."

"A couple of towels to put over him would be great. Something to lie on as well, if you have it."

Michael opened a locker and pulled out two well-stuffed sail bags while Tamara went down into the cabin. Michael dropped the bags and stepped on them to partially flatten them out.

I pointed to the bags. "Here you go, Spot." He stepped onto the sail bags, squatted down on his haunches and lowered until his elbows touched. His teeth began a new beat to their chattering.

Tamara came back up with two blankets. She wrapped them around Spot and held him, whispering into his ear.

I sat numb and useless while Michael and Tamara untied the two boats and then hoisted the sails. We headed back to Glenbrook. When I'd warmed enough to speak clearly, I used Michael's cell phone to put in a call to Diamond Martinez of the Douglas County Sheriff's Department. When he answered I had to ask him to talk louder three times, unconsciously raising my own voice until I was shouting myself. Eventually, we communicated and he was at the pier looking through binoculars when we docked a half hour later.

"You said a boat blew up when it was near you?" Diamond said.

"Yeah. About twenty yards away."

"Why so close in the middle of the lake?"

"I was meeting the person in the other boat. She was about to pull alongside when it happened."

"This a person you know?"

"Never met her before."

"You know her name?"

"Faith Runyon."

I gave Diamond all the details beginning with Faith's phone call the day before. Diamond took careful notes and asked dozens of questions.

"You're thorough," I said when he was done.

"I'm going for Sergeant," he said. "Don't want to screw up." He looked again through the glasses, then handed them to me. I trained the binoculars out at the lake. There were two Sheriff's Patrol boats and a Coast Guard boat all near Jennifer's overturned boat. A man leaned out holding a pole with a net on the end, scooping up pieces of debris.

Spot and I had drip-dried by the time Diamond finished taking my statement, although Spot still shivered. We got into Diamond's Explorer for a ride to the Salazar mansion so we could switch to my Jeep.

"Some of the marinas have large boat hoists," Diamond said. "I'll see if Jennifer's boat can be lifted out. Nice boat like that would be worth trying to save."

I thanked Diamond, and he drove away. Spot and I got into the Jeep and headed home.

FIVE

It was a warm afternoon. When we got to my cabin Spot walked out onto the deck and lay down in the sun. I joined him. We were soon baking. I moved into the shade while Spot flopped over onto his side, his huge tongue protruding onto the deck as he panted.

The phone rang. It was Mallory from the South Lake Tahoe PD.

"Yes, captain," I said.

"They call us commanders, now," he said.

"That's right. I keep forgetting."

"I got a call. You and your hound okay?"

"Except for our ears."

"What happened?"

I filled Mallory in beginning with Faith's first call.

"It's all on the Nevada side, which means Diamond's jurisdiction, but call me if I can help."

"I will," I said. "Thanks."

Spot was still lying in the sun.

"Spot, you should move to the shade." I pointed.

He ignored me and panted.

I kept seeing Faith Runyon standing in her boat, giving me a wave just before her boat exploded. I couldn't grasp the magnitude of what had happened.

My ears still rang. I reached up and rubbed them. A sharp pain pricked my temple. I felt the skin and pulled out a splinter. It was a white needle of fiberglass, part of Faith's boat.

She had said almost nothing that hinted of who she was or what she knew about Glory. I thought she had the classic symptoms of paranoia, being watched, followed and having her phone line tapped.

Faith said she lived in Squaw Valley. I looked in the book, but there was no listing under Runyon. I called Information. They had nothing. I looked in the Yellow Pages. There were no Personal Consultants.

Maybe there were other things I should look up. But my brain was too foggy. I dialed Street and got her machine. Not wanting to alarm her about the explosion, I left a vague message.

My head had begun to pound, so I ate some aspirin. I sat out on the deck with Spot as the sun settled in the west. Eventually, the cold of evening drove us inside and I went to bed without fixing dinner for either of us.

Sleep came fast in the beginning. But I awoke in the middle of the night and couldn't shake the image of Faith standing there, blue eyes radiant, as she was engulfed in the fireball. She hadn't officially hired me. But she'd called for help. I owed her.

SIX

The phone was chirping. It wouldn't stop. I looked at the clock. It was early in the morning.

"Owen, are you all right?" Street said when I mumbled hello. "I heard about the boat exploding on the news. I was so worried! I called several times."

"Sorry, I had the ringer on low and didn't hear it. Yes, I'm okay. Spot, too. We have some ringing in our ears, but no other injuries." I told Street about the previous day, and she eventually calmed.

"I can tell you were sleeping," she said. "I'll let you go back to bed. Call me, okay?"

Later, I got up and found Spot lying under the living room window in a ray of sun. His tongue was flopped out on the floor boards. He appeared to be baking. Dying by fire was preferable to dying by ice-cold water.

"Hey, large one, wanna take a ride to Squaw?" I said in my cheeriest voice.

Spot didn't move, didn't even raise his eyes.

"It's a road trip. It's true that you'll be able to see the lake, but we won't go near a boat. Promise."

No reaction.

"Okay, suit yourself."

I took Spot out on the deck, hooked up the long chain so that he could get to shade and his water bowl, then drove up the shore.

It was a typical August afternoon. A cool breeze cut the hot sun. When I came around the north side of the lake I drove into the shadow of a fast-growing thunderhead. The cloud was pink and orange and yellow. It looked like Turner's storm.

Hail started pummeling the windshield as I drove into Tahoe City. It started as pea-sized and soon grew to the size of marbles. Wind rocked my Jeep. If I were on the lake I'd get a glimmer of what Turner's storm was like. I was envisioning golf balls falling from the sky when it abruptly stopped.

I joined the Truckee River where it begins at the dam in Tahoe City and followed it along 89 to the Olympic Rings that mark the Squaw Valley turnoff.

The hail stones had left a white coating on the landscape, but as I rolled into the spectacular valley the sun poked through and the road began steaming.

The new village at the base of the ski lifts is a collection of expensive condos and exclusive shops and restaurants and art galleries all grouped around a set of pedestrian-only streets. Although the village has a garage hidden underneath, it is for the rich condo owners and their guests. I parked out in the far lot amongst the other proles.

The walkways of the village were crowded with people strolling along, sipping cappuccinos and window shopping. I looked for the kind of place that every resident and vacationer alike would stop in and found it in a bakery.

A long line led up to the counter. I waited behind two girls wearing Stanford sweatshirts and talking about one of their mom's stock options. When I got up to the counter I pointed to a tray under the glass. "Two Danishes, please." Because my ears were partly deafened, my voice was unnaturally loud.

The woman leaned back a bit. "Here or to go?"

"One of each," I said, thinking of Spot's latest favorite food. "I'm looking for Faith Runyon," I said, as the woman rang up my purchase. "She lives someplace in Squaw." I spoke as if she were still alive. "Any idea how I might find her?"

The woman shook her head and handed me my change and the tray with one Danish on a fancy paper plate and a dressy waxed bag containing the other.

"She's young, tall, pretty, long black hair, blue eyes," I said. "Sound familiar?"

The woman shook her head again. She looked past me toward the person behind me. "Next," she said. I took my food.

After I ate I walked around to the check-in office for vacation rentals. A small, bald, middle-aged man who was all smiles was eager to help me with my dream vacation. He was eating a poppy seed bagel when I walked in. He quickly put it in a desk drawer. He smiled, straining to keep his lips closed as he chewed.

"Do you know Faith Runyon?" I said. "She lives around here, and I'm trying to locate her."

"I'm sorry, sir. We are very respectful of our owners' privacy." He was still chewing. He swallowed, then slurped tea out of a foam cup.

"She lives in one of these condos?" I said.

"I don't know. But even if she did, I wouldn't be at liberty to tell you which one."

"She's young, tall, pretty, long black hair, blue eyes. Sound familiar?" I said for the second time.

He shook his head. "I don't know a woman of that description." The man grinned. There were two poppy seeds stuck in his teeth. "Sorry," he said.

I checked a restaurant nearby, then another, then another. No one knew Faith Runyon. I went to the hotels and inns, spoke to the receptionists, the concierges, the bartenders. I found coffee shops and a sandwich shop. There was a sunglasses shop, a hat shop, two art galleries and a cyber café. There were ski shops and snowboard shops.

No one knew Faith Runyon.

I was about to leave the valley when I saw one more place that nearly every resident would visit. The cable car building.

The attendant was an older woman. I asked her about Faith. She pursed her lips and shook her head and didn't say a word.

I looked around and saw a young man loitering near the big windows that faced the mountain. He was in his twenties and had two silver safety-pins stuck through his left nostril and two more through his left eyebrow. His left ear was heavy with rings. I didn't want to see the left side of his tongue.

"Excuse me," I said. "I'm looking for a woman named Faith Runyon. About your age, tall, pretty, black hair, blue eyes?"

"Who's asking?"

"Owen McKenna." I reached out my hand.

"Paul Johnson." His grip was strong. Up close, he looked like he'd been dug out of a peat bog. There were chunks of debris in his dreadlocks. He regarded me for a moment. "This girl you're asking about, does she have really blue eyes? Like Lake Tahoe? Like they're almost lit up from inside?"

"That would be her. Ring a bell?"

"Been awhile since my bell got rung. But she'd ring anyone's bell, let me tell you."

SEVEN

"I never knew her name," Paul said. "Faith. I like that."

"She talk to you much?"

"I wish. All those rides she takes on the cable car, but she never notices any of us. Even when I rode up on the same car. She just stares out at the cliff. Thoughtful, I guess. And sad. More sad than anything. She's dressed to kill and she's probably got enough money to last forever, but she's sad. She your friend?"

"Acquaintance."

"Oh. You're one of them. She puts away the sadness for you guys. When she comes back down the cable car with you she's always smiling and laughing and making like everything you say is the funniest and smartest. All because you've got the bucks."

"She's a prostitute?"

"Oh," the young man said. "I thought you were a client. Sorry. You're the first one to call her that. Usually it's call girl. Or what did that one guy call her? A courtesan. Now there's a word."

"How does one contact her?"

"Now you want to go out with her?"

"I just want to talk to her," I said.

"Yeah, right. I don't know how to contact her." He turned and looked out the tall windows of the cable car building. He spoke toward the mountain. "She's probably the most gorgeous girl I've ever seen. The way she carries herself is so... what's the word? Elegant. She could be a model. Instead, she sells herself to rich men."

"That bother you?" I said.

"I know, you think I'm some kind of innocent idealist. My friend Bobby Crash said that to me." Paul was still facing the mountain.

"He calls me Iowa. Like I'm so innocent I'm an Iowa farm boy. But I'm from L.A. I've seen it all. So no, it doesn't really bother me that she sells herself." He turned away from the mountain and looked at me. "What bothers me is that she's so sad."

"Has Bobby met Faith?"

"I think so. But I don't think they are close friends." He pointed out the window toward where the cables arced up the cliff. "He goes up to High Camp after work, sits by the pool and works on his choreography. It's like a meditation. He closes his eyes and moves his hand through the air, like he's visualizing his aerials off the halfpipe." Paul moved his hand around in front of his face as he spoke. "Then he sketches the routine on bar napkins. Come winter, he'll put the moves to the test. The guy never goofs off. Either he's out riding or he's thinking about riding. After he won the last championship, he got an agent. And Company Twenty-Five is starting to take off so they've got the bucks. Bobby says his next endorsement contract is going to be ten times the last."

"What's he endorse?"

"Ride Twenty-Five snowboards. The Bobby Crash model."

"Haven't heard of him," I said.

"You've never heard of Bobby Crash?"

"Sorry."

Paul Johnson looked at me with astonishment. "He's only about the best rider in the country. Bobby Crash rocks. Rails, pipes, boardercross, free-riding."

"Where would I meet him?"

"Actually, he's up at High Camp now. He works at the local sports shop and goes up to High Camp everyday after his shift. He rode the car up a few minutes ago. The next car's leaving in a couple minutes. If you hurry you can find him up there."

I got a ticket at the window and was in the line a minute later. Paul Johnson was still standing at the windows.

I called out to him. "What do you do here, Paul?"

"Me? Nothing, yet. I just moved up to Squaw to do some riding. This is an awesome mountain. I'm trying to find work, but I haven't had any luck so far." He turned and the sun sparkled on the pins in his nose. "So I come and watch the cable car. Kill some time. Meet some other snowboarders."

The older woman began taking tickets. "Thanks for your help, Paul," I said.

"You're welcome," he said with a politeness that belied his grunge look.

There were a dozen tourists with me on my trip up the mountain. They plastered themselves against the windows as the big box swung out from the base station and began its ascent.

At first, the cable car went up at a gradual angle. Then it approached the giant cliff and climbed almost vertically up 2000 feet. A man said, "Cheaper than Disneyland and better, too. Huh, honey?" There was no response.

At the top of the cliff the car swung past one of the towers. I heard a gasp, but no other sounds of distress.

We eventually slowed and pulled into High Camp, easing into the docking bay. I walked past the bungie-jumping towers and around toward the pool. Up in the cirques on the mountains were snowfields left over from the previous winter. The afternoon sun was lowering in the sky. Nevertheless, a group of young adults lay on lounge chairs working on their tans. They spoke about security problems with their company's latest software. Nobody sketched on bar napkins.

"I'm looking for the bar?" I said to a pool worker.

He pointed. "See over there toward the ice-skating rink? Take a left. It's in the lodge."

I did as told.

The bar was large and well-lit and nearly empty in the summer. Bobby Crash was at a corner table. A beer sat on the bare table while he sketched on a napkin. I sat at the bar and waited while a bartender at the far end washed and rinsed wine glasses.

Six video screens showed a Cessna flying above the ocean coastline. As a sometime pilot, I guessed the altitude at 10,000 feet. Three men appeared at the open door of the Cessna. They had para-chute packs on their backs and snowboards on their feet. One of the men hurled himself out of the plane into space. Another followed immediately. The third man carried a video camera. He jumped out after them.

The snowboarders fell through the sky, tumbling end over end. They righted themselves and surfed on the air. Angling their boards just so, they shot back and forth while falling through the sky at 120 miles per hour.

"You like sky surfing?" a voice said.

I turned and saw Bobby Crash standing nearby. He set his empty glass on the bar. He was a big, solid guy in his mid-twenties, wearing baggy, olive shorts that came down below his knees and looked like a skirt. On his feet were over-sized athletic shoes open and unlaced on sockless feet. He had on a baggy shirt with the sleeves rolled up. His forearms bulged.

His hair was blond and carefully shaped like a thatched roof overhanging his ears. An inch-long tuft of hair hung from the edge of his lower lip and dangled over a clean-shaven chin. He was handsome in spite of himself, tan and squared-jawed.

"I'd love to try sky surfing sometime," I said.

He smiled and suddenly looked like an unkempt movie star. "My friends the Nostrum brothers in Brentwood took me up twice. Dad's a Dreamworks guy. Owns a Beechcraft."

"I bet it was rad," I said.

He didn't even notice how hip I was.

"Totally," he said. He took hold of the lip tuft, pulled it so his lower lip came down, then let go so his lip snapped shut with a little smack. "But sky surfing's still not as good as riding snow. Deep powder in the trees is the best."

I was watching the little lip tuft bounce as he spoke. "You're Bobby Crash, aren't you?"

He nodded and beamed at me. "Ever since the Ride Twenty-Five TV campaign I've been getting recognized. But you're the oldest dude yet, I'll give you that."

"Actually, I didn't recognize you. Paul Johnson told me you were up here working on your choreography."

Crash's happy face collapsed. "Iowa has a problem with his mouth."

"He told me you rock."

"Yeah?" He smiled again and leaned on the bar. "I've been talking to a producer. I might do a film. At the right price, of course."

"Of course," I said.

Bobby Crash glanced at himself in the mirror behind the bar. He gritted his teeth and angled his head to see his jaw muscles bulge.

"Johnson says not only are you the raddest rider, but you get all the girls, too."

"Being the champion doesn't hurt with the ladies," he said.

I glanced at the video screen. Girls on Rollerblades were flying up the sides of a giant halfpipe, arcing through the air and rocketing back down. "I'm wondering about one of the ladies," I said. "Faith Runyon?"

Bobby Crash had turned to look at the video screen. At the sound of Faith's name he snapped his head back to me. "I told Iowa not to..." He stopped and took a deep breath. "I didn't think you were a client." He gave me a grin that made me think of crocodiles.

"I'm not."

"Then who are you?"

"I'm the last guy she spoke to before she died," I said, watching him closely.

Crash took a moment before he reacted. He put both hands on the bar, spread them wide and leaned onto his arms. He let his head hang and gave it a slow, exaggerated shake. "That's terrible," he said. He gritted his teeth again, swallowing elaborately. "How did she die?"

"Violently."

Again I watched his reaction. I saw nothing but a slight delay.

"Whoa. Did some dude kill her?"

"Interesting that you don't assume an accident," I said. "Your first thought is murder?"

Crash looked at the floor then at me. "I don't know. I guess it just seems that girls, you know, get killed sometimes. Instead of dying in accidents."

"How did it work?" I said.

He turned back toward me, biting the side of his lower lip.

"What do you mean?"

"She met her johns up here, right? Were you her pimp?"

Crash's eyes grew wide. "Hell, no! Like I would be a pimp!" He made a snorting sound. "Besides, I just come up here to work. I had nothing to do with her. I'm a professional athlete."

"You didn't like her?"

He looked at me, calmer, back in control. "What's not to like about her?" He forced another smile, a fakey "say cheese" grin that needed practice.

"So how did it work?" I said again.

"I have no idea."

"Of course you do. You saw her. You talked to her. No doubt you saw her johns."

"Sorry, I never noticed."

"Maybe one of the bartenders was her pimp?"

He shook his head. "Like I said, I work on my choreography. I'm an artist. Some girl comes up here to meet guys who can't get laid without paying for it, I could care less."

"You weren't one of her johns?"

Crash threw his head back and laughed. "Me? You're joking, right? Like I'm going to pay for it when I've got more groupies than I can count."

"She wasn't interested in you, was she?"

Crash squinted his eyes at me. "Actually, she thought I was hot. I saw her looking at me."

"So you did notice. I want some information about her. Who she knew. What her johns were like."

Crash suddenly steeled himself. "What I noticed was none of your business."

Maybe Crash knew something that would incriminate himself. "You wanted her," I said, "but she didn't pay you any attention. You're the big-shot, champion snowboarder, but she only had eyes for guys with big bucks. For a self-centered brat who is used to getting everything he wants, that could almost be motive for murder, couldn't it." I said.

Crash's tan face turned crimson. He shouted at me. "I don't take shit like that from anybody!"

I stretched one foot out behind my barstool, bracing myself as he slammed his hands into my chest.

The blow made me jerk, but I stayed put. He tried to shove me again. I stepped sideways, took his arm and twisted it around behind his back. He was strong, and it took a lot of effort to make it seem like holding him was effortless.

The bartender who'd been rinsing glasses behind the bar had come up. "Is, ah, everything all right?"

"Just cleaning out some detritus," I said. "He pay his bill?"

The bartender nodded. He looked worried. Probably was Crash's friend.

I pulled out a ten and tossed it on the counter. "Here's for the commotion. Sorry."

I took Bobby Crash outside and around the building out of sight from the tourists playing in the swimming pool. There was a big, flat rock next to a dumpster. I turned Crash around and laid him down on the rock so that the sun was in his eyes.

I leaned over him, my knuckles pressing onto his ribs and sternum.

"She met her johns in the bar?"

Crash made a little nod.

"Why? Did she know someone here?"

"I don't think so." His voice was small. "I can't breathe with you leaning on me."

I let up the pressure a bit.

"I think it was a safety thing," Crash said. "She could talk to them over a drink. If she got the creeps, there is a ladies room by the rear entrance. She could leave out the back to get away. In the winter she could have a board and clothes stashed in a locker. In the summer, she could keep a mountain bike up here. The client has to wait for the next cable car."

"You saw that happen?"

"Once, yeah."

"Who was her pimp?"

"I dunno."

"Recognize any of her johns?"

"No."

"Know any of Faith's friends?"

"No."

"You know where she lived?"

"I have no idea. Squaw, Truckee, Tahoe City. I don't know."

"Then tell me something helpful."

"What do you mean?" he said, whining.

I leaned on him. "A conversation you overheard. Something that would tell me the identity of one of her johns. What they drank. Their clothes or cars."

"I didn't hear anything. They always sat in the corner. The clients came up on the cable car, so how am I gonna know what they drove?"

"Was she always here first? Waiting for them?"

"Yeah. She'd wait by the end of the bar where it was hard to see her. They'd come in and go to the corner table, sit and wait for her."

"How often?"

"Like how many clients a week?"

I nodded.

"Not that often. Maybe once a week. That's just what I saw. I don't know how many times she'd meet guys when I wasn't here. It seemed like late afternoon was her regular time, you know. That way she could size the guy up, they could go to dinner at a normal hour and then, you know."

"Why do you think they'd go to dinner? You hear something about dinner?"

"No. You could just tell. She was so... You'd want to take her to dinner, talk to her, look into her eyes. Any guy would."

"I need something else."

"I don't have something else!"

"Yes you do." I leaned onto his chest.

"I can't remember anything... Let me breathe!"

I let off the pressure.

"One time when she was waiting at the end of the bar, a big

fat guy came in and went over to the corner table. He was like, you know, he waddled more than he walked. I heard her mutter under her breath."

"What did she say?"

"Something like, 'Lady Katy, I said I don't do fatsos!'"

"Who's Lady Katy?"

"I don't know."

"You're sure about the name?"

"Yeah. It rhymed, and I remembered it."

"You think Lady Katy is a madam?"

"I didn't think it at the time. I guess I thought it was a figure of speech. But I suppose Lady Katy could be her pimp."

"Tell me about the johns."

"I already did! They came in and sat at the corner table. She'd go and sit down and after a couple drinks, they'd leave. I didn't recognize them."

"But you can characterize them."

"What do you mean?"

"You saw their clothes, heard them talk."

"I didn't hear them talk. They mostly just stared at her. They kept their voices low. And they had different clothes. Most wore sweaters and nice pants. A few wore jeans, and one or two even wore suits. I remember that fatso wore a suit. They were all expensive clothes. Polo, Armani, stuff like that. These guys reeked of money, that much was obvious."

"Any idea how much Faith charged?"

"Christ, how am I gonna know that? More than you can afford, I can tell you that."

EIGHT

It was twilight when I got home. Spot was curled up on his cushion at the corner of the deck. He jumped up as my headlights swept over him. I got out carrying the paper bag with the Danish in it. I held it up and shook it.

Even though Spot was 40 feet away and it was nearly dark out, I could see his eyes grow intense and his ears quiver. His chain vibrated against the deck.

I took the Danish out of the bag, held it like a Frisbee and gave it a hard shot. It came in high. Spot leaped up and snatched it out of the air with a loud clicking thump of teeth snapping on pastry.

I sucked glaze off my fingers, walked over and unhooked his chain. Spot followed me indoors, his tongue making slurping noises as he licked his chops, his nose reaching out to sniff the empty paper bag.

The cabin was dark inside, but I didn't hit the switch. A numbing weariness came over me. I got a beer out of the fridge and sat down on my rocker in the dark. There was still a pale orange glow in the western sky. The mountains were a dark silhouette. In front of them was the broad sweep of lake reflecting the twilight. Not far out there would still be floating debris, bits and pieces of boat and...

I downed my beer. Then I went back to the fridge, pulled out three more and lined them up on the little table next to the rocker. I put on Samuel Barber's Adagio For Strings, then sat down in the dark and listened to the progression of major sevenths while I made up epitaphs for a frightened woman who died young because she overheard something deadly.

Or maybe hearing it wasn't deadly. Maybe the deadly part was deciding to take the information to McKenna.

The phone rang. It was probably Street. Ever since I'd met her I'd tried to get her to spend every hour with me. I didn't care if it happened through benefit of marriage or as an exercise in saving on mortgage costs. I just wanted her with me and had only succeeded for a few short months after she'd been kidnapped a year ago. Now the phone was ringing, and it was probably Street, and all I could think of was another woman on an exploding boat and that fraction of an instant when a life vanishes.

I let the phone ring and drank more beer.

NINE

I was in my office early the next morning. Spot found the sun and lay down in it. He watched with great interest when I opened the donut bag.

"Donuts are for people," I said.

He sighed and put his head down. He didn't look up as I ate, but his ears turned toward me. They twitched when I slurped more coffee. When I was done, I crumpled up the bag and threw it in the basket. Spot sighed again and rolled over onto his side.

I spent an hour paying bills. Turner's storm raged.

Spot never moved. What was the point if there were no donuts.

The phone rang.

"McKenna Investigations," I said.

"Hey, Owen, Upton here." A voice from the past. A good guy who helped me during the stress when I left the SFPD.

"Upton. Good to hear from you. Still in homicide?"

"Four more years and I'm outta here. Pam and I got a little cabin near Mendocino where we plan to retire. White picket fence, vegetable garden out back, the whole nine yards. We're going to sell the house here, and with Bay Area prices what they are, we should be in good shape. How's the hound? Still full of life?"

I looked over at Spot. "Oh, yeah. Bursting. What's up?"

"I saw a news item on that boat explosion up in Tahoe. It said you were there. You okay?"

"My ears still ring, but yeah."

"First the singer Glory dies mountain biking, then the woman in the explosion. What's going on?"

"I don't know. A woman named Faith Runyon called me. She wanted to meet on the lake to tell me something she'd heard about Glory. But her boat blew up before she told me anything."

Upton's breathing was loud in the phone. "Part of the reason I called is because of Glory. You know much about it?"

"Only what I read in the paper. She was bicycling on the Flume Trail and went off the cliff. Probably an accident, but I understand her bodyguard is getting some close attention because he was bicycling with her at the time. Why do you ask?"

"Remember years back when you and I participated in that bi-city outreach program?"

"Sure. House calls to the families of chronic juvenile offenders. Show them that cops are actually real people." I could still visualize the scummy dumps that most problem kids called home. Drug-addicted moms making babies and collecting whatever handouts came their way. Never a dad to be found.

"Do you recall Luther Washington? A dozen years ago?"

"Tall, skinny kid? Could run like a deer?" I said.

"That's him. Came into San Francisco on BART everyday and boosted motorcycles for a parts outfit run by Jimmy D. Luther died not long after the last time we brought him in."

"Figures," I said as it came back to me. "What a waste."

"Remember his mama's homemade cookies?"

"That's right," I said. After we'd brought Luther in several times, we went to his mother's place in Oakland. I remembered how unusual the apartment was, neat and clean, pictures on the wall, a book or two lying around. I said, "Luther's mother even played us a few tunes on an old upright piano."

"Do you recall Luther's little sister?"

"Yeah. I forget her name, but she could sing like Aretha."

"That's why I called," Upton said. "Her name was Glorene. Glorene Washington grew up and started performing as Glory. I thought you'd want to know."

TEN

After we said goodbye, I sat at my desk.

I hadn't thought of Glorene Washington in the years since, but still the news hit me hard. She'd been eleven or twelve, skinny as her brother Luther. I could still see her wide-set brown eyes, shiny as polished agates. She was a shy girl with a rare but electric smile. Yet the eyes and smile were nothing compared to the voice.

The time we visited, she hummed constantly, warm, round tones that were more like what one would expect from a woodwind than from a kid. When her mother played the piano, the bashful girl sang like the star she became.

I'd never seen Glory perform, but I'd heard her on the radio. Her voice was deeper than most, reminiscent of the great jazz singers. She had less vocal pyrotechnics than the other stars, but was more soulful. While the other singers sometimes wore you out, you could listen to Glory all night.

It was a terrible loss, a young woman with a huge talent going off the mountain on a bicycle. I'd bicycled the Flume Trail with its dangerous drop-offs. It was easy to see how someone could accidentally die. But there is a statistic about young women that dogs me and all cops alike whenever the subject comes up.

The number one cause of death for young women isn't accidents or drugs or suicide, but murder at the hands of their husbands and boyfriends. Glory was with her bodyguard when she died. Could he have been a jealous boyfriend?

Then Faith called saying she heard something. And Faith was killed.

I picked up the phone and dialed Diamond.

"Sí," he answered.

"I thought you were into French these days."

"I meant oui," Diamond said. "Been learning Deutsch, though. I've been reading philosophers. Lotta them are German. Nietzsche, Kant, Marx. Be good if I could read them in Deutsch."

"Plus, you still have the Karmann Ghia, don't you?"

"Ya. Even got it running again. What's up?" he asked.

"When are you going to make rank?"

"Hoping to by my birthday. Sergeant Bellamy is retiring then. I'm numero uno on the list after taking the exams. And the sheriff likes me. So it's looking good. But you didn't call for that."

"I'm wondering about evidence on the explosion."

"Nothing definitive," Diamond said. "Couple of our guys helped the Coast Guard fish a bunch of debris out of the water. Biggest piece they found was a twelve-inch chunk of teak. Looks like a trim board. Mostly, they just found fragments. A piece of the fabric roof over the bridge. Some plastic off the seat cushions. And a bunch of pieces of green paper. Stuff that floats. Everything's at a lab in Reno. They're checking for traces of explosive."

"Call me when you get the results?"

"Sure," he said, though it didn't sound like his first priority.

"I've learned a few things about the victim on the boat."

"Should I get my tape recorder?" Diamond said.

"A pencil should do." I told him about going to Squaw and finding out that Faith was a prostitute and that she may have had a madam who went by the name Lady Katy. I also mentioned that the information came from a champion snowboarder named Bobby Crash who seemed to be hiding something.

When I was done, Diamond said, "Got it. Anything else?"

"Have you learned anything about Glory's death?"

"Not much. The Flume Trail is in Washoe County, so it's out of my jurisdiction. The coroner's report said that death was caused by head trauma received in the fall from the trail. I told them what you said about Faith contacting you because she supposedly knew something about Glory's death. Then I got a call from a Sergeant

Ralph Cardoza. After I told him about you, he said he'd give you a call."

"I haven't heard from him yet."

"Let me give you the number. I think I put it here in my Palm Pilot." After a few seconds Diamond said, "Then again, maybe not."

"No problem. I can find it." I thanked Diamond and hung up. I got out the Reno book and looked it up.

"Washoe Sheriff's Office," a cheerful female voice said.

"Hello, this is Owen McKenna calling for Sergeant Cardoza."

"I'm sorry, he's on vacation. Would you like his voice mail?"

"Sure, but first can you tell me if he has a cell number? Apparently, he's been trying to reach me."

"Ralph? When the fish are biting? That's a first. But, no, I don't have a cell for him."

"Okay, I'll just leave a message."

She put me through and I left my name and number.

He called a few minutes later.

"That was fast," I said.

"How's that?" Cardoza said. He sounded irritated.

"I just left the message and you called in a few minutes."

"Now there's a coincidence. I didn't get the message, yet. Just thought I'd try you." His voice had the thick rasp of a long time smoker.

"Catch anything?" I asked.

"What?"

"They said you were on vacation. Sounded like a fishing trip."

"Oh," he said. "You mean have I caught any fish. Let me tell you, I'd have more luck using my cat's hairballs than these flies. I swear trout used to hit on anything green. Not anymore. It's like they had a seminar and decided green was dangerous. Hey, guys, stay away from green, ha, ha. Cousin Guido got his lip yanked out. And Tony? He took a nibble on a green meanie, and he disappeared. Flew right out of the water. Anyway, I always work on vacation, McKenna."

"Dedication," I said. "What can I do for you?"

"I wanted to get the details of this woman who called you about Glory. Deputy Diamond Martinez said you're an ex-cop. Said you'd be helpful."

"Certainly." I proceeded to give Cardoza the whole report starting with Faith Runyon's phone call.

When we were done Cardoza said, "What's your take on the Runyon woman's story?"

"Hard to say. Her stress and worry was real. As to whether she really had heard something about Glory's death, I don't know. I made a few inquiries about her, but haven't found anyone who knew her well enough to give me a sense of her. Right now, her credibility is in her death. Not often someone says they have information about a death and then are killed in a violent explosion."

"You think the boat explosion was intentional? That she was murdered?" Cardoza said.

"It looks suspicious. Rare for a boat to explode," I said.

"And right when she's going to spill some beans," Cardoza added.

"Rarer still for a boat to explode so violently," I said.

"You're thinking high explosives?"

"Yeah. And Faith's death suggests that Glory's death wasn't an accident, either. You've talked to the bodyguard?"

"We brought him in," Cardoza said. "Gave him the routine. Name is Tyrone Handkins. He didn't cave. But he's a big, strong guy with shifty eyes. He had the means and opportunity and motive. But we've got no real evidence on him."

"What do you mean, motive?" I said.

"Guy was in love with the singer. It's all over his face. He practically melts at the mention of her."

"How does love translate to motive?"

"Oh, come on, McKenna. You know how it works. A sexy broad becomes a star. She gets rich and famous. Her opportunities expand exponentially. The media goes crazy. Meanwhile, her poor bodyguard is just a kid who came out of the projects and thought he had a chance. But he sits on the sidelines while every big cheese between here and Paris wants a piece of her. Her brain goes all dreamy under the attention, and the bodyguard can't take it. Once he was the big guy in her world. Now he's just an employee. Fill in the blanks. It adds up to motive."

I thought about it. "You think you can build a case against him?"

"I don't know. No matter what kind of boy Handkins is, it still looks like an accident. It appears he only loses by Glory's death. His job, his stature, his lover. Everyone else we talked to said he wasn't a hothead. So we couldn't hold him."

"Maybe it wasn't the bodyguard that Faith called me about. Maybe someone else was up there to push Glory off the cliff."

"But Handkins said they were alone. Said Glory swerved all of a sudden and went off the trail. If someone else was up there he'd be sure to mention it. He'd do anything to save his ass. I can read a guy like that."

"If you think the bodyguard was Glory's killer, that would imply that he was behind Faith's death, too. Anything about him or his background that could connect him to a source for explosives?"

"I don't know. We talked to him before the explosion. But a guy like that was probably in the army. He could've gotten some bomb training there. One thing I learned from my dad was how to judge character. He taught me how to tell which guys are straight shooters and which ones aren't. Some guys, they look you in the eye and tell it like it is. You can see the sincerity. Other guys, they look around, anywhere but in your eyes. Those are the liars. You go talk to Handkins. Watch his eyes."

"Any idea where Handkins is now?" I asked.

"Glory's whole entourage was staying at the hotel where she was going to perform. Maybe he's still around. Hey, you let me know if you learn anything more about the woman on the boat, okay? Let me give you my cell number." He recited it.

Cardoza thanked me for my time and said goodbye.

ELEVEN

I sat and thought about Glory and Faith Runyon and Tyrone Handkins and Turner.

I'd read about Turner and the Snowstorm painting in my art books. He had convinced some sailors to tie him to a spar of the steamboat 'Ariel' as a raging snowstorm came in off the ocean. He wanted to know what a blizzard was really like. They left him tied up there for four hours, and he was whipped back and forth as the boat was thrown about like a cork. The storm was so ferocious, Turner thought he was going to die.

Either he was exceptionally dedicated to doing research for his paintings or he was crazy. Or both. It turned out that he survived, and he painted a picture of the experience. It was unveiled in 1842 and caused a sensation.

I was wondering about ferocious storms when my door opened and Street Casey walked in. As always, it was like I'd opened a window to a fresh breeze. Street smelled clean and looked beautiful in tight jeans and a loose white shirt of thin fabric that was buttoned all the way up to the collar. Street often did that, dressing counter to what I expected. If it were a freezing day in February instead of a hot day in August, she'd come in and take off her coat to reveal shorts and a tank top.

Spot jumped up, finally acting alive. His tail knocked the tape dispenser off the corner of my desk. The roll came out when it hit, and it rolled across the floor. Spot saw it, ran and grabbed it and brought it over to Street. He wagged again. Proud.

Street came over and kissed me. Her lips were luscious, and a tremor ran through my body.

She gestured at my feet up on the desk. "Working hard as always?"

"I was just thinking about Turner's storm."

Street pushed my legs off the desk, turned my chair and sat on my lap.

"And I wondered how it is that people get caught in storms that overwhelm them," I said.

"People like the singer on the Flume Trail and the woman on the boat?" Street asked.

"Yeah."

"Have you ever read Sontag's Against Interpretation?" Street said.

"Sontag?"

"Yeah. Susan. It's one of her essays."

"Hey, Dr. Casey, I'm an ex-cop, remember? Maybe you entomologists read that stuff for excitement, but guys like me stick with Dr. Seuss."

"Nothing wrong with Dr. Seuss. Especially now that The Cat In The Hat is available in Latin. I saw it in a bookstore. Cattus Petasatus."

I looked at her.

"Anyway," Street continued, turning back to Turner's painting. "Sontag basically says don't try to figure art out. Just enjoy it."

I ran my hands along Street's thighs, then felt her waist. "But what about all those metaphors that great artists put in their paintings?"

"You mean the ones that illuminate our troubled souls?" Street said. She pushed against the desk to make the chair spin. "Or the ones that make you think about sex?"

"Yeah. Those ones," I said. I stopped the turning chair.

"Sontag would probably say that Turner painted a snowstorm and not a metaphor. Take from it what you can about snowstorms, but don't use it to try to understand why those women died."

We sat in silence for a while, both looking at the painting.

"What would Sontag say about romantic love?" I asked.

"Probably that you can't figure it out with paintings of boats."

"Same for sex?"

Street nodded.

"So," I said, "looking at the boat in the snowstorm doesn't make you think of the great will to survive in the face of Mother Nature's singular fury?"

Street rolled her eyes.

"A will," I continued, "that often manifests itself in procreative energy? Sometimes on a rolling boat deck? In snowstorms?"

Street made a delicate little snort. She got up off my lap, leaned against the edge of the desk and unhitched the top button on her shirt. "Even a hard, bare desktop would be better than a boat deck in a snowstorm," she said.

TWELVE

After Street left, Spot and I drove over to the Nevada-California state line. There was a truck parked in front of one of the hotel signs. High above, a guy was in the little box at the end of a long, telescoping arm. He was taking down the letters of Glory's name. I parked in a shady place out back.

Juan Carrera was working the reception desk. "Mr. Owen McKenna," he said, smiling, shaking my hand. "So good to see you." He was a small well-built man, too handsome for his own good. His flashing eyes and the neat little mustache above a bright smile attracted an endless string of young women.

"The pleasure is all mine," I said. "Juan, I need a favor."

"Of course, my friend. You helped me with my green card problem. I am forever indebted."

His green card problem was that he didn't have one until a few months ago. Several times he was picked up in South Lake Tahoe for trivial reasons and deported. Two weeks later he'd be back. Jobs were easy to find. The machismo-imbued work ethic the Mexicans bring to low paying jobs makes for many employers willing to overlook the risks of missing paperwork.

But the periodic deportations were a huge hassle, and Juan, who'd done some landscaping for me, asked me to help. I became his advocate. Juan filled out the forms, I made a lot of calls, and, after far too long, he became a legal resident.

"You know about Glory," I said.

"Yes. It is a terrible thing. A tragic loss."

"Are her people still staying here?"

"Some are. Most have left."

"I'm looking for her bodyguard. Tyrone Handkins."

"He is still here," Juan said. "He had breakfast an hour ago and went back up to his room."

"Can you give me his room number?"

Juan grinned. "You know I would need to have Mr. Handkins' permission. Perhaps I can call up?"

"Please. Tell him I have information about Glory."

Juan looked in the computer and punched buttons on the phone. "Hello. Juan Carrera at the front desk. Is this Mr. Handkins? Oh? Thank you. I'll try her room." Juan turned to me. "A man said to try the room Glory was staying in." He dialed another number and introduced himself again. "Mr. Handkins, Mr. Owen McKenna is here to see you." Juan was silent for a moment. "No, he is not a salesman. I understand that he has information about Glory." Another pause. "Thank you, sir. I'll send him up." Juan wrote the room number on a piece of paper.

"Thanks," I said, and headed for the elevators.

I rode up to the 12th floor. Glory's door was down to the left. My knock was answered by a large black man, about 30 years old, dressed in gray sweats.

"Tyrone Handkins?"

"Yes."

"Owen McKenna. I'd like to speak to you about Glory if you have a few minutes."

Handkins took a deep breath and let it out. He turned, and I followed him through the entry foyer into a large suite.

I sat on an upholstered chair. Tyrone sat on a leather couch next to a copy of the New York Times. He crossed his legs, and a reflective patch on his white running shoe caught the light. His eyes were red and puffy as if he'd been up all night. They glanced left, then right, then shut, like a cat's, for a long moment. When they reopened, I could see a deep weariness in them.

He picked up the paper and folded it carefully, hard muscles bulging under his sweatshirt. "Are you a cop?" His enunciation was crisp and precise.

"Private."

"Who are you working for?"

"Nobody."

His eyes narrowed for a moment. "The desk man said you had info about Glory."

"I just said that so you would talk to me. I met Glorene Washington when she was a little girl."

"So?" he said.

"Young woman like that dies in the presence of her boyfriend, I want to ask some questions."

"I was her bodyguard, not her boyfriend."

"I've heard otherwise."

"Rumors. Look, I've been over all this with the Reno police." He looked down at the floor.

"I understand they were interested in what you might gain by pushing Glory off the cliff," I said.

"What difference does it make to you?" he said.

"Same difference it made to the other cops."

"I didn't kill her."

"You say it was an accident?" I said.

"Maybe. Maybe not."

"If it wasn't an accident, what was it?"

"I don't know. She was an excellent rider. It wasn't like her to swerve off a cliff."

"You think it was suicide?" I said.

"No." Tyrone was shaking his head. He shut his eyes and rubbed them. "She wouldn't do that."

"How do you know? Sometimes people kill themselves and their friends say they never knew the person was depressed."

"I knew Glory well."

"Like a lover?" I said.

Tyrone's eyes flicked up to me, then sideways. He looked out the window. I could see what Sergeant Cardoza meant when he said that Handkins had shifty eyes. "I told you, I wasn't her lover. We were close, but not like that." He picked up the newspaper, stood up and walked over to the window. He was only a couple inches shy of my six-six, and he outweighed me. He looked out at the lake, then turned back. "It could be that someone did something to her to make her swerve." He set the newspaper down on top of the TV, then unzipped a small black briefcase and reached inside.

"Like what?" I said.

"Some kind of time-delay drug." Tyrone felt for something in the briefcase. He moved his fingers as if working a calculator, then pulled his hand out. "Or maybe someone shined a laser beam in her eyes."

"You're suggesting she was murdered."

"I don't know. I just know she wouldn't swerve off the cliff unless something made her do it. She was totally focused. She concentrated well."

"You have an idea who would want to kill Glory?"

"No. Maybe someone wanted to kill me instead."

"And they got her by mistake? She grow up so big and tough a killer could mistake her for you?

"No," Tyrone said.

"So a killer tried to put the time-delay drug in your coffee, but she drank it instead?"

"Don't mock me." Tyrone's eyes flickered left and right, then settled on me. He looked dangerous.

"I'm not mocking you. I'm asking the obvious questions. What makes you think someone wanted to kill you?"

"Because no one would want to hurt her. She was the sweetest person alive."

"Great reasoning," I said.

"It's the only thing that makes sense."

It seemed that nothing made sense. "Was Glory riding behind you or in front?" I asked.

"In front."

"Was she close to you?"

He nodded.

"So if anyone shined a light in her eyes, wouldn't you have seen it?"

"Probably."

"It would be much easier for the killer to just run out as you bicycled past and push you off the cliff. More accurate, too, if the real target was you instead of Glory."

"Then her death, or mine for that matter, couldn't be mistaken for an accident. And he'd have to kill us both to make certain there were no witnesses."

"Who knew you and Glory were going to be on the trail?"

Tyrone looked out the window again. Lake Tahoe shimmered under a hot sun. "The whole crew knew we went out for a run or a ride every morning. It wasn't any secret where we were going. The Flume Trail has a reputation. We were excited and talked about it." A phone rang softly from a small desk. Tyrone walked over and picked it up. "Hello? Yeah. The sooner, the better." He hung up, turned and looked at me.

"Did you see anyone near the trail during your ride?" I asked.

"No. It was early in the morning."

"Let's say you are correct that someone wanted to kill you. They knew you were going to be bicycling the Flume Trail. Could they have hidden near the place where Glory went off?"

"Certainly. The guy would have several places to choose from. Lots of rocks and trees up there."

"You say guy. It couldn't be a woman? Someone jealous of your attentions to Glory?"

Tyrone looked at me like I was drooling. "Women don't kill people. Not like that. It was obviously a guy."

"Tell me about your relationship with Glory."

"It's none of your business," he said.

"Did she have any life insurance?"

"Not that I know of." Tyrone shook his head. "She asked me about insurance once. I tried to talk her out of it."

"Why?"

"I explained that it made no sense. If you are rich enough, you don't need any insurance."

"She was that rich?"

"Of course." Tyrone said it as if I weren't paying attention. "I explained that she only needed to detail her beneficiaries in her will."

"Did she do that?"

"I don't know. You'd have to ask her lawyer."

"Who is that?" I asked.

"I don't know."

"Maybe a beneficiary wanted her dead so he or she could inherit."

"I doubt it. She told me that she was leaving most of her money to the California Conservancy for preservation of wetlands."

"Why would someone want you dead?"

"Lots of reasons. I get in people's faces sometimes. I'm not always delicate."

"What a good reason to commit murder," I said.

Tyrone's eyes narrowed again. He reached down and smoothed his sweats on his muscular thighs. He walked over to me. Under the sadness I could see the inner calm of someone who is supremely self-confident. When he spoke, it was with a soft voice.

"I told you not to mock me. I'm tired of you. It's time for you to leave."

"Let's just say you're right, that it wasn't an accident, that Glory was killed by someone who intended to kill you. Maybe I can help."

Tyrone scoffed. "I don't need help," he said. "Glory's dead. I don't care much about anything anymore. Now get out."

I walked back through the living room and into the entry foyer. I noticed there was a shadow under the door to the hotel hallway. I stopped and watched.

The shadow moved.

I looked through the peephole. It was dark as if someone had put tape over it.

THIRTEEN

I heard the soft sound of a room key card being slid into the lock, then the click of the lock releasing. I yanked the door open.

A man wearing tan leather gloves held a room key card in his left hand. His right hand gripped something that was concealed in a shopping bag. From the shape, it looked like a police baton. The man had on khaki pants and a white long-sleeved dress shirt.

And a ski mask.

The man saw me and kicked me in the stomach. He turned and sprinted down the hall. I stumbled back against the wall of the entry foyer, then ran after him.

He came to a T in the hallway and turned right.

I pounded after him and saw him enter a utility door. I got to the door and jerked it open.

There were two employee elevators. The doors on the left one were just beginning to shut. I couldn't get to him in time. The man stared at me from behind the ski mask as the elevator doors closed. He was solidly built. In the eye holes of the mask there was only darkness. No glimmer of reflection, no color, no movement.

The floor numbers above the elevator went from 12 to 11.

Behind a cart of towels was a metal fire door with a red exit sign above. The cart tipped over as I banged it out of the way. I plunged down the stairs three at a time.

At the 9th floor I jerked open the door to the utility area. The light above the left elevator said 7. He was gaining on me.

The steps blurred as I descended. I went down to the 3rd floor and pulled open the door. The elevator light said 2. Now I was gaining on him.

I counted off the floors to the lobby and burst out into an employee entrance area. The letter L was lit above the left elevator, but the doors had not yet opened. I waited, lungs heaving.

The doors didn't open. He was going to the basement.

I sprinted down the stairwell, almost knocking over a small Hispanic women in a blue dress and white apron. I jerked open the door at the bottom and ran out into a wide hallway. The left elevator was standing open and empty.

The hallway had a couple dozen people in it. A woman pushed a rolling cart. A man had a two-wheeler loaded with boxes. I saw a darting movement thirty feet down the hall.

A security guard put a key into a door. The man with the shopping bag ran up behind him and pushed his way into the room after the guard. Someone said, "What the..." and was cut off. I heard a grunt, then a thud.

I reached the door just as it was shutting. I kicked it open.

Inside the door was a row of metal lockers. The guard was on the floor in front of them.

I ran around the far side of the lockers and looked out.

I was in the core of the hotel, the steel and concrete structure exposed. The space was the size of a racquetball court.

To one side were two rows of TV screens, six across. Each screen showed a different picture of the casino floor. The pictures changed every few seconds. Below the bank of screens was a long desk. Another security guard was on the floor in front of the desk. Blood was coming from his temple. I grabbed a phone and dialed 0.

"Front desk," a woman answered.

"Two security men are wounded in the video monitor room on the basement level," I said between panting breaths. "Call an ambulance."

The sound of receding footsteps came from behind another fire door. I hung up the phone and pulled the door open. Another stairwell.

I went up three steps at a time. The staircase climbed into the center of the hotel. Several flights up, I went through a door into a large, dark, horizontal space. A metal walkway forked into two walkways going left and right, one of which forked again and went around to the side. The dimly lit space was laced with steel trusses and ductwork and cables.

I was above the casino ceiling, a hidden floor reached only through unmarked access points. Catwalks allowed security personnel to look down on gamblers from above. I realized that the gold and silver metallic panels that decorated the casino ceiling were actually one-way mirrors. The ceiling below me had long rows of angled glass. Mounted along these strips were video cameras. They pointed down at the gaming tables and slot machines, the chip piles next to the dealers.

Bubbles of one-way mirror protruded a foot below the ceiling height. In each bubble was a motorized camera that could swivel in any direction.

I crouched near a duct that provided some cover. The only movement was from the gamblers below. A clink of metal came from the left. I sprinted down the catwalk toward a dark area where several of the walkways intersected.

The walkways echoed the layout of the tables below. Structural columns and beams interrupted the grid. Short flights of stairs went up and over the big I-beams like large stepladders.

I bounded up and over one of the step-ladder stairs. He ran down one of the diagonals. I turned, trying to cut him off.

He stopped to see which way I was going, then went left. I ran after him. He came to the end of the catwalk where it stopped at the far wall. I had him trapped.

Like a gymnast, he vaulted over the railing and dropped toward the ceiling below. He crashed through one of the bubbles, his feet blasting the video camera out of the way.

The sound was like an explosion. People screamed.

The man landed feet first on a Blackjack table. He rolled expertly, jumped to the floor and sprinted down the aisle through the panicked crowd. The shopping bag was gone, but he still held his weapon, a dark object that looked like a piece of painted wood.

FOURTEEN

I thought of jumping after him, but the drop was far enough that I'd likely break an ankle. I watched through the glass ceiling as he ran out the door to the street and sprinted away. I heard shouting, then a muffled crack like a car backfiring. Or a gunshot.

There was an exit door down one of the catwalks. I stepped out into one of the employee-only corridors and let the door lock shut behind me.

I went back down to the lobby and waited while Juan spoke with a hotel guest. Around the corner a crowd had assembled in the casino where the man had jumped through the ceiling. Several Douglas County Sheriff's Deputies ran toward the commotion.

"Hello, Mr. McKenna," Juan said to me. "I saw you come from the elevators over by the crowd. Can you tell what is going on?" He leaned over the reception counter trying to see.

"I have no idea," I said.

"Were you able to speak with Mr. Handkins?"

"I was. Thank you. Can you call up to Glory's room again? There is something I forgot to ask him."

Juan pressed the phone buttons and waited. "No answer," he said, shaking his head.

"Maybe try his room in case he went there."

Juan dialed. "No answer there, either."

"What about Glory's crew members? Any idea where I might find them?"

"The roadies? If you hurry you might catch them backstage or outside. They've had their truck backed up to the loading dock all morning."

"Thanks." I went through the casino and out the rear doors. The loading dock was around to the side.

The truck was easy to spot. It had a red Peterbilt tractor. The chrome was polished to a high sheen. Swirling yellow pinstripes decorated the fenders. Each pinstripe loop had a little airbrushed scene in it. Storms predominated. I wondered what Turner would have thought of an 80,000 pound, rolling, metallic canvas. Probably would have traded his father for the opportunity.

The trailer was stainless steel. In flowing red script, ten feet high and forty feet long, was the word Glory. There were curlicues in the letters. Each enclosed loop featured another storm.

The trailer was backed up to the loading dock. The roadies were hard at work, pushing carts with large black components. Amps, mixing boards, huge speaker cabinets, recording equipment.

There were four men and one woman, all wearing black leather jackets and ratty blue jeans. They were in their twenties and collectively had enough metallic body piercings to interest a scrap metal dealer.

I walked up and said, "Afternoon. My name is Owen McKenna. I wonder if I could ask you a question."

Two of the guys were pushing a four-wheeled dolly loaded with black instrument cases. They ignored me.

I turned toward the woman and gave her my most charming smile.

She seemed to look through me. "Hey, Mike," she called out to one of the guys in the trailer. "Hold up until I get some blankets behind those cases." She turned and trotted after them.

The fourth guy was cinching straps around several monitor speakers. I walked over to him. "Excuse me," I said.

He, too ignored me.

I put my hand on his shoulder.

He straightened up fast, tensing his shoulders as if to strike. Then he thought better of it. "Look, mister, Tyrone called down, said not to talk to you."

"Answer one question and I'll get out of here. Who's in charge?"

"Tyrone."

"I mean, who's at the top of Glory's show? Who does Tyrone report to?"

"I don't know. Glory's company is based in Vegas. Remake Productions. Maybe somebody there."

I told him thanks and left.

That evening, I called Diamond. I tried three different numbers before I got him on his cell phone.

"Hello," he said. His voice sounded somber and echoed like he was in an empty room.

"It's me," I said. "Any news yet on the debris from the boat explosion?"

"The, uh, lab called. What they said doesn't fit with your description of a powerful blast." Diamond spoke with spaces between his words like when he was first learning English.

"They didn't find any residue of explosive?"

"No, they didn't. The debris was permeated with traces of gasoline, nothing else."

"Then how could a thirty-three foot cruiser be reduced to splinters?" I said. "It doesn't make sense. The shock wave alone indicates a high explosive."

"Sorry," Diamond said. "The boat was old. Maybe it was infirm and ready to give it up."

"Even so, common sense suggests that an exploding gas tank wouldn't do more than break up an old boat of that size. You said the largest piece left was a twelve-inch piece of trim board."

"The largest piece left floating. I double-checked with the lab. I asked if they could miss traces of high explosive. They said no way." Diamond's voice was monotone.

"Diamond, what's wrong?" I said.

"We had some excitement at one of the casinos."

"I know," I said, then told him how I pursued the man in the ski mask through the hidden floor above the casino. "The guy I was chasing, he seemed dangerous," I said. "Like a wild animal. I'm not sure how to describe him."

"Feral," Diamond said.

"Huh? Yeah, feral."

"How did you come upon the guy?" Diamond asked.

"He'd been about to enter Glory's suite where I'd been talking to Glory's bodyguard, Tyrone Handkins. I don't know if the guy I chased was after Tyrone or after me."

"Why would he be after you? How could he even know you were there?"

"When I was talking to Tyrone, he reached into a briefcase and did something that looked like speed-dialing a cell phone. Maybe he was paging the guy in the ski mask. A few minutes later, Tyrone got a phone call. He said a few words including, 'the sooner the better.' Could be he was setting me up."

"Doesn't seem like the bodyguard would immediately hire someone to ace you. But if the feral guy is trying to ace the bodyguard instead, it adds credence to the bodyguard's claim that it was him, not Glory, who was the target up on the Flume Trail."

"Also would take him off the list for Faith," I said.

"Yeah," Diamond said. "Did you see a weapon?" The question sounded very important.

"Just a piece of wood."

"Wood? What did it look like?"

"Like a child's baseball bat. Eighteen or twenty inches long. Dark gray."

Diamond was silent a long time. "I was there," he said. "At the casino. Not my best day."

"What happened?"

"I pulled up just as the guy in the ski mask came running out of the casino. I did the routine, shouted the warning. He spun toward me as he ran and brought his arm up. He was sixty, seventy feet away. I thought he had a sawed-off shotgun.

I felt nauseous. "The piece of wood," I said.

"I suppose. I warned him again, but he pointed it at me. Sure looked like a piece. I squeezed off one round and missed. Perp turned and ran down the sidewalk into a crowd."

"Don't worry," I said, trying to think of a way to reassure him. "There'll be some hard grilling, but you'll come through okay."

"Maybe not. It gets worse. My round ricocheted. Apparently, it hit a doll a little girl was carrying."

"What? Diamond, I'm sorry. You didn't see the girl?"

"No. There was no one nearby. I swear. But the next thing I knew, a woman and her little girl were there. The woman was hysterical, screaming that I almost killed them. Her daughter was crying, too."

"The daughter was holding a doll?"

"No. The doll was on the sidewalk some distance away. The mother said it flew out of the girl's hand. I was sure it couldn't be true, so I went and got the doll and brought it over to them. I handed it to the girl to calm them down."

"But you said your round had hit the doll?"

"Right. The girl took the doll, turned it over, and there was the hole. In the side of the doll's head."

I was breathing hard as Diamond spoke. "It was your round?" I said.

"They're not sure, yet. Rockport and Linetco were there. They took the woman's statement. Took the doll as well. There was no exit hole, and the doll rattled, so the round was still inside. It's being tested to see if it matches my sidearm."

"What did the sheriff say?"

"The usual. He put me on administrative leave."

"Suspension with pay?" I said.

"Right. I'm at the mercy of the shooting review board. And however the sheriff responds to their report."

We were both silent.

"I'm sorry, Diamond," I said.

"Me, too," he said.

"Let me know when you hear anything?"

"Yeah."

FIFTEEN

The following day I drove to my office to get the mail and check messages. Once again, Spot was already asleep when I pulled into the parking lot. The boat explosion and brush with hypothermia seemed to make him crave sleep. Especially if he could be in the hot sun or the hot car. I got out and opened the back door. Spot didn't appear to notice.

"You coming? No? Okay, get your beauty sleep." I left Spot in the Jeep. I pulled open the door to the office building and trotted up the stairs.

The mail that had been pushed through the slot covered a large section of floor. As I got down on my knees and was scooping it up, I bumped the Butterfly palm. It tipped over and dirt spilled across the carpet. One of those days.

I pulled the vacuum out of the closet. The outlet by the door is so old it won't take grounded plugs, so I stretched the cord over to another one. I was down on my hands and knees working the vacuum hose over the dirt when the door exploded inward.

The door just missed my forehead and hit me on the shoulder. I did a shoulder roll sideways. A man stepped in. His outfit was the same as yesterday, khaki pants, white shirt, tan gloves and a ski mask.

His weapon was a wooden section of handrail. Painted gray, no shopping bag to conceal it. He leaped toward me. Swung at my head with a ferocity that made my adrenaline squirt. I jerked sideways. The blow hit the thickest part of my trapezius muscle just down from the neckline of my shirt. It was a savage impact. Fire burned in my shoulder and numbed my right arm.

I jumped past the roaring vacuum and grabbed my desk lamp with my left arm. He swung. I blocked with the lamp. The metal shade ripped away, dented and ringing like a bell. The bulb shattered into a cloud of glass chips. He stepped in and swung again. I moved sideways and held the lamp base up. His blow cut the tubular metal in half. The part with the switch broke away. Sparks flew. Electricity coursed up my arm. I wasn't touching any grounding metal, so the shock wasn't severe. I dropped it onto my desk chair.

He came around the desk. My right arm was still numb. I grabbed the fax with my left hand and threw it at him. He slapped it away like a bug. I leaped back and to the side and got the desk between us. He feinted left, then right, trying to get me to move.

I thought he was going to come around the desk. Instead, he suddenly bent forward at the waist, reached out and swung at my midsection.

My reflexes were too slow. The handrail caught the front of my abdomen.

It felt like I'd been eviscerated. I went down to the side of my desk.

He was on me as I hit the floor. He swung toward my head. I jerked sideways. The wood hit a hammer blow to my upper arm. He swung again, and I tried to bend away. The handrail struck my abdomen like a baseball bat. I gasped. He struck me again, this time across my chest.

I kicked my leg out to trip him. He stepped over it like he'd spent hours jumping rope. His next move was so smooth he should teach it to cops. He danced a quick step inside my calf. With my leg held in place for a fraction of a second, he swung the wood at the inside of my knee. I jerked at the last moment, but he still managed a grazing blow.

It's like the funny bone on the elbow only worse. I was paralyzed with pain. Electric agony shot through my leg. Muscles twitched out of control. I grabbed the leg, stifling a grunt. He swung again at my head, but my jerking made him miss. He pulled back to swing again. I rolled and got my elbow under the front corner of the desk. I heaved it up. The man stepped back and away and hit the chair.

He sat down on the electrified lamp base. The desk kept tipping and fell toward him, pinning him in the chair for a moment. I knew he was getting a small shock from the lamp base under his butt. If I could ground him, the shock would be incapacitating.

The vacuum was still running. It had a metal housing. I rolled over and grabbed it.

The man pushed the desk off of his lap. Then, muscles jerking with mild shock, he tried to get off the chair and broken lamp. I gritted my teeth against the pain in my knee and hurled the vacuum up and through the air toward the man. He reached his arms up protectively and caught it, his hands gripping the metal housing.

It was like he had a seizure. He jerked and thrashed. I pulled myself up to my feet. He jerked so hard, the chair fell over sideways. The vacuum fell away and the man slumped away from the electrified lamp. I limped over toward him and kicked at the wooden handrail. It flew across my office. I was bending down to pull off his ski mask when he kicked up hard. His foot caught me in the groin. I bent like a pretzel, unable to breathe. It took all my concentration to reach across the desk and grab the phone cord. The man was standing up, staggering. I swung the phone by the cord, and it wrapped around his neck and hit him on the head.

He'd had enough. He ran out of the office, ripping the phone off his head and out of the wall at the same time.

I fell over onto the floor, pain ripping through my body, and I lay there listening to the vacuum run.

SIXTEEN

I sucked air in short, panting breaths. Each tiny expansion of my lungs felt like I was ripping chest muscles. Every bone was a sharpened instrument, piercing through red-hot, swollen muscle.

Eventually, I moved an arm. The shoulder joint squeaked. Liquid seemed to ooze through the space between the bones. I bent a leg a few degrees and dug down with the edge of my shoe. Straightening the leg pushed me forward a couple inches. I inched my way toward the vacuum. I felt for the cord and yanked it out of the wall.

With the vacuum off I heard the loud beeping of a phone off the hook. But he'd ripped it out of the wall.

The fax.

I crawled toward the beeping. I pulled the handset off the machine and dialed Street at her insect lab.

"Hello," she said.

"Street, it's me." My voice was a rough whisper.

"Owen, what's wrong?"

"Come to my office. Call Diamond."

"Do you need an ambulance?"

"No. But maybe Doc Lee can come over."

"Are you certain? Owen, you might not..."

"No ambulance," I wheezed again. "Call Diamond."

"Okay. I'll be right over."

I got the phone hung up, then lay there.

Street's lab is only a couple blocks away. She ran in a few minutes later. She'd gotten Spot out of my Jeep. "Owen, what happened?!!" She rushed over, bent down and put her hands on me. Spot sniffed me hard. Their touches burned.

"Don't," I said.

"What?"

"Hurts." I struggled for air.

"Oh. Spot, c'mere." She pulled him back.

"When Diamond comes..." I said.

"I'm here," he said as he walked in. "Was ist das? Sometimes Mexicans take siesta on the floor, now you? It's not that hot out." His words were sarcastic, but his tone was without spirit. He was in civilian clothes, frayed jeans and dirty, worn-out running shoes, a sharp contrast to his normal uniform.

"He's hurt," Street said. "Something happened, but he didn't want an ambulance. Could it be a heart attack?"

"No, look at this place," Diamond said. "Must have been a fight. Where is the pain?" Diamond squatted next to me.

"Everywhere. He..." I stopped to breathe again.

"You got yourself worked over. Guy in the ski mask?"

I tried to nod.

"How did I know that," he said, his voice monotone. Diamond lifted the edge of my collar with his fingertip and looked underneath. "You're going to have more color than a rainbow."

"You got beat up!" Street was horrified. "You should go to the hospital. You could have internal bleeding."

Diamond used a tissue to pick up the piece of handrail. "Break any bones?" Diamond said, hefting the wood.

"I don't think so," I said.

"Even so, the muscle and organ bruising could be severe. Street's right. We should take you to the hospital."

"No," I said. "Help me sit?"

Diamond and Street each took an arm. With much effort they got me into my desk chair.

Spot was sniffing all over the office.

Street got a beer from my mini fridge and found aspirin in my drawer. I knew it would thin my blood and make any hemorrhaging worse. But the pain was too much. I took four tablets. Swallowing didn't hurt at all. Life is good.

"Did you call Doc Lee?" I said.

"Yes," Street said. "He's golfing at Edgewood. Said he'd be over as soon as possible."

"Just one bruiser?" Diamond asked.

"Yeah," I said.

"You get a good look at him?"

"No. But it was the same guy I chased at the casino."

"He was here to warn you off something."

I gave Diamond a feeble head shake.

Street saw it. "What do you mean?" She said.

Diamond looked at me.

I shut my eyes and concentrated on breathing.

"Owen," Street said, alarmed. "Why was he beating you?"

I didn't answer.

"She's going to find out anyway, Owen," Diamond said. "May as well be honest."

"Okay."

"Guy was going to kill him," Diamond said.

Street's eyes were panicked. "Then you should have police protection." She looked at Diamond.

"I can't help," he said. "I'm on administrative leave. I only came up from the valley to... hang out at the beach."

"I don't understand," Street said.

"Had a problem at the casino yesterday, involving the same guy who worked on Owen." He held up the handrail. "I took a shot at him. My round ricocheted and hit a girl's doll."

Street's eyes grew. "Oh, Diamond, I..."

"Now I'm a civilian." He looked out the window. "I can't work any protection for Owen. I'm here only as a friend."

"How's that going?" I said.

"Bad. It turns out the mother of the little girl with the doll is Violet Verona."

"I've heard that name," Street said.

Diamond nodded. "She owns the Scents Of Love perfume chain. A thousand boutique stores nationwide. Very rich, very connected. Rockport told me that the sheriff got a call from Senator Stensen's office. They're saying the senator is very concerned about

Nevada's reputation for having cops who abridge the civil liberties of innocent civilians. Their wording. The senator wants to be assured that the Douglas County Sheriff will show no benefit of the doubt to a rogue cop. Their words again." Diamond took a deep breath and let it out. "And I thought I was going to make Sergeant. Now it looks like I'm going to lose my job. Maybe worse."

I got a decent breath in me. "Do you think the sheriff's decision will be affected by what the senator says?" I asked.

"I think the sheriff is a straight shooter. He will go by what the shooting review board says. But this is one of those big gray areas where they are making a subjective analysis about my judgment. In that situation, how can a sheriff stand up to the senator?"

Street said, "I'm so sorry, Diamond." The air in the room seemed thick. The only sound was my labored breathing.

Street went over to the little sink, found a cloth and moistened it. She used the cloth to wipe my forehead. "Owen, you belong in a hospital. What's the point of being so stubborn?"

"Couple reasons," Diamond said. "First, hospitals are expensive. Isn't Owen still doing that pay-his-own-way thing?"

Street said, "You're going to worry about money when you've been beaten half to death?" She bent over and looked at me.

"Plus," Diamond said, "going to the hospital communicates that you've been beaten down. That you can't take it. Whereas, Owen is a tough guy. A tough guy eats some aspirin, then goes to the ball game."

Street said, "Owen, tell me this macho bullshit has nothing to do with you."

I didn't have the energy to speak.

Diamond said, "It's not just macho bullshit. If the enemy thinks Owen is tougher than nails, he's less likely to come back soon. He knows that Owen will fight. The guy won't try him again until he has a really good opportunity. Like if Owen were lying in a hospital bed with Valium in his system."

Street turned to me, anger and confusion on her face. "There won't be a good opportunity if you get police protection."

The door opened and John Lee walked in. He had on tan pants and a tan golf shirt. His watch was the kind where you can switch watchbands. Today, it was tan. He looked around, a fierce intelligence behind small, dark eyes. "You got in a tussle," he said. Doc Lee was a master of understatement. "Concussion?"

"No. He missed my head," I said.

"Any major injury?"

"I don't think so."

Doc Lee poked and prodded and looked under my clothes. "What did he hit you with?"

Diamond held up the handrail. "This," he said.

Doc Lee nodded. "Tell me the places of impact."

"Traps, deltoid, abdomen, chest. My knee was the worst."

Doc Lee carefully lifted my pant leg up to the knee and looked at the swollen, purple bulge. Then he inspected the other places I'd mentioned. "Owen, I know you understand the difference between muscle damage and injury to other organs. If we need to repair muscles we have some time. But if you have intestinal damage we may need to address it immediately. You took major blows to your belly. What's your assessment?"

"If I make any tension in my abdominal muscles the pain is significant. But I don't feel intestinal trauma."

Doc Lee looked at me, wondering if I was as lucid as I sounded. "The sit-ups paid off?"

"I think so."

"Doc Lee pulled a prescription pad out of his pocket, scrawled on it and tore off the sheet. "You're going to be sore. Take one of these every four hours." He glanced out the window toward Edgewood golf course. "It's a nice day, and even cardiac surgery is usually scheduled in advance."

"You better get back to your golf game," Diamond said. "We'll watch over his carcass and feed him beer."

SEVENTEEN

After Doc Lee left, Diamond said, "How come this guy runs from you at the casino, but isn't afraid of you here?"

"Probably because the casino is crowded and my office is not. And here he had the element of surprise."

"Why you figure he wants to kill you?"

"The most likely answer is Tyrone is worried I'm going to uncover evidence that implicates him in Glory's death. Maybe Faith's, too. So he hired the guy with the mask."

"You got a less likely answer?"

"The masked guy didn't like me chasing him at the casino, so he came to teach me a lesson?"

"First theory sounds better," Diamond said. "So we'll concentrate on Tyrone."

"I'll concentrate," I said. "You already made it clear you are out of it."

Street said, "If talking to Tyrone brought on this beating, then you should stay away from him. The police should take care of it." She looked at Diamond. "Right?"

"You want the official or unofficial answer?" Diamond said.

Street waited.

"Officially," he said, "I'd tell Owen to leave this problem to Tahoe's finest. He should go home and take up a hobby. Bonsai trees. Model railroads."

"Unofficially?" Street said.

"There's no point in cops going to interrogate Tyrone. He'll be gone."

"Does that mean you're not going to press charges?" she said to me.

"I'll get Rockport to file a police report," Diamond answered, "but my guess is we won't find any suspects to press charges against."

"If this guy wanted to kill Owen, why didn't he use a gun?" Street said.

"Makes a lotta noise," Diamond said. "Bullets can be traced. But a stick of wood can be burned. Murders are hard to prosecute when there's no murder weapon."

Street looked horrified.

Diamond turned to me, "You said this guy wore a ski mask. Could you tell what color he is?" He got out a pad and started writing.

"White."

"Way he talked, or skin peeking through the mask?"

"He didn't talk. But even if he did, that wouldn't necessarily indicate his color."

Diamond stopped writing. "Don't give me that politically correct bullshit."

I shrugged. That hurt.

"You saw skin?"

"Yeah. On his neck."

"He wore gloves?" Diamond said.

I nodded.

"Size?"

"Good-sized. Six-two. Two-ten."

"Eye color?"

I shook my head. That hurt, too.

"Any other observations?"

"He smelled of mouthwash, but I could still tell he's a smoker. He ate garlic last night. And he was tense and nervous. He had bad B.O."

"Well, ain't you a Perry Mason," Diamond said. "Why do you figure he didn't talk?"

"Who knows? Maybe he thought I'd recognize his voice. Either that, or he's a deaf mute."

"Right. Okay, let's get you home," Diamond said.

He and Street each took an arm and with much effort got me down the stairs. Spot thought it was fun, three people abreast on the stairs. He tried to nose in between us. We eventually made it out to my Jeep. The beer and aspirin had begun to take effect.

Street left her VW Bug in the lot and drove my Jeep with Spot in it. Diamond followed with me in the passenger seat of his old blue pickup. It was a painful journey to my bed. Once there, Street brought me another beer. Diamond had me go through the beating once again.

"How did he move?" Diamond asked.

"Fluid and strong. He's an athlete." I stopped to breathe. "He's had some fight training. Something useful in the street."

"Karate?"

I shrugged again and winced. When was I going to learn. "I think I'll try and sleep a little," I said.

Street frowned. "He didn't hit you on the head, did he?"

"No."

"You're certain? Concussion can make you sleepy." She was remembering last winter when the doctor in Kauai admonished me not to ever bump my head again.

"I'm certain," I said.

Diamond gestured with his pad. "I'll give this and the handrail to Rockport. He'll probably call you for confirmation. Oh, one more thing. I got some of the explosion debris back from the lab. I'll get it out of the car." Diamond left and returned a minute later. He handed me a bag with a bunch of pieces of green paper in it. "This'll keep you occupied. Jig-saw puzzle for your convalescence."

"Thanks," I said.

EIGHTEEN

I barely moved out of bed for the first two days. Street brought me meals and newspapers and walked Spot. When I had enough energy I reached for the bag Diamond had brought and poured the green pieces of paper out onto a piece of cardboard.

There were hundreds of pieces, all deformed by their time in the water. They had ragged edges. Most were green. A few were tan and gray. The color looked like it had been applied with felt marker. Some pieces had printing on them, carefully-formed block letters similar to the way architects print. None of the groups of letters made any sense. I spent a couple of hours on it, but could not fit any of the pieces together.

The second evening after Street left, she called me shortly afterward. "Owen, as I drove away I saw a van parked in the dark over by Mrs. Duchamp's. Could someone be watching you?"

"Maybe. But there isn't a lot of excitement in staring at this cabin with me in bed. I'll call Diamond, though."

"You'll stay inside?"

"With Spot next to me," I said.

We said goodbye and I dialed Diamond. "Are you up at the lake or down in the valley?"

"Up at Roundhill, doing a little side work at the new Company Twenty-Five grand opening."

I remembered the name from my talk with Bobby Crash who endorsed Company Twenty-Five snowboards. "Isn't that pushing the terms of your suspension?"

"I don't think so. No gun, no uniform. It's like being a retail clerk. I stay outside and help with traffic and such. You should see the crowds. People buy tickets for twenty-five bucks. Every ticket wins something. Either a Ride Twenty-Five snowboard, a Skate Twenty-Five skateboard or a twenty-five percent discount coupon to Club Twenty-Five in Cabo."

"Sounds like an expensive promotion."

"Ya. But it is sehr gut promotion. TV crews are here from Reno and Sacramento. Even Senator Stensen put in an appearance. Made a little speech about the new Camp Twenty-Five for disabled kids that Company Twenty-Five is sponsoring. Hold on a sec," Diamond said. I heard a big party in the background, a DJ making announcements over a loud rap track, a car horn, kids shouting. "Hey, I gotta go," Diamond said.

"When do you get off?"

"They said they'd need me until they shut the doors at midnight."

"Want to swing by? I've got cerveza."

"Sure."

"When you come, look for a van near my cabin."

"Will do." Diamond hung up.

I went back to work on my green puzzle. I managed to find four pieces that seemed to fit together. I joined them with tape.

Spot gave a woof shortly after midnight. He lifted his head off the floor and stared at the wall. His ears turned one way, then the other. I eased my way out of bed. Spot stood up and trotted to the front door. I kept my hands on the walls to steady myself as I followed him. Spot didn't make any other sound, so I knew he recognized my visitor. I don't know how it works. The sound of footsteps or something.

Spot pushed forward to greet Diamond as I opened the door. Diamond did the requisite ear rub as I turned and worked my way toward the kitchen nook to fetch us beers.

"Last time I saw anything move that slow, it had four legs and a shell," he said.

"Would have helped when he tested his handrail on me." I handed him a beer. "How'd the grand opening turn out?"

"There was a mob. You should have seen the kids swarming around Bobby Crash."

"The snowboarder."

"Yeah. About twenty-five years old, of course. It's like an art, the way he dresses. So carefully attired to make it look like he just threw on any old thing." Diamond sipped his beer. "They paid me my hourly rate and tipped me twenty-five bucks."

"You can upgrade your brand of Scotch."

"Naw, I'll add it to the next money order I send my mama in Mexico City. She already thinks she's a greenback queen. Told me her new TV made her the hot spot of the barrio."

Spot swung his head around at the sound of his name.

"Not you, Spot," Diamond said. "A barrio spot."

Spot stared at him, ears focused, nostrils twitching.

"Help me with the puzzle?" I said.

"Sure. Where is it?"

"In the bedroom."

Diamond got the bag of pieces. We spread them out on the kitchen counter.

"See a van outside?" I asked.

"No. I also cruised Street's condo. No van."

"Thanks for checking," I said. "This camp for disabled kids that Senator Stensen is promoting. That doesn't sound like a big profit center for a sports company."

Diamond picked up one of the green pieces and looked at it. "I read a thing about the camp in the paper. Company Twenty-Five is trying to change their image. Until now they've been fixated on profit. Their market share among kids twenty-five and under is huge. Snowboards and skateboards. Wall Street loves the company. But there is a growing backlash. A group of mothers was so upset over their kids getting tattoos that say twenty-five, that they've started a protest group. Mothers Against Company Twenty-Five. The camp for disabled kids is just the thing to help. And Senator Stensen is big on helping disabled kids. The camp is supposed to go in somewhere on the North Shore. According to his speech, the idea is to tear down some old cabins and a motel and apply those water and sewer units to the new complex. Even so, they need some major rule bending from the Tahoe Regional Planning Agency. But Senator Stensen can probably apply some pressure."

"Any idea what the T.R.P.A. thinks?"

"Don't know." Diamond frowned. "But I can't imagine they'd be amenable to a big development right on the lake. Probably want some serious environmental mitigation fees." He held his hand out palm up and rubbed his fingertips together.

I drank some beer. "You're quite the cynic for someone who came here for the American Dream."

Diamond shrugged. "Learning gringo speak and gringo ways makes for gringo attitudes. Not like we don't grease palms back home."

"You're suggesting that Camp Twenty-Five is going to bribe T.R.P.A. officials?"

"Not personally. It's institutionalized, here. The bureaucracy makes an assessment of how bad your project is for the lake. How susceptible your steep lot is to erosion and such. Then you have to buy other lots, tear down old cabins or whatever, and return the lots to indigenous condition. Then you can apply additional coverage to your steep lot that you shouldn't be allowed to build on in the first place. Hey, here's one that fits." Diamond assembled one piece onto another.

He continued, "But the bottom line is, rich people and rich companies can do what they want even if their project is bad for the lake. Take golf courses. That's where the real money is these days. If the T.R.P.A. did their job, there'd be no golf courses in the basin. Massive amounts of watering leaches fertilizer and other nutrients down through the sod and eventually into the lake. But the T.R.P.A. looks the other way. Meanwhile, they make the little people put erosion control and infiltration trenches around their houses even if they live on a flat lot. It all gets back to who can pay."

I said, "Whereas, in Mexico..."

"In Mexico, if you pay money to be allowed to do something bad, we call it what it is."

"You would have Camp Twenty-Five build down in the valley of, let's say, Douglas County?"

"Yeah. We could use the jobs. And they could still donate some of their profits to environmental projects for the good of Lake Tahoe."

"Diamond," I said slowly, not sure how to proceed, "I've never known you to be very interested in American politics. But you are suddenly tuned into Company Twenty-Five and their proposed Camp Twenty-Five and Senator Stensen's involvement. All this comes a couple of days after he and his office intervened in your situation to try to get you fired. You're taking a big risk if anyone thinks you're investigating. If the senator's office were to get the idea that you were..."

"What, an uppity immigrant with brown skin?"

"Yeah. They could probably make things a lot worse for you. You can get into some deep shit when you mess with politicians at the senate level."

Diamond frowned and looked at me hard. He drank some beer, set the bottle down and traced the label with his forefinger. He stood up and walked across my tiny living room, stopping to bend down and pet Spot who was lying on the rug.

"Something smells, Owen. I don't know what it is. But I don't see how my round could have hit that little girl's doll."

We were silent.

"You don't believe me," he said.

"Yes, I do. But you sound paranoid. Why would Violet Verona be after you? Or, for that matter, why would a U.S. Senator persecute you? Racism? It doesn't make sense."

"I know it doesn't make sense. That's why it smells."

NINETEEN

My aching body woke me up early. I managed pills and coffee all by myself and then, after my aches had diminished, a careful shower. The coloring on my torso would give a meat inspector bad dreams.

I went back to bed and called Street. "Your favorite patient calling," I said when she answered.

"Feeling any better?"

"Like a steak left too long in tenderizer. Worse than the helicopter crash in Kauai. You coming over?"

"Somebody has to rescue Spot from the nursing home."

"Wondering if you can bring your laptop. I think I can do a little work in bed."

Street said she'd be over in a couple of hours.

I used the time to leave a message about the boat explosion on Jennifer Salazar's voice mail. Then I worked on my green puzzle. Maybe it was the morning light, but in less than fifteen minutes I'd found four more pieces that fit together. The next twenty minutes were without success. An hour after that I fit two more into my tiny green patch. Only a couple hundred more to go.

The phone rang. It was Jennifer.

"I just wanted to tell you I ruined your boat," I said.

"I got a message about it from the caretaker. I tried to call two different times, but couldn't get through. The caretaker said you and Spot are okay?"

"Yes."

"Thank God. That's all that counts. Forget about the boat."

"But that boat was very expensive."

"Don't worry. Anyway, when you've got as much money as I do, a boat is nothing. For that matter, if you ever get in a financial jam, I'll cover for you. I don't want to intrude, but don't worry about money."

"Jennifer, you shouldn't say things that..."

"Owen, stop it. I was fourteen when you met me. Now I'm sixteen. Have I changed my resolve about anything in that time?"

"No, but..."

"Then stop wondering if I'm going to grow up and be a different person. I didn't even earn my money. You and Street are almost my only close friends. You saved my life and my mother's life. So I'm going to be your patron if you ever need it. No matter how many boats I buy, I'll still be rich."

Neither of us spoke for a moment.

"Thank you," I said.

We said goodbye, and I went back to my puzzle. I found another piece that fit by the time Street arrived with her laptop.

"Look at you. The puzzle master," she said. "I'd offer to help, but Spot is waiting."

I went online to research Glory's company while Street walked Spot. The roadie at the loading dock had said it was a Las Vegas outfit called Remake Productions. They turned out to be a management company that handled promotion and bookings for three different acts.

I was still perusing the website when Street came back smelling of pine trees and summer. She said she left Spot chained on the deck.

"What's the project?" she asked as she sat on the edge of the bed.

"I'm checking into the company that handled Glory's band. Remake Productions out of Las Vegas. They manage three bands. Here's the first one." I turned the laptop so that Street could see. "A Hip-Hop band called Meen Tyme." I pointed to the picture of four black kids in their early twenties wearing baggy clothes and big gold chains around their necks. "The description says that Meen Tyme loves women," I said.

"Codespeak for lyrics that aren't misogynist?"

"One can hope. The second group is female, called Hot Summerz." I clicked on their link. "They have a certain look. Silver metallic clothing with lavender accents. Even their hair is lavender."

"What kind of music do they play?" Street asked.

"Don't know. They are singers. Some of the pictures show a three-piece band behind them, long-haired white guys in their 30s. Guitar, bass and drums. They open for big acts like Glory."

"What about Glory?"

"Most of the Remake Productions website is devoted to her. The pictures show her progression from singing at weddings and bars in Oakland to large arenas across the country." I clicked on a few. Each picture was accompanied by a hand-written note where Glory told of shyness, stage fright and insecurities.

"Check out her backup musicians," I said. "This band member played for Nancy Wilson. One guy did a stint for Wynton Marsalis. One did studio work for the Stones."

"Pretty impressive for a shy girl."

"While you were walking Spot, I did some multiplying in my head. Arena sizes, ticket prices, number of CDs Glory sold, and roughly figured that the Glory enterprise was grossing upwards of thirty million a year."

"Serious money," Street said.

"Yeah. If her death was not an accident, one would think that her money would be the logical starting point in finding a motive. But Tyrone thought she was giving most of her money to the California Conservancy to preserve wetlands. Without a major beneficiary, there wouldn't be motive. It's not as if some other singer would benefit from her death."

"Right," Street said. "Glory's death would probably only increase the sales of her own CDs."

We talked some more, then Street said she had work to do. She kissed me goodbye and was walking out the door when she stopped and came back in. "Owen, what if Glory's death and Faith's death have nothing to do with Glory's career? Maybe the only connection between them is that a psycho is killing beautiful young women. Maybe he's making them look like accidents to throw off the cops?"

"Then why would he come after me? It doesn't fit the pattern."

"Because you're the first person to worry him about getting caught."

I thought about it. "Maybe Glenda Gorman could look into it. See if any other young women have died recently."

"It would be worth a try," Street said. She made a kissing motion and left.

I called Glennie at the paper.

"Owen, you bad boy, you haven't called me for practically ever. I know I should just be glad you're alive after what you've been through. But how's a girl supposed to keep her spirits up if she doesn't get a little attention from a guy like you?"

"You mean, from a guy with a dog like mine."

"That, too. How is my little polka dot baby?"

I looked out at Spot on the deck. He was on his back in a crescent curve, all four feet up in the air. His jowls had flopped open under the tug of gravity, exposing pink flesh and large fangs. "He's out in the sun practicing a yoga position," I said.

"Give him a hug and a kiss for me?"

"Maybe a hug."

"So what do you need? Lemme guess, you're assuming the boat explosion wasn't an accident, which makes that poor girl's death a murder."

"Correct. Same for Glory's death on the Flume."

"Which means," Glennie said, "that you're wondering if there are other such accidents."

"Yes. Especially if the victims are young women."

"And I, being an investigative ace, am the one to search the archives and find out."

"My thought, too. I'll owe you."

For the next few days I used Street's laptop to do some research when I wasn't assembling my green puzzle. I went back to the Remake Productions website and noticed something unusual.

There was no information about Remake's whereabouts. No address, no phone number. The only contact information was an email address.

Most businesses provide you with many avenues to purchase their goods or services. Toll-free phone numbers, fax numbers, email, snail mail, walk-in locations, names and contact information. Did the pressures of show business make it necessary to hide?

To check I looked at several other music sites. Individual stars had sites that also offered little or no contact information. But management sites were the opposite, inviting contact, doing everything they could to make it easy to book a band.

But Remake requested that all inquiries be directed to their email address.

There are other routes to acquiring data.

After more digging I learned that Remake Productions was a corporation. The contact name was Tony Nova and the address was in Las Vegas.

TWENTY

The morning of the seventh day I was able to walk the entire twelve foot distance to the kitchen nook and pour my coffee without wincing. I could again inhale a decent breath without ripping chest muscles. It was time to visit Remake Productions in Las Vegas.

I was grabbing my toothbrush and a few other items when Spot turned toward the back door and growled. "What is it, boy?" I looked out the kitchen window but didn't see anything. Spot stared at the door and growled again. I went around the counter, opened the door a crack and looked out. Nothing caught my eye.

A sound came from the front. Spot turned and walked across the room to the front door, sniffing the air, his nostrils flexing. I opened the front door to see Diamond pulling up in his old, blue pickup. Spot pushed out past me, trotted toward Diamond, then ran past his pickup and around the side of my cabin.

I hurried after him as fast as my sore muscles would allow. Spot barked and growled as I came around the corner.

A shout came from the woods. "Easy boy. Easy! Christ, don't make me!"

"Spot!" I called. "Stay!"

Diamond joined me as I pushed through a stand of red fir. "I saw a Douglas County Jeep Cherokee turn up your road," Diamond said. "So I turned, too."

"Speak of the devil," Diamond muttered as we came upon a young deputy with his arms outstretched, holding his sidearm in both hands. The automatic was pointed at Spot who stood ten feet away. The fur on Spot's back was up like a brush. His legs were slightly bent as if ready to attack. The rumbling growl in his throat was deep and loud.

"You can put the gun down," I said. "Spot, it's okay."

The man lowered his gun. Spot stopped growling, but didn't move.

"What are you doing here, Rockport?" Diamond said.

"I finally got a break in my schedule. So I came up to ask Mr. McKenna a couple questions about the casino chase."

"Why park so far off the road?" Diamond said.

"I was slowing as I got close and I saw movement in the woods." Rockport looked over his shoulder. "I knew Mr. McKenna had been attacked, so I wanted to check it out. Next thing I know this dog comes after me. Christ, he's got some size on him."

"You can relax, Rockport," Diamond said. "Meet McKenna. McKenna, Deputy Rockport."

We shook. He had a strong grip. Up close, I could smell cologne and breath mints.

"Sorry about startling you," Rockport said. He gave me a nervous smile. He looked like he came from the casting office. He was tall and thick and stood like a Marine at attention. His brown hair was cut in a flattop, and his tan was deep enough to stress a dermatologist.

"I doubt anyone was in the woods," I said. "Spot didn't bark until he heard you. Maybe it was a bear. There are so many that Spot has started to ignore them. Come, Spot, meet Deputy Rockport." Spot came slowly, acting suspicious. Rockport bravely held his hand out for Spot to sniff. I led Diamond and Rockport through the trees back to the cabin.

"Hey, thanks for calling your dog off," Rockport said, grinning nervously. He had one of those Covergirl smiles where they pull down their bottom lips for maximum tooth exposure. His teeth were wide and flat like miniature bathroom tiles, and he had enough of them to complete a small shower.

"Any time," I said.

"Now that I know the sheriff's vehicle is Rockport's, I guess I'll head off," Diamond said. He got in his pickup and left.

I didn't feel like inviting Rockport inside, so we spoke in the driveway. He asked me a few questions about the casino chase and the beating I'd received at my office. He was particularly interested in every detail I could remember about my assailant, and he took careful notes on a small spiral pad.

"Let me know if you think of anything else," he said, then he thanked me for my time and left.

I got my puzzle pieces from the cabin and let Spot into the back seat of the Jeep. The long drive down to the highway has several hairpin curves, and I took it slow because the jostling of the Jeep made my body throb.

I drove south into town and turned up Kingsbury Grade. There would be a pile of mail at my office and enough messages on the machine to freeze it up, but I didn't stop. Ever since the man in the ski mask had worked me over, my office seemed as appealing as one of those basement rooms in the Tower of London.

It was another perfect summer day in Tahoe. The sun was hot, the air cool, and the sky impossibly blue. But I was leaving for the desert, and it was August. I hoped my air conditioning was in good shape.

TWENTY-ONE

I took back roads from Carson Valley over to 95, headed down past Walker Lake and the big military installation at Hawthorne. From there it was south to Tonopah where the highway dropped down to the starkest desert landscape I've ever seen.

The road went straight for dozens of miles across white ground that was parched and cracked and lifeless. Mountains of black rock rose here and there like what an artist might imagine exists on an alien planet. To the west loomed White Mountain, its snow-caked summit more than fourteen thousand feet in the air. I was cruising alone on the highway when my cell phone rang.

"Owen? It's Glennie. I've found a couple of deaths that look funny."

"Accidents that could be murders?" I said.

"Right. I've copied all the newspaper stories and printed some other relevant stuff. You want me to read this over the phone, or do you want to pick it up and read it yourself?"

"I'll pick it up. But not for a day or two. I'm out of town."

We made some small talk, then signed off.

After driving most of the day, I went by the turnoff to Hollybrook. I still had vivid memories of breaking into the sanitarium where Jennifer Salazar's mother had been imprisoned against her will. I continued on south. Soon, the giant hotels of the Las Vegas Strip appeared in the distance, shimmering in the afternoon sun.

I'd turned the air conditioning up to high speed, yet the inside of the Jeep was getting uncomfortably warm. It took a couple of minutes poking around the radio dial before I heard that the temperature downtown was 113 degrees. I realized that I couldn't leave

Spot in the Jeep even for the shortest time. Eventually, I found street numbers approaching those for Remake Productions. The address appeared to be in one of the hotels. There was a parking place a couple blocks away.

"Hey, doggie, wanna go see what a music management company looks like?"

He was asleep in back. What a surprise. I got out into blast-furnace heat, opened the rear door and repeated myself. Spot lifted up his head, eyelids drooping. He sniffed at the hot air coming in and put his head back down with a sigh of satisfaction.

"C'mon, Spot. Time to go."

He ignored me.

I reached in and tugged on his collar.

He resisted, but soon realized he didn't have a choice. He groaned and finally got to his feet.

Spot has been in downtown Reno, Sacramento, Oakland and San Francisco, so I knew what the reaction would be. People stopped and stared. I concentrated on finding a path that stayed in the shade of buildings so he wouldn't burn his feet. At one point, we were faced with a hundred foot stretch of sun-baked sidewalk that was hot enough to sear a pot roast. On the other side was a giant hotel with a tropical garden of lush plants like those in Kauai and graceful palm trees arcing over a man-made waterfall. Above the waterfall, a monorail emerged from an opening in one side of the glass wall of the hotel and curved off around to the other side. Why walk across the lobby when you can take the train?

"Okay, Spot, time to run." I pulled him into a trot across the cement, my sore muscles aching. After a couple of steps he started doing a weird, prancing dance. "Faster, Spot."

He didn't need convincing. We sprinted to the tropical rain forest. Spot jumped over the plantings at the edge of the stream and into the water. A crowd assembled as Spot ran up and down the man-made stream, doing his best to splash all the water out.

A security guard came up to me. "Is that your dog? Your dog can't go in the water."

"Oh, sorry," I said. I called out, "Spot! Out of that water."

Spot ran down the stream, did a quick stop and sprayed water all over us. The guard gasped. I pulled Spot toward the hotel entrance. He was too long to fit in the revolving doors, so we went to the side where the regular doors were.

"Hey, you can't take a dog in there," the guard yelled from behind us.

We pushed inside to a breeze of cooled air that smelled like carpet cleaner and popcorn.

The cacophony of beeping slots and electronic poker machines and other games was overwhelming. Crowds of people ambled through the gaming tables. A clown juggling orange balls went by on a unicycle.

"Sir, dogs aren't allowed in the hotel," a loud voice called out. Another security man.

"I have an appointment at Remake Productions. They called about a Seeing Eye dog. Where would their offices be? Up on the mezzanine?"

"No one except the blind are allowed to have a Seeing Eye dog."

"I am blind." I walked Spot toward an escalator that went up in a curve toward the monorail station.

"I'm calling the police," the guard said. He ran over to an office with walls that were mirrored on the outside and, no doubt, one-way glass on the inside.

I was certain that Spot had never been on an escalator, but he pulled me onto the moving steps without hesitation. The monorail train floated by above us as we neared the mezzanine. I looked up at the mirrored ceiling and waved.

A shopping arcade stretched off in one direction. The first shop was a boutique with R-rated lingerie in the display window.

I stuck my head in. "Can you tell me where the business offices would be? I'm looking for Remake Productions."

A young woman chewed on her gum, blew a pink bubble, popped it, then sucked it back in her mouth. "Next floor up."

We took another escalator ride and found Remake Productions down a wide hall. I opened the door, and we walked into a small room with tan suede wallpaper and brown carpet. A large man slouched at a desk, a computer keyboard in his lap. He wore a T-shirt and blue jeans just like the roadies who'd been loading Glory's truck. Maybe it was the Remake uniform. A cigarette dangled from his lips. He had three-day whiskers on his chin.

"Be with you in a minute," he said without looking up. The cigarette waggled as he spoke and an ash fell off on the front of his T-shirt, but he didn't notice. He reached out, moved the mouse, clicked a couple times, then typed on the keyboard.

"Okay, that looks better," he said. He clicked the mouse again and turned toward me. "Big dog," he said, cigarette bouncing. There was no surprise on his face or in his voice. Probably had Great Danes in his office every day. "Lots of spots," the man said. "Be a good name for a dog like that. Spot."

"Yes," I said as Spot looked from him to me.

The man squinted against the cigarette smoke. "Oh, almost forgot." He turned back to the computer screen and did some more tapping on the keyboard. "There. Better still. Not great. But better."

"I'm looking for Tyrone," I said.

"Who?" The man was scowling at the screen, moving the mouse, clicking it like he was sending Morse Code.

"Tyrone Handkins. Works here."

"Oh, Handy. Worked. Like me. We're flirting with the past tense around here. Bossanova may want him to switch over and work with Hot Summerz, but don't bet on it. Glory was the tap root for this little money tree. Without her it's time for some pruning."

"Bossanova?"

"Tony Nova, the boss."

"Where do I find Handkins?" I said.

"Beats me. He never comes to Vegas. Gets his marching papers from Bossanova and hits the road." The man's cigarette was unfiltered and had burned almost to his lips. He shook out another, lit it off the end of the stub and dropped the stub in a foam cup half full of coffee. It hissed.

"Where does he live?" I asked.

"Handy? Got me. L.A., I think. I only met him just once. It's not like he's gonna invite me to his next slumber party." He sucked down hard on the new cigarette and the end glowed orange.

"Do you have his phone number?"

"No. Bossanova's secretary handles personnel questions." He turned back to the computer monitor.

"What do you do here?" I said.

"What is this, the Rockford Files? I do the ad layouts and handle the bookings. You want Hot Summerz for your wedding party? Let's talk. It'll cost, but you'll have a wedding no guest will ever forget. Or maybe our boy band is more your style."

"Let me think about it," I said. "What about Tony Nova's number?"

The man reached a card out of a small holder on the edge of the desk. "The numbers that come first, where it says bookings, are me. Phone and fax. My name's Bill Banes. The ones down below are the business office." The cigarette bounced violently in his lips.

"Where is that?" I said, looking at the numbers. I was surprised to see the Northern Nevada area code.

"Where is the business office?" The man turned from the computer and squinted at me through cigarette smoke. "Bossanova isn't a real public guy. I gave you the phone number, okay?"

"Thanks for your help. I'll give him a call. C'mon, Spot. Let's go." I turned to leave.

"Hey, you're joking, right? I mean, about the name Spot. He's not really..." his voice faded away as the door shut behind me.

When Spot and I were almost down to the lobby, two cops pushed their way through the crowd onto the up escalator. People got on behind them. We got off at the bottom. One cop saw us and started yelling. He tried to work his way back down through the people, but he couldn't move down fast enough. Spot and I were out onto the broiling street in seconds.

"The sidewalk's still hot," I said, putting my hand in his collar. "You wanna get your feet wet again before we run?" This time I held onto his collar. He jumped into the stream and nearly pulled me over. I pulled him back out and we ran to the Jeep.

TWENTY-TWO

I stopped at a sandwich shop and got a jumbo sub. Out at the end of the strip was a motel with a sign that said "Air-conditioning!" and "Pool!" and "Pets Okay!"

Once inside, I put all the tomatoes and lettuce on one half of the sandwich and gave Spot the other half. The way he Hoovered it, I envisioned moving to Southern California and opening a chain of sub shops for dogs.

I got on the phone and dialed the office number on the business card for Remake Productions. A pleasant, recorded voice said to please call back during business hours. I worked on my puzzle late into the evening. At times it seemed futile, but I added several more pieces.

The next morning I fixed coffee in the in-room machine and dialed Remake Productions. The same voice answered live. "Remake Productions."

"Hello," I said. "May I speak to Tony Nova, please."

"I'm sorry, sir, he's out. May I take a message?"

"How about Tyrone Handkins?"

"I'm sorry, there is no one of that name here."

"When will Tony Nova be in?"

"I can't say, sir. All you can do is leave your number."

"What about your address? I'd like to stop by."

"We don't give out Mr. Nova's office address for security reasons. I can give you the address of our Las Vegas office."

"Thanks for your help," I said and hung up.

I remembered Watt Waitsfield, a guy in Reno who works for a database company. One of their clients is the phone company.

Watt had called me when a loan shark was squeezing him about his gambling problem. I couldn't do anything to scare the lender away, but I got them to restructure the debt. Watt was very grateful.

It had come in handy a couple times since.

His side business required the anonymity of a pay phone, so I took another cup of coffee with me to the phone across the street, called Watt and left the pay phone number on his pager. I drank the coffee and waited. I could see Spot standing at the motel room window, chin resting on the windowsill, while he watched me on the other side of an endless stream of trucks and cars.

Watt called back in a few minutes. He must have been in his car to find a pay phone so fast.

"Hello, my friend. What's happenin'?"

"I'm vacationing in Vegas. It's great. Only things missing are my friends Tony Nova and Tyrone Handkins. I thought I'd stop by their office and personally ask them to join me. But I can't remember where it is."

"Let me see if I can help. What have you got?"

I read off the business office number from the bottom of the Remake Productions card.

"Great. Give me ten minutes."

Twenty minutes later, the phone rang again.

"Did you find my friends?" I said.

"One of them. The number rings at fourteen, twenty-two, twenty-nine, Desert View Highway in Reno. Suite G. The number is billed to Remake Productions, with Tony Nova on the data record. He also has an unlisted number that rings at sixty-nine Windemere Glen in Reno."

"What about Tyrone Handkins?"

"M.I.A."

"Okay, thanks."

"My pleasure."

I hung up, checked out of the motel and headed out of town. I tried not to let it bother me that I'd driven all the way to Vegas only to find out that what I wanted was in Reno.

TWENTY-THREE

It was dark by the time I arrived back in the Carson Valley. I drove north into Reno and turned into the Wild Oats supermarket. I ordered a large pepperoni pizza and grabbed a six-pack of Sierra Nevada. I took the beer and the pizza box back to the Jeep and set them on the hood. I hitched a foot up on the bumper, ate a piece and opened a beer. Spot leaned forward from the back seat, staring at me with laser eyes and radar ears.

When the pizza had cooled enough that the cheese wouldn't burn, I let him out onto the blacktop parking lot and had him sit. I tossed him a piece.

I always wonder what the point is of having such large teeth when they don't get used. The pizza disappeared like a wayward duck into the intake of a 747 jet engine. Spot looked up at me and licked his chops. His tail swept the asphalt. I tossed him another piece. Same disappearing act, same sound effects.

I poured a beer into the plastic ice cream bucket I keep in the Jeep. I held it steady while he drank it. When he was done he carefully ran his tongue around the bucket, getting every drop. Then he looked at the remaining bottles.

"No," I said. "One beer is enough." I got a pliers out of the glove box, took Spot around to the side of the building and used the pliers to turn on the tiny square faucet shaft. Spot drank with gusto.

"Okay, Spot, libations are over. Let's go find Tony Nova."

I drove to the office address first. Suite G was the seventh door down a plain, sprawling building in a new office park. Suites A and C had lights on, but all the others were dark. I peered through the glass of G. The only light inside was a computer screen saver.

I stopped at a gas station and bought a map of Reno. The street called Windemere Glen was a little curlicue.

South and west of Reno is a broad expanse of land that slopes up toward the mountains. I headed up the long incline of the Mt. Rose Highway. The houses got fancier the higher up I went. Near the exclusive golf course neighborhood called Montreaux on the left, I found the turnoff on the right.

Three turns later, I came to Windermere Glen. It went north a few blocks and then turned west and headed up toward the mountains.

The brass numerals were set into a panel on the big iron gate. On either side of the gate were imposing walls of brick that swept up like an angel's wings. Where the brick stopped the tall, wooden fence began, stretching off across the desert. There was no view of Tony Nova's house from the road.

I continued upslope for a half mile before I found a turnoff. I turned onto gravel and climbed into empty desert that would one day be filled with mansions. I kept watch for a glimpse of Tony Nova's house down below me. But Nova's spread was well-planned. His house never popped into view.

The gravel came to a stop at a 50-foot-tall water tank that, in a fit of smart design, had been painted in patterns of sienna and beige and sagebrush-blue-green, the better to blend into the desert. I parked behind the tank. Spot and I got out into one of those perfect desert evenings. The air was cool and thick with the scent of sage. The million lights of Reno sparkled in the valley below. I got out the old-fashioned tire iron.

"C'mon, Spot," I said as I marched off into the desert.

We still hadn't glimpsed Tony Nova's house when we came to his fence. I pried off some boards and made an opening. Spot and I stepped through.

We continued across the desert. I tripped on a succession of sagebrush and unseen rocks. Spot had no problem. Maybe he can smell rocks.

We came over another rise and saw Tony Nova's house. Concealed lights lit tan, adobe walls. A swimming pool shaped like a kidney bean glowed blue in the night. Nearby were artful plantings with yellow garden lights. A small, cascading stream came down through the rocks and plunged into the pool.

On the opposite side of the house was the entrance with a curving drive that looped around a fountain. Water shot up in four, graceful curves and splashed down into a blue reflecting pool. In the center of the fountain was a marble sculpture of a nude, muscular man. It looked like a Bernini.

To the sides of the house were more gardens. There was a small pond that probably held fish. I'd seen hotels on Maui with less water.

Near the fountain was parked a Burgundy-colored Mercedes with smoked windows. Nova could come and go and his distant neighbors would never even know what he looked like. On the other side of the Mercedes was a five-car garage.

I touched Spot on the nose, a gesture that meant silence. We approached from the side where there seemed to be the fewest windows. The garden plantings were thick and we were able to get close to the house. A small lawn in front of us was well lit.

I whispered, "Stay," to Spot and ran to a small window set in the adobe wall. I stood in the floodlights and peeked in the window.

Inside was a study, with a red Navajo rug on a cream-colored tile floor. On one wall were bookshelves with what looked like actual books in them. In the corner was a kiva with logs stacked in a wall nook.

I tried the window. Locked. I moved sideways to the next one. It, too, was locked.

"Spot," I whispered as I approached the corner of the house. "Come."

We went around the corner and tried other windows, working toward the front door. Tony Nova was security conscious. Every window was shut and locked.

We got to the front door in the full glare of the floodlights. The wedge of the tire iron slipped a short way into the crack between the solid oak door and the steel jamb. A little flexing suggested it wouldn't give at all. I was about to move back to a window when I thought to try the knob.

It was unlocked. Spot and I walked inside.

I knew Spot would alert like a search dog the moment he sensed human presence, so I kept my hand on his collar, the better to feel his tension. There was a mountain bike parked in the entrance hall. It had a lot of chrome and burgundy metallic paint.

We went through the entrance hallway, looked in on the living room and dining room and continued on to the kitchen. Spot did not alert. We walked softly down toward the bedrooms.

All were empty.

Back in the center of the house was an enclosed courtyard with a glass roof. We walked across the courtyard and looked into a large great room. Spot went rigid at my side.

The room was artfully lit with down-lighting from recessed ceiling cans. At one end, a conversation pit was sunk three feet below the floor. The curved leather seating wrapped around a fireplace with a huge copper hood above it. Nearby was a gun case displaying several hunting rifles.

A framed replica of a famous painting hung on the adjacent wall. I knew it from one of my art books. It was "The Banjo Lesson" by Henry Ossawa Tanner and showed a black man teaching a young boy how to play.

At the other end of the room was a home theater system, with an eight-foot screen in front of brown leather couches. Spot's tension was directed at the far wall which was glass. A slider was open. On the dark deck outside was a hot tub, the water churned into a froth by underwater jets. I saw the shape of a man sitting in the tub facing away from us, toward Reno. We walked across the room and out the open slider.

"Who are you," the man said before we got to him. "And what are you doing in this house." His voice was deep and resonant, and I recognized it. He didn't turn around.

"I'm from the water police, Tyrone."

TWENTY-FOUR

I walked around the far side of the hot tub where I could face Tyrone Handkins. I sat down on a planter. Spot looked at Tyrone, then me, sensed there was no immediate danger and relaxed. He walked over to the tub and lowered his head to lap at the roiling water. The hot foamy water bubbled over his nose, and Spot jerked back. He shook his head, stared at the water, then shook his head again as he licked chlorine off his nose.

"Does the Bossanova know you're here enjoying the place?" I asked. "Or is this a benefit he is unaware of when he's out of town?"

"Bossanova?" Tyrone didn't move from his seated position. The foaming water came to just below his shoulders. He could be holding a weapon under the water, and I'd be unable to see it. He looked at me, then glanced away. Shifty eyes.

"Tony Nova. Your boss. The Remake Productions computer guy in Vegas called him that."

"Banes said that? I hadn't heard that."

"Where do I find Nova?" I said.

"What for?" Tyrone's eyes went to the lights of Reno, then down to the foaming water.

"I want to ask him some questions."

"Questions like what?"

"Like why did the guy in the ski mask come to Glory's hotel room while I was there talking to you? Was he the guy you paged?"

"I don't know what you're talking about."

"I saw his shadow under the door and surprised him before he could surprise me. I chased him through the casino. The next day he succeeded in surprising me, this time at my office. He almost killed me with a handrail."

"You look alive to me."

"Does he work directly for you? Or for Tony Nova?"

"Neither," Tyrone said. "I have no idea who you're referring to."

"You want me to think he was there to surprise you, instead?"

Tyrone glanced up. "I don't know. Maybe he was."

"Then who did you page?"

"I don't recall paging anyone."

"You reached inside a black briefcase. It looked like you were pushing buttons on a cell phone. A minute later, you got a call to which you responded, 'the sooner, the better.' Sounded like I was being set up."

Tyrone's eyes darted up and down. "Look, I don't know what you're talking about. I get a lot of calls."

"Then what were you doing with your hand inside the briefcase?"

His head went back and forth in a slow shake. "I don't remember. Are you sure? Maybe I... Wait, I remember." Tyrone's eyes met mine for a moment. "I have a travel alarm. I'd set it because I was going to take a nap. But I couldn't fall asleep. I remembered it was still on when you were talking to me. So I reached in to turn it off. Here, I'll show you."

He stood up and climbed out of the hot tub. He reached for a terry cloth bathrobe that was hanging nearby and pulled it on. Still dripping, Tyrone walked barefoot through the sliding glass door into the great room.

Spot and I followed him into the indoor courtyard, then out to the master suite. Tyrone walked over to a dresser and lifted a briefcase off the top. He handed it to me. "It's inside. Have a look."

I pulled out a travel alarm and a cell phone. "The alarm makes for a good explanation. But there's a cell phone as well."

Spot was inspecting the carpet. He found a good place, circled once and lay down.

"I haven't used the alarm since," Tyrone said. "Check the alarm time. It's probably set for two o'clock."

I found the button and pressed it. The display read 2:30 p.m. "Where is Tony Nova?"

"Gone."

"Where?" I said.

"I don't know."

"When will he be back?"

Tyrone looked around the room, exasperated. "I don't know."

"The guy at Remake Productions said that you and he and maybe everybody else may end up out of work now that Glory is dead. He said she was the main revenue source for the company. Is that true?"

"You don't..." Tyrone stopped himself.

I tried to provoke him. "Maybe you dealt with the worry of your boss firing you by getting rid of him. Or he already fired you, and you killed him in revenge."

Tyrone stared at me, a severe frown on his face. "You're like the rest, aren't you," he said. "I'm guilty from the beginning. There's nothing I can do." His voice had the same wounded sincerity that I'd heard a dozen times before from ruthless killers.

"I'd like to think not," I said. "But you were present at her death. You had means and opportunity and possibly motive. I came to ask you questions at the hotel and got jumped and nearly killed as a result. You told your roadies not to talk to me, then you disappeared. Now I find you at your boss's house and you evade my questions about him." I was raising my voice. "If he didn't come to the same fate as Glory, where is he?"

"I told you!" Tyrone shouted. "I don't know."

Spot jumped to his feet, concern on his face.

Tyrone stepped toward me. "Get out!" His hands were clenched into fists. He wanted to take a swing. I couldn't tell if self-restraint or Spot's presence held him back.

"Get out of your boss's house?" I said. "Let's call him and ask. Prove to me that he knows you're here. Let him tell me to leave."

Tyrone's face was flushed and his eyes seemed afire. He walked out of the master suite, moving fast. Spot and I followed. Tyrone marched through the courtyard, into the great room and over to the gun case. He opened the glass door and pulled a rifle off the rack. It looked like a Remington 700. Tyrone worked the bolt action, lifted it up and aimed it at my chest. I was only 20 feet away across the room. He was shaking with anger, but there wasn't much chance that he would miss.

"You are a trespasser," he said, rage in his voice. "The gate was locked. Somewhere there will be evidence that you forced your way in. I am authorized to be here. Even a black man would be acquitted in that situation."

"Easy, Tyrone." I put my hands up. "No more killings. I'm leaving." I backed up several paces, turned and left.

TWENTY-FIVE

The next morning I drove over to Emerald Bay Road and stopped at the local FBI field office. Special Agent Ramos was in.

I'd met Ramos when the arsonist was lighting forest fires in Tahoe. My memory of him was that he was an irritating, self-important jerk. He was a short man of Mexican heritage who spoke like Dan Rather. His shoes were polished, his pants had sharp creases ironed into them, and his short hair was thick and black and combed with a part on the left side. Except for a large mole on his forehead, he looked like a model for a film about the immigrants who made this country great.

"Good to meet you, Mr. McKenna," he said as if he'd never seen me before. "What can I help you with?" He sat down in his desk chair.

"I'm looking for a guy who beats people up with a wooden handrail. Wears a ski mask."

"The guy who came to your office. I saw the report." Ramos leaned back in his desk chair, his hands gripping the chair arms. After a moment he said, "You said you are a licensed investigator?"

I nodded, trying to repress the immediate resentment you feel when someone asks what they already know.

"Mr. McKenna, there are many components in our system of jurisprudence," Ramos said, his words heavy with arrogance. "The FBI was conceived to be the top layer of..."

"Cut with the bullshit, Ramos. I don't need your song and dance about need-to-know. I saved your ass last fall when I found out where the arsonist was going to light the next forest fire. If I hadn't, how many lives would have burned on your watch? You owe me, and you know it. Either you can pay your bill now and sleep at night, or you can lie awake counting how many ways you are an insult to your job."

Ramos colored a deep red. "Are you threatening me?"

"With your sense of right and wrong, yes."

Ramos reached over and pulled a cigar out of a box on the corner of his desk. He peeled the wrapper, cut the end off with a silver pocket knife and lit it with a silver lighter. His color was returning to normal. When he had the cigar burning he spoke.

"It is disturbing that the man in the mask came to your office. As far as we know, he's only operated in Vegas and L.A. prior to this."

"Who is he?"

"We don't know. We call him the shape-shifter because he presents himself in different ways."

"You mean disguises," I said.

"Disguises, yes. And methods. We believe he operates through the Internet in a manner that is nearly impossible to trace. If a person wants his services, the person posts a cryptic message on a particular bulletin board with an email address and a code word. The code is apparently obtained through referrals from previous clients. The shape-shifter watches the bulletin boards and responds only if he wants to. Both parties use email addresses with one of the big web-based services like Yahoo so that they can be accessed from anywhere. They continuously change the addresses and use public computers at libraries or cybercafes to log onto the email accounts. We've intercepted several communications, but the email accounts had already been abandoned by the time we moved in."

"These services you mention. They are...?"

"We're not sure, however we believe the shape-shifter is an assassin. One of the emails we intercepted was traced to a report of a man in a mask leaving the scene of a murder in Vegas."

"How was the victim killed?"

"He was beaten to death with a wooden stick. We analyzed some fibers and determined they were Douglas fir. Presumably, the shape-shifter used wood so he could burn the murder weapon. Having him show up at your office, however, is a break from the one-use doctrine."

"You mean using a weapon only once."

"Yes. As you know," Ramos said, puffing on his cigar, his voice thick with condescension, "many murders are solved when the murder weapon is found and traced to the killer. The one-use doctrine is a simple and effective way a murderer can avoid detection. Specifically, a murderer destroys whatever weapon is used in the crime. It could be burning a wooden stick, or dropping a gun over a boat into the depths of Lake Tahoe. Of course, most killers are fools and don't think of this. Or, even more stupid, they remember that the rifle cost a thousand dollars and they resist the impulse to dispose of it."

"So the guy in the mask is breaking his rule by using the mask and the wooden stick multiple times."

"Possibly. As soon as a weapon is used again, a pattern emerges. However, the original killing with the stick might have been done by someone else, and the shape-shifter was adopting that as a disguise when he came after you. For him, it is a one-use situation. But law enforcement will think it is the former killer they are after. Or turn it around. A new killer could be copying the shape-shifter. Either way, the confusion of evidence and clues is an effective screen."

"Most professional killers just use a gun. Much more effective."

"I agree," Ramos said. "And this guy may well use a gun, too. But there is another side to the shape-shifter. In addition to his one-use approach, which demands variety, he likes flair."

"Death by stick has more flair than death by gun?"

"Yes. More exciting and, better yet, riskier. Risk equals excitement, which is nectar to some killers." Ramos sucked on his cigar and blew a cloud of blue smoke. "One of the emails had a code we deciphered as an address of a tire store in Thousand Oaks. A car was serviced there and left in the lot overnight. The next morning the owner picked it up. A doctor who lived up in the Santa Monica mountains. He drove it off a curve on the Mulholland Highway and plunged five hundred feet to his death."

"Why do you think it was murder?"

"Two reasons. First, the guy owed the Vegas mob close to a half-million and wasn't paying. Second, a couple of our forensic guys spent some time with the burnt wreckage. They think the back seat was rigged so that a man could come out of the trunk."

"And do what, grab the wheel and cause the accident?"

"Yes," Ramos said. "Steer the guy off the cliff and roll out the door at the last moment. Like a Hollywood stuntman."

I thought about it. "You're thinking of the boat explosion?"

Ramos nodded. "We went over all the debris the Coast Guard found. We didn't find anything specific to connect to this guy. But the boat explosion had flair. This guy loves that he can kill in outrageous ways and in a wide variety of ways. No doubt, he also loves that he can take enormous risks and still not get caught.

"If the people hiring him don't know his identity, how does he get paid?"

Ramos puffed on the cigar. "We can only guess."

I waited.

"Eighteen months ago a woman came to us with a story. She'd been on a tour bus outside of Las Vegas. It was a bus with windows that open. They were in the middle of the desert when she dropped a postcard. She got out of her seat and was looking for it on the floor when she saw a man in the back seat reach into his jacket pocket and pull out a pager. It hadn't beeped, so it must have been on vibration mode. He opened the window and threw a canvas bag out of the window just as the bus was on a bridge. The bag went over the bridge to the canyon below. We've looked in the area and there are a couple of spots where someone below could have driven out on back roads."

"She get a description?"

"No. He had a baseball cap pulled down low over his face. She didn't think much of it until later when she was watching a movie on TV and realized she'd witnessed a perfect cash-drop."

"You figure a guy sits some distance away with binoculars and makes the call," I said.

"Right. Even if we'd been following the guy making the payoff, we couldn't have caught the recipient unless we'd had a helicopter. And if we did have a chopper, the guy might have spotted it and not made the phone call. That kind of drop can be made from a bus or train or boat or even a private plane. If it is unmarked cash, it is a hard system to bust."

"You have an idea why someone would pay a professional to come to Tahoe to kill me?"

Ramos shook his head.

"Anything else unusual happening around here, lately? Something the FBI would pay attention to?"

"No. Only the incidents in your office and the casino, and the boat explosion. We've seen nothing else unusual. The death of the singer Glory is still being treated as an accident."

"What do you know about her bodyguard?" I asked.

"Tyrone Handkins? The coroner ruled that the cause of death was her fall from the Flume Trail."

"Are you looking at anyone else besides this shape-shifter?"

"No. But that doesn't mean much. As I said, for all the evidence we have, the shape-shifter might be long gone and this is a new dog using old tricks."

"The boat explosion and the beating involved me, but you never thought to ask me about it or tell me about this guy in Vegas."

"Like I said, we've been looking at it, but we've found nothing that would merit a conference with you. If that changes, perhaps you and I will have further communication. Now, have I paid my bill?"

TWENTY-SIX

As I drove away I called the Washoe County Sheriff's Office and asked for Sergeant Ralph Cardoza.

"I'm sorry, he's on vacation," the receptionist said.

"Still? He was on vacation almost two weeks ago."

"I know. We're all jealous. He had a lot of extra days saved up."

"Okay. I'll try his cell." I had the number on a Post-it note in my wallet.

"Any luck fishing?" I said when he answered.

"No, I gave up on that reservoir. I'm going down to Hope Valley, maybe try Blue Lakes. You talk to Tyrone Handkins?"

"Yeah. I found him at his boss's house outside of Reno."

"No kidding. Who's that?"

"Tony Nova. Lives just off the Mt. Rose Highway. You were right about Handkins having shifty eyes. But I didn't get anything out of him except a temper."

"I'm going to keep him in my sights, just the same. Hey, where are you at?" Cardoza asked.

"I'm driving up the east shore."

"Then we probably went past each other. I'm north of Cave Rock, heading south."

"Why don't you pull off at the boat launch just south of Cave Rock. I'll meet you there."

There were many parked cars at the launch, but only one man standing there when I pulled in.

"Sergeant?" I said when I got out of my Jeep.

"Good to meet you, McKenna." We shook. Cardoza radiated swagger and confidence. He stood straight and chewed his gum the way a kid does, lips parted, his jaw moving up and down with the insistence of assembly-line machinery. I guessed him at a fit 40, although his faded jeans and worn running shoes made him look younger. He had expensive sunglasses parked on top of his head. Behind him was an old Audi that looked to be in great condition.

"I heard you had a guy come after you," he said. "Must have took some balls. What are you, six and a half?"

"Yeah. He surprised me at my office."

"The report said he wore a ski mask?"

"Right."

"Think it could have been Handkins?"

I shook my head. "The guy was white."

"Maybe Handkins hired him."

"That's what I wondered. The guy was outside Glory's hotel room after I'd questioned Handkins. It seemed like Handkins had set me up. I chased the guy, but he got away. He showed up at my office the next day."

"Anything about him stand out?"

"He was professional. Wore gloves. Didn't utter a word."

Cardoza nodded. He squinted out at the lake. "I still think Handkins is our man. Hires muscle to work for him, is my guess."

"Could be," I said. "I thought I'd have a look at the Flume Trail. See if the area squares with what Handkins told me. Do you know if the place Glory died is still marked?"

"Maybe. Call the Incline Village office. They would know. Tell me, McKenna. Your client was the girl on the boat?"

"Yes. Faith Runyon."

"But she's dead. So who're you working for?"

"My conscience."

Cardoza frowned at me, then turned to the Audi.

"Hard to get to a lot of good fishing lakes in a low clearance car," I said.

"That's why I thought of Blue Lakes. They paved it not long ago. You should check it out if you haven't been out there."

Cardoza left, and I called the Incline Village office of the Washoe Sheriff. A deputy named Doug Minney came on the line. I explained who I was.

"I want to go check out the Flume Trail where Glory died," I said. "I was wondering if the place is still marked."

"Why? You think you can learn something we missed?" His voice was higher than his natural register. Tense. Defensive.

"I doubt it," I said. "But it'd be easier to visualize if I saw the place where she went off. I thought I'd go up there with a mountain bike expert. Look at the tracks, stuff like that. Be good if I could do it before other bikers come through."

"It's been over a week since she went off."

"I know. But the only storm since then went north of the Flume. The tracks might still be there."

"Well, the crime scene tape is still there. Same with the logs the Forest Service put down to divert bicyclists to the side. But we reopened the trail some time ago, so who knows if anybody has messed up the tracks. Steve was going to go up in the morning and take down our tape and move the logs."

"Any chance you could delay it a little?"

"Delay official business for you?"

"Just a few hours is all I'd need."

There was a long pause before Minney spoke. "We left three Dayglo orange streamers to mark where she went off. They're tied to a branch on a Lodgepole pine on the mountain side of the trail. The singer went off directly opposite. You can't miss it." His breathing was audible over the phone. "We put tape on stakes along both sides of the trail about a foot off the ground. We had the deputies step over them so as to not disturb any tracks, foot tracks or bike tracks. But even so, there isn't much to look at. We also brought a guy up there from a bike shop in Incline. He couldn't tell us anything. He saw one type of tread that comes from the Velociraptor brand of tire. That's the kind the singer's bodyguard has. There was another bike track from a guy who came along after the accident. His tracks obscured much of what had been there before."

"What kind of tire did he have?"

"I forget. But it's kind of a generic tread that doesn't leave a recognizable track."

"What about the tracks from Glory's bike?" I asked.

"She had a tire called an El Gato. It leaves distinct tracks, but since she rode in front, her tracks were mostly covered up by the bodyguard's tracks and the other guy who came along."

"And others after him, I suppose," I said. "August has to be the busiest month on the Flume."

"Yeah, but the accident was early in the morning and the guy who came along called nine-one-one on his cell. One of our guys, Jackson, called the guy back right away. Got him to block off the trail some distance away in both directions. The guy dragged branches across the trail and told everyone who came along to turn back, that he was under order from the cops. The guy was real careful about staying off the trail. Meanwhile, the bodyguard was climbing down the cliff toward the girl."

"I've met him. Tyrone Handkins."

"Right. Jackson and another deputy, Monasset, got up there before Handkins climbed back up. So they were able to keep him and anyone else from walking on the trail."

"Which way were Glory and Tyrone going?"

"North, from Marlette Lake toward Incline. They didn't have a shuttle car. The bodyguard said they planned to loop back over the mountain and head back to Spooner."

I thought about that. Glory must have been in great shape that she could plan a 20-mile ride at high elevation, and then perform back-to-back concerts.

"Let's just say you did notice something," Minney said. "First thing you'd do is call us, right?"

"Of course."

"I'll talk to Steve," he said. "See if he can wait until noon to take down the crime scene tape."

TWENTY-SEVEN

After lunch, I drove across town to a bike shop.

There were two young men working in the repair area. One was explaining brake design to a customer. The other had a bike frame up in a bike stand so that he could work on the derailleur. The man's hands were covered in black lubricant.

"Afternoon," he said when he saw me. He clicked the shifter, held the pedal and turned the crank. The chain climbed up to the largest sprocket, click by click, and then started back down.

"I'm an investigator, and I'm looking to hire a mountain bike expert," I said.

He stopped and looked at me. "Investigator."

"Yes. Owen McKenna."

"You mean a detective?"

"Yeah."

"Joey Dickson." He held up his blackened hand to show that he couldn't shake. "I guess I'm what you'd call an expert. But I'm slammed here at the shop in August."

"I was hoping to find someone who could go out with me tomorrow morning. Can you give me a referral?"

He resumed turning the crank. "You need a guide?"

"Yes. Someone who can read trail marks and tread patterns. That kind of thing."

He grinned at me. "Like a mountain man who can follow deer tracks, only for mountain bikes?"

"Exactly," I said.

"Cool. A tracker. Well, I wish I was your guy. But to be honest, the guy you want is Wheels."

"Wheels?"

"Wheels Washburn." He wiped his hands on a rag and picked up a well-worn mountain biking magazine. The pages automatically opened to a center photo spread. "Check it out," he said. "Here's Wheels up on Mr. Toad's Wild Ride."

The picture showed a popular trail that runs from Luther Pass down toward South Lake Tahoe. The look on the long-haired guy's face was maniacal glee as he launched off a rock. His bicycle was six feet off the ground. He floated above it.

"He's an awesome rider," Joey said. "Knows the technical stuff, too. Here, I'll write down his number." He scratched out a number on a card. "Only I should kinda warn you about him."

"What's that?"

"He's got this thing where he jerks and grunts. Almost like barking. It's called Tourette's syndrome. Anyway, don't let it bug you. Wheels is a real nice guy. We call him the Tourette tornado."

I got Wheels Washburn on the phone late that afternoon. There was a loud racket in the background.

"Hold on a sec," he shouted. In a moment, the noise slowed and stopped. "Sorry about that. I was running a log splitter." Other than a single grunt his speech sounded normal.

"So you want, like, crime deconstruction based on tread marks," he said after I explained my request to go up to the Flume Trail and look at the place where Glory went off.

I said, "I'm just thinking that if I went up there alone, I'd see a bunch of bike tracks and they wouldn't mean anything. But they might suggest something to you."

"Sherlock o'er the Flume," Wheels said. "Conan Doyle wouldn'ta thunk it, mountain bikes, would he?" His phrasing was interspersed with grunts.

"Maybe not," I said.

"Essay project in college. Conan Doyle and Sherlock. Title was 'Alter Ego, Ergo, Ego Altered?' Don't think the prof bought my thesis. Got an A, though. Then she pressures me about the grad program at UC Irvine. Creative writing. What's it gonna be? Words or wheels? My name is Wheels. What was she thinking?"

"Will you do it?"

"Sure. I was going to ride the Chan, anyway. May the Flume it be instead."

"The Chan?" I said.

"Short for Jackie Chan. A bitchin' ride from the top of Kingsbury down. Gonna get closed because the Forest Service thinks it causes erosion. Bunch of weenies, those guys."

"How much do you charge?"

"To play Sherlock? Enough for dinner at the Cantina?"

"Sounds fair," I said. "Are you free at nine a.m.?"

"Oh," he said. "Late riser? Remember Shakespeare, Ben Franklin, Jimmy Carter, Paul McCartney. Note the premiums that fall to early birdies."

"I was taking it easy on you. McCartney is an early riser?"

"Got me. Good guess, though, doncha think?"

"Seven o'clock, then?"

"Better," he grunted. "Meet at Spooner Lake Campground? You're not a shuttle boy, are you? I always do the loop."

I understood that he meant disdain for anyone who parked a second car near the bottom of Tunnel Creek Road for an easy ride back to Spooner Lake. Instead, he'd ride to the end of the Flume Trail and loop back up and over the mountains above Marlette Lake, riding a much longer and strenuous route.

"Shuttle boy?" I said. "Next thing, you'll be asking if I like classical music and go to museums."

"Please," Wheels said. "I had to read Capote in college. Been watching John Wayne movies ever since."

"Seven it is," I said.

Street and I got take-out Chinese and drove out to Emerald Bay. We parked at the Bayview Trailhead and hiked to the rocky cliff above the west end of Cascade Lake. Even in August, there were enough snow patches in the mountains to keep a steady flow of icy water rushing to Cascade Falls. We sat next to where the water tumbled over the edge. Below us was the indigo oval of Cascade

Lake and behind it the huge blue swath of Tahoe. Spot lapped some water, then lay down next to the stream. He stretched out his head so that his nose was only inches from the flowing water.

"You said you talked to the FBI man today?" Street said as she reached chopsticks into one of the white paper boxes and picked up a Sugar Snap pea. With delicate precision she placed it in her mouth. Spot strained his eyes upward to watch.

"Agent Ramos," I nodded, digging in with my plastic fork. "Same jerk as before." I ate peas and chicken, then forked rice out of the other box. I cranked off the screw cap on a Big House Red, pulled glasses out of my pack and poured. I handed one to Street. "He thinks the killer is a professional who has a thing for flair and variety."

"Meaning?" Street dipped her chopsticks into the rice box and came out with five, maybe six grains. She chewed them carefully. I watched the thin edge of her jaw and the smooth skin of her neck as she swallowed. I didn't understand why the way she ate gave me lascivious thoughts.

"Meaning," I said, "that it would explain why he used the handrail in my office or the bomb on Faith's boat or figured out how to get Glory to ride off the Flume Trail when it would be much more efficient just to shoot us with a rifle."

"Maybe he doesn't like rifles." Street pulled a piece of chicken off the chopsticks with her lips.

Spot gave up watching us. His eyes tracked a floating bug as it went past his nose.

"Maybe. My guess is that he avoids firearms because they are easy to track. Then again, Ramos thought that there was no reason why the killer wouldn't use a rifle if it suited him."

"You're scaring me," Street said.

"I don't mean to do that." I rubbed her thigh. "I'm only saying that the killer's taste for the unusual probably wouldn't be exclusionary. If a rifle was appropriate for a job, he might use it." I put my arm around her shoulders. "I'll be careful."

We ate for a while.

"Do you still think Tyrone hired this guy?"

"Maybe."

Street maneuvered another speck of food onto her chopsticks. "Are you getting enough? I feel like I'm hogging it all."

"Yes, quite the glutton you are." I took the box and ate the rest.

She said, "It sounds like killing is a game for this guy. Like he's not just doing a job for money."

"Could be."

We drank wine and looked out at the scenery.

Street said, "Remember that psychologist you met when the arsonist was lighting the forest fires? The one who did work for the FBI in San Francisco?"

"Yes. George something."

"Morrell," Street said.

"I'm the guy who met him. You recall his name."

"One tends to remember the details leading up to one's kidnapping."

I gave her shoulders another squeeze.

Street shivered. "What was it he said about serial killers?"

"The homicidal trinity," I said. "Many serial killers have a background of firestarting, animal torture and bed-wetting."

"I meant, what is the reason they kill?"

"They don't kill because they want a particular person dead. They kill because it gives them a thrill."

"You think this guy could be like that?"

"No. It would suggest that the victims have no connection to one another. Faith called me about Glory, so that suggests some kind of connection. When I got involved, the killer came after me."

"But this concept of variety and flair would suggest that something about it is fun for him," Street said. "A thrill. That's not how I would imagine the motivations of a paid killer."

I drank the last of the wine.

"Maybe you should call Morrell and ask him," Street said.

On the drive home, we stopped off at Street's insect lab so she could pick up some homework. I poked around while she dug in a file cabinet.

Street often did forensic consulting, taking maggot samples from bodies and using them to make time-of-death estimates. So I usually expected to see some gross-looking bugs at her office. Even so, I was surprised when I looked into a see-through container over on a darkened counter. Inside were very large cockroach specimens. I thought they were dead, and I flipped on a light for a closer look. There was an explosion of movement. I jerked back as they climbed over each other in an attempt to get out of the light.

"I thought the only live bugs you had here were maggots and bark beetles." My breath was short.

"Oh, you found my little darlings. You know the Intro to Entomology class I teach at the community college. Well, one of my students, Theresa something, once told me they had two-inch cockroaches in the apartment where she grew up in San Francisco. I must have seemed doubtful of the size."

"So she dropped by with proof?" I said.

"Yeah. Two days ago. The infamous American Cockroach. Periplaneta americana. Common from Florida to Mexico. And apparently in some less-than-savory buildings in the Bay Area. I can't decide what to do with them."

"Just don't let them out."

Spot and I said goodbye to Street at the door of her condo and headed up the mountain to my cabin. It was 9:30 p.m. when I got Morrell on the phone.

"Sorry to bother you this late," I said after I reminded him that he'd been a consultant to me on the forest fire case.

"No problem. Being retired means that my evening is no longer more precious than my day. Call any time."

"Do you know of the singer named Glory?"

"Yes, I have her third CD, Born Of Jazz. Listened to it twice since I heard about her death."

"I'm looking for her killer."

"I thought her death was an accident."

"It's looking like murder." I went over the events since Faith first called me. When I was done I said, "My assumption is that the man who attacked me with the handrail is the same man who murdered Faith Runyon and Glory. If the FBI is correct, he may be a hired killer. My question is in regard to his motivations."

"I don't mean to sound flip," Morrell said, "but most hired killers are motivated by the money."

"That makes sense. So why would he go to such lengths as using a bomb to blow up Faith's boat, or try to kill me with a handrail? As for Glory's death, we don't yet know why she rode off the cliff. But in any event, a gun is much easier and usually more effective. Why not use it if the goal is the money?"

"I can only speculate," Morrell said. "First, there are the practical reasons, which you've no doubt considered. Bombs destroy evidence. Bicycles going off cliffs look like accidents. A wooden stick is an easy weapon to burn. Then come the impractical reasons, which is to say, the reasons of the psyche. Think of the bus driver who drives too fast, the pilot who likes to push the performance limits of a jet, the cardiac surgeon who tries a daring but unnecessary new technique. All have nothing to do with the supposed reasons they go to work, which is to provide a useful service and get paid for it. Yet, people routinely engage in behavior that by some measures is stupid. This killer may be doing the same thing."

"You don't think this guy is just a thrill-killer?"

"No. The typical serial, thrill-killer is likely to be disconnected enough from reality that we would call him psychotic. He's murdering just for kicks. And his victims are not connected to each other. That doesn't fit this killer. This guy may have been paid to kill both Glory and Faith. And you, for that matter. Or perhaps he was only paid to kill Glory, and his pursuit of you and Faith is merely to cover his tracks."

"So he's seeking variety in his methods just because it makes life more exciting."

"Yes, crass as it sounds."

"Taking risks is universal even if it isn't rational?" I said.

"Yes. In fact, we're starting to discover that our brain isn't organized according to rational principles at all. More and more, it appears that our behavior follows emotional principles. Think how many times you've seen someone do something that appears ineffective or dangerous or needlessly repetitive and you've thought to yourself, 'Why would someone do that? It makes no sense.' The answer is that, viewed through an emotional lens, such behavior may make perfect sense."

"And make the person feel good."

"Or give the person some release. Like scratching an emotional itch."

"Any thoughts on how to find this guy?"

Morrell was silent for a moment. "You don't know why he killed the young prostitute or the singer. But he's after you because you are interfering with his plans." Morrell paused again. "I think the killer will keep coming after you as long as you pursue him. So, if you want to catch him, keep the pressure on and he will present himself, one way or another. But be very careful. He may kill you first. He has obviously been successful in the past."

"I appreciate the information," I said. "If I have more questions about him, can I call you?"

"Please do," Morrell said.

TWENTY-EIGHT

The next morning I was waiting at the Spooner Lake Campground when an old rusted Subaru flew into the lot. I knew it was Wheels when he got out. The guy shook and jerked and twitched. His right foot slapped the ground as he walked.

He came over to me and introduced himself. His long brown hair flipped around a weathered face about 30 years old. He had a thin, hard build and probably weighed 150, 20 pounds less than Spot who stood to the side. Watching. Wary.

"Good of you to come," I said.

"Forgot me double-brimmed cap and me pipe. But sage and discerning me middle names, mate." He saw Spot. "Hello!"

"Wheels, meet Spot."

Spot stood his ground as Wheels jerked his way over to him. The guy obviously knew dogs and, save for the twitching, had mastered the art of approaching a canine. Showing no fear, but also showing no threat, Wheels sidled up to Spot and held out his hand for Spot to sniff. He didn't look Spot in the eyes. "Big guy," he said.

"I can see you know how dogs think," I said.

"Had a Mastiff once. Called him Bull. Bull was a big dog, too. But not as big as this guy."

Wheels left Spot and opened the back of his car. The inside was littered with splinters of wood. Wheels dragged out his mountain bike. "Been splitting and hauling wood," he said as he pulled a piece of bark out of his rear spokes.

I'd expected a gleaming, high-tech bicycle. His machine looked like it'd been dipped in mud. Wheels walked his bike over toward Spot. "Spot, my man," Wheels said. "Ready to run?"

Spot looked at Wheels, then over at me.

"Heeeaaahh!" Wheels screamed into the early morning air and took off, spinning his rear tire as if he'd popped the clutch on a motorcycle. His legs churned, his pedals spun, and he shot up the trail. Spot ran after him. Wheels went past a patch of woody brush, grabbed a dead branch and broke it off as he went by.

"Yo, Dr. Watson!" he shouted at Spot. "I think it's a clue!" He hurled it far off the trail.

Spot ran after it, picked it up and ran back to Wheels. Spot crunched on the stick, and nothing but pieces fell out of his mouth.

The trail to the Flume rose 1100 feet to a crest and then made a short descent to Marlette Lake. On the west side was the ridge that held Marlette Lake in place. Below that was the blue mass of Lake Tahoe looking like an ocean in the mountains.

Back during the heyday of the Comstock Lode in Virginia City, there was a huge demand for logs to shore up the mine tunnels. The mining companies looked with lust on the forests of Tahoe and schemed up ways to get logs from Tahoe to the mines.

A wooden, trough-like flume was built starting from Marlette Lake. Essentially an aqueduct designed to float huge logs, the flume used water from Marlette Lake to carry the logs north along the mountainside to a spot above what is now Incline Village. There, the mountain was narrow enough that they dug a tunnel through it. The flume was extended through the tunnel to the east side of the mountain. From there the flume went down the mountain at a steep angle. The logs slid at high speed down to the Washoe Valley, sometimes with daredevil loggers riding on them.

Wheels and Spot were waiting for me at the beginning of the Flume Trail. Wheels had one foot on a pedal, ready to ride.

"We should walk our bikes off to the side of the trail so we don't mess up the tracks," I said.

"But the, ah, accident was close to a half mile from here, so we can ride the first part, right?"

"How do you know where it happened?"

Wheels hesitated. "Lemme see. Heard about it when the news first went around. Bunch of us mountain bikers were talking about it. I can ask Spider, see if he remembers."

"Could you call him tonight?"

His eyes glanced out at Tahoe. "Sure. Don't see why not."

We walked our bicycles along the narrow trail, and watched for the three streamers that marked the place where Glory went off.

"Let's stop here," I said when I saw them 50 yards ahead.

We leaned our bicycles against a boulder. I took hold of Spot's collar, and we walked down the path, carefully stepping on the tiny edge to the side of the worn trail. Wheels followed.

"What do you want me to look for?" he said, grunting. Now that we were off our bikes I heard his right foot flopping.

"Just tell me what you see."

We came to a line of logs that had been placed to divert bike riders to the mountain side of the trail. Just inside the logs was crime scene tape marking a long, narrow portion of the trail.

Wheels bent over and studied the trail. "First thing I see is a Velociraptor. Makes a distinctive track in soft dirt. The marks won't hold in sand, but then nothing does." He pointed. "The Velociraptor's been obscured by another track that came later. Can't tell what it is. Lot of tires like that."

"Why do some leave recognizable marks and others don't?"

"Knobbies are just like car tires that way. If the tread is bold and unusual in its shape, then you can tell what it is by the tracks. With less bold tread, it gets harder to tell." Wheels walked along the side of the trail, studying the dirt.

He made a grunting noise and pointed. "Here's another one. El Gato markings peeking out from under other tracks."

I turned and resumed walking. Spot was on my left. If my dog felt any qualms about being on the edge of the drop-off, he didn't telegraph it.

When we were 20 yards away from the three plastic ribbons, I stopped and told Spot to sit. I pulled his leash out of my pocket, hooked it from his collar to a skinny Lodgepole pine that grew where the ground dropped away toward Lake Tahoe. "Sorry, Spot, but I can't have you pawing up the trail."

"I'll go on ahead and check it out," Wheels said. He headed down the edge of the trail, careful to not step in the tracks.

Spot sat watching Wheels, his ears perked up high.

When I got to Wheels, he was squatting down on his haunches, twenty feet before the three ribbons. I let him look at the dirt uninterrupted. He stood, walked slowly alongside the trail toward the ribbons, squatted down again. Next, he about-faced and traced his way back. He went past me almost to Spot.

Wheels twitched and flopped his foot. He scowled at the dirt. I worried that his flopping gate would mark up the trail, but he remained off to the side. Soon, he turned and came back. "Trail is better back by your dog. It gets worse where she went off. More sand. Doesn't want to hold a tread mark." He got to the ribbons and grunted. "But here you can see a bit of El Gato mark. Goes at an angle, right off the trail into the air." He looked down over the drop-off and winced. "Definitely not a good place to go off."

Wheels turned back toward me. "So we know she had the El Gato tires. The guy followed on Velociraptors."

"What makes you think he followed? Maybe he went before her on something that doesn't make a track."

Wheels shook his head. "Look here." He pointed to the trail just past the point where Glory went off. "The Velociraptor marks go into a skid, just like what would happen if she were in front and suddenly went off. He would hit his brakes."

"But the Velociraptor tracks go past the point where the El Gato marks go off the cliff?"

"Yeah."

"Doesn't that seem strange? If I were riding behind someone who went off the cliff, I'd stop immediately."

"You'd *brake* immediately," Wheels said. "But if you were going fast, you'd skid for moment before you came to a stop."

"You are presuming they were going fast," I said.

"Not presuming. Come back here, I'll show you."

Wheels walked back down the side of the trail. He stopped and pointed to a depression in the trail. "They gapped this dip, so they were obviously booking."

"Gapped the dip?"

"Yeah," he grunted. "Their tread marks stop at the edge of the dip and then reconnect on the other side. Four feet through the air. Means they jumped up with their bikes as they approached the dip and they were going fast enough to completely gap it. Not a lotta girls do that. She must have been hot on her wheels. She went first. Then her boyfriend followed."

"Her bodyguard. Who said he was her boyfriend?"

Wheels fidgeted, but I couldn't tell whether from nervousness or from Tourettes. "Boyfriend? Just a figure of speech, I guess."

"No one said that to you?"

He frowned, thinking. His left eye blinked and his left cheek twitched. "Like I said, Spider and the boys were talking about her death and how it happened. Maybe one of them referred to the guy as her boyfriend. But I'm not sure. Anyway, you can rule him out as a murderer."

"You can tell that from tire marks?"

"'Course. Her tracks swerve before she went off the cliff. Probably took a good blow on her right side. His tracks show that he was riding behind her, not on her side. He couldn't have delivered the blow."

"You said he was close behind, based on him going past where she went off before he was able to stop."

"Right," Wheels said.

"Then couldn't he have reached out and struck her rear tire? Or swung a stick at her shoulder?"

"Sure, but I don't think that would be sufficient to drive her off the trail." Wheels was shaking his head. "A fast-moving bike has a lot of gyroscopic stability in the rotating wheels. The way her tracks suddenly careen to the side suggest the kind of blow you could only get from something else."

"Like a person jumping out and pushing her?"

"Yeah."

"Except," I said, "that the bodyguard would have seen such a person."

"Quite the scenario, eh?" Wheels grunted. "Bodyguard didn't push her, and didn't see anyone else push her, either. So what made her go off the cliff?"

I looked down at the drop-off. The best answer I could think of was that Tyrone hired someone else to come up the trail in advance of their ride and run out at the precise moment to give Glory a shove. I walked over to the place where it would have had to happen, squatted down and pointed at the tracks. "This is where the El Gato tires first swerved before she went off?"

"Yeah." Wheels squatted next to me. "It's an S-shape. Here and here."

I looked at the trail.

Wheels knew what I was thinking. He said, "If someone ran out from those trees and pushed her, they'd leave tracks. Unless they got a branch and rubbed them out, huh?"

I couldn't see any marks to the side of the trail, footprints or erasure marks. The trees on the mountain side of the trail were a short distance away. I ducked under the stiff, scratchy branches of red firs, bent down and crawled into a little space that was darkened by the thick canopy. A red squirrel screamed at me from somewhere above my head.

I heard Spot whine as I waited for my eyes to adjust. The depression under the trees was a perfect hiding place. It was surrounded by drooping branches, yet had several sight-lines to the Flume Trail. The ground looked as if something, a deer or bear or maybe a human had spent some time lying in the dirt. I scanned the ground looking for a boot imprint or cigarette butt or Jim Bowie knife. There was nothing.

"Hello?" Wheels called out. "You lost?"

I crawled back out from under the thick, heavy boughs.

TWENTY-NINE

That night I thought of pulling out some candles and making Street a romantic dinner. She rarely has her cell phone on, so I tried both her condo and her lab. I got her machines at both. Maybe she was in transit between the two.

I opened a Silver Rose cab in case she came to join me and poured myself a glass to drink now in case she didn't. I made a teriyaki stir fry. Spot was lying on the rug in front of the woodstove as if it were fired up on a January night instead of sitting cold during the relative heat of August. Street still hadn't called back when the stir fry was ready, so I served it up. Spot lifted his head and sniffed the air. His ears were perked up high and taut. One of them flicked toward the window, then turned back.

I pointed to his food bowl which I'd earlier filled to the rim with dog food. "Mmmm!" I said. "Tantalizing treat of savory sawdust! Compressed into delicious bite-sized nuggets!"

Spot looked at me, ears relaxing and eyes drooping with disappointment. He glanced toward the microwave, then shifted into a peculiar position he favors, front leg curled, elbow tucked under. He stuck his snout into the crook of his wrist, nose jammed straight into the rug.

His deep breathing became forced, sucking air through the rug fibers. I tried to ignore him as I ate. But his breathing became more labored until I felt out of breath just listening to it.

Finally, I couldn't take it any longer. "Spot. Stop it." He kept up the sucking sound. "Spot!" He lifted his head and looked at me with sad eyes. His ears perked up again. But this time they swiveled sideways.

Spot swung his head around, suddenly alert, hearing something outside the cabin.

I was about to speak when he jumped to his feet, a deep rumble in his chest. He trotted to the big window that faces the deck. Because the view falls off to the lake a thousand feet below I have no blinds there. Spot growled louder. I could see nothing in the black glass other than his reflection.

The phone rang. I reached it off the kitchen wall.

"Hello?" I said as Spot turned and ran to the window in the front wall of the cabin. I'd shut the blinds on that one when we came home. Spot forcefully nosed the blinds aside, bending the strips to get to the glass, although I doubted that he could see out at the black night any better than I could.

The voice on the other end of the phone made my skin prick up into goose bumps. "You've really irritated me, McKenna." It was a non-human voice, synthetic and metallic. "Now it's time for your punishment."

I shouted. "SPOT! COME! GET AWAY FROM THE..."

The window exploded.

Spot screamed. Sparks flew from the woodstove as a round from a high-velocity rifle struck the iron and ricocheted into one of the kitchen cabinets. My old police instincts took over. I dove to the floor, my hand flicking at the kitchen light switch as I dropped the phone.

Spot was still turning sideways from the impact. He was out of balance and went down onto his rear. My wine glass seemed to fall in slow-motion. It hit the floor after I did and shattered. I belly-crawled toward the living room light switch. Pieces of window glass glinted on the floor. A mist of glass dust hung in the air. Wine had splashed across the room. But the shade of color was off. I realized it was Spot's blood. I reached up and turned off the light switch.

Spot had gone silent. "Spot! You okay?" I said, my throat so dry that my words were a rasp.

The only sound in the dark cabin was his wheezing breath. I scurried on my hands and knees over to him. He pushed up off of the floor, his legs quivering. "Come into the bathroom," I said, pulling on his collar. I got him into the bathroom and shut the door. There is a night light that stays on. In the dim glow of the tiny light I could see that the bullet had creased Spot's side. It was an ugly eight-inch gash down the side of his back that parted fur and flesh like a farmer's plow. There was no pulsing from a severed artery, but blood flowed profusely. I had to slow the bleeding, or he'd go into shock.

"Stay here," I said. Spot sat still, his front legs spread wide and shaking violently. His eyes were dazed.

I scrambled on hands and knees through the dark to the kitchen. The phone dangled on its cord. I pressed the button several times, but got no dial tone. The caller was still on the other end. I hung it up. My cell was off and would take too long to boot up.

The roll of duct tape was in a drawer. Paper towels were on the counter. Back in the bathroom, I folded several towels into a narrow strip and laid it along Spot's wound. He cried. I covered the towels with two strips of duct tape. Blood had soaked the fur below the wound and the tape wouldn't stick. I ran three loops of tape all the way around his chest. It would be hard for him to breathe, but it would compress the wound.

Spot looked at me, alarm and worry in his eyes. He needed surgery and plenty of stitches, but this was going to have to suffice for now.

It's difficult to judge a shooter's position when you're being shot at, but my cop's sense told me he was up my neighbors' communal driveway.

Bandaging Spot had taken long enough that the shooter could have come up to the cabin. He could be waiting just out the front door or out on the deck. Maybe I could make him think I was staying inside.

There was a broom in the closet nook. I draped a towel over the bristles. With my back against the heavy log wall, I reached out with the broom and pushed aside the window blinds. Nothing happened. Maybe the ambient light from Mrs. Duchamp's yard light wasn't enough to illuminate the moving towel. I moved it some more.

The next shot came with frightening precision as if the shooter had a night scope. The round blew through the towel-covered broom. It exploded the floor lamp by the rocker and thudded into the log wall above the woodstove.

My breath was short. A shooter at night is like a punch in the gut. I struggled to breathe.

I grabbed my cell phone and pen light and hustled Spot out the back door. His movements were slow and stiff. Blood ran out from under the duct tape that encircled his chest.

We headed for the dark forest behind my cabin. The forest fire burn from the year before left us exposed in the dull moonlight that was coming through a cloud bank to the west. I ran through the open burn. Spot lagged behind. He whimpered. On the far side of the burn, we plunged into dense blackness under the pine and fir. I knew the path well and followed it by instinct into the forest.

The trail went down at a shallow angle. It followed the contours of the land until it reconnected with the communal driveway several hundred yards below my cabin. I stopped before the drive and touched Spot on the nose to signal silence. The shooter may already have checked the cabin and discovered me gone. He could be walking down the drive, looking through night-vision goggles, waiting for us to step out.

Spot's left front leg shook. His ears were down and back. He telegraphed none of his usual power. He was weak from the trauma of the gunshot and the loss of blood.

I took his collar and jogged to the drive, dragging him with me. We sprinted across what felt like a flood-lit stage, and ran into the forest on the other side. Spot limped.

No shots were fired.

When we were out of range from anybody listening, I turned on the cell, dialed Street's numbers and left messages.

"Street, sweetheart. Someone is after me, and I'm concerned they may come after you. You should get in your car and leave. Don't answer the door and don't let anyone stop you in your car. Try to get Diamond or Mallory on your cell. Go to one of the hotels and check in. Stay there until I can reach you."

I hung up and called Diamond.

"What you got?" he said.

"A shooter at my cabin. Missed me, but winged Spot pretty bad. He's got a deep groove in his flesh. We got out the back door. We're on the bike trail that traverses the mountain to the north."

"Okay, hold that," Diamond said. I heard him talking on his radio, the radio he wasn't supposed to be using, telling dispatch to send deputies up to my cabin although we both knew the shooter would be gone.

"I'm back," Diamond said. "What's your plan?"

"I need to get Spot to Doc Siker fast. Can you pick me up?"

"Where?"

"This trail goes down at a slight angle and intersects Highway Fifty just south of Glenbrook. It'll take me awhile to walk it in the dark. Give me an hour. If you come along slowly with your turn signal on, I'll know it's you. I'll give you three flashes on my penlight."

THIRTY

Spot and I were in the trees just off the highway when Diamond came along in his pickup, his feeble yellow turn signal flashing.

I hit the button on the penlight. He pulled over and jumped out. Spot was too weak or in too much pain to climb into the pickup. Diamond helped me get him up into the seat, lying on his right side. I got in, then pulled him over my lap so Diamond could get in behind the wheel. We three packed the seat wall-to-wall.

Diamond said, "I called Doc Siker and asked if he could work on Spot down at Solomon Reed's place. Safer to get you and your hound out of the Tahoe Basin."

"Siker okay with that?"

"Yeah. He says the equipment for horses and cows is a little different, but the procedures are the same. He'll meet us there."

Diamond headed over Spooner Summit, then coasted down the long slope toward the glittering lights of Carson City 3000 feet below.

"I got a phone call right before the shooting," I said.

"From the shooter?"

"Yeah." I told Diamond what the caller said and tried to describe the strange voice quality.

"A computer voice?"

"No. Less real."

"Male?"

"No. Not female, either. Medium high, metallic sounding."

"Like a robot in a sci-fi movie?"

"Exactly."

"Hard to figure it out," Diamond said. "The shooter is outside your cabin, calls you on his cell and what, plays a tape recording of a robot voice into the phone just before he shoots?"

"Or else there were two people."

"Could the caller have a kazoo in his mouth as he spoke? Or something that would buzz like waxed paper?"

"I don't think so. The sound was more synthetic," I said.

We got to the bottom of the desert valley, turned south toward Minden and Gardnerville and eventually turned into a dark parking lot in front of a building with blue metal siding. A small sign said Solomon Reed, Large Animal Veterinary Hospital.

Dick Siker's SUV was already parked by the door.

I opened the door and squeezed out from under Spot. He cried.

I heard a door open and turned to see Dick Siker approaching. "Owen. Diamond," he said. He came around to look in on Spot. "Duct tape," he muttered.

Spot looked up at the words, concern on his face.

"Going to be fun getting duct tape off, huh, Spot?" Dick leaned into the pickup and ran his hands over Spot, checking those things that vets check.

Spot looked worried.

Dick turned on a flashlight, lifted up Spot's jowls, pressed on his gums and watched the color slowly return. He placed a stethoscope on Spot's chest and listened. "He's pale, but he's breathing okay." Dick gestured toward the duct tape. "Last time I tried to remove a bandage like that it was packing tape wrapped around the leg of a Jack Russell terrier. Almost lost a couple fingers that day. This is going to be harder to get off. Duct tape bonds to fur."

"I was in a hurry," I said.

"So I see. Let me go get a sedative."

He went inside and returned with a syringe. Spot didn't budge as Dick, working under the pickup's dome light, found a place to make the injection.

Five minutes later, Spot was placid, and the three of us walked him inside and helped him up onto a table. Doc Siker began to try to pull the duck tape off. It didn't come. He pulled harder. A corner came loose along with the ripping sound of hair pulling out. Spot cried again.

"Okay," Dick said. "We'll go to plan B. Have to be careful, though, when I get to the wound. You think it is pretty much centered under the tape?"

"Not sure," I said. "It was dark. A guy was shooting at us."

"I understand. You better hold Spot's head."

I came around the table and held Spot while Dick started working a hair clipper under the edge of the duct tape. Spot cried louder. As soon as a portion of the tape was loosened, Dick cut it off and held it out for Spot to smell.

"See, boy? Nothing to be alarmed at."

Spot sniffed it, then turned away. He cried out twice more as Dick worked with the clipper. Dick gradually worked the tape, and the blood-soaked paper towel underneath it, free.

"Ouch," Dick said when he saw the wound. "Sorry, Spot, but the duct tape was the easy part. You're not going to like me working on this at all. Owen, maybe you should hold this guy's head a little tighter. Never know when he gets hungry for my arm."

I held Spot's head while Dick washed the wound and applied disinfectant. He injected anesthetic in several places, then hooked up an IV. In another five minutes, he began stitching. Despite the sedative and numbing injections, Spot squirmed. Dick used a big needle and pulled coarse thread through my dog's hide like he was stitching the thick leather on a baseball glove. Maybe that was what made us talk about baseball in our effort to sound calm for Spot.

Our conversation moved from the Yankees to the Dodgers and then to Sandy Koufax and whether he was merely the best pitcher of his day or the greatest pitcher ever. By the time we'd decided on the latter, Dick had made repairs to Spot's muscle down to his rib bones, and Spot sported more stitches over his shaved hide than a baseball.

When we were done, we discussed whether or not I should leave Spot at the vet hospital. Dick said I could take him, but only if I were very careful of the wound and made certain that Spot got plenty to eat and drink. He stressed that Spot had lost significant blood and would take a long time to heal. I thanked Dick and made myself a mental note to include some fine wine when I paid the bill.

Diamond and I got Spot back into the pickup.

"Where to?" Diamond said.

"We need a place to stay."

"Hotels don't like dogs," Diamond said. "The guy could find you if you stayed in a motel."

"If he's determined," I said.

My cell phone rang. I looked at Diamond as I answered it.

"Hello?" I said.

"I have your cell number, too," the robot voice said.

I motioned to Diamond and leaned toward him so he could put his ear next to mine and listen in.

I said, "I'm going to nail your ass to the wall."

The synthetic voice made a witch-like cackle. "Oh, that's good, McKenna. You're a funny guy to say that when I own your future. I own your dog's future, too, and your girlfriend's future." The voice cackled again, a harsh, chattering laugh that rose to a crescendo before the caller hung up.

I dialed Street's numbers again. She answered her cell. "Owen, I got your message. What happened?" She sounded frantic.

I explained about Spot.

"Spot got shot?!"

"He's okay. Dick Siker stitched him up. Where are you?"

"I checked into Caesars."

"Good. Be very careful. Don't answer your door for anyone you don't know. Not even room service."

"You think I'm really in danger?" she asked.

"I don't want to take any chances. I had a caller. He referred to my girlfriend. I don't know if he would actually come after you, but he's obviously dangerous."

"Okay, I'll stay here until you think otherwise."

"Sorry," I said. "Not what you bargained for, being with me."

"You're worth it. Spot, too. Where will you stay?"

"I'll figure out something."

We spoke for some time. Eventually, she calmed. I reassured her that Spot and I would be safe.

After we hung up, I set my phone on the dashboard.

"Dude on the phone was creepy," Diamond said.

We sat in silence for a moment.

"Could give a guy bad dreams," he said.

"Only if a guy has a place to sleep," I said.

"You need to go into hiding."

"Right. In a place where this guy would be reluctant to break into if he found out."

There was a pause.

"Like a sheriff's deputy's house," Diamond said.

"He wouldn't even know I was there."

"But if he did..." Diamond trailed off.

"Back in San Francisco we had a saying, 'Shoot a cop, start a war.' This guy probably doesn't want a war."

Diamond started the pickup and turned south toward Minden. We stopped at a supermarket where I bought several cans of dog food. Then we went to Diamond's house. It was off a little street that was off another little street.

Diamond pulled into a narrow driveway that ran between a thick hedge and the side of his small, stucco house. Diamond's backyard was dark and private. He turned behind the house, parked under a cottonwood tree and next to a car wrapped in a tarp.

I gestured toward the tarp. "Is that your Karmann Ghia?"

Diamond nodded. "The terror of Carson Valley. Kids in their Camaros hide when I go cruising in the Orange Flame."

Diamond let us in the back door. He showed Spot a thick rug that lay on top of the living room carpet. Spot carefully lowered himself down onto his right side so the wound on the left faced up.

I pet his head. "You want some dinner?"

Spot ignored me. Diamond opened a can, scooped some food out onto a plate and put it in front of Spot's nose. He moaned and turned his head away.

"Okay, maybe later," I said.

"Your Jeep is at your cabin," Diamond said as he handed me a Pacifico beer. "Probably the shooter knows what it looks like. You can use the Orange Flame if you want."

"How's it running?"

"Like a border jumper trying to make it to Tucson before dawn."

"Last I recall, it was up on blocks."

"I had to weld in a patch for part of the floor pan that rusted away," Diamond said. He looked at me like he was sizing up my length. "Only problem is, you'll have to slouch. And don't stomp on the brake or your foot may go through my floor repair and hit the road." Diamond picked up his radio. "Let me see what's happening at your cabin."

He spoke for some time, then turned to me. "Rockport and Linetco and a couple other deputies are about done up there. They didn't find anything but the mess. They're short on lights, so they'll look for shell casings in the morning. Rockport is coming down to the valley and is wondering if you want anything."

"Can he bring the puzzle?"

Diamond relayed my request and turned off the radio.

"You think the shooter will try to get at me through Street?" I said.

"Like during the forest fires? Maybe. But kidnapping is messy business and leaves lots of evidence. My guess is he'll keep a low profile. A single killshot to your head when you are alone is the best way to get you."

"Reassuring," I said.

Diamond nodded. He got out some tortillas, black beans, salsa, cheddar cheese and ground beef. He went to work shredding the cheese while the ground beef browned on the stove. "You think the shooter had a night scope?"

"Yeah. The lights were on in my cabin when the first shot came. But the second shot came with the lights off. I moved a broom in front of the window. The shot was accurate."

I drank some beer.

Diamond was rolling enchiladas. "Even with a good night scope, you'd have to be a trained shooter to make a shot at night," he said.

"Did Rockport ever serve in the military?"

Diamond shook his head. "Don't know. Could be. He's into guns." He slid the enchiladas into the oven.

"What do you mean? He collects them?"

"I don't know that he collects them. But he knows all about weapons. He talks about them. Zip guns, assault rifles, exotics. Ammunition, too. Why? You think he's a candidate for the shooter?"

"Crossed my mind."

"Wonder if he owns a ski mask," Diamond said.

"Right size," I said. "Athletic, too. Probably eats garlic."

"Lot of people eat garlic."

"Does he smoke?"

"No," Diamond said.

"Of course, if this guy is as clever as Agent Ramos says, he probably puffed on a cigarette right before he came to beat me up, just on the off-chance that I would survive and think my attacker was a smoker. Any chance Rockport has a dark van?" I said.

"Actually, he does have a van, but it is gray."

"Gray could look dark at night."

"Maybe," Diamond said.

Diamond pulled out the enchiladas and set them on the table. He got out two more beers and we ate. The food was delicious. "Maybe Spot would prefer this over that canned stuff," he said.

I cut off a bit and mixed it into the uneaten dog food. Spot didn't inhale it with his usual gusto, but he ate.

My cell phone rang. It was Mallory. "Some excitement at the homestead?" he said.

"Yeah," I said.

"You okay?"

"I am. But Spot's got a bad groove on him."

"You gonna go back to carrying a gun?"

"I'm at Diamond's. He's got one."

"You mean, he's got a Glock. That ain't a real gun," Mallory said. "It's plastic. Combat Tupperware."

"It'll have to do," I said.

"Okay, but somebody wants you bad. Keep a low profile."

"Yes, commander."

He hung up.

I drank some beer. "Mallory calls your gun combat Tupperware," I said.

Diamond grunted. "He thinks if the antecedents to modern firearms are metallic, then modern firearms should be, too. I think Mallory would look good in a white wig and knickers."

"Good point," I said.

"Besides, my nine's got a metal barrel. Although, someday they'll modernize that."

Diamond and I moved to the living room. Diamond took the big arm chair near Spot and let his arm dangle down so his hand could rest on Spot's head. I sat on the couch. We set the case of beer between us. There was a knock at the door. Diamond got up and opened it.

Rockport stood there holding the puzzle and the bag with the green pieces of paper. He grinned at us, every one of his big teeth visible. "First, it's gunfire up on the mountain," he said. "Now it's a jig-saw puzzle party. Hard to keep up with you guys."

"Want to come in for a beer?" Diamond said.

"No thanks. Bedtime for me. I better be going."

"Thanks for dropping off the puzzle," I said.

"You're welcome." He stopped as he was leaving and turned back toward Spot. "How's your dog?"

"He'll live."

"That's good. The shooter was probably aiming at you, not your hound, don't you think?" Rockport grinned and left.

I spread puzzle pieces out on the coffee table.

"At least the guy trying to kill you hasn't gone after Street," Diamond said as he pawed over the green pieces of paper. "Suggests he might not want to kill me, either."

"I wouldn't think so," I said.

"But I could get caught in the crossfire."

I drank more beer, dark thoughts intruding. "If he'd been up on the highway, watching the right stretch, he might have seen you pick me up."

Diamond looked at me.

"In which case," I said, "he could have followed us to the vet hospital and then here, to your house."

"But you said, 'Shoot a cop, start a war?' Just the thought would attenuate bad boy behavior, eh?"

"Yeah," I said. "First thing that came to mind. Attenuate."

Diamond looked at the puzzle pieces. He grabbed one out of the pile. "Look at this. It goes right here. And here's another. I thought you said this was difficult."

"It is. But I've been concentrating on the hard ones so you could find the easy ones."

"Of course," Diamond said.

"Have you ever thought about intruders?" I said as I found a piece, this one brown with the letters 'CL' on it.

"In this little hamlet," Diamond said, looking around at the house, his eyes pausing on the two narrow, double-hung windows near where we were sitting. The windows had white, plastic roller shades pulled down to the sill. There was a narrow slit between the shades and the window frames where I could see black window glass. The spaces weren't wide enough to see much from the outside. But even from a distance you could maybe tell where people were sitting.

I picked up an empty beer bottle, walked over and set it on the window sill. The sill was narrow and the bottle just barely balanced in place. But it did a good job of holding the shade close to the window frame, making it so no one could see in. I used another bottle on the other side of the shade, then did the same on the other window.

I glanced across to the kitchen where tiny slits were visible on either side of those window shades. "Would it be paranoid to put bottles on all the window sills in the house?" I said.

Diamond shrugged and fitted another piece of green paper onto the puzzle. "In Mexico, the rich people build walls with broken glass embedded along the top. Maybe they know something."

"You're not rich," I said.

"So bottles on the sills is the next best thing?"

"How many windows does this house have?" I said.

Diamond looked into space and counted. Then he looked at the empty beer bottles scattered around. "We'd have to drink some more beer."

I pulled two more bottles out of the case and handed one to Diamond. "Good to have a mission."

We did our best to produce empties. Much of the time we sat in silence, working on the puzzle. It had grown to an oblong shape about six by nine inches, perforated by several holes. There were light green areas surrounded by darker areas, also green. The one brown piece looked like it had a hard edge, as if it were a portion of a building out on a field.

I said, "I was thinking about Violet Verona and your round hitting her little girl's doll. Remember you were saying you thought it was fishy?"

"Yeah."

"You think Rockport has somehow manipulated that? If not the round in the doll, then the aftermath?"

Diamond was quiet for a minute. "He's ambitious. Told me once he wants to be sheriff some day. I remember when we got the results from the exams. He was pretty bent out of shape at coming in number two."

"With you number one."

"Yeah."

"If Rockport is unethical, he might try to screw your promotion."

Diamond sipped some beer.

"He could also be doing some muscle work on the side," I said. "If so, he'd have some money to show for it, right? Notice any extravagance on his part? A new car? Coke habit?"

Diamond made a slow shake with his head. "More I think about Rockport, he's so earnest and focused that I can't see him for it. It's like he really wants to be perfect. Everything with him is just so. Kind of guy who irons his jeans. He gets what he wants. He'll probably make sergeant now that I'm out of the way. Probably be sheriff one day, too."

We were quiet some more, drinking, working on the puzzle. Diamond had assembled a small sub-group. He suddenly saw how it fit into the main group. I helped him tape it in place.

"You know what it looks like," I said. "A golf course."

"You're right. This brown thing could be the clubhouse. Would explain the letters CL."

"The course is shaped like a mitten," I said.

"Yeah. Like the state of Michigan," Diamond said.

We kept working and drinking. In time it became clear that it was, in fact, a drawing of a golf course. It had nine holes, an assortment of sand traps, a clubhouse and many houses scattered throughout.

"You think this is what Faith Runyon wanted to show you?" Diamond said.

"I don't know. Doesn't seem like anyone would kill her to keep her from showing me a golf course."

We kept sorting the pieces, trying to fill in the many gaps. We drank more beer.

"Big mistake, squeezing off that round," Diamond said.

"You made the best decision you could at the time," I said.

"Still a big mistake. But then you know how that works." Diamond's voice was thick.

"Yeah," I said, trying not to think about the worst moment of my life.

"I coulda hit that girl."

"No, Diamond, don't think that way. You said no one was nearby. Just you and the guy in the mask. He had a handrail, looked like a sawed-off. It was a freak ricochet."

"Freak or not, I hit the doll. I coulda hit Violet's girl." Diamond leaned forward, elbows on his knees, beer bottle hanging from a curve of forefinger. "It was a terrible thing to do. Makes me wonder what kind of guy I am."

"Don't focus on it," I said. "A capacity for self-critique is a good thing, but you want to keep it in check."

Diamond swigged beer. "Nietzsche said the most contemptible man is one who can't ever feel self-contempt. So I should be glad, huh?" In the dark I could see the glint of tears in his eyes. "But what if I'd hit the girl, Owen? What then?"

I knew the answer but kept my mouth shut.

Later, I took Spot out for fresh air. The desert had cooled and the sweet scent of sage wafted through the neighborhood. Spot walked stiffly, favoring his left front leg. Dick Siker hadn't said anything about whether there could be nerve damage. He'd only mentioned that Spot wouldn't like breathing for the next month or so, and that the pain that accompanied chest expansion would worsen over the next few days.

I watched for any sign of a murderous rifleman, but saw no one.

Diamond had gone to bed by the time I got back. Spot and I were staying upstairs in the narrow, attic bedroom. Spot didn't like climbing the steep stairs.

There were two gable dormers with a window in each. I snugged up the shades with more beer bottles and put my clothes on a small wooden chair.

It took a long time for me to doze, lying there in a place that seemed vulnerable. Worse, I made Diamond vulnerable just by my presence.

I was dreaming about Turner being tied to the mast when the first beer bottle fell.

THIRTY-ONE

I sat up fast. My breath came in short gasps.
          Spot growled.

"No, Spot!" I whispered. I swung my feet out of bed, reached out and put my open palm on his nose. He tried to jerk to his feet, but was slowed by pain. A low growl came from his throat. I tapped my palm against his nose again. The rumble stopped, but the vibration in his body continued.

Once again, I rued my decision to give up guns. But just as quickly, I realized that the intruder could be a kid. Better to be helpless against an armed man than to risk that again.

I didn't know where the bottle had fallen, but I thought it was downstairs. I was about to head down when I stopped. If I could get outside from one of the upstairs windows, I could have surprise on my side.

The roof shingles were too rough for bare skin, so I pulled on my pants and shoes. I was reaching to remove the beer bottles from one of the windows when I sensed movement outside.

I froze and waited. The shade was dark, but a tiny bit of light came in where the beer bottles held the shade against the window frame. Something moved. A shadow on the roof, just outside the dormer window.

I stepped back, grabbed the wooden chair and took two fast steps toward the glass. The chair crashed through the glass. I kept up the speed, my upper body going through the window.

The chair hit a man, hard to his middle. The guy made a high-pitched grunt. I gave the chair a final heave as my thighs hit the wall under the window. The intruder went down the roof backward. A pistol arced up and back as the man rolled, scrambling to grab onto the edge of the roof.

Gunfire erupted from downstairs. A torrent of angry Spanish. More gunshots, more Spanish.

The man rolling down the roof couldn't get a grip. His shirt caught on the gutter and ripped. He went off the roof and fell to the ground.

Two weapons fired downstairs. Booming cracks shook the neighborhood. Barking erupted from a dozen dogs at once.

It stopped as fast as it started. I heard movement out toward the back of the dark yard. The fence gate opened and someone yelled 'hurry' in a rough whisper.

"Diamond!" I called out.

"I'm okay!" he yelled back. "You?"

"Okay," I said as I ran down the stairs.

Diamond squatted in the hallway, his legs and bare feet dark brown under white boxers. He held his Glock up toward the kitchen windows.

"I think they left," I whispered.

Holding his gun with one hand, Diamond grabbed his radio off the kitchen counter, called in and gave them the details.

"My guy ran," he said when he clicked off the radio. His voice was a hiss of anger. "You had one upstairs?"

"Yeah. Fell off the roof into the side yard."

Diamond went out the kitchen door, both hands holding his gun. Spot and I went out the front door. We stayed against the house. I peeked around the house's front corner and waited while Diamond came around the back corner.

The yard was empty. In the distance, an engine started up and a vehicle raced away.

"The roof guy had a pistol," I said. "It went into the air and fell toward where you're standing."

Diamond looked around at the dark grass. "I'll turn on the lights when we get some backup."

"You got off, what, six or seven rounds?"

"Six," Diamond said. "Which meant he got off four."

I was thinking four at the same time Diamond said it. Like many cops, my subconscious tallies gunfire automatically, something I acquired at the range when I was at the academy.

"Where'd the bottle fall?"

"Kitchen window. Guy broke the glass. Next thing I knew, you were destroying my upstairs." Diamond was pacing, fast angry steps. "What'd you do, kick through the upstairs wall?"

"Chair through the window," I said.

Diamond looked at me. "American dream for a brown boy is first get your citizenship, then buy a house. I finally got both. Now you're ripping my house apart. Perps are shooting it full of holes. I wanted to make sergeant by my birthday, but after the shooting review board finishes my inquisition, they'll probably revoke my citizenship." He turned his head and spit. I'd never seen Diamond spit.

"I don't think they can do that," I said. "You get a look at either of them?"

"No. I was ready when the guy busted through the kitchen window. I fired a warning shot into the kitchen ceiling. He returned fire, so I aimed at him. He moved to the side, poked his gun back in the window. I fired at the wall by the stove, hoping my round had enough punch to get him on the other side. But he still reached in and fired in at me. I kept shooting and he finally ran off. But I never saw his face. Sonofabitch."

"I didn't see the guy on the roof, either."

Sirens came from two different directions, stimulating more dog barking, then finally overwhelming the dogs.

It took three hours to complete official business, including a search of the yard and alley, which did not turn up a handgun or shell casings. I didn't know Douglas County had so many deputies, red-faced middle-aged guys with thick chests and thicker stomachs, young, eager men with trim middles and hard arms and shoulders. Rockport was one of them. He was quiet and efficient as he gathered evidence. The sheriff was there as well. Shoot at one of them, they all rally round. Even if the guy being shot at is a Mexican on administrative leave.

They retrieved slugs from walls while other deputies double and triple-searched the yard and surrounding area.

By the time Diamond and I were alone again, it was dawn.

"Back to bed?" I said.

"Being a victim of attempted murder makes me want to take a nap, sure." He was pacing again. I'd never seen him so mad.

"I could make some breakfast," I said. "Leftover enchiladas?"

Diamond was inspecting bullet holes in his wall. "Mi casa, my castle!" He smacked the wall with the palm of his hand.

I heated up the leftovers in the microwave. Diamond cut off a chunk with a fork and blew on it to cool it off.

"You've got some focused canine attention trained on you," I said, trying to reduce the tension.

"To be expected with a Great Dane and an enchilada in the same room." He tossed it to Spot.

We ate, not mentioning again what had happened. At 8:00 a.m., Diamond handed me the keys to the Karmann Ghia that was under the tarp in the backyard. I understood that he'd rather I leave in his beloved sports car than stay and put him and his beloved house at further risk. "I gotta go," Diamond said.

"Not to work, Diamond? You'll make things a lot worse."

"I could spend my day interviewing contractors who specialize in tear-downs with a bulldozer?"

"Diamond, it's not that much damage. A few bullet holes, couple windows to replace. I could do the repairs myself when I get some time. Anyway, you need to stay away from work. Play some golf or something."

"Right, I show up at the last bastion of rich, white Republicans, I'd probably meet Violet Verona and Senator Stensen on the links." He opened the front door, then turned back and walked into the kitchen. He handed me my cell phone and a battery. "I recharged it last night. Same brand as mine. Here's my spare battery. Take it with you." He walked back to the door. "Don't worry about Street. I'll check in on her at Caesars."

THIRTY-TWO

Spot and I became pariahs. Exile was the only choice that made sense considering the danger I presented to anyone near me.

I was about to leave when I remembered that the guy had torn his shirt on the gutter when he fell off the roof. Maybe there were some threads that I could take to a lab for analysis.

I found a plastic Ziplock bag in the kitchen, took it upstairs and climbed out the broken window. The roof was steep. I eased my way down the shingles. I found far more than a few threads. Wedged into a gutter seam was a sizable portion of shirttail. I turned the plastic bag inside out and got the shirttail inside it without touching it. Back in the kitchen, I double-bagged it.

The last thing I needed to find was Diamond's camping equipment. I'd been on a fly fishing trip with him in the past and knew he had the basics. I figured he'd rather I borrow some gear without asking him than presume to stay in his house another night. I found his stuff jammed on shelves up high in the coat closet.

I took the camp stove and cookpot combo, a sleeping bag, flashlight and backpack and carried it out to the backyard. I untied the tarp and lifted it off the car. The orange Karmann Ghia glowed in the morning light. I stowed the tarp behind the driver's seat.

I put the puzzle and camping gear in back, then urged Spot into the front seat. I eventually got him situated so his butt was over against the shifter and his right side was against the seat back. I got the door shut and went around to squeeze into the driver's seat. My knees came up on either side of the steering wheel.

Spot was trying to shift into a more comfortable position. He pushed with his front feet and twisted against the seatback.

There was a loud snap and the singing sound of tearing metal. The seatback fell down to a level position. Spot lay down on his right side, happy that the now-broken seat was much more like a bed.

"Forgive me, Diamond," I muttered and turned the key.

The Karmann Ghia cranked and fired, then killed. I tried it again and it only cranked. The smell of gas wafted in the window. Flooded. I floored the pedal and cranked some more to clear out the carburetor. It fired, coughed blue smoke, then smoothed out.

I briefly considered driving to Canada, changing my name and starting my life over. But that would make visits from Street few and far between, so Spot and I headed back toward Tahoe.

The old VW barely went 40 mph during the long climb up the mountain, and I worried that the engine would blow its gaskets. I was grateful for the distraction when my cell phone rang.

It was Street.

"Sweetheart," I said. "When this is over, will you go with me to a deserted beach far away?"

"It sounds like you are already there. I hear a dull roar in the background."

"It's the Orange Flame cresting Kingsbury Grade."

"Did it go all right at Diamond's house?"

"No. From now on, I'm on the move."

"What do you mean?"

"Two shooters came last night."

I heard Street inhale. "What happened?"

"We scared them away. But the message was clear. I'm marked goods. I dare not stay with anyone."

"Where are you going to stay?"

"I've got Diamond's camping gear. I can hide out or bounce around motels and such. I'll be okay. You'll be safer if you don't know my whereabouts. Did you get any sleep last night?"

"Yes. I think I'll stay at Caesars for the time being."

"Good. Can I see you?" Unless they were watching Diamond's house, they wouldn't know that I was in his old car.

"Of course. Come to the front of the lobby?"

"Give me twenty minutes."

I pulled into Caesars and parked behind a white stretch limo and next to a silver Rolls Royce. The bellhop stared at Spot and me in Diamond's little orange car. Street ran out. She reached in and hugged Spot, careful not to bump his wound, then crawled over him and wedged herself behind my seat with her legs draped over Spot. She caressed him with a touch so soft I wondered if he could even feel it. But his eyes closed in bliss.

I drove off, leaving a blue cloud of exhaust swirling around the Rolls and the limo.

We went to Nevada Beach, a large stretch of sand near Roundhill. Spot lay down in the hot sand. Street and I sat facing the water. Waves lapped at our feet. Across the blue water was Mt. Tallac. A snowfield glowed brilliant white on its northeast side.

I told Street about our night at Diamond's and about the man who'd called me twice.

She asked about the voice. I did my best to describe its robotic quality.

Street frowned. "I once met a man who'd had throat cancer. They'd done an operation that took out his voice box. He couldn't speak normally. But he had a little device like a remote control that he held against his throat. It made it so he could talk."

"He sounded like a robot?" I said.

"Yes. I don't know how it worked. Some kind of sound generator."

"So my caller could be a throat cancer victim."

"Didn't you say the man who came in your office with the stick never uttered a word?"

"Yes," I said, raising my eyebrows, "I did."

An hour later, confident we hadn't been followed, I dropped Street off at Caesars and headed over to the hospital. Doctor John Lee was on duty in the ER, but the desk man said he'd be taking lunch in less than half an hour. I waited.

"Feeling better?" Doc Lee said when he saw me from behind the check-in counter. He hung up a clipboard, took off his white coat and came through the door.

"Yes, much, thanks." I walked with him outside.

"I'm just going to lunch. Want to come along?"

"Sure." Across the parking lot, Spot craned his head out the window and watched me get into Doc Lee's little black Mitsubishi sports car. Doc Lee had it revving by the time I crammed myself into a passenger compartment that was even smaller than that in the Orange Flame. He raced out of the lot and down the street.

"Serious G-forces in this crate," I said as my head bobbed with the acceleration.

"Zero to sixty, four seconds. Top speed, one forty-five."

"Which is useful on our curvy mountain roads."

"Useful in the Washoe Valley," he said as he raced up to a stop sign, braked, then shot out onto Highway 50, tires squealing as he shifted into second. He ran the engine up to about 7000 RPM, a powerful whine coming from under the hood. Just as I thought he'd go airborne, he hit the brakes and turned into a fast food joint.

"Burger for lunch okay?" he said, jerking to a stop.

"I didn't think a scientific-type, health professional would suck down saturated fat and salt for lunch."

"Salt and fat is why it tastes so good. What's wrong? The carnivore has turned into a tofu boy?"

I thought of Wheels calling me a shuttle boy. "Still a carnivore," I said. "Unabashed. I eat tofu boys for lunch."

"Sweet," Doc Lee said, giggling. "I could be your tofu boy."

"I didn't mean it that way," I said.

"So I figured. But it never hurts to ask, right?"

"Right."

We went in, ordered and took our food to a little round table. "Anyway," he said, chewing a mouthful of burger and fries, "if this fat gives me heart disease, I'm in the right business."

"Which is why I stopped by." I told him about the man who'd called and spoke in the robot voice. "Street said she'd once met a guy who had throat cancer and he used some kind of device to speak. Do you know about that?"

"Electrolarynx," he mumbled as he sucked on the straw in his chocolate shake. "Hold it to your throat for sound generation. The sound resonates in your oral cavity just like sound from vocal cords. Well, not exactly just like. More like a robot. Anyway, you make speaking motions to form words." Doc Lee swallowed. He held his fist against his throat and silently mouthed a series of words. "Like that," he said. "But most laryngectomees get implants or learn esophageal speech."

"What are those?"

"We can implant an artificial voice box, a tube that makes sound when air goes through it. It's like having a saxophone reed in your throat. Otherwise, patients can learn esophageal speech, which is swallowing air, then making words as you belch it back out."

I set the rest of my burger down. "Maybe I won't take up cigars after all."

"Good idea."

I sipped some Coke. "A normal person could use an electrolarynx, right?"

"Just to sound funny? I don't see why not."

"Where would you buy one?"

"Lots of places. Medical supply houses. The Internet. Or steal one from a hospital."

I thanked the doctor for his time and he dropped me back at the hospital.

I drove over to the Lake Tahoe Community College. In spite of summer, the lot was jammed as always. The Orange Flame backfired as I turned it off, kicking out a loud cloud of blue smoke. I leashed Spot to a Jeffrey pine with a large area of shade.

Diamond's young cousin Juanita was working at the Admissions and Records counter.

"Oh, Mr. Owen," she said, beaming, her teeth white and a little crooked in her pretty, pixie face.

"Hi, Juanita. I came here to ask a science question."

"Oh," she said. Eyes wide. Grin wider. "I'm sorry. I know accounting. And computers. I'm very good at computers. But science... I'm not good at science."

"I was thinking of a science teacher. Physics or chemistry."

"Oh, of course," she said again, blushing. Oh was her favorite word. "I thought...," she turned to the computer. Her face was approaching the color of a tomato. She tapped a few keys. "Mr. Johansen teaches chemistry. But not during the summer. Same for his lab tech. Oh, here we are. Mr. Kebler. Physics. He teaches in the summer. Oh, but he's in class until 11:30."

I looked at the clock. "I'll wait. Where is his classroom?"

Juanita told me and I thanked her.

"Bye, Mr. Owen," she grinned.

I was outside the classroom when a dozen kids streamed out. The only two adult students stayed behind to ask questions. The difference between school by default and school by choice.

When they were done, I introduced myself.

"Bill Kebler," he said. "Good to meet you." He was a scrawny, bald man with a pleasant smile and squinty eyes. He wore baggy khaki trousers that bunched around his waist where they were held in a strangle-hold by a belt made of leather loops.

"I've heard of you," he said. "From your reputation, I would have predicted you'd be an out-sized individual. The observation verifies the hypothesis." He laughed nervously.

"I wonder if I can ask you a question."

"Of course. I work for the state. Your tax dollars at work. Ask away." Another nervous laugh.

"I'd like to ask about explosives."

"Really! Didn't see that one coming! Should we sit down? This could be fun!"

We sat on student chairs.

"I witnessed a boat explosion on the lake," I said.

"Yes, of course. A girl died. Terrible."

"It was a powerful explosion. It blew the boat into splinters. There was a fireball, and the shock wave overturned the boat I was in. I'm wondering what kind of explosives could do that."

Kebler frowned. "Not really my area. I just teach the basics. I start with Newton's laws of motion, go to gravity, electro-magnetism, the properties of matter and energy, then touch on thermodynamics, relativity and so forth. But explosives? Probably best if I don't go there with kids, don't you think? But back to your question. I suppose any type of high explosive would do it. Dynamite. Nitro. A plastic military explosive like C-four. Even a homemade bomb using the right combo of fertilizer and some hydrocarbon like oil or gas. I could look it up and get back to you, if you like."

"Would any of those explosives be untraceable?"

Kebler shook his head. "Can't imagine that. All explosives would leave behind their reactive by-products."

"When you say 'high explosives,' what exactly do you mean?"

"Again, explosives aren't my area. But some are really just very combustible materials that are tightly compacted. Pack them into a container like a pipe and you get a crude but effective bomb. When they are ignited, you get extremely fast combustion that generates a great amount of hot gas. The combination will explode the pipe with a large release of energy."

"What do you mean when you say very combustible?"

"I wasn't thinking specifics. But I suppose something like the powder in firecrackers. Even match heads might do the job. You'd have to get the right amount of air mixed in to make it effective. But a bomb made with those materials wouldn't cause the destruction you describe."

"High explosives are different?"

"Yes. High explosives don't simply burn fast. Instead, they consist of organic nitrates that are self-oxidizing and hence inherently unstable. When they are exposed to a very strong shock, such as what you get from a blasting cap, the chemical undergoes an exothermic reaction. The resulting shock wave travels through the explosive at very high speed." Kebler gazed up at the ceiling. "We're talking a shock wave that travels at maybe tens of thousands of miles per hour. In effect, all of the material undergoes the reaction at once. Because of the high velocity shockwave, and because of the amount of energy released, a high explosive is much more powerful than other explosives." Kebler stopped, frowned as if he were examining what he just said, then nodded with satisfaction.

"The way I described the boat explosion, do you think a high explosive would be necessary?"

Kebler thought a moment. "A large boat blowing into splinters? Yes, a high explosive seems the likely candidate."

"The Coast Guard collected the remaining boat splinters that were floating on the water. They sent them to a lab for analysis and all that was found were traces of gasoline. No explosives of any kind. That's why I asked if any explosives were untraceable."

Kebler shook his head. "It doesn't make sense. They'd find traces. A gas tank blowing up couldn't do that to a boat. Not even a smallish boat. And you said this was a big boat, right?"

"Yes. Thirty-some feet long. A good-sized cabin."

"Something's wrong. The lab made a mistake."

I said, "Could the splinters they pulled out of the water have soaked too long?"

"No. That's the thing about explosives. The force of the blast drives explosive residue into any materials nearby." Kebler was still shaking his head. "The lab has to be inept. That's the only explanation." He stood up. "I'm running out of time. I have to meet someone for a noon appointment." He started walking toward the door. "I'm sure the Coast Guard would use a qualified lab."

"Yes," I said.

Kebler reached the door and stepped out into the hall. I stayed at his side.

"You're certain they only found gasoline?"

I nodded.

Kebler and I rounded a corner, went past a coffee counter and down another corridor.

"Just gasoline," Kebler muttered. He stared at the floor. "It's basic physics. Every explosive would leave by-products. Testing for them is not complicated. The lab would... Wait!" Kebler jerked to a stop and swung his arm out sideways. His hand hit my forearm. "I've got it!" He rubbed his hand.

"What? A high explosive that leaves gasoline traces?"

"No! A mist bomb!"

"What is that?"

Kebler turned and stepped in front of me. "I remember reading about mist bombs long ago. The military developed them. The way it works is that you have a device that sprays gasoline mist in just the right manner with the exact gas-to-air mixture."

"Like what happens when the fuel injectors spray gas into the cylinders of an engine," I said.

"Yes. But they no doubt tinker with the gas and air, probably upping the oxygen level. Although they couldn't use pure oxygen because it would spontaneously combust. I don't know how a mist bomb is containerized. But the main thing is that when a mist bomb is ignited the shock wave travels not like bombs made of highly combustible material, but much faster."

"Like a high explosive."

"Yes." Kebler held his hands out in front of him, palms facing each other about a foot apart. "Take an ordinary hydrocarbon, mist it just so and... Kaboom!" Kebler threw his hands apart. A woman walking by ducked, then scurried away.

"How would one go about making a mist bomb?" I asked.

"Well, it wouldn't be as simple as taking auto parts and hooking them up. Like most things, the effectiveness is in the details. The military guards its secrets pretty well. But let's say you could steal the device from the military and put it on some kind of radio control. Maybe the container would fit in the cabin or bilge. Or maybe the device just fills the bilge and cabin with mist. The boat is out on the lake. The result is still like that of a high explosive. And all that is left behind are traces of gas in the wood splinters." Kebler's enthusiasm was unsettling.

"If the misting device was made of metal, it would sink to the bottom along with the engine," I said.

"Yes! Divers could search and bring it up!"

"Except that the explosion was out where the lake is sixteen hundred feet deep. It would never be recoverable."

Kebler was disappointed. "Even so, I believe that is your answer."

I thanked Kebler and left.

THIRTY-THREE

Back in the college parking lot I sat on the grass next to Spot and called Agent Ramos.

"A mist bomb," I said after explaining why I was calling. "A professor named Kebler at the college knows about them. He said the military developed them. The device atomizes gas such that it explodes very much like a high explosive. He believed such a bomb could be what blew up Faith Runyon's boat."

"That would fit the shape-shifter's tendency for the unusual."

"Yes, and the one-use concept as well. But it would have to be stolen from the military. Does the FBI keep that kind of data?"

"I'll check into it," Ramos said.

"Will you let me know if you find out anything?"

"Thing is," Ramos said, "the military is very tight about breaches of security. They don't like to admit that thefts occur."

"Right. Makes them look lax. But two shooters tried to kill me last night at Deputy Martinez's home in Minden. I'd appreciate any information."

"I heard about that," Ramos said. "And the caller with the strange voice."

"Yes. I spoke to Doc Lee over at the hospital. He said it could be an electrolarynx. Either someone who has had throat cancer, or someone who just uses it to make strange speech so they wouldn't be recognized."

"The man who used the handrail on you at your office didn't speak, correct?"

"Correct."

"So we could have someone who is mute. Or it could be part of the shape-shifter's M.O."

"Or someone impersonating the shape-shifter," I said. "One more thing. Diamond Martinez and I put together most of the bits of paper the Coast Guard pulled out of the water when Faith's boat blew up. They make a picture of a nine-hole golf course. Does that sound familiar?"

"No."

I said goodbye and called Wheels Washburn.

"Hello?" More of a grunt than a spoken word.

"Wheels? Owen McKenna. Remember I was wondering where you got the idea about the location of where Glory went off the trail?"

"Yes. Good little detective that I am, I called Spider just after you and I got down from the mountain. Told him that I had two bees in my bonnet. One was that I knew the accident happened about a half mile down the trail from the Marlette Lake dam. The other was thinking the man with Glory was her boyfriend, not her bodyguard. Thorough, aren't I?"

"Spider have an idea?"

"Yeah." Another grunt. "He said it was Bob Metan who knew about the accident. Soon as he said it, I remembered Bob talking about the singer Glory and some prostitute named Faith who died in that boat explosion. Seemed to know all about their deaths."

"How do I get hold of Bob?"

"He works up at Squaw. I forget the name of the shop. Near the cable car. Only don't ask for Bob Metan. He's becoming well-known in snowboard circles and uses a professional name. Bobby Crash."

"Thanks, Wheels. I'll be in touch."

I hung up and made several phone calls trying to track down Bobby Crash. Eventually, I got routed to the marketing department of Company Twenty-Five. They said they weren't at liberty to give out contact information. Next, I went through Information to contact sports shops in Squaw Valley. After many calls, I finally happened on the shop where he worked.

"Bobby Crash? I can't tell you where he is," a high, shrill female voice said. "Can you tell me? I'd sure like to know. Didn't show up yesterday, didn't call, neither. His shift started today at one, but it's a quarter after and he isn't here."

"Can you give me his home phone?"

"No way, mister. There's rules about that."

I dialed the Herald and asked for Glenda Gorman.

"Owen," she said, her voice tense, "I heard the police report about the shooting. Is Spot..."

"He'll be fine, eventually."

"Thank God. I was so worried. I left messages at your office and cabin."

"Sorry. Takes me awhile to return messages. Any chance we can get together today?"

"Sure. Where do you want to meet?"

I was thinking about risks to Glennie as she spoke. The killers had probably seen the draped car in Diamond's back yard. Did one of them lift up the edge of the tarp to see the make and color? I thought it was safest to meet her away from the newspaper building, away from her house and away from Diamond's Orange Flame. "Maybe we could meet at Tallac Estates?"

"Sure."

"You know where the Baldwin Mansion is. Why don't you park near there and walk toward Baldwin Beach. There's a great place just off the trail."

"Okay. Give me an hour," Glennie said.

Glennie showed up just after Spot had found a pile of pine needles to lie on. She ran over to him. "Spot, you poor baby." She pet him, careful to avoid his wound. He turned his head when she rubbed around his ears.

"I checked every death near Tahoe in the last few months and found one or two that you might want to look at," Glennie said. She opened a file folder, pulled out the first paper and handed it to me.

I looked at her notes while she spoke.

"The first one is Monica Lakeman. She was thirty-nine years old, never married, no kids. She owns, I should say owned, a property management company specializing in vacation rentals. She was active in the Truckee business community, was on the Board of Directors at the Chamber of Commerce."

"How'd she die?"

"There's a long stairway down from the deck at one of her rentals near Tahoe City. It is a property she owned herself, and she took special pride in its maintenance. She was doing a last-minute inspection before a corporate group came from Miami. She fell down the stairs, hit her head and broke her neck."

"She was alone at the time?"

"Supposedly. The coroner's conclusion was that the broken neck from the fall killed her."

"But there was a question about what caused the fall?" I said.

"Yes. The stairs were in good condition and there was nothing unusual that would cause a person to trip. She fell during daylight. There was no rain or anything else to make the stairs slippery."

"They do any analysis?"

"Yes. The results were consistent with what would have happened in a typical fall. They found some skin and pant fibers on the third tread down and skin and makeup on the seventh tread down. There were abrasions on her knee and a bad scrape on her face."

"Who inherited?"

"The company and her property are being sold. All proceeds go to a charity that specializes in helping disabled kids. Apparently, her only sibling was a disabled brother who died very young."

"Not a promising case," I said.

"No, but it fits what you asked for. A woman whose death could have been a murder."

"Yes, it does." My attention went to a plane doing big S-turns in the sky. It was a small, high-wing plane, white with blue stripes, probably a Cessna 150. I watched it for a minute, thinking back to my last flying escapade when I broke Jennifer's mother out of the asylum on the Nevada desert.

The plane came out of its steep banking turn to the starboard, rolled over to port and arced the other direction. "You said you found another death?" I said.

"Yes, a strange one."

"Who was it?"

"A banker named Eduardo Valdez. Forty-five years old. He was the senior loan officer at Fidelity Trust and Security in Incline Village. He was hit by a drunk driver at about one in the morning."

"Happens all the time."

"Not like this. The driver hit him on the Mt. Rose Highway about two-thirds of the way up from the desert to the Mt. Rose Ski Area."

I realized it was not far from where Tyrone's boss Tony Nova lived. "He was out walking the Mt. Rose Highway late at night? His car break down?"

"Not according to the driver. The guy said the victim wasn't walking. Said he fell from the sky."

"Some drunks are imaginative," I said, laughing.

"I'll say," Glennie laughed with me. "That's terrible, isn't it. A prominent banker dies and we're laughing about it like it was roadkill."

"Yeah, but he was a prominent, *flying* banker. How'd they catch the drunk?"

"The guy called nine, one, one on his cell. He was waiting when the cops got there."

"They find the banker's car?"

"Yeah, it was at home in his garage."

"Of course," I said. "Who needs a car when you can fly?"

Glennie giggled and slugged me on the shoulder. "Stop it, you're horrible."

"The guy change his story after he sobered up?"

"No, that's the thing. The next morning he stuck with the story. Said he was driving up the mountain, going slow because he'd had too much. It was dark and he didn't want to miss any of the switchbacks. Next thing he knows, a body falls out of the sky in front of his car." Glennie stifled another giggle. "The driver never changed his story. He's still in jail in Reno in case you want to talk to him."

"Eduardo have a family?"

"He divorced eight years ago, left his job at CitiBank and moved here. His ex stayed in New Jersey. No kids, just like Monica Lakeman. A socialite in Incline said she can't imagine divorcing him. She gave him an eleven on the one-to-ten bachelor scale. She said, quote, he had M.E.L.S. coming out his ears."

"M.E.L.S.?"

"My question, too. She said that's how her Incline friends rate men. Money, Education, Looks, Style. The order is important. She said his death had to be some kind of accident. Like, he got a ride from someone who let him out to walk, then the drunk hit him on the road. She said there was no possible reason why anyone would want to kill him."

"Except for excessive M.E.L.S.?" I said.

"Except for that," Glennie said.

I stood up. "Glennie, I owe you."

Glennie stood and walked over to where Spot was still sprawled on the mat of pine needles. He had assumed what I'd come to think of as the duct tape position, stretched out on his right side, bandaged side up, left front leg held out straight so that the elbow and shoulder joints didn't flex.

Glennie bent down and pet Spot. "You don't have to thank me," she said. She came over and looked up at me. "Just don't forget about me, okay?"

I knew what she meant. I was in love with a woman who wouldn't commit to me. Yet, here was a good woman who would. "I won't, Glennie."

"Be good to Spot," she said as she walked away.

THIRTY-FOUR

I got Spot folded back into the broken Karmann Ghia seat and we drove across town to the bike shop. It was getting late, but I still had errands to run before I went to my next hiding place.

"Hey," Joey said when I walked in. "You get hold of Wheels on that guide thing you wanted?"

"Yes, I did. He was very helpful. Any idea where I could find Bobby Crash?"

"The snowboarder? I don't know where he lives, but he works up at Squaw. You could check there."

"Thanks. I also wanted to rent a mountain bike."

"What happened, you crash yours?"

"No," I said, thinking that I couldn't risk picking it up at my cabin. "I've got a friend coming to visit and we wanted to go for a ride. He's a tall guy like me, so whatever fits me will work."

Joey scanned the rack. "I've got one large frame left. Lemme give it a turn through the parking lot, check the derailleur."

He pulled the bike from the rack and rode it around the blacktop, shifting up and down through the gears. "Looks good," he said as he braked to a stop.

"Let me adjust the seat post." He wheeled it over next to me, opened the quick-release and pulled the seat up to its highest position. "What do you think?"

I got on, put my foot on the pedal. "Feels good."

Joey was staring at the little Karmann Ghia. "How you gonna get this bike home?" He walked over to the car. The passenger window was open. Spot had cranked his head around and rested his jaw on the door.

"Big dog," Joey said as he gave Spot a pet.

"I thought I could lash the bike to the little luggage rack," I said.

"Be like tying it to a paper clip," he said.

I purchased some bungie cords and Joey found some foam padding. We jammed the padding under the pedal and the axle points, then lashed the bike down to the luggage rack. It was wobbly, but seemed to hold. I thanked him and left.

I stopped at the supermarket and bought a couple of days worth of food, human type and dog type. I found a small daypack to put it in.

My biggest concern was driving up the east shore past the driveway to my cabin without being seen. A Harlequin Great Dane in an orange Karmann Ghia was not the best way to be incognito. But I had no choice.

I made it unaccosted to the Spooner Lake Campground where I'd met Wheels Washburn. I parked in one of the less-visible spaces. There were other cars and pickups and campers around, but the only people I was aware of were making noise inside of a tent.

When you wear a pack on your front, the straps want to slip off your shoulders. So I put the daypack on my front first, followed by the backpack. The straps of the backpack held the straps of the front pack in place. Last, I pulled out the tarp and tied it in place over the car.

I climbed onto the bike, called to Spot, and pedaled into the woods. I stayed in the trees and headed back out toward the highway. Spot followed. He moved slowly.

Cars sped by on the highway. When a break came in the heavy traffic of summer tourists, I pedaled out of the woods and across the road.

There is an old Forest Service trail some distance away that heads down toward the lake. I angled through the woods toward it.

The east side of Tahoe gets only a third the moisture of the west side because it is farther from the Sierra Crest, the topographic feature that wrings precipitation from the clouds. As a result, the forest is much thinner and I was able to ride much of the way.

I was riding across an open meadow when I heard a familiar sound, a low drone from the sky. I looked up to see a plane, a blue and white Cessna 150 coming just over the treetops.

"Spot!" I called out. "Come!" I turned and pedaled fast to a stand of fir trees. I plowed into the boughs of the tree, falling purposefully to the side. My bike went down and I slid on my stomach up to the tree trunk like I was diving for second base.

"Spot!" I yelled again. He loped in after me, favoring his left front leg. I pulled him down under the thick branches as the plane came over the meadow.

Maybe I was being paranoid, but twice I'd underestimated the men pursuing me. I wasn't going to make that mistake again. It was the same plane that had circled overhead when I was talking to Glennie on the South Shore. If the killers were in the plane, Spot and I would be an easy shot with a rifle.

The plane went into a big S-turn. It looped around and came over the meadow twice. It continued on, back out over the treetops and disappeared. I waited, thinking about the banker falling from the sky. The drone of the plane eventually went silent.

"Okay, Spot," I said, getting on the bike.

The old Forest Service road was rutted and overgrown. We followed it for a couple of miles as it angled down toward the lake. A half mile before the water, we came to a tree where a blaze mark had been cut decades before. We turned and followed a trail across a steep forested slope and through a boulder field. Just after we crossed a dry creekbed, we came to a broken-down structure that I'd discovered years before. The one-room cabin had been made of small logs. The roof had fallen in and the ground had eroded under one side, leading to the collapse of one of the walls. It remained a broken, three-sided structure with a great view of the lake.

I cleaned out the clutter of pine cones and fallen branches, laid out Diamond's sleeping bag on the sand floor and set about making some dinner before it got completely dark.

I opened the dog food bag and let Spot eat out of it. I got Diamond's stove fired up and heated a couple cans of soup directly in the cans. When we were done eating, Spot and I walked in the twilight down through the forest to the lake a half mile below. Spot walked into the water and drank for a long time. I splashed water on my face and drank from cupped hands.

It was dark as we walked up to our campsite. But the moon was brighter than the previous night. Back at the broken-down cabin, I showed Spot where to lie.

"C'mon, boy. We gotta share Diamond's sleeping bag."

At high altitude, it often gets down into the 30s during summer nights. Even if Spot weren't half-shaved, his thin fur couldn't keep him warm. I put the sleeping bag over the two of us. Our shelter had no roof. The stars twinkled through the branches of the Jeffrey pines. A cool breeze rolled down the slope from above. The birds had gone silent. I lifted my head and looked out at the lake. A single light moved across the water. No one knew where we were, not even Street. If the killer was as smart as I thought, he'd realize I wouldn't let her know where I was staying. Thus, he couldn't use her to get the information. But he could use her to force me to come in from the cold. The thought made me nauseous. I called her on my cell.

We spoke for fifteen minutes, each of us reassuring the other that we would be safe. Then we said goodnight.

It was getting late, but George Morrell, the psychologist, said evening consults were okay. He answered on the fourth ring.

"The killer called me," I said. "I wondered if I could ask you about it."

"Certainly."

I told George about the attacks at my cabin and at Diamond's house. I described the phone call just before Spot got shot and the other phone call where the killer said he owned Street's and Spot's and my future. When I was done, I said, "Any thoughts come to mind?"

George spoke slowly. "I don't imagine I can add much to what you already know, but I'll go through it anyway.

"Obviously, the assaults by gun suggest that these men are serious about killing you. Although, my guess is that you are primarily dealing with one individual."

"You mean, one guy is calling the shots?"

"Yes. Only one guy is motivated to kill you. Any others who come along are support troops to the general. The fact that he is departing from methods that can look like accidents, or even from the handrail that can be easily destroyed by burning, makes it clear that he is getting desperate."

"That's why he brought help when he came to Diamond's," I said.

"Yes. Your pursuit of him is pushing him into riskier behavior. This is both good news and bad, the good being that these tactics make him more likely to get caught."

"And the bad?"

"The bad being that you are much more likely to get killed. Think of the suicide bomber analogy. The less the killer cares about consequences to himself, the more success he has at his mission. And because you have a girlfriend, he is also likely to get at you through her, putting her in serious danger.

"As for the synthetic voice, if he really is mute for reasons of cancer or otherwise, this would be an excellent indication. I'm not familiar with the electronic device you describe, but my guess is that he can speak normally and is using it as a disguise."

"You think I shouldn't spend time trying to track down throat cancer victims?"

"Correct. Someone who uses an electronic larynx in real life would be loathe to speak during the commission of a crime. It would make them an obvious suspect."

"I might be more successful looking at recent sales of electrolarynxes," I said. "Better yet, I might look for an oncologist who specializes in throat tumors. One who also knew the young women who died."

"Yes," Morrell said. "That's the direction I'd take."

A great idea, I thought, except that I'd been unsuccessful in learning anything about Faith and had only uncovered the barest bits of Glory's life.

"Why do you think he is calling me?" I said.

"To taunt you. It gives him excitement, and it cranks up the tension so that killing you will be a bigger release for him."

I thanked George for his help.

"Owen," he said before he hung up.

"Yeah?"

"You don't yet know why he killed the two young women. But you know why he wants you. Death is a game to him. He also appears to be shrewd and intelligent and, I think, entirely sane. I've seen that combination before." He paused.

"You were going to say something else."

"I don't want to sound melodramatic. But this is the most dangerous kind of killer you can face. Unless you change your name and move away, he's probably going to succeed in killing you. I can't stress how careful you need to be."

"Message received," I said. "Thanks."

In the middle of the night I woke up to a noise. Spot was awake, too. He didn't growl, but his head was up, pointed toward the forest. I lay motionless and silent. My chest was tight, breaths short. The forest made little sounds. Spot listened. Five long minutes later, Spot put his head down. I tried to relax. I went over the Turner painting in my mind, hoping the focus would make me sleepy. Instead, my mental picture of the froth and fury of wave and wind made me more agitated.

Why would Turner voluntarily submit to such a dangerous stunt as being lashed to the mast in a storm? Was it because he wanted to confront his worst fears, drowning or freezing or being pummeled to death by the elements? Did he record the experience with paint and canvas so that future viewers could draw on his harrowing experience? Or was it, as Susan Sontag might argue, merely a depiction of nature's fury? Nothing more than a snapshot of a weather phenomenon. Nothing that would throw illumination on what drives a sane man to kill two young women and possibly more, then target me.

I lay there, tense and stressed, wishing I were with Street.

I broke camp at the first hint of dawn.

THIRTY-FIVE

Spot and I hiked down to the lake for a morning drink, then headed back up toward the car. I left the bike hidden in the woods.

A woman and two children noticed me unwrapping the Karmann Ghia. Her kids were fixated on Spot. I envisioned the men hunting me eating at the same McDonald's as the kids. If the men heard the kids talking about the huge, spotted dog, a few questions would give the men a starting point to search for me.

It was a risk I couldn't avoid.

Spot and I drove north up the east shore. Glennie had told me about Eduardo Valdez, the banker who'd fallen from the sky. His bank, Fidelity Trust and Security, was in Incline Village. I found a shady parking place on the back side, left Spot in the Karmann Ghia and walked around to the front door.

The receptionist forced a smile and said, "Good morning, sir. How may I help you?" She was a big, tall blonde with a jaw and brow so heavy I'd have thought her a transvestite if her voice weren't so high and delicate.

I pulled out my wallet and showed her my license. "My name's Owen McKenna. I'm investigating a matter that may connect with the death of Eduardo Valdez. May I speak to someone who worked with him?"

Her eyes got wide. "I suppose you could talk to Mr. Lamb." She glanced over toward an empty desk in the corner. "He's a loan officer, too. But he's out. Would you like to make an appointment?"

"I'm not sure what my schedule will be, so maybe I'll just stop back later?" I thanked her and left.

The other person Glennie told me about was Monica Lakeman, who died falling down a flight of stairs. I drove to Truckee and found Lakeman Property Management in the historic downtown area. There was a sign with a picture of a cabin and pine trees and Lake Tahoe in the background.

The door was locked. Cupping my hands around my eyes, I peered in through the little windowpanes. The lights were off. I recalled that Glennie had said that everything was being sold and given to charity.

I went to the Truckee Chamber of Commerce. Inside, a cheerful woman was quoting statistics about the area to a caller on the phone. When she was done with her glowing report, I was ready to move to Truckee myself.

"Yes, sir," she said after she hung up.

I introduced myself and explained that I was inquiring about Monica Lakeman's death.

Her face became very serious. "Mr. McKenna, I'm sure you are very wrong to even consider that her death wasn't an accident. Wouldn't that suggest that Monica was involved in something illegal?"

"Not at all. Was Monica married?"

The woman shook her head.

"Then perhaps Monica had a lover?"

"Oh, no, I'm certain that she didn't. I'm not a busy-body, but I happen to know that Monica hasn't been involved with anyone for many years."

"Maybe Monica had a passion that someone else took exception to."

The woman was shaking her head. "Monica wasn't the passionate type. She had a simple life. She took care of her properties. Ran her business. Served on our Board of Directors."

"The properties she managed," I said. "I understand that most were vacation homes that she rented out when the owners weren't in the area?"

"Yes."

"She also owned some herself?"

"Yes, I believe she owned three houses. One here in Truckee and two near Tahoe City. One was just across the highway from the lake. It has a great view. She could have retired on that house alone."

"Was that the house where she fell?"

The woman closed her eyes for a moment. "Yes."

"Can you think of anyone who disliked Monica or had a strong disagreement with her?"

The woman shook her head.

"Did Monica ever take an unpopular position in her role on the chamber's Board of Directors?"

Another shake.

"Let me know if you think of anything else?" I handed her my card.

The woman nodded. She was obviously upset by my questions. I thanked her and left.

I drove down Interstate 80, through the canyon and into Reno where I found the Washoe County Jail.

After showing my ID, explaining my purpose and offering both Mallory and Diamond for referral, they let me in to see Tom Johnson, the man who drove over Eduardo Valdez on the Mt. Rose Highway.

He sat alone on a wooden bench in a jail cell. His feet were pulled up, heels on the edge of the bench, hands locked around his bent knees. His chin rested on his right knee, his eyes to the wall.

"Man here to see you, Johnson," the deputy sheriff on duty said.

Tom Johnson swung his head around and looked at me. He was skinny, and his eyes drooped.

The deputy opened the cell, let me inside and locked it behind me. "I'll be right here in the hallway," he said. "Holler when you want out."

I nodded at him and he moved away.

I sat down on the bench three feet away from the prisoner. He watched me, then turned and looked back at the wall.

"I'm Owen McKenna. I'm looking into a matter that concerns Eduardo Valdez. I'd like to ask you a few questions if I may."

"Go ahead," he said. His throat needed clearing.

"You hit him with your car," I said.

"Yes."

"Can you tell me about it?"

It was a long time before he spoke. "I ran him over. I'm sorry, if it makes any difference. I guess I pretty much screwed myself. I did the twelve step thing for a long time, but things changed on me. Now I've killed a man, and I can never take that back."

"How did it happen?" I said.

"What's to tell? I was driving up the Mt. Rose Highway. It was late at night, about one in the morning. I'd had maybe eight or nine beers at Finnegan's. I know, I know. You don't need to give me the lecture. I was in the wrong place at the wrong time. Mr. Valdez, too. I can't turn back the clock. No one will ever know how sorry I am. But I guess that doesn't matter." He stopped and took a deep breath.

"They assigned me a lawyer," he continued. "Mr. Bronfman. I don't know if he's any good. Awfully young. But it's not like I can call up Johnnie Cochran. I'm a meat cutter at a local market. We're not unionized. I'm doing great if I can just make the rent. But it doesn't matter how good my lawyer is. I deserve whatever is coming to me."

"How was it that you hit Valdez?"

Johnson was facing the wall. "It was dark and... He was in the road."

"What do you mean, in the road?"

Johnson turned and looked at me. "In the road. Is that a problem?"

"I've heard that you claimed he fell out of the sky."

The man turned away from me and stared at the wall.

"Were you drunk when you said that?" I said.

"Yes. No. What does it matter?"

I stood up, walked a few steps away. "Did you make that up about him falling out of the sky?"

"Yeah, sure. I made it up."

I turned back to him, grabbed his shirt with both hands, yanked him up to his feet, then raised him into the air. He trembled as his shirt bit into his armpits. "Tell me the truth," I said.

"Okay! No! I didn't make it up."

I lowered him down.

He sat on the bench and rubbed his armpits. "He fell out of the sky."

"Give me some details."

Johnson sighed. "Up where the highway starts doing all those switchbacks. I came around a sharp curve. The highway is dark, so it's hard to see. I was leaning forward, concentrating on the painted lines. I was about halfway through this tight curve when he fell out of the sky." Johnson was breathing hard. "It was terrible. I saw him for a split second in my headlights before he hit. His eyes were open. Maybe he was already dead. I've heard that happens, eyes staying open after you die. But maybe he was still alive. I don't know. Then he hit the pavement and..." Tom Johnson stopped speaking. He panted and swallowed and went silent.

"What happened?" I said.

It took him some time before he spoke. "He bounced."

"What do you mean?"

"Just like I said. He hit the road, and his body bounced. He came back up to about the level of my headlights when I hit him. My bumper slammed him back down onto the road. I tried to stop. But I was slow on the brakes. My wheels went over him." Johnson stopped talking. A tremor shook his body.

"You think you might have imagined this whole thing?" I said. "Falling out of the sky?"

"Look, I understand if you don't believe me. I know it sounds ridiculous. But that's what happened."

"You've been a drinker a long time?" I said.

"Yes. I was sober a long time, too."

"Gotten picked up for drunk driving before?"

He nodded again. "Twice. Fifteen years ago. I did my time and stayed sober until a month ago. Then my girl left me. Rita and me were together over four years. All of a sudden, she's involved with a guy who owns a lawn care company. He has a lot more money than I'll ever have. Maybe it isn't the money. But I can't help thinking he's buying her stuff she'd never get from me. I heard they went to Hawaii. I know Rita's never been there before. It hurts pretty bad."

"So you started drinking."

"Yeah. Only friend I've got."

"How many times have you hallucinated before?"

Johnson was staring at the floor. He shook his head. "Never."

"But you've passed out before. A guy who drinks himself to oblivion usually sees things."

He was still shaking his head. "I'm not that kind of a drunk. I probably average a twelve-pack a day, but I don't pass out in the gutter. I go to bed like anyone else." He lifted his head and looked at me. "I've never hallucinated."

I leaned against the wall, hands in my pockets. "Give me a better idea about where this happened."

THIRTY-SIX

The Mt. Rose Highway departs at the south edge of Reno and climbs up the slope toward the mountains on the north side of Tahoe. Diamond's Karmann Ghia held 37 mph with the gas pedal floored as we climbed at a steep angle up past where we'd previously turned off to find Tyrone Handkins sitting in Tony Nova's hot tub.

The desert ends near the famous Montreaux links. Microclimates don't get more obvious. It's as if somebody drew a line in the dirt, planted sagebrush on one side and Jeffrey pine on the other.

I followed Tom Johnson's instructions until I came to the switchback where I believed he'd run over Eduardo Valdez. I was somewhere over 7000 feet of elevation. Slide Mountain and the slopes of the Mt. Rose ski area towered above me. There was a faint rubber mark on the pavement. I pulled over and got out.

A truck went by, its engine and gears whining as it went up the long incline. After it passed, the road was empty. I walked into the middle of the asphalt and looked around.

To the east side of the highway the world dropped away in a steep canyon that stretched 2000 feet down to the Washoe Valley and the broad splash of Washoe Lake. To the west, the mountain rose up at a sharp angle. The slope was forested and had two huge boulders projecting through the trees. But the boulders were too far back from the highway for a man to jump off and hit the road.

I spent a few moments considering Tom Johnson's story. After years of questioning suspects as a homicide detective in San Francisco, I'd developed a sixth sense about their stories. Many times I'd heard outlandish tales, and I'd learned to distinguish which ones had a possibility of truth. If a guy says he found the drugs or gun or money lying in the street, you know he is probably lying. But if a reasonable-sounding guy says the man he ran over fell out of the sky, the very fact that it is so implausible makes you think no one would make it up, and you begin to suspect that somewhere in his addled brain is a germ of truth.

But when I again looked up at the slope above me, I realized there was no way Eduardo Valdez could have fallen in front of Johnson's car unless he'd been dropped from a plane.

I thought about the Cessna flying above me on the South Shore and then later on the East Shore. If the plane belonged to the killers, they could well have dropped Eduardo Valdez from the sky. But it seemed too incredible to think that, in all the vastness of the landscape, he would end up under Tom Johnson's wheels.

I got back in the Orange Flame and continued up the highway, over the pass and down to Incline Village.

The big blond receptionist at Fidelity Trust and Security pretended that she didn't recognize me. I said that I was here to see Lamb who was in full view over at the corner desk.

"Oh, yes! Of course!" She picked up the phone and pushed a button. We both heard the buzz of his phone from across the room. Lamb picked up his phone and they spoke in soft tones. They hung up. "He said he'd be happy to see you. You can just walk over." She pointed toward his desk.

"Thank you." I walked over to where Lamb sat at a large wooden desk. The desk had a blotter that was printed with a Green Bay Packers logo. Next to the blotter was a large pigskin paperweight. Miniature golden goal posts were stuck into the football, one on each end. The crosspiece on the left goalpost was a gold pen, the crosspiece on the right, a gold pencil. Near Lamb's elbow was a Vince Lombardi coffee cup.

Lamb stood up to greet me. "Morning," he said in an airy voice. He shook my hand. "Al Lamb." He had a Band-Aid on the crest of his forehead. At six-three or so, he wasn't as tall as me, but he probably outweighed my 215 by 85 pounds. He was pink and thick from his ears to his nose to his lips to his neck and all parts south.

His hand on mine felt like a boxing glove. His chest was the size of my washing machine. There were 120-foot-tall Jeffrey pines near my cabin whose trunks weren't any bigger than his thighs.

"Owen McKenna," I said.

He didn't smile as we shook. He gestured to one of the chairs in front of his desk and we both sat down. We considered each other for a moment.

It is an automatic, alpha-male thing that women and smaller men don't do or understand. The process is encoded in our genes, a social mechanism that served us well back when we were hunters and gatherers. Everyone in the tribe benefited from a mutual understanding of which guy was numero uno, the guy who held the trump card when it came to giving orders or bedding the women.

Then again, maybe it was just stupid, testosterone bullshit. Probably, the same skinny geeks who start the Microsofts of today were romping the girls in the caves while the beefcakes were out butting heads.

Either way, Lamb and I came to a nearly instant, unspoken understanding. I might be taller, but he had alpha tattooed on his balls.

"I'm an investigator looking into a situation that may have something to do with the death of your colleague, Eduardo Valdez. I'm wondering if you can tell me anything about him?"

Lamb's eyes lost their friendliness. He spoke slowly, his airy voice like Marlon Brando's in The Godfather. "What's to tell? Guy worked with me. Guy died. It was a real shame."

"A real shame, huh?"

"Yeah," he said. "What? It's a problem I think it's a shame when a guy dies?"

"You call Eduardo 'guy,'" I said. "That your pet name for him?"

Lamb shook his head. "You're a guy, too. Tonight I'll tell my buddies, 'Guy came in the bank today. Guy with a thing about names.' You never used the word guy?"

"Most people who worked with someone who died wouldn't. They'd say, 'I was so sorry about what happened. Eddy Valdez was my best bud. He and I were like twins, we were so close.'"

Lamb looked at me. "Yeah, right, me and a Mexican best friends."

"Eduardo was a Mex?" I said. "And they let him work in a bank?"

"Go figure," Lamb said, his face unchanged. "We've got all those gardens, but they give him a desk."

"Any idea why someone would want to kill him?"

Lamb snorted. "It was an accident. He was hit by a drunk driver. Or don't you read the police report before you start investigating?" He said the word investigating with a sneer.

"The driver said he couldn't avoid hitting your colleague. Said Eduardo fell out of the sky in front of his car."

Lamb didn't smile, didn't respond.

I said, "So I thought maybe Eduardo got pushed in front of the car. A drunk could sort of expand on that, don't you think?"

Lamb didn't speak.

"You ever hear anything that would suggest that Eduardo was in trouble? He ever say something revealing?"

"Revealing? What's that, detective speak?"

"Yeah. Did he?"

"No," Lamb said.

"He didn't say, 'Golly, Al, I'm worried someone might drop me out of the sky in front of a car?'"

Lamb's eyes were getting smaller which made his other features look even thicker. He pushed on his lips with the eraser end of a wooden pencil. I once saw a cow that was mouthing a fence post. They had similar lips.

"You want to open an account?" Lamb said. "Otherwise, get out of the bank."

I stood up and turned to leave. "Later, amigo."

I had an hour before the bank closed. Spot and I waited. Five minutes after closing, Lamb came out and got into a Buick. He pulled out of the lot and turned left. I followed as Lamb made more turns and climbed up into one of the rich neighborhoods above

Incline Village. Lucky for me, Diamond's Orange Flame was invisible. Lamb never seemed to notice me tailgating him.

We crawled around sharp switch-backs and came to two expensive houses that were side-by-side. Lamb turned in at the second one. The drive was made of red brick laid in an elaborate floral design. The house was stone and cedar shakes and had a little garden just out from the front entry. There was a sculpture in the garden, a full-sized bronze of a quarterback throwing a pass. I wasn't sure what the house would cost, but it would require an income about eight hundred times larger than the salary of a banker. Maybe there was a rich, young woman in the picture who ran a mutual fund and was attracted to an alpha male with bovine lips.

Lamb parked the Buick behind a gleaming pearl-colored Lexus. I pulled in after him, boxing him in.

"Spot," I said. "Guard me. Understand?" I tapped my chest with my index finger.

I leaned over and opened the passenger door. Spot got out slowly. He was stiff and in pain, and he showed it.

I climbed out just as Lamb did. Spot came around and stood near my side, but didn't seem too alert.

Lamb turned toward us. "You are a pest. A gangly, stubborn pest." He seemed to ignore Spot.

"That airy voice of yours, you talk like that on purpose?"

He looked at me without emotion. Which meant lots of emotion.

I said, "I bet you tell the girls you played for the Packers, took a forearm block across the throat and that's why you sound so funny."

His face went from pink to red. "I did play for the Packers, you sumbitch."

A man came out of the house next door. He walked toward his car in the driveway next to us.

"Oh, now I remember," I said. "Allen Lamb, the Benchwarmer Man. Still had a clean uniform at the end of the season."

Lamb might have been a great football player, but any good middleweight could have taken him in the ring. He telegraphed the coming swing so much that both Spot and I were ready. It was easy to dodge, and Spot made a little jump and grabbed his wrist on the follow-through.

Lamb yelled as Spot pulled down, his jaws like a bear trap with 170 pounds attached. Spot growled deep and loud.

"GET HIM OFF ME!" Lamb yelled. He was bent at the waist and Spot was pulling his arm out like tug-of-war. "Tell him to let go, or I'll swing him around and crush him against that tree!"

"Lamb," I said. "Maybe you don't know dogs, but they have an instinctive response. If you don't resist, they'll just hang on to you. Puncture your skin, but nothing more. But if you do resist, they bite harder, maybe break some bones. I know you're big and strong enough to swing Spot off his feet and around in circles. But the problem is, before you get him around, he'll bite your arm off."

Lamb's beady eyes had grown large. They flicked from me to Spot hanging onto his forearm. "I'm going to sue! This is assault with a deadly weapon! You're going to jail!"

I felt a tap on my shoulder and turned to see the neighbor who'd been watching from behind his car. He was shaky with tension and looked ready to run. "I'll be your witness," he said. He handed me his card. "I saw him attack you first. Your dog was only protecting you. You want me to sign something, let me know." The neighbor stared at Lamb who was still bent over, his arm stretched out to Spot's jaws. "Over a year now, since that guy moved in next to us. I kept telling my wife the guy's a hothead. It was only a matter of time, something like this happens." He turned and got into his car. He called out, "You give me a call." He started the car and sped off.

"Tell your dog to let go!" Lamb said.

Spot still held his outstretched arm.

"After you answer some questions."

"What, dammit? Ask your questions!"

"Why are you so hostile about Eduardo Valdez?"

"I'm not!"

"Lamb, you need medical treatment. Answer my questions and I'll tell my dog to let you go."

"It's just that... They made him vice president instead of me. I deserved it. I've been at the bank longer."

"Plus, you're a native-born American and a football hero."

Lamb looked up at me. "Yeah. It's unfair."

"So unfair you dragged him out to the highway one night?"

"No way. What kind of guy do you take me for?"

"Anybody else at the bank who felt like you? Somebody who might help Eduardo get run over by a car?"

"I don't know. They're taking our jobs. Taking our women, too. Could be lotsa other guys who'd like Eduardo gone."

"Eduardo that smooth with the ladies?" I was remembering the Incline Village rating system. Money, Education, Looks, Style.

"He had investments," Lamb said. "Some ladies, they're blind or something. Go out with any guy who has a bankroll."

"What kind of investments?"

"Real estate. He owned a bunch of rentals."

"Where?"

"Neighborhoods along the north shore. Little cabins he bought for seventy, eighty thousand each. Now they're each worth four or five hundred. Now tell your dog to let me go!"

"What did he do at the bank?"

"Mostly real estate loans."

"There's something that would drive someone to murder."

"Sure, the way he did it." Lamb's voice was a hiss. "He was into activist banking. Green banking, he called it."

"Meaning?"

"Where loan decisions aren't just based on the financial qualifications of the buyer and the viability of the project. If Eduardo didn't think the project was good for the environment, he wouldn't approve the loan. Guy deserved to die."

"Can you think of any other reason that someone would want to murder Eduardo, aside from the fact that he was a greenie and a successful Mexican who is stealing our jobs and our women?"

Lamb narrowed his eyes. "Isn't that enough?"

THIRTY-SEVEN

Spot and I camped again, hidden in the woods above the east side of the lake. I cleaned up as best I could in the morning, but still looked rumpled and dirty. I got Glennie on my cell.

"Remember you were telling me about Monica Lakeman and how she died? You said she left her estate to a charity for disabled kids."

"Right. Hard to find motive in that, huh?" Glennie said.

"Yeah, but I'm trying to be thorough. Any chance you learned which charity it was?"

"I don't think so. But hold on and let me get my notes out of the file."

I waited a long time. Lots of boats were out crisscrossing the lake. They were so far away that even the speedboats seemed to creep along.

"Owen, you still there?"

"Yeah."

"I found it. Sometimes I surprise even myself. It is called the Camp Twenty-Five Foundation. Must be connected to Company Twenty-Five, that outfit that just opened a store in Roundhill. Want me to look up the address?"

"Yes, please."

I cruised by the Camp Twenty-Five Foundation office. It was in an old, two-room cabin on the lake side of North Lake Blvd., near the area known as Tahoe Vista. The cabin was the old Tahoe Style that had tree bark siding. It sat under the canopy of pines.

There was an access road that ran past the cabin to the lake's edge. Between the cabin and the lake were majestic Incense cedars. Nearby, was a similar log cabin. Farther down, three new mansions stood side-by-side, facing the lake like beauty pageant contestants lined up for the judges.

An orange Karmann Ghia with a Harlequin Great Dane couldn't have been more noticeable if I'd outfitted it with blinking neon signs. So I parked on a deserted back street behind a motel several blocks from the Camp Twenty-Five cabin.

"Time to play deaf and dumb," I said to Spot as I opened my door. He was sprawled across the broken seat, his rear legs in the back of the car, his front paws hanging off the edge of the seat. He lifted his head up and rested his jaw on the dash. "Dogs who don't bark make for happy owners. Comprende?"

He ignored me.

A half-block down the street a woman was getting out of her minivan. Her black eyeliner was so heavy she looked ready for the Halloween Freaker's Ball. She stopped when she noticed me and then stared at Spot for several seconds. So much for a deserted street.

I cut through the motel parking lot and jogged across the highway, dodging the heavy tourist traffic.

A small hand-painted sign hung next to the cabin door. It said Camp Twenty-Five in green script over rough brown wood. Through a window I saw two women at desks, both on the phone. I made a soft rap rap with my knuckles, turned the knob and stepped inside.

The warm, humid air of the cabin was thick with scents of coffee and perfume. There were three desks. A small fan sat on the vacant one. A strand of yellow yarn tied to the metal grill verified that it was moving air, although I couldn't feel it.

One of the women said goodbye to the phone, hung up and turned to me. She had a red beehive hairdo and glasses from the fifties with red rims that came to points at the outside. "Welcome to Camp Twenty-Five Foundation, sir." She smiled. Her cuspids were very sharp. Some of her red lipstick had gotten on one. Or maybe she'd sucked the blood out of the last visitor and forgot to neaten up afterward.

"Good afternoon," I said. "I'm Jim Boyle from the Johnsrud Foundation down in Merced."

"Suzanne Stock." She reached out her hand to shake. She had soft, moist skin and long red nails that looked dangerous.

"Pleasure, Ms. Stock."

"You can just call me Suz," she said.

"Then Suz it is." Red Hues Suz, I thought. "And Jim works for me. Suz, this spring our board decided to increase our grants for disabled children programs and your foundation came up as a promising vehicle. So I'm here, one foundation to another."

The woman grinned at me. She picked up a pen and wrote Johnsrud Foundation on a Post-it note. "Well, well, Mr. Boyle," she said. "Jim. Anything I can do, just ask." The tip of her tongue made a slow journey along the edge of her top lip.

"I'd like to make some inquiries about your new camp."

"Of course. Anything you want." She raised her eyebrows and arched her back. "Please have a seat." She gestured toward two stick-legged chairs with embroidered cushions.

I pulled one up and sat down. "Correct me if I'm wrong," I said. "Our understanding is that you intend to build a camp for disabled kids?"

She nodded. "Yes, indeed. Right on the shore of Lake Tahoe." She pointed to a sign on the wall and read it aloud.

"Special Children.

God's Gift to the World."

It may have been brochure-speak, but she said it with sincerity.

"Excuse me," I said, "but isn't that terribly expensive? I mean, Tahoe lakeshore is some of the priciest real estate in the world."

Red Hues Suz gave me her biggest smile. There was lipstick on one of her lower teeth as well. "We feel that disabled kids from all backgrounds have the right to enjoy the unique environment of Tahoe just as the privileged children of the rich and famous do."

"But how would you ever raise that much money?"

"Thanks to the fundraising efforts of good people from all over, people like Senator Stensen, Camp Twenty-Five Foundation already owns eleven lakeshore lots." She grinned and paused to let me absorb this important detail. "We also have over a dozen lots that aren't on the lake. The foundation is attempting to purchase enough contiguous lots so that we can satisfy the T.R.P.A. requirements. We have commitments from sellers on dozens more. If all goes according to plan, we should be able to break ground in another year."

I glanced at the other woman. She was still on the phone and was drawing a small file along the edge of a long thumbnail. She didn't appear to notice me.

"Tell me," I said, speaking slowly. "This camp. How big will it be?"

"Our goal is to be able to invite one hundred Special Children at any one time, with no disability ignored. That means that many of the children will need personal attendants. However, our plan is for a Camp Twenty-Five endowment that is large enough to fund all eventualities. Even a quadriplegic child on a ventilator could be flown in with his or her full-time nurse." The woman stopped to smile some more. "Mr. Boyle, I mean Jim, you can tell your foundation that Camp Twenty-Five will be the premier destination playground for Special Children."

"What about the physical aspects of the camp. How many lots, how many buildings and such?"

She turned and reached over to the top of a floor safe, picked up a map that was mounted on foam board and set it on the desk so that it faced me. "Here is a parcel map. The parcels marked in green are already owned outright by the Camp Twenty-Five Foundation. The parcels in light green are ones where the owners have signed letters of intent stating that they are willing in principle to sell to the foundation. We just have to work out the details."

"Like price," I said.

Her smile disappeared for a moment, then came back full force.

"Correct," she said. "The parcels marked in yellow are the ones where we believe the owners will eventually agree to sell to us."

"What makes you think they will?"

"It's more or less a personal assessment by our executive director. She has an uncanny ability to predict these things. There are some owners I thought would never sell because their homes had been in the family for generations. Our director felt otherwise. Sure enough, they eventually sold. Like I said, she can tell which ones will cave." The woman suddenly put her hand to her mouth. "Oh! Did I say that?! Sorry, it is just a little joke we have around here!" Her face got red.

"No problem. I didn't hear it."

She reached out and patted my hand. "Thank you, Jim. You know how it is. Office banter and such."

"Of course." I was trying to see any of the parcel numbers on the map, but they'd been covered with whiteout. I pointed to the map. "These parcels marked in red. Let me guess. They are the problems, aren't they?"

"Yes. As you can see, among the many properties we've designated as necessary for the project are a few whose owners have stated that they refuse to sell."

"Could we make a copy of that map? I could take it back to my board and show them how much progress you've made."

"Oh, no, I'm sorry." She picked up the map, turned and set it back on the safe. "That is private information. We must respect the privacy of the sellers."

"Perhaps you have a list of their names? I'd like to talk to the people who don't want to sell."

Suzanne shook her head in alarm. "They have a right not to be bothered."

"I didn't mean I'd bother them. Just talk to them for another perspective on Camp Twenty-Five."

"Well, I suppose I could ask our director. But I don't think she would agree."

"What will you do about the people who don't want to sell?"

She smiled. "Eventually, they'll see the writing on the wall and realize that they don't want to stand in the way of one of the worthiest projects ever to come to the Tahoe Basin. Special children must come before property owners' concerns."

"Can you tell me about the programs that the camp will provide?"

"Actually, we have a prospectus that we hand out to our donors. Let me get you one." She stood up, opened a cabinet and handed me a large, glossy booklet. I flipped through it and saw that it was filled with pictures of handicapped children in wheelchairs and on crutches. They had happy grins on their faces as they chased beach balls in front of the lake, roasted hotdogs in a roaring campfire, and rode on sailboats with the wind in their hair and sun on their faces.

"Here are some more handouts," she said, handing me another brochure and several sheets of colored paper with fine printing. "The one on yellow paper is a letter of intent. You need not specify an actual amount. Just have your board look it over and pledge within one of the ranges printed on the sheet. You know how these things work. It isn't binding. But it will be invaluable when we approach other funding sources. We'll be able to say that..." she glanced down at the Post-it note where she'd written the name I gave her, "...that the prestigious Johnsrud Foundation has signed on to support us."

"Thanks, Suz," I said. "You can be sure we'll look this over carefully. And when we have questions...?"

"You can call me." She handed me two cards with gold embossed printing on a deep blue background. "Or you or your board members can speak to our executive director."

I looked at the cards. One said, Suzanne Stock, Consultant. The other one said, K.D. Scarrone, Executive Director.

Red Hues Suz gave me a shy grin. "Our cards make us look kind of fancy. I'm not really a consultant in the professional sense. But I do believe in my job."

"What about..." I read the other name, "K.D. Scarrone?"

"It's the same for K.D. She's so enthusiastic and good at fundraising that they gave her the director title. In truth, the board makes all the decisions. We're just the worker bees."

"Does she go by Ms. Scarrone?"

"She's real informal. You can call her by her initials. K.D. Around here, you'll hear her nickname. Lady K.D. You'll definitely have to meet her. Our most enthusiastic fundraiser, Lady K.D. is." Suzanne grinned some more.

"I'd like to talk to K.D. Where would I reach her?"

"Actually, she's rarely in this office. She owns the Hard Body Workout gym in Incline Village. You'll find her there most days. Here, I'll give you that card as well."

The other woman was still on the phone. I stood up and was turning to go when the door opened. "My God, the traffic!" a woman said as she entered. "I had to park way over behind the motel..." She turned and saw me. Up close, the eyeliner looked like it had been applied with a Magic Marker. "Oh, it's you," she said. "With the giant dog in the little orange car."

"You know Mr. Boyle?" Suzanne said.

"No, I just saw him getting out of his car a while ago. He's got this huge spotted dog. Like a Dalmatian, only about four times as big. What kind of dog is that, anyway?"

"Sounds like a Harlequin Great Dane," Red Hues Suz said.

I grinned at her. "You know your dogs," I said, then I left fast.

Back in the car, Spot barely lifted his head in greeting. He was wounded and hungry and homeless, and it affected him as much as it would the next person. I drove away thinking about the big heavy safe and the parcel map with the parcel numbers whited out, and Lady K.D. Scarrone, the Camp Twenty-Five Foundation director, the same Lady K.D., probably, who was Faith Runyon's madam.

For the first time since Faith's boat had exploded, I had the sense that I was getting somewhere.

THIRTY-EIGHT

I found the Hard Body Workout gym on a side street in Incline Village. It was in a three-story, contemporary building just behind one of the shopping centers. I parked and walked into the foyer. The deep booming sound of music heavy with bass thudded through the building. There was a sign listing the occupants, and it read more like it was in Berkeley than in Nevada's richest community. The top two floors had an herbalist, a psychic, an alchemist, an aroma-therapist and a feng shui artist. The basement floor was devoted to the Hard Body Workout. I went down the stairs.

I pushed in through glass doors and walked into a wall of sound. It was a cavernous room lined with floor-to-ceiling mirrors. Half the room was filled with shiny chrome workout equipment on vinyl flooring. The other half had a hardwood floor. Music boomed from speakers in all four corners.

A group of about two dozen women in bright spandex with bold patterns jumped and danced to the beat. There was a hierarchy to their position. The fat women were at the back, the skinny women just in front of the fat ones. The front two rows had the showgirls and showgirl wannabes.

The leader of the group was an athletic woman in her early forties. She wore a glossy black suit with a lacy, pink design across the shoulders and down at the top of her butt. She had on pink high-top athletic shoes and big, bouncy, strawberry blonde hair. She called out commands as she danced, but the commands were lost in the music. Unable to hear, the sweating group watched and tried to imitate her. The music was deafening and the scent was suffocating, perfume and sweat and a touch of patchouli.

It was the kind of gym I'd expect in the inner city, surrounded by the steel and concrete jungle. But in the outdoor recreation capital of California and Nevada it seemed surreal.

I walked up to the front desk where a teenage girl sat on a stool. She looked up at me, her lips stuck in a petulant pout. "Yeah?" she shouted over the music.

"I just stopped by to see Lady K.D.," I shouted, hoping the phrasing would work regardless of whether K.D. was in or not.

The girl glanced over at the woman who was leading the group, then scowled at her nails. "Well, she's gonna be awhile."

"I'll catch up with her later," I said.

"Whatever," the girl said without looking up.

I left.

I took Spot for a walk around the area, always listening for the boom boom of the dance music. When it stopped, I put Spot back in the Karmann Ghia and loitered near the building. K.D. Scarrone came out, walking fast. She'd changed into a business suit, gray jacket, gray pants, low, black pumps and a black leather briefcase that hung from a shoulder strap. Her hair was pulled back in a tight bun. She walked over to a polished black Mercedes.

"Lady K.D.?" I said, approaching.

She opened her car door and stood behind it, ready to jump in and lock the door. "And you are...?"

"Owen McKenna. I'm a private investigator. You and I have some business in common that I'd like to speak to you about."

"What business is that?"

"Faith Runyon."

"I don't know any Faith Runyon."

I leaned on the fender of her Mercedes. She glared at where I was touching her car. "K.D.," I said, "I don't play games, and I don't like to waste time. Either I get the information from you or I start asking around town until someone else can help me. I'm discreet, and I have no desire to tell others about your other business, but I imagine it will get out. Maybe you don't mind that."

It took her two seconds to make a decision. "Get in. We'll talk in the car." I rode shotgun as K.D. Scarrone drove her polished black Mercedes through Incline Village. We took some back roads and ended up on Lakeshore Blvd. Her perfume had a hint of pepper, and it mixed with the leather of the car's interior.

"I know you were Faith Runyon's madam," I said after we'd driven a mile.

K.D. glanced at me. The Mercedes drifted toward the edge of the road. I gestured toward the windshield. She looked and corrected the car's direction with a jerk of the wheel. She drove straight for a moment, then pulled over and parked in front of a mansion with a "for sale" sign out front.

I waited for her to speak. The big metal sign was stuck into the grass near my passenger window. It said WOODS REAL ESTATE. Below the title were the words Can't See The Real Estate Forest For The Trees? Call Daniel Woods.

She didn't speak, so I decided to provoke her. "How could you do that?" I said. "Selling Faith like a commodity. She was well-spoken, beautiful, no doubt intelligent. She could have earned a living doing countless other things." My voice had a bite to it. "What kind of person are you?"

"Don't you dare to judge me without knowing what my circumstances are!" K.D. Scarrone glared at me across the front seat, her fingers white on the black leather steering wheel. Her nails were perfectly shaped and painted with little songbirds. A different species for each nail.

"What are your circumstances?"

K.D. stared out through the windshield. Her lower lip twitched once. She stopped it and tensed her lips together.

I waited half a minute. An automatic sprinkling system turned on in the yard next to us. A dozen black, sprinkling heads spit and crackled and then sprayed half-circles of water over thick, green grass. A red Porsche flashed by, going twice the speed limit. The Mercedes made the slightest of rocking motions in the wake of the Porsche. She still didn't speak.

"K.D.," I said, "Faith knew something about Glory, the singer who died. She was going to tell me what it was, but she died when she was coming to meet me out on the lake. Since she contacted me, someone has been trying to kill me. They will try again. If they think you knew whatever Faith knew, they will come after you as well. The more I know about Faith and you, the better I'll understand what I'm dealing with." I shifted in the car seat, cocked my left knee to the side and turned toward K.D. Her tension had added a bitter edge to her perfume. Her hands still gripped the wheel.

When she finally spoke, her words were slow and measured. "I first saw Faith ten years ago on South Virginia in Reno. The worst section of the street. I was driving back from a party. It was maybe two in the morning."

K.D. paused and closed her eyes, remembering.

"She was walking down the sidewalk, wearing these little white hot-pant shorts with nylons and high-heeled boots. I slowed and pulled over. This girl kept coming down the sidewalk toward my car. She listed, not like a drunk, but worse. Like a drug addict. She came up to the passenger window and shouted at me. Her words were slurred and I couldn't understand. She shouted again. I realized she was asking if I wanted sex. I hit the button to roll the window down."

K.D.'s eyes were still closed, tighter now with the memory. "When she saw that I was a woman, she leaned against the car and started sobbing and mumbling about needing money. Her shorts were filthy with dirt and her nylons were run. She was skinny as an eyeliner pencil. I unlocked the door, opened it and told her to get in. She looked at me with suspicion and moved away. So I told her I'd give her money if she got in. She was wary, but helpless with drugs and hunger. She got in."

K.D. opened her eyes and turned to look at me. "I turned on the inside lights. Up close I could see that she was a child. Fifteen or sixteen years old. Her makeup was thick to try to cover up a black eye and bruises on the side of her head. She shook with withdrawal symptoms.

"I took her home and got her cleaned up," K.D. continued. "She cried and shook all night. At one point she screamed that I had to take her back to her man who would give her a fix. I had to physically restrain her. In the morning I got my doctor to come to my house. He gave her something and said she'd be okay if I could keep her in one place for a week and get some food into her. He said that's how long she'd wrestle with the physical craving for drugs."

K.D. sighed. "That was the hardest week of my life. But I got her calmed down. I learned that she was a runaway from Idaho. She'd had a terrible childhood. The worst kind of abuse. So I told her I was going to take care of her, get her back into school and, if she wanted, teach her the gym business."

"But she was still a hooker ten years later," I said. "What happened?"

"After she'd been with me for two weeks, she ran away. I found her three days later, back down in Reno, walking the street. I brought her home again and tried to keep a tighter watch on her, but she ran away again."

"If you gave her a better opportunity, a chance at a better life, why did she keep going back to the street?"

"I'm not sure. I imagine it was because that was the only world she knew. It was how she had always earned her keep, and more importantly, how she found approval."

"And how she got her drugs," I said.

"Yes," K.D. said, nodding. "It took me longer to find her the second time. I put the word out to streetwalkers, paid them, called their pimps. Eventually, I got a call that Faith was working a different neighborhood. I found her and brought her to my home one more time. This time, I decided that if she was going to be a hooker, at least I could show her how to do it a much better way."

"That is heartless. You sold a young woman for profit?"

K.D. didn't respond. She sat there, gritting her teeth.

"What made you do such a thing?"

K.D. stared out the windshield. She glanced over at the sprinklers, then looked across the street where the lake was just visible between the mansions.

I was getting very irritated. "K.D..."

She finally shouted at me, "Because that was the world that I knew best, too!"

THIRTY-NINE

K.D. brought me back to the gym. I transferred to the Orange Flame where Spot waited. I followed her up to her house.

It was a small, dramatic structure that clung to the mountain up above Incline Village. We sat in her living room. It had floor-to-ceiling windows that provided a grand view of the lake. In one corner of the room was a large cobblestone fireplace with a natural gas insert. On the mantle was a picture of a man who was made up to look like Charlie Chaplin. He was mugging for the camera. The resemblance was impressive. I picked it up.

"My old boyfriend," K.D. said. "Baker Camden."

"Quite the name," I said.

"Quite the cutup. I was introduced to him by my father. Baker was a disaster by every measure. Only reason I still have the photo is I thought it was funny. He liked to play dress up. Pretend he was someone famous."

Evening had come and there was a chill in the air. K.D. touched a thermostat and the gas fireplace grew a blue flame among the ceramic logs. Spot was already lying in front of the fireplace. K.D. walked over to a small bar and poured us each a drink, a beer for me in a tall glass, bourbon on the rocks for her. She sat on the hearth and pet Spot near his wound.

"What happened to your dog?"

"The guy who is trying to kill me shot into my cabin one night. He got Spot instead of me."

K.D. gasped, her eyes huge. "That is terrible! The poor thing!" She pet Spot tenderly, running a finger up his nose and over his head. A big, long-haired tabby cat came out from under a couch and walked toward them. Spot lifted his head to look. The cat paused, then continued forward and sniffed Spot, nose to nose.

"Animals can always tell who is safe, don't you think?" K.D. said. "Whether it's people or other animals."

I nodded. In the warm evening light, I saw that K.D. was quite pretty, with high cheekbones and green, almond-shaped eyes.

"I was an only child," she said. "My mother died in a car accident when I was three. My father tried to raise me. But he didn't know how to be a father, never mind be a decent human being. He wanted to be a Navy fighter jock but didn't make the cut. He spent his career fixing air conditioning systems on aircraft carriers. I was left with a neighbor lady whenever he shipped out. Dad paid her a few bucks a day, and she spent it on smack. Low-grade, street heroin. I was eleven years old the first time I shot up." K.D. gripped the inside of her elbow. "I almost died. But I was the strongest-willed kid you ever saw. If it didn't kill me, I'd try it again.

"Dad would come home and find me strung out. He'd beat me up, tell me I was no better than a street whore. Then he'd leave me again. I hated him more than I can say. Still do."

"So you became what he detested to spite him."

"Partly, yes. And partly because I came to hate myself just as much as him."

"Is he still alive?"

"Yes. The jerk popped a vessel in his brain and ended up in a home in Fresno. He can't talk, but his brain is still there. I can see it in his eyes."

"Now you're a successful businesswoman. Can't you leave him behind and focus on the rest of your life?"

"No. I'm going to be sticking my success in that bastard's face as long as he is still drooling on himself. Sometimes I'd like to hit him the way he hit me. I'm strong and physical." She put her arms up like a karate student and turned on the ball of one foot and the heel of the other. "I could kick him from here into the next life."

"What about Faith? Why let her go the same route?"

"Her childhood was not unlike mine," she said. "Never mind the sordid details. All I wanted was to teach her the lessons I'd acquired the hard way. But it seemed hopeless. The girl was stubborn and willful. Hell, I'm beating around the bush. The truth is she was the most impossible little witch you can imagine."

K.D. stood up, walked over to the windows and looked out at the darkness. She started crying. "I still can't believe she died." K.D.'s tears grew until she was sobbing. She pressed her hand to her face and bounced her forehead against the window glass. I waited while she cried.

"You know how life presents you with choices every day," she said with her back to me. "It seems so simple for most of us, making the right choices. By the age of twenty-one I'd come around and was making choices in my own best interest, accepting that they included working in the sex trade. I steadily upgraded my pimps, then found a madam who specialized in a higher-class clientele." K.D. turned to face me. "But with Faith, it was the opposite. She made the wrong choices at every opportunity. It was as if everything she did was designed to make her life more difficult."

K.D. took a long drink, the ice cubes piling up around her upper lip as she drained the last drops of amber from her glass. "It was seeing that incredibly self-destructive behavior that made me start to understand myself." She shook her head as if still amazed. "There I was in my early thirties, trying to straighten out a broken girl, and I was only beginning to understand that I still hated what I'd been, where I'd come from. I was still broken myself. Maybe I still am. But I'm trying." K.D. swallowed.

"So I taught her how to present herself. How to talk, how to listen, how to walk. I taught her bedroom tricks, what to do with clients to keep them calling back." K.D. paced in front of the windows. "Lady K.D.'s finishing school for street whores." Her voice was hard and derisive. "I knew there should be a better way to keep Faith off the street and away from the pimps and their drugs. I just didn't know what that way was. So I figured that if she was going to be a whore anyway, I'd teach her how to be a high-class whore.

"Within a few years," K.D. continued, "Faith was very successful. She had a regular clientele of some of the richest and most powerful men on the West Coast, men who were willing to pay a fee that, frankly, was exorbitant. But these are multi-millionaires, even billionaires, so cost didn't matter. They would pay anything to have Faith with them for an evening. She was that captivating. The more obscure clients would take Faith out on the town, either here in Tahoe or down in Reno. The famous clients who didn't want to be recognized would go to their private estates, gated mansions on the lake where only the butler and wait-staff would see them."

"Faith must have been getting rich."

"Yes, she was. But she still hated herself, just like I did. I tried to talk her into changing her life. She had more than enough money to quit. I talked to her about self-respect. But she wouldn't hear it. I think she hated me as well. And I guess I don't blame her considering I kept her going in the profession. I got her cleaned up, got her off drugs, made her rich, but none of that mattered to her."

"What makes you think she hated you?"

"It wasn't anything direct. Just her pride, mostly, in having my ex-husband as a client. She liked to have that subject come up."

"Who's your ex?"

"Doesn't matter anymore. Just one more of those rich clients of hers. I first met him as a john before he became the big guy on the block. It was dreamy, the way he took me on as a personal project, romanced me, treated me to a nice life. We married and had a few good years. I think he even loved me a little. First time I'd ever experienced that. Then I turned thirty and he moved on to younger women.

"It wasn't until Faith had been with me for years that my ex called me up and wanted a date with her. One of his famous friends had recommended her."

"That must have been painful," I said.

K.D. made an exaggerated nod. "And as a personal insult, he offered such a ridiculous sum to have Faith that I thought it was a joke. The next day I discovered he'd deposited half the money in my account. He called back and said it was a down payment."

"He knew your bank and account number?"

"It wouldn't make any difference with him whether he did or

not. He has people who can find out."

"So you accepted," I said.

K.D. nodded. "He became one of Faith's best customers, and he put a lot of other rich men onto her."

"Didn't some of them want to do like your ex did with you? Take her off to their own private island?"

"Absolutely. She got a proposal from about a third of her clients."

"Why wouldn't she take one of them up on it?"

"Because she thought she was too vile to deserve a real life."

"But she never let her clients see that side of herself," I said.

"No. She was the consummate actor. What she did was a masterful performance designed to get huge dollars and have them begging for more. She was far more successful at it than I ever was." K.D. appeared to study her glass. "Far more beautiful, too."

"You stayed out of the business after your divorce?"

"Yes. In the years just before I met my ex, I'd been doing quite well and I put a good amount away. When he left me I was able to buy this house and start my gym."

"Sounds awfully sensible for a prostitute."

"You'd be surprised how practical sex workers are. The ones who stay off drugs, anyway. Many of them want to get into a better business, but don't have the capital. And all of them realize that there is an age where the business begins to wane and the clients turn to younger product. The practical girl makes plans for some-thing else by the time she turns thirty."

"You make it sound respectable."

K.D. sat down on the edge of one of the leather chairs. "The sex trade is incredibly demeaning to girls at the bottom end, the ones who work the streets and seedy clubs. But for someone like Faith, someone who is able to be picky about her clients, it can be acceptable work. Some girls even enjoy the business. Not the sex, but the business. The money can be great, and it is flattering to have important men want to be with you. But do any of them have self-respect? I doubt it."

I looked at K.D., trying to envision the neatly-dressed, middle-aged businesswoman as a young prostitute.

"You disapprove," she said.

"Yes, I do. But I also believe most any activity between con-senting adults is none of my business."

"You think you wouldn't hire a call girl."

"No, I wouldn't."

"I've seen men like you melt when they saw Faith in an evening gown."

"I don't melt."

"You have a mate?"

"Yes."

"What if you were rich and single?"

"What I think isn't germane to investigating Faith's death."

"You're avoiding the question," K.D. said.

"I think sex is sacred. It's not something I would purchase."

"You are a Puritan."

"No. It's a personal point of view. No Bible attached. Anyway, if Faith was rich, and she hated herself, I would think you could have succeeded at getting her into a more legitimate business."

"You're thinking that it was in my interest to keep her working the trade so that I could get richer as well. But I wanted her to quit. She would not hear of it." K.D. stood up and walked a few paces away. "You don't believe me."

"Yes, I do," I said.

"Why?"

"Because you sound sincere."

K.D. stared at me. "You know, Mr. McKenna, you are a piece of work. Where were you about twenty years ago?"

"Working for the San Francisco Police Department."

"You were a cop? Figures." She got up and walked over to refill her drink. "Want another beer? Or do people who think sex is sacred stop at one? Oh, I'm sorry. I shouldn't have said that."

"Don't worry about it. Yes, I'll have another."

She brought our drinks over and sat down. "So what do we need to do to find Faith's killer?"

FORTY

"I need Faith's client list."

"I was afraid of that." She shook her head. "I can't."

"You must. Almost for certain, it was a client she overheard. That doesn't mean the client killed her. But it is the only place I have to start."

"But the rest of her clients are innocent. Maybe even the client she heard this thing from – whatever it is – is also innocent. I can't have you going around asking embarrassing questions. Those men have reputations at stake. You could ruin them."

"You're afraid I'll ruin you in the process."

K.D. looked infuriated. "No, I'm afraid for them! I have principles, too, Mr. McKenna! Maybe my principles aren't the same as yours, but that doesn't mean I don't have them!" Her voice reverberated in the room.

"I can call the sheriff. They'll get a search warrant."

"They won't find anything. Only I know the information. One thing I learned long ago is that what isn't written down can't be found. The little that is written down is noted in a manner that is meaningless to anyone but me."

"Maybe there are other things you can tell me that would help."

She didn't speak.

"How did Faith's clients find out about her? Did you put the word out in certain circles?"

"No. At least, not since the very beginning. It was all referrals. One of her clients would tell another man about her and pass on my phone number."

"They always called you?"

"Yes, that is the rule. Everything about Faith was kept private. Her clients never knew her phone number, or where she lived or even her real name. We made up the name Faith Runyon. She had a pretend occupation as well. Modeling. It gave her something to say, and it fit with how she looked."

"What is her real name?"

"I never knew. When I first met her, she called herself both Faye Taylor and Raye Thomas."

I watched K.D., wondering if she was telling the truth.

"How did it work? The arrangements."

"Clients would call a number and leave a message. I would call them back, and, in the beginning when many of them were new, ask some qualifying questions. We were especially careful about disease and vice and the police. If the potential client wasn't completely forthcoming, I would hang up and refuse future calls.

"If I was satisfied with their answers, they would pay in advance by credit card. In later years, all of her customers were repeats."

"You have a bank account for this business?"

"The income goes to my gym, and Faith's cut went to her as a salaried personal trainer. People pay lots of money for that. With a little help from one of her clients who had political connections, Faith got a Social Security number in the name of Faith Runyon. The IRS never audited either one of us. Everything was handled honestly, and we always paid our full taxes."

"How many clients did she have?"

"I won't say."

"Where did she meet them?"

"I won't say," she repeated.

"I've already learned that she met some of them at Squaw Valley."

"Good for you."

"How much did she charge?"

"I won't say."

"What was your cut?"

K.D. looked at me and didn't speak.

"What was the average age of her clients?"

K.D. bent down and pet Spot.

"Let's try it this way," I said. "I can go over the relevant facts. They may suggest a particular individual to you. If so, you can consider telling me that person's name without giving me Faith's entire client list. If not, at least we may be able to rule out some of her clients."

K.D. looked at me. "I'll think about it."

"Okay. Let's start with what she told me, that she overheard someone say something. That suggests that one of her clients had other people around when he was with Faith. Or he spoke on the phone when he was with Faith. Can you think of anyone where Faith had mentioned such activity? Where she wasn't alone with a man?"

"There were many times when Faith would have had an opportunity to overhear something. I don't know the specifics, but she made comments here and there. At times she accompanied her client to small private gatherings. There were also occasional parties where a client wanted her to be on his arm. And of course there were shows and restaurants, sometimes in Reno, sometimes in South Lake Tahoe. I suppose she could overhear something sensitive at any of those places. It could have been any number of clients."

"True. But you probably have an idea of the men who were loners or else were very secretive. The men who would be very discreet about every meeting with Faith and equally discreet about everything they would say. My guess is that those men can be ruled out."

K.D. gave a slight nod.

"Ruling out those men," I continued, "would leave how many others?"

K.D. shook her head.

I tried a different tack. "Many men have lives without any component that would induce murder. They may be rich, but it is because they own a nuts and bolts company. The biggest secrets in their lives are their email passwords. On the other hand, there are men who are connected to the mob or political figures or are simply so wealthy that they are constantly exposed to information that could never be allowed to get into the wrong hands without creating murderous implications. Considering those two different kinds of individuals, do any of Faith's clients stand out?"

K.D. gave Spot another pet.

I was getting nowhere. I finished my second beer. "You're the executive director of the Camp Twenty-Five Foundation. How did that come about?"

K.D. seemed to relax. "I was looking for a way to give back to the community. One of my customers mentioned it, and I got involved in fundraising for them. I thought I was doing an okay job. I even called some of my old clients and some of Faith's clients as well. Turns out I blew the doors off their previous fundraising efforts. The board asked me to be their executive director. It is mostly a cheerleader position. But I guess I'm good at it. It makes me feel good to be involved in such a good charity."

I took that in. She was smooth, and it sounded sincere. "K.D., several names have come up in my investigation. I wonder if you have ever heard of them?"

"Shoot."

"There's a Deputy Rockport who works for Douglas County Sheriff's Office. Ring a bell?"

She shook her head.

"What about a snowboarder named Bobby Crash?"

"Oh, sure. Where did I hear that name? Isn't he the one who rides for Company Twenty-Five?"

"Yes. Know anything about him?"

"No. Just heard his name, that's all."

"What about Tyrone Handkins?"

K.D. frowned. "I feel like I've heard that name somewhere. Or read it in the paper?"

"He was Glory's bodyguard."

"That's right. The paper did a big article on her death up on the Flume Trail. They mentioned him as a possible suspect."

"K.D., when I spoke to Faith, she said she had something to

show me. After the boat explosion, the Coast guard fished a lot of pieces of paper out of the water. We've assembled them together like a jig-saw puzzle, and they made a picture of a golf course. Can you think of why Faith might want to show me a picture of a golf course?"

K.D. looked surprised. "I have no idea. As far as I know, Faith never played golf in her life. She certainly never mentioned anything about golf to me."

"Do you know what the connection is between Company Twenty-Five and Camp Twenty-Five?"

"One of the Camp Twenty-Five board members was talking about it once," K.D. said. "He said there wasn't any legal connection between the two. Apparently, Company Twenty-Five let Camp Twenty-Five use their name concept because they felt it was beneficial to their image."

"Who was the board member who told you that?"

"Eduardo Valdez. He was killed in a terrible accident not long ago."

"The man who was run over."

"Yes. We couldn't believe it. He was a wonderful man."

"Can you give me the names of the other board members?"

"I only met about half of them at a cocktail party fundraiser. Suzanne Stock knows them much better. She could give you a list. Frankly, I'm not at the Camp Twenty-Five office much. My director title is just a title they gave me to honor my fundraising. Suz and Betty are much more hands-on than I am."

I stood up. "If I have any other questions, may I call?"

"Of course." K.D. stood up and smiled. She held out her hand. "I hope I've been helpful."

Spot and I were out the door when she called out to me in the dark. "Mr. McKenna?"

"Yeah?"

"I just want you to know that Faith was a good kid."

I nodded as I wedged Spot and myself into the Orange Flame.

FORTY-ONE

I got Street on my phone as I drove away. She was still safe at Caesars. I gave her an update and we whispered sweet nothings before we hung up.

I continued south and was turning into the Spooner Lake Campground when my phone rang.

"Hello?"

"Owen McKenna?" The peculiar grunts were unmistakable.

"Wheels. What's happening?"

"Something came up. Thought I should call. Of course, it may be nothing, but one never knows, eh?" He grunted. "I was over at the bike shop, the one that referred you to me? Anyway, a customer came in, said he wanted to rent a good mountain bike. Wanted to do the Flume Trail."

"Lot of people doing the Flume at the height of the tourist season."

"Yeah, but get this." Another grunt. "He mentioned...Oh, hold on, that's the doorbell. I've been waiting on my pizza delivery."

I heard the phone being set down. I waited half a minute. I thought I could hear Wheels speaking in the distance. Then the phone was picked up. "This old cabin has thin walls, McKenna. I heard everything from outside." The metallic robot voice, high in pitch, androgynous terror. "Wheels is still alive, but I don't know if you can get here fast enough to save him. Do you even know where he lives? I'll give you a clue. Zephyr Heights." The line went dead.

I glanced in the rearview mirror. No one was close. I jerked the wheel and hit the brakes hard. The Orange Flame spun around in the campground road. The car came to a rest facing toward the highway. I jammed it into first, revved the little engine, popped the clutch and sped back down the road. Spot moaned with the sudden motion. We shot out onto the highway, skidding sideways. I dialed 9-1-1 as I raced south and rattled off the information to the emergency operator. Then I hit the speed dial code for Diamond. He answered on the third ring.

"I was talking to Wheels Washburn when robot voice arrived at Washburn's door. He's going to kill him. I'm near Spooner Lake, heading south. The killer said Washburn lives in Zephyr Heights. Taunting me. I don't know what the street address is, or even if Zephyr Heights is accurate."

"I can find out," Diamond said. I heard him on his radio. When he came back on the phone, he barked out Washburn's address in Zephyr Heights. "I'm at Roundhill," he said. "I'll be there in a couple of minutes. See you there."

There were two sheriff's Jeeps parked in the dark drive when I arrived 15 minutes later. Diamond's pickup was in the street. I left Spot in the Orange Flame and found Diamond, Rockport and another deputy in the narrow backyard which was lit up by a flood on the back corner of the house.

There was a pile of split wood stacked on one side of the yard. On the other side was a pile of rounds, cut into 16-inch lengths, unsplit and unstacked. A chain saw rested on the pile. There were also some uncut logs 8 feet in length. In the middle was a hydraulic log splitter. The body was pinned down on the splitter rail, held in place by one of the heavy 8-foot logs. A branch had been wedged against the hydraulic pump lever. The piston had pushed the body onto the splitting wedge, cutting it in half just above the hips.

Diamond jerked his head toward the victim. "Recognize him?"

"It's Wheels Washburn," I said.

He nodded. "Major contusion on his head. Looks like he was knocked out, then dragged out here."

"The neighbors didn't see anything?"

"Only one neighbor is home. She said that Washburn had been cutting and splitting wood earlier in the day. Then she heard the splitter engine fire up again about ten minutes ago. When it stayed constant for a long time, she came to look, just as Linetco pulled up. She's in her house, pretty hysterical."

"Who got here first?" I said.

Rockport said, "Linetco did. He said that..."

"Let's let him speak for himself," Diamond said.

Rockport turned red.

Linetco was a small, compact man in his late twenties, with dense black hair cut very short on top and nearly shaved on the sides. He stood at attention, chest out. His hands were clenched at his sides. They opened, fingers spread wide, then clenched again. "I was down on the highway at Zephyr Cove when the call came from dispatch. I came up straight away. Knocked on the door. No answer. Heard the splitter. Came around and found him like this. Then Rockport came, then Diamond."

"Did you see anyone driving away as you came up from the highway?"

Linetco shook his head. "No, sir."

"Rockport?" I said. He was still red. "No. No one on the road at all."

Two more Douglas County deputies arrived. They were Linetco's age, young guys pulling the evening shift. Then Sergeant Cardoza from Washoe County came around the side of the house.

"I heard a call about a killing," Cardoza said. He chewed gum like he was trying to pulverize it. "Was in the area, thought I'd stop by." When he saw the body he paled. His Adam's apple bobbed as he tried to fight the nausea by swallowing. He recovered fast, looking away from the body. He approached the others.

"Ralph Cardoza, Washoe County," he said. About my age, he was older than the other deputies. Although he was out of his jurisdiction, he seemed to command some respect. Linetco and Rockport went through the scenario again for his benefit. Diamond, in his civvies like Cardoza, but, unlike Cardoza, on suspension, stayed to the side. I excused myself and walked around to the front of the house as a Honda Civic pulled up. It had a lighted pizza sign on the roof. A pimply kid got out with a pizza box. "Pizza for

Washburn," he said. "That you?"

"I can take it," I said. I paid him. He handed me the pizza and drove off. I walked over and stuffed it into the garbage can next to Cardoza's Audi.

Cardoza came around. "McKenna, right? Couldn't recognize you in the dark except for your height."

We shook.

"Cold out here at night," I said. "Talk in the car?"

He nodded. We squeezed into his Audi.

The sergeant sat in the driver's seat, leaned his elbows on the steering wheel and put his palms on the front corners of his head as if to hold in the pressure. He took a deep breath. "That was tough back there. Never seen anything like it."

"Me neither."

"Is this the work of our guy?" he said. "The singer's boyfriend? Or someone working for him?"

"This is our killer," I said. "Whether or not he's Tyrone Handkins, I don't know."

"I heard about the shooting at your house. And the break-in at Deputy Martinez's house."

I told Cardoza about the phone calls from the killer.

"A robot voice, huh? What a sick bastard. Well, keep me informed. I got a singer's murder on my beat. Not just any singer, either. I want her killer."

"So how do you read this murder?" I said.

"I don't know. It's like this perp thinks it's a game. It's not enough just to kill somebody. It's gotta be in some twisted way."

"You think it's all about thrill?" I said. "Or a sex thing?"

"Could be," he said. He put his hands on the wheel, ten and two, and he rotated them like twisting motorcycle grips. Back and forth, twice, three times. "More likely, he just gets a rush out of making people die in unusual ways. Why shoot someone when you can cut them in half."

We were quiet for a minute.

"Some vacation you're having," I said.

"Yeah. What's the point of even trying to take time off."

"Stay in touch?" I said.

He lifted a closed fist and did a soft, slow hammer-motion on my thigh. "You too, bud."

I got out of the car, and he drove away.

I went and told Diamond I was leaving, then got back into the Orange Flame with Spot. It was a long, lonely drive back up the dark highway to the North Shore.

I tried to forget the image of Wheels Washburn. Forget that the helpful, innocent young man didn't know the depravity of the world he lived in. Pretend that we were a species whose focus was to build peaceful civilizations, compose grand symphonies, write love sonnets, paint great art. Our worst enemies were mother grizzly bears, great white sharks, aliens and asteroids. Not other men. Humans were special. We would never do what I kept seeing over and over.

Think about something else, any thoughts to stave off the demons. Water-skiing in the high-altitude sun. Chips and salsa and Sierra Nevada Pale Ale. Long hikes through the Desolation Wilderness. Street's bra strap across her shoulder blade. Liftoff in a small airplane. A Mountain Chickadee climbing around the trunk of a Jeffrey pine. Emerald Bay from the top of Maggie's Peaks. Oscar Peterson on the piano with Ray Brown on bass. Cross-country skiing at night under a full moon. Jimmy Stewart doing his Mr. Smith soliloquy. Turner's paintings.

Being tied to the mast while the boat was tossed about in a storm would bring on a nauseating vertigo. But at least you'd know you're alive. And you wouldn't think about psychopaths.

But it would remind you that you're alone.

We find for a moment, here and there, those amazing times where the companionship of another resists the aloneness. It can be as simple as the grace note of a stranger holding the door for you. Or it can be as deep and complex as the bond of a soul mate who understands every nuance of your struggle with the world and gives you complete love of mind and body.

Yet, in the end we're still alone.

The worst part of being on the run was missing Street. Although

I was comfortable spending time by myself and didn't pal around with buddies, I was still a loner by default, not by choice. I'd much rather be with Street. But she always kept a distance between us. It wasn't that she saw other men. For as long as I'd known her, I was the only man in her life. As best I could tell, she was afraid to get too close in case something happened to me. A result of a childhood where the people she depended on betrayed her.

I slowed as I came to a patch of fog that swirled thick, yellow tendrils past my headlights. It looked like something Turner would have painted.

I wondered if he'd been a lonely man. While he'd found great success with his art career, and he had a modest social circle, I hadn't read of any close relationships other than that with his father.

Turner did have a liaison with a woman named Sarah Danby. Some people thought he fathered her children. But Turner never married her. Why?

Had Sarah Danby refused him? If so, why would she be unwilling to commit to a successful artist and businessman? Had she, like Street, been scarred by an abusive childhood? Was she afraid of developing too much dependence on someone who could one day disappear?

How common was it that people were afraid to get too close to someone they loved?

I didn't know the answer. But I knew I was in a line of work where people shot at me and targeted those closest to me.

Anyone would want to keep their distance.

FORTY-TWO

I drove a few blocks past the Camp Twenty-Five cabin and pulled into the parking lot of a restaurant and lounge. Although it was midnight, there were still cars in the lot. If anybody saw the Karmann Ghia, they would think it belonged to a bar patron.

I had to leave Spot in the car because, even though Danes don't shed much, it would only take a few black and white hairs and paw prints to give away our identity.

I looked in Diamond's glove box for a fingerprint suppressor but found nothing useful. I didn't want to check the trunk because passersby, usually oblivious to people getting in and out of cars, are much more likely to notice someone digging around the trunk in the dark of night. Maybe I could tear up my shirt.

Spot lifted his head as I opened the door. I gave him a quick pet. "Just go to sleep," I said.

As I got out I swept my hand under the seat and found a dirty blue paper towel of the kind that gas stations provide for checking the oil. I stuffed it in my pocket, leaned on the door until it quietly clicked shut, then walked to the dark trees at the edge of the parking lot. I stayed off the highway, in the trees, skirting old cabins, vacation homes and the newer mansions that were taking over the area.

Soon, the dark outline of the Camp Twenty-Five cabin came into view. I came up behind it. Just as I ran up to the cabin, headlights flashed my direction.

I threw myself up against the cabin wall. The vehicle paused as its headlights caught me. If I didn't move...

The vehicle started moving, completing its turn. It drove along the shoulder of the highway, going slower than the rest of the traffic. In the dim light I saw that it was a van. It slowed almost to a stop. There was no light or sign of movement from behind its windows. The van stopped and turned off its lights. It was a good distance from me, but in clear line of sight. If they had binoculars, they could see me. I didn't move. After a long minute, the van's lights came on and it sped away. I waited another minute, wondering if it was coming back. But it did not return.

From my visit earlier that day, I thought the front door would be easy to jimmy, but I didn't want to leave marks. The large windows were modern, with tempered panes that have to be struck hard to break them. And when they break they sound like a bomb.

The back wall had a single window set up in one corner. Probably a bathroom window. It looked easy to open, but was small and high.

I found an empty metal garbage can at a nearby house. I carried it back to the cabin and set it below the little window. The can's bottom was old and corroded. I didn't dare put my weight directly on it. Gripping the cabin wall for balance, I stepped up onto the rim of the can.

The little window had hinges on the top edge and swung up and out. It was open about six inches. There was a support arm on one side that locked it into place. Using the paper towel, I reached in and unhooked it.

I pushed against the log wall with my feet, angled my shoulders and squeezed through the window frame. My hands hit the top of a toilet tank.

I did a handstand on the toilet tank, worrying that it would break off, then stepped down with my hands until I was doing a handstand on the toilet seat. From there I crumpled to the floor. I used the blue towel to wipe down the toilet tank and seat.

The only light in the cabin came from outside, broken rays that filtered in from car lights on the highway. I pulled out my penlight and turned it on.

Nothing appeared to have changed in the cabin since earlier in the day, except that the safe was locked. There were many files and desk drawers I could go through and perhaps somewhere in them I would find something revealing. But anything sensitive would probably be in the safe. Of course, a devious person might use the safe as a decoy and put the most significant documents in full view on a desktop, but I doubted it. Furthermore, Red Hues Suz had lifted the parcel map from the top of the safe. It was reasonable to think it was now locked inside.

I squatted down in front of the safe. It was a name brand and, despite what we see in the movies, nearly impossible to break into without resorting to methods that would destroy its contents.

Even so, there is often an easier way.

Years ago I went to a SFPD seminar on safecracking. A representative from one of the big safe manufacturers told us about a study that showed that 50% of people with safes put the combination in an obvious place near the safe. Like hiding a house key near the front door, it is a stupid thing to do, but people do it anyway.

I started on the safe itself. Holding the penlight in my mouth, I felt along the sides and edges of the safe, behind it against the wall and baseboard. The hand towel reduced my sensitivity, but I thought I'd still be able to detect a piece of paper taped out of sight. But I found nothing.

There was a potted plant on the floor next to the safe. I looked in the dirt and ran my hands around the pot.

Moving farther from the safe, I started in on the closest desk, pulling out drawers to look at their undersides, flipping through files, checking the computer keyboard and monitor, the paperweights and knickknacks. I looked for any written numbers that could be a combination.

After a half hour, I started in on the second desk, then widened my search to the entire cabin. After two hours I was ready to give up. My penlight had dimmed to yellow. I switched it off.

I didn't want to climb back through the window, so I went into the bathroom and reattached the window support arm. I could walk around to get the garbage can later.

I was about to leave when something caught my eye. I turned

on the penlight once again and shined it on the wall.

Next to the door jamb, was writing on the wall. It was in pencil. It said, "Before closing, turn off the space heater and coffee pot."

I'd been blind to the obvious. The note about closing was not written on a piece of paper, but in pencil directly on the wall.

I went back to the safe. I shined the penlight on the wall next to the safe, but it was too dim. I'd have to take the chance. The desk light was on a short cord, so I angled it toward the safe. It was in plain view of the window that faced the highway. But there was nothing I could see to hang in front of the window or in front of the desk lamp. I saw no cars nearby, so I flipped on the light.

The glare was blinding and it took me a moment to adjust. I checked the wall above and around the safe. Nothing. I looked over the floor and on the safe itself. There was no writing that I could see. I moved back and tried to see the setting from a larger perspective. I looked at it the way I'd learned to look at a painting. I let my eye follow one line to another, roaming around the scene, gradually going from the most important objects to the least. But all I saw was the safe and the wall and the plant. You can't write very well on a plant.

But you can write on the pot.

I grabbed it and leaned it back. The pencil marks were clear under the direct glow of the desk light.

Holding the plant with my left hand, I spun the dial with my blue towel. The mechanism was smooth and precise. I ran through the numbers, turned the handle, and the heavy door swung open.

Inside was a shelf with a blue three-ring binder and a stack of manila file folders. Each folder contained a sheaf of papers and was held together with a heavy rubber band. I lifted all of them out.

In the bottom of the safe was the parcel map Red Hues Suz had shown me earlier that day. I added it to my pile.

Just then headlights flashed in the window from the direction of the highway.

I flipped the desk light off.

The headlights came down the access road. It was a van, and it was driving fast.

I shut the safe and spun the dial. If the people in the van didn't know the combination, it could be hours before anyone knew what I'd taken. There was a Diet Coke twelve-pack box sitting next to the coffee maker. I dumped out the remaining cans and stuffed the manila folders and the binder into it, corner to corner. The map was too big, so I smacked it down on the edge of the counter, forced the foam board to bend in the middle, then slid it into the Coke box.

The van was almost to the cabin. I turned the deadbolt, jerked the door open and ran out into their headlights.

The van hit the brakes and skidded on the dirt. I sprinted around the corner of the cabin, into the shadows.

The van came to a stop. There was quick movement behind me. Footsteps pounded in the gravel, then went silent when they hit the soft mat of pine needles that surrounded the cabin. I slid as I turned the far corner and raced under the bathroom window. Maybe only one person had chased after me and someone else was waiting on the other side. Only one way to find out.

I turned the final corner and sprinted behind the van, illuminated only by the red tail lights. Then I was in the dark forest, running blind. After 50 yards, I stopped. The sound of the van's revving engine came through the trees.

Light shown on the three mansions by the lake, then headlights moved in the trees. I glimpsed the van through the foliage. It went down the access road toward the mansions, then did a slow U-turn and drove back out and stopped in front of the cabin.

The smartest thing for me to do was escape while I had the chance. But I couldn't resist the opportunity to see the killers.

I walked back through the trees toward the cabin. The van was parked in front, engine running, lights off. I came up through the trees, parted some branches and peered out.

It was a Chevy panel van from the late 70s, painted a dark tone, maybe gray, maybe brown, dented in several places. No one was in either front seat. Still holding the Coke box, I stepped out of the trees and walked around the rear end. The van's back doors had windows. I cupped my hands and peered in. The faint outlines of a few boxes were visible on the floor. There were no people.

I looked toward the cabin. The door was shut. Light spilled from the big windows. I moved up against the cabin wall and was crossing in front of the door when the cabin lights went out.

I sprinted toward the far side of the van as the cabin door opened. I peeked around. The killer was in the shadows, walking toward me. Either he wore a mask or his face was darkened. I saw the glint of a large handgun with a long barrel. If I ran into the woods he'd have a good chance of hitting me.

I jerked open the driver's door and jumped up into the seat. I pulled the shift down into drive as I floored the accelerator.

The old engine roared. It took a moment for the transmission to shift. The killer's gun spit fire. The passenger window and windshield exploded. The gears finally engaged with a huge jerk, rocking the van and spinning the wheels. I fishtailed away as more shots punctured the metal skin of the van.

The access road was a narrow stripe of darkness through the forest. I felt around for the headlight switch as I rocketed toward the highway. It was a pullout knob on the dash. I yanked it out so hard the knob came off. The headlights came on, but the dash lights were burned out.

When I got to North Lake Blvd., I turned right, away from the restaurant where I'd left Spot in the Karmann Ghia. I realized that my legs were bent up. I found the seat lever and slid the seat all the way back. A mile down, I turned left off the main road and doubled back through neighborhood roads, out of sight from the Camp Twenty-Five cabin. A narrow turnoff appeared. I took it and bounced down a rutted path into the woods for a quarter mile. I stopped and felt for the light switch, found the little pin that once held the knob and pushed it in. I turned off the ignition, got out and threw the keys into the woods.

FORTY-THREE

It was 2:00 a.m. by the time I got the Orange Flame wrapped up in its tarp at the Spooner Lake Campground. An hour later, Spot and I finished eating an insufficient dinner. We finally lay down on the ground and went to sleep without water or wine.

In the morning I inspected the documents I stole and discovered they were nothing but legal mumbo jumbo. They were filled with phrases like, 'Whereas the first party of the second part and the second party of the second part do hereby agree to addendum B, except that such proceeding shall be non-binding on the first party.' I realized I would need a legal translator.

We drove into South Lake Tahoe where I stopped at my friend Conan Reynolds' office. Conan runs a little law practice when he isn't hiking or skiing, which means he's in the office two or three days a week when the weather is bad and maybe not at all when it is good. His specialty is divorce which, as he likes to point out, isn't glamorous, but half the population eventually needs him. The papers in my possession had nothing to do with divorce, but I thought he'd be better than me at translating which party belonged to which part. He was in and was very busy watching the Cubs get vivisected by the Yankees. I dumped the Diet Coke box out on his desk.

"Where did you get this stuff?" he said as he rifled through the documents.

"A little bird dropped them by. I thought that before I pop them in the woodstove to heat the cabin, I'd see what they mean. Think you could do a quick translation?"

"Not now, I'm busy." He glanced at the TV. "I can look at them tonight. Stop by tomorrow?"

"Sure." I thanked him and went back out to where Spot waited in the Orange Flame.

I didn't know what my next move was, although I very much wanted a shower and fresh set of clothes. I decided to head out of town for the Bay Area and see if I could start at the other end of Glory's life. Unlike Faith, at least Glory came from somewhere. I could find a motel on the way.

I pushed the Orange Flame up and over Echo Summit and let her roll down the long hill toward the Central Valley. I gassed up in Placerville and continued on until I started to fall asleep near the coastal range.

There was an exit in Vallejo that promised lodging and shopping options. I got a change of clothes at a K-mart, found food for both of us at the Safeway, then turned into the closest motel. I told the desk woman that there were two of us, forgetting to mention that one of us had two extra legs and very large teeth. Shows what fatigue will do.

At three o'clock in the afternoon, Spot took one bed and I took the other. Eighteen hours later we woke up much refreshed. I showered and dressed and we headed into The City.

I found Upton in a cubicle at one of the San Francisco precincts. We exchanged handshakes and a little shoulder slapping.

"I had a question about Glory Washington's mother and brother."

"Anne and Luther," Upton said. He pointed to a chair. I sat.

"You said the brother died. What happened?"

"Don't know," he said, shaking his head.

"What about the mother? Any idea where she is now?"

"Nope," he said. "Let me make a call over to Oakland, see what I can find out." I pulled a familiar catalog off the corner of his desk and flipped through it as Upton worked his way through several layers at the Oakland PD. The catalog was for books and videos marketed to cops. Everything from how to disarm street thugs to the best way to make a high-risk vehicle stop.

Eventually, Upton got through to a cop in charge. They had a short conversation. Upton said, "Maybe I better send McKenna over to talk to you in person." After a few more words, he hung up and turned to me. "They don't know anything about Glory's mother. As for the brother's death, Lieutenant Reddenburg seems to know the situation well. He said feel free to stop by."

I thanked Upton and left. I headed back over the Bay Bridge, found a parking garage where Spot would be in the shade, and was soon in Reddenburg's office.

Reddenburg leaned back in his desk chair and laced his fingers behind his head. His short-sleeves revealed large biceps.

I sat on a gray metal chair with a ripped, green padded seat.

"So you were in homicide with Upton some years back," Reddenburg said after I'd introduced myself. "Why'd you quit?"

It was a question I'd been getting ever since, but I still dreaded it. "I was involved in a shooting. A kid was killed."

Reddenburg looked at me. "They clear you?"

"Yeah."

"But that doesn't make it easier."

"No," I said.

Finally Reddenburg said, "You came about Glory's family. I don't have much. The mother is Anne Washington. A good woman. Didn't deserve what happened. The brother was Luther Washington. Now there's a sad one. No surprise, him dying young, considering the crowd he ran with. But it sure was unfortunate. Luther was a really smart kid. I spent time with him, bringing him in now and then. Later, I spoke with one of his teachers and he had the same impression of Luther that I did. We both saw a potential in that kid that we rarely see in the other kids filling up our facilities."

"How'd he die?"

"Drowning. We pulled him out of the Bay one morning after a call from a dock worker."

"What was Luther involved in before he died?" I asked.

"Same as always. Motorcycle theft. The last time we brought him in, we had a good case. A witness to the theft of a Honda race bike picked Luther's mug out of the book. We found Luther's prints on the bike which we recovered from a chop shop we busted. So we charged him. His mother posted bail."

"And he ran."

"Right," Reddenburg said. "Now, here's the strange part. There was a gang killing right before we picked up Luther on the grand theft charge. A man got shot in one of the disputed turf areas. His wallet and watch were gone. After Luther jumped bail, we got an anonymous tip to look at Luther for the killing. So we got a warrant and went through his things at his mama's apartment. And there was the firearm under Luther's mattress. A little Saturday night popgun. Twenty-two caliber. Tests showed a match with the slug we took out of the victim's head."

"You think Luther was the killer," I said.

"It sure looked like it."

"What was strange about it?"

"First, the gun had been wiped of prints. If you're going to hide a gun under your bed, why bother wiping it down? Second, I didn't see Luther as the type. You get to know these things after working with kids for years. The kids who kill have cold eyes. Like something already died back in there. But that wasn't Luther."

"Maybe he was framed."

"I wondered that. Of course, his mama said no way did the gun belong to Luther. So I spent some effort on the idea, but nothing came of it."

"His jumping bail on the motorcycle theft charge might suggest he figured you'd make him for the shooting. But the gun under his bed doesn't make sense. Why not throw it away?"

"I don't know. Some killers don't think of the obvious." Reddenburg said.

"Did Luther's death look accidental?"

"Actually, it was hard to tell at first. The body had been in the water a while. Looked pretty bad. I didn't recognize him. The coroner eventually came back with drowning as the cause of death. There were no other signs of trauma to the body. But just because someone dies of drowning doesn't always mean it's accidental."

"He have ID on him?" I said.

"No. He had clothes on, but he'd been stripped of all valuables. Rings, wallet, necklace."

"If there was no ID, how'd you know it was Luther?"

"After he jumped bail, his mother reported him missing. Said he'd been calling and suddenly stopped. When we got a body that was skinny and looked like it could possibly be Luther, we called her in and she said it was her boy. Broke her heart, I think."

I could still visualize Mrs. Washington. Poor woman. First Luther. Now Glory.

"Glory's death," Reddenburg said, frowning. "They still think it was an accident?"

"Officially, yes. But that's why I'm asking about Luther."

"You got something on it?"

"Not much," I said. "Hearsay, innuendo. Another young woman called me to say she knew something. Then she was killed."

"The boat explosion I heard about."

I nodded. "I wonder if you can look in Luther's file and give me the address of his mother?"

Reddenburg stood up and dug in a tall, gray four-drawer cabinet. He pulled out a file and wrote down the address for me. I thanked him for his time.

I went to Anne Washington's apartment and found it full of kids and a young mom.

"Mrs. Washington?" she said, a blank look on her face. "You got the wrong apartment."

I knocked on three different doors down the hallway before I found someone who knew Mrs. Washington.

"Anne Washington was the sweetest person on the floor," a wizened, white-haired black woman said. She leaned against the doorway for support. "Years and years we lived in this building. I helped with her kids. We baked together. Cookies and breads. For the church bake sales. I was so sorry to see her go."

"When did she leave?"

"Some years back. After her boy died. She kind of fell apart. Started forgetting things like turning off the stovetop. I check the

stovetop every other minute, myself. You just can't have stovetops
left on. I worried about her. But then her daughter got rich. She's a
famous singer. Lord, can that girl sing. She came to help. But she put
her mama in an old folks home. Now maybe that's help according
to some, but not me." The woman shook her head. "'Course, Anne
would go crazy brain sometimes. But that doesn't mean she had to
leave her apartment. I'm older than Anne. But I'm not going to no
old folks home. Not me. I'll chain myself to the radiator."

"Do you know what home Mrs. Washington is in?"

"No. Someplace near Walnut Creek. All I know is you have to
be rich. But her daughter pays the bills." She leaned toward me and
spoke in a low voice. "Just between you and me, I don't think it's
right. All those white people. Mind you, you seem nice enough. But
Anne Washington should be with her own."

Back in the Orange Flame, I drove around until I found a
phone booth with a Yellow Pages. I jotted down the numbers for
nursing homes and assisted living facilities near Walnut Creek and
surrounding communities.

I called each and asked for Anne Washington. After seven
negatives, I finally got a positive at the Pleasant Acres Residences. A
woman said visiting hours were from 3:00 p.m. to 5:00 p.m.

It was already 3:00 and rush hour was starting, so I hurried.

The Oakland tunnel was backed up a mile, but the traffic,
while slow, was moving. I made it through the mountain and found
Pleasant Acres up on a steep hillside.

They directed me out to a large lawn behind the main building.
Artful gardens thick with flowers made it seem more like an
arboretum.

I introduced myself to a young woman in a blue business suit
and asked if she could tell me where Anne Washington was.

She brought me out across the grass to a spot of shade with a
beautiful view of the valley.

A woman sat in a wicker chair, facing the view, a sweet look on
her face. She wore an ankle-length yellow skirt and a yellow blouse
with lace trim at the neckline. The yellow fabric cast a warm glow

up onto her face which, despite the years, I still recognized.

"Mrs. Washington," the young woman said, "I've brought you a visitor. Mr. Owen McKenna is here to see you." The young woman smiled at both of us, then left.

"So nice to meet you again, Mrs. Washington," I said.

The woman turned her head a little and looked up at me. She kept smiling and gave me the tiniest of nods.

I sat cross-legged on the grass in front of Anne Washington, in what seemed like the glow of her yellow clothes and warm smile.

"We met some years ago, Mrs. Washington. I was a cop, and my partner and I came to your apartment to meet Luther."

She smiled at me. She had healthy, clear skin and a pretty face below thick hair, which was brushed up and back. Her eyes were deep brown and crinkled at the corners. They looked at me, not focusing perfectly, but still, I thought, taking me in.

"You gave us homemade cookies and you even played the piano. Your daughter Glorene sang. She had a wonderful voice."

Anne Washington started humming, her smile as warm as ever. Her voice was rich and deep. It was obvious where Glory had gotten her talent. I didn't recognize the tune. A blues. Mournful. Emotive. Yet still she smiled.

"I came to ask you about Luther and Glorene," I said.

She hummed and smiled.

"I'm a private investigator and I'm looking into Glory's death. I wanted to ask if you were aware of anything unusual about your daughter before she died."

She kept humming.

"Did she contact you? Did she say anything strange?"

No response. A gray squirrel ran by, and the woman's eyes followed it for a bit. Then she looked out over the valley. Then back at me. Her smile was undiminished. She was humming a new tune, now.

"Mrs. Washington, I'm interested in any thoughts you have about Glorene. Anything at all that comes into your mind about recent events. Any concerns? Anyone else asking you questions? Is anything worrying you?"

It was obvious that the woman was gone, in a happy place. The rest of us should be so content.

I stood up to leave. I decided to try one more approach. "It's been nice talking to you, Mrs. Washington, on such a cloudy day."

"It's a sunny day."

I sat back down. "Are you so happy because it is a sunny day? Or are you happy for a different reason?"

She smiled. Her eyes looked at the sky, slightly out-of-focus.

It was frustrating. I didn't think she was trying to be difficult. Nor did it seem like it was a game to her. She wouldn't respond. Except when I provoked her.

"Now that your daughter has died," I said, "I would think you would be sad. How can you be happy?"

"My son died, too." She still smiled.

"So why are you smiling and humming?"

She hummed a few bars, then stopped. "My son came back." She looked at me. Her smile was radiant.

"Your son came back?"

She nodded.

"But he died years ago," I said.

"I know. But he comes late at night when everyone is asleep. It's my best dream ever."

I looked out over the valley, wondering if there was anything I could learn from her.

"Do you think your daughter will come back, too?"

"Of course," she said, beaming. "Maybe tonight or tomorrow night. Or next month. It could be years, but she'll come."

"That would make one happy," I said.

She started humming again.

"Thank you very much for talking to me, Mrs. Washington." I stood up and left her smiling out across the valley.

I was near Placerville when I had a thought. I dialed Lieutenant Reddenburg. A woman asked me to wait. I drove by a billboard with a picture of a rose. Underneath it said, "Scents Of Love." The curvy words were shaped like a woman lying on her side. I remembered it was the perfume chain owned by Violet Verona.

"Reddenburg here," a voice barked.

"Owen McKenna. I had another question."

"Shoot."

"The guy Luther shot. Do you know who he was?"

"Not off the top of my head. You want to hold on?"

"Please." I was driving up into the foothills toward Cameron Park. The highway got steeper and I had to downshift again. The engine roared as the speed gradually crept from 38 to 40 to 45.

"Here it is," Reddenburg said. "The victim was a guy named Willard Kilpatrick. Lived in Oakland near where he died."

"Any idea what he did for a living?"

"Lemme see. It might be in here. Oh, right in front of my face. He was with the Sierra Club. Doesn't say what he did. Maybe one of those trust fund babies, watching the environment for the rest of us working stiffs."

"Thanks, I appreciate it."

"Wait, here's something else." I heard papers flipping over the phone. "It says he was also the Governor's appointee for one of the at-large seats on the T.R.P.A. That's Tahoe Regional…"

"Planning Agency," I finished for him.

"Right. You must know about them, huh?"

"Yeah."

FORTY-FOUR

I dialed the newspaper and got Glenda Gorman on the line.
"Did you learn anything about those people who died?"
she said.

"Not much. But I have another death I'm hoping you can look up. This one was clearly a murder. A man named Willard Kilpatrick was shot to death in Oakland about twelve years ago. The police thought he was killed by an Oakland gang member. Kilpatrick worked for the Sierra Club and was appointed by the governor to serve on the T.R.P.A. as one of the at-large members."

"Okay, I'll see what I can do. How do I get hold of you? I can't seem to get you at your office or your cabin."

"I'm out of town. I'll call you later today."

"You think I can learn this guy's life story that soon?"

"If not you, who?" I said.

"Nobody!" she said with enthusiasm, then hung up.

I stopped at Conan Reynolds' law office on my way back into South Lake Tahoe.

His secretary said, "Go right in, but don't expect him to be in a good mood. He's still mad over yesterday's game."

"What's the matter," I said as I pushed in through his door.

Conan was digging in a desk drawer. "Whassa matter?" Conan said. "Yankees killed 'em. Eighteen zip. What kind of game is that, eighteen zip? That's not a game."

"But you knew it would happen."

"Doesn't make it hurt less. If the doctor says to you, 'hold on, this is going to hurt,' it'll probably hurt even more, not less."

"True," I said as I sat in one of his chairs.

Conan reached a stack of folders off a nearby table. "This is the stuff you brought in."

"Were you able to get anything out of it?" I said.

He steepled his fingers and leaned forward, elbows on his desk. "So," he said. "You're wondering about the legitimacy of Camp Twenty-Five."

"Maybe."

"What do you know about it?" he asked.

"Very little," I said. "A non-profit group that plans to build a camp for disabled kids."

"What made you wonder about its legitimacy?"

"I was looking into the deaths of the singer Glory and of Faith Runyon, the girl who died in the boat explosion. One of the first people I met was a kid who is sponsored by Company Twenty-Five, a snowboarder named Bobby Crash. I also met a mountain biker named Wheels Washburn. Turns out he knew just where Glory had gone off the Flume Trail. That was not public information. Wheels said he heard it from his friend Bobby Crash. Bobby Crash doesn't seem to be around. And Wheels was killed two days ago. You know Glenda Gorman, the reporter?"

Conan nodded.

"Glennie found out that a woman named Monica Lakeman recently died in a fall down the stairs of one of her rental houses. The stairs were in good condition and the weather was dry. Monica left her entire estate to Camp Twenty-Five."

Conan raised one eyebrow.

"Faith Runyon was a prostitute. I tracked down her madam, a woman named K.D. Scarrone. Turns out she is executive director of Camp Twenty-Five. I went to the Camp Twenty-Five office and noticed they were using a parcel map to indicate which properties were theirs, which ones they were about to acquire, and which ones were owned by people who were unwilling to sell. The map had the parcel numbers whited out. It struck me as strange. You want more?"

"There's more?"

"From the time I first started asking questions, a couple of guys have been trying to kill me."

"I heard about a shooting up at your cabin," Conan said.

"I chased one of them at the casino. Diamond Martinez responded to the call. He thought the guy was taking aim at him. Diamond fired a shot. His round ricocheted and hit a girl's doll. Diamond said there was no girl nearby. Nevertheless, the mother raised a ruckus. Her name is Violet Verona, a rich businesswoman. Next thing Diamond knew, the sheriff got a call from Senator Stensen's office. They were urging the sheriff to make an example of Diamond, referring to him as a rogue cop. The sheriff suspended Diamond. But Diamond is a straight cop. If he says that no mother and girl were nearby during the shooting, then I believe him. Diamond thinks it is fishy. Especially with Senator Stensen getting involved."

"What does this have to do with Company Twenty-Five?"

"Maybe nothing. But Stensen has recently become an advocate of sorts for Camp Twenty-Five. He gave a little speech about it at the Company Twenty-Five grand opening in Roundhill."

Conan said, "Camp Twenty-Five keeps popping up in a lot of places, huh?"

"Right. Made me want to look at some of their papers." I pointed to the stack on his desk. "You didn't see any reference to a Tyrone Handkins, did you?"

"Nope. Who's he?"

"Glory's bodyguard. What about Tony Nova, the owner of Glory's management company?"

Conan shook his head.

"Willard Kilpatrick?" I said.

Another head shake.

I said, "He worked for the Sierra Club and was appointed to the T.R.P.A. board years back. He was killed in Oakland." I gestured at the files again. "What do you make of this stuff?"

"First of all, it doesn't look like there is any ownership connection between Camp Twenty-Five and Company Twenty-Five. I think Company Twenty-Five is letting Camp Twenty-Five use their trademark because it softens their image. They're perceived as a corporate shark, gobbling up small sporting goods stores, manufacturing product with child labor in developing countries..." Conan waved his hand through the air. "But you probably know all that." He pointed at the stack of files. "In that pile are contracts for the sale of almost three dozen lots purchased by Camp Twenty-Five. All but four are seller-financed. Camp Twenty-Five put a small amount of money down and is paying off the balance over ten or fifteen years or even thirty years in some cases. Some sellers financed one hundred percent of the sale. The four that weren't seller-financed were purchased outright with cash. But I suspect that the appraisals that determined the prices were below market. Most homeowners don't realize how much Tahoe property has gone up in recent years."

I said, "Even those sellers who were aware of the full value of their property probably cut Camp Twenty-Five a good deal anyway, just because they thought it a good cause."

"Yeah, sure," Conan said.

"You're not a believer?"

"Put it this way. This paperwork would make more sense if the whole business is a sham. A lot of this paperwork refers to the Camp Twenty-Five Foundation. But on the contracts the buyer is simply Camp Twenty-Five, Inc."

"Is Camp Twenty-Five, Inc. a non-profit company?"

Conan was shaking his head. "I got curious about it, so I made some calls. Camp Twenty-Five, Inc. is a for-profit corporation, incorporated in Delaware, and it has two stockholders. A Martin Z. Elgin in Palo Alto, and an Adelina S. Kercher in Denver. I did an online search and turned up nothing on either name."

"So when someone sells their Tahoe lot to Camp Twenty-Five, they're actually selling it to two unknown people from out of town?"

"Right. I called up one of the title companies on the north shore that handled some of the sales. They had no contact information other than the local Camp Twenty-Five office. The women in the Camp Twenty-Five office brought them the information on the various sellers along with a Camp Twenty-Five check in the amount specified on each purchase agreement. The check was drawn on a bank in South Dakota and the Camp Twenty-Five address printed on the check was a post office box in Delaware, no doubt serviced by one of those businesses that forward mail to the real address, wherever that is. The title company handled the sales and the mortgage contracts. The deeds of trust were recorded in the county recorder's office."

"Showing Camp Twenty-Five, Inc. as the new owner," I said.

"Correct."

"Was there anything in those papers that binds Camp Twenty-Five, Inc. to actually building a camp for disabled kids?"

Conan gave me a wry smile. He picked up the bent foam board parcel map, straightened it out and held it up for emphasis. "All I saw is a company acquiring a fortune in land at cheap prices and almost no cash outlay."

Seeing the map at a distance, I saw clearly what I'd suspected. The Camp Twenty-Five lots formed a large mass that looked like a mitten balanced on the north side of Lake Tahoe. The shape was identical to the golf course picture that Diamond had helped me assemble.

I said, "What would keep Camp Twenty-Five from doing something else with the land, something much more profitable than a camp for disabled kids?"

"As far as these documents indicate, nothing."

"If Camp Twenty-Five doesn't build the camp, wouldn't they be open to lawsuits?"

"On charges that they misrepresented their purpose? Maybe. But who would bring the suit? One of the sellers? If so, Camp Twenty-Five would probably be able to settle for a fee that would look large to the seller and small from the perspective of their current land portfolio."

"Wouldn't the Attorney General get very interested in such a scam?"

"Maybe, but there wouldn't be much to go on. Who was hurt? The sellers for selling cheap? Yes, but many of them don't know it. More than half are from out of town themselves, and they are probably ecstatic that they multiplied their investment in Tahoe several times over. Never mind that they could have done even better with a different buyer. As for the Camp Twenty-Five brochures and such, if you look closely at the wording, you'll see that it is nothing but clever suggestion." Conan pulled a brochure out of the pile and held it up, flipping through its pages. "None of the promo literature specifically states that the land they're acquiring will actually become a camp. The Camp Twenty-Five brochures just imply that some day disabled kids will be able to romp in a mountain lake." He pointed to a couple of paragraphs of fine print at the bottom of the last page. "Let me read some of this. If I hold it close enough to my lamp I can make it out without a magnifying glass.

"'With proper financial management of Tahoe property, Camp Twenty-Five's goals of building a camp for disabled kids come closer to reality every year. We'll never lose sight of our dream that Special Children may one day run and play, swim and sail in God's Country.'"

"And then there is an asterisk," Conan continued. "So I looked all over the brochure and finally found another one below this photograph of a kid in a wheelchair next to a mountain lake." He held it up and pointed it out to me. "Want to know what it says in even finer micro-print? It says, 'A Special Child enjoying the splendor of a proposed location for Camp Twenty-Five on Leech Lake, Montana.'"

Conan smacked the brochure with his other hand. "Can you believe that?"

"Yes, I'm sorry to say, I can."

"So," Conan said, "unless a seller actually tape records contrary information given out at the Camp Twenty-Five office, I don't imagine the Attorney General would have much of a case. Put it before a Grand Jury and I can guess what would happen. The jury members, all much poorer than the rich people selling their Tahoe lakeshore, would have a hard time finding enough sympathy for them to bring an indictment against a company that may, in fact, actually plan to build a camp. Here, or in Montana."

FORTY-FIVE

I picked up the parcel map and asked Conan Reynolds if I could leave the files with him. He nodded, and I left.

Outside, I leaned past Spot and slipped the parcel map under the seat where I'd been keeping the golf course puzzle.

I drove over to the Herald. I knew the risk, but I was making progress and I needed information fast. Glennie was in.

"Where is Spot? How is he healing?" she said, worried.

"I parked behind the building. Come see." I pointed.

We went around to the back where Spot had his head hanging out the window of the Orange Flame. He was standing in a half-crouch, his body pushing up against the ceiling and filling the entire car. Glennie wrapped her arms around his head and cooed into his ear. "Ooooh, poor wounded baby, forced to live all alone with this detective who never spoils you rotten like I would."

Spot wagged so hard I thought his tail was going to break the windows of Diamond's car.

Glennie turned to me, pulled a little notebook out of her back pocket and flipped some pages. "Okay. Willard Kilpatrick. Worked for the Sierra Club like you said and was appointed by the governor to serve on the T.R.P.A. board. He was a left-wing political operative. A hero to some on the left, but those on the right said he was into dirty politics. Kilpatrick Consulting's clients were a Who's Who of politicians with environmentalist leanings."

"What is dirty about that?"

Glennie gave me one of those wide-eyed looks that means she's learned something exciting. "What Kilpatrick specialized in was finding companies and divisions of companies that were committing serious environmental crimes, like dumping toxic chemicals where they would get into reservoirs or ground water that is used for drinking water. So, if you were a politician with environmentalist leanings and you were running against someone who was less than eager to make environmental protection a high priority, you'd hire Kilpatrick's firm to essentially connect your opponent to some company's toxic waste. It could be as simple as discovering that your opponent owned a bunch of stock in a company. Kilpatrick had an amazing ability to find a money trail that led from their toxic site into your opponent's pocket."

"Was he successful in influencing any elections?"

Glennie grinned. "He's credited with actually changing the outcomes of three different senatorial races over the years and five congressional races. He was becoming very big when he died."

"Where were these races?"

Glennie paged through her notes. "Senate races in Georgia, Wisconsin and New Mexico and congressional races in Arizona, Vermont, South Carolina and two in Florida."

"What was he working on when he died?"

"It had been a year since he was appointed to the T.R.P.A. He'd become very involved in development issues. He was using his post to try to stop all development in the Tahoe Basin until much stricter environmental impact rules were put in place."

"Were there any singular projects he focused on?"

"Not as far as I can tell," Glennie said. "He focused on all of them. Anyway, you said he was shot by a gang member in Oakland? It's not like he was killed over a Tahoe dispute."

I thought about it. "You didn't find any major disagreements he had with anyone in Tahoe or about Tahoe?"

"No. But if he'd lived any longer he might have. Apparently, he'd been hired by Joanne Pasadena, Nevada's Democratic senate candidate thirteen years ago. The assumption was that Kilpatrick would find some environmental dirt on Pasadena's opponent. But then Kilpatrick was killed and Pasadena's opponent went on to win."

"Senator Stensen."

"Right. The man who made headlines years ago by moving from California to Nevada to run for the Senate."

"A close race, wasn't it?"

Glennie guffawed. "They don't get much closer. His margin of victory was less than two hundred votes. If Kilpatrick had lived, who knows what might have happened."

"I wonder what kind of environmental skeletons are in Stensen's closet."

"Implying that the senator might have had Kilpatrick killed?" Glennie raised her eyebrows.

"Maybe."

"I didn't find anything that would suggest that. Of course, his voting record has always been pro business and development. And he's done lots of little things that have outraged environmentalists."

"Was Stensen involved in any Tahoe land development?"

"Not that I know of. But not long after Kilpatrick was killed, Senator Stensen intervened on a golf course and housing development down in the Carson Valley. The Douglas County Commissioners were debating a zoning variance that the golf course needed. Many in the local community were against it because of the population growth it was going to create."

"What did he do?"

"Just the standard political horse trading. The Senator let it be known that he was aware of a water project that the Douglas County Commissioners wanted federal funding for. He also let it be known that the golf course would be good for both the county and Nevada. It turned out later that one of the biggest investors in the golf course was Whitehorse Valley Ranches, a developer in Vegas."

"And the senator is in bed with them?" I said.

"Very much so, according to the rumors." Glennie turned back to Spot and rubbed his ears.

"Maybe Stensen was trying to clean up his image by supporting Camp Twenty-Five."

"Maybe. One more thing you should know." Glennie flipped through her notebook. "I read about a fundraiser that Stensen is having."

"For his next election campaign?"

"No. For Camp Twenty-Five. Where did I write the date down?" She turned some more pages. "I must have forgotten. Come back inside. It's on my desk."

We walked into the building and down an aisle to her desk. "Here it is," she said, handing me a sticky note. "Saturday at eight o'clock at his house on the lake."

"The big fenced spread near Marla Bay, right?"

"Fenced is an understatement. It's like a fortress. The only way you can get in is with a private invitation and photo ID. I once heard from an aide to one of California's senators that a personal invitation to Stensen's Tahoe palace is a highly coveted sign that you've achieved stature in the senate power structure."

As soon as she stopped talking I heard a distant, repeating sound. Like a dog barking. Deep in pitch.

Spot.

I turned and sprinted for the door. I spun outside. My feet slid on grit in the parking lot as I turned at full speed, heading for the street at the back of the building.

Spot's barking grew louder. Ragged with anger.

The man in the ski mask was on his back, lying half under the rear bumper of Diamond's car, reaching up into the engine compartment. Spot had his head out the window, straining to see the man, barking ferociously. I pounded toward the man.

On the other side of the Karmann Ghia, a dark sedan was in the street. The man in the mask rolled out from under the bumper and jumped to his feet. He took two running steps and jumped into the open back door of the sedan. The sedan sped off. Spinning wheels kicked up gravel and dirt.

I was still sprinting toward Diamond's car when I realized what had happened.

The man had planted a bomb.

FORTY-SIX

I jerked to a stop twenty yards from the Orange Flame. Spot turned away from the speeding vehicle and swung his head around toward me. I started backing up.

Glennie came rushing up to me. "What's wrong?"

"Car bomb," I said, panting. "Two men. One put it up in the engine compartment." I pointed toward the Karmann Ghia.

"No!" Glennie turned and stared at the car. "But Spot is..." She started toward the car.

"Glennie, stop! There are lots of ways to trigger a car bomb, one of which is motion. You can't go near the car. We mustn't do anything that would make Spot jump around." Glennie looked horrified as I pulled my phone out of my pocket and dialed Mallory. "Stay calm," I said. "And watch to make certain that no one else goes near the car."

"But as long as we don't touch the car..."

"A bomb can also be triggered by remote-control radio. The men who planted it could double back and watch from a distance. I'm the target, but that doesn't mean they won't decide to detonate it just to destroy the evidence."

Glennie hugged herself, her arms shaking as she stared at Spot.

"Yeah?" Mallory's voice barked in my phone.

"This is McKenna. I'm at the Herald. I've got Diamond's car, an orange Karmann Ghia. I just saw the man in the ski mask rolling out from under the car. He escaped in a dark sedan. I'm reasonably certain he planted a bomb."

"Christ," Mallory said. "Okay, keep everyone away. I'll call Newt Engel. I'll be there in a minute."

I heard the first siren in a few seconds, followed by a second and third. They grew into an emergency chorus that seemed to rip the air and made Glennie cover up her ears.

In less than ten minutes the highway and all the nearby streets were closed off by South Lake Tahoe and El Dorado County Sheriff's vehicles. Fire trucks pulled into three different positions on the street. Men ran with fire hoses. Others hooked them up to hydrants. Someone shouted over a bullhorn. CHP cruisers joined the mix. Traffic was rerouted. Nearby buildings were evacuated.

The authorities created an empty zone fifty yards in diameter. The perimeter was a ring of vehicles. Officers stayed hunkered down on the far side of the cars and trucks, peeking through at the little orange car in the center of the circle.

Spot looked back and forth, his neck pushing against the half-opened window. His brow was furrowed with worry. He couldn't see me on the other side of a fire truck.

"McKenna," Mallory said, appearing at my side, "you didn't tell me your hound was in the car."

"Can you get everyone to turn off the sirens and the bullhorns? Spot is moving around too much. He could set off the bomb. I have to call out to him, but he can't hear me."

Mallory shouted into his radio. A siren abruptly stopped. Then another. The cacophony lessened a bit, then softened substantially. I heard some men shushing others. In a minute, there was an unearthly hush, quieter than ever without the normal traffic on the main road in front of the Herald.

"Hey, your largeness," I called out. Spot swung his head around hard at the sound of my voice. I winced as the little car rocked with the motion. "It's okay, boy." I struggled to make my voice calm. Dogs don't need to know the words to understand the tone. "Nothing to worry about. We'll get you out of the car in few minutes and go run on the beach."

"McKenna," Mallory said. A short, stocky guy with a little red mustache and puffy cheeks stood at Mallory's side. "This is Newton Engel. Closest thing we got to a bomb expert. Took that course up at the Herlong army base. Wanna give him what you've got?"

I took Engel through the details of what I'd seen.

"Did you see the package?" Engel asked when I was done.

"No. But he had his hand way under the car and he was reaching up. My guess is he stuck it on the front side of the engine."

Engel looked out at the Karmann Ghia. "Engine's in the rear on those, right?"

"Right."

"What were his movements?"

"Just reaching up. Then he rolled out from the car and ran to a waiting sedan."

"No," Engel said. "What I mean is, think about the difference between seeing a mechanic doing some fine manipulation under your car like threading the plug back into the oil pan versus taking a rag and blotting up some spilled oil. All you see is his arm under the car, but the movement is different. Could be this guy was stringing a wire or setting a timer? Or maybe he was just jamming a package next to the engine?"

I thought about it. "More like the latter. It didn't look like he was manipulating anything."

A huge front-end loader roared up, gears grinding, and came to a stop facing the Karmann Ghia, ten yards away. The driver turned to look at the Herald building behind him. He jockeyed forward and back, moving sideways toward a streetlight, then stopped. The driver worked the hydraulic levers and moved the giant bucket up and down until he was satisfied. He turned off the monster, climbed out and shouted to Mallory. "Sucker blows now, this baby will pretty much protect the left side of the newspaper building from the blast. But you gotta promise the city will cover my tractor, 'cause my insurance don't cover acts of God. I swear, you gotta promise."

"Mayor's word of honor," Mallory said.

"How long was the car unattended?" Engel asked me.

"I'd only been away from it for a couple of minutes. I heard my dog start barking, and I immediately ran out. The man couldn't have been at the car for more than fifteen seconds."

"How soon would your dog start barking after the man came up to the car?"

"Immediately."

Engel stared at the car. "Then that probably rules out most triggers. He wouldn't have had time to wire the door or the ignition."

"No," I said. "I figure it has to be a motion device or a radio device. It could be a timer, but that wouldn't be reliable."

"Yeah. A timer's out. Who knows when you would stop at a store or something." Engel pondered as another front-end loader drove up. The driver did the same as the first, positioning the tractor between the Karmann Ghia and another building and adjusting the big bucket to deflect any blast.

"Problem is going to be getting your dog out," Engel said as he stared out at Spot. "A gentle rocking won't trigger a motion device like this. But a sharp shake like your dog jumping out will." Spot was looking from one tractor to the next.

"It's okay, boy," I called out. "You hang in there."

Engel got on his radio and started talking bomb lingo and requesting equipment and expert reinforcement. "I'm thinking plastic," he said into the radio. "With a detonator on a motion sensor. Package is on the front side of the engine. It's one of those rear engine VWs from the seventies. The engine block will direct the blast forward into the passenger compartment. I know. Doesn't take much explosive to be effective." Engel listened for awhile, then handed the radio to Mallory.

I talked to Spot while Mallory spoke on the radio.

Mallory finished and turned to Engel. "Sac says they're sending men and gear up in a CHP chopper. What kind of gear?"

Engel shrugged. "I'm still learning. They've got suits and video robots and some other techie stuff. Main thing is to keep that dog calm until they get here."

As he said it, Spot was turning around inside the car. He stuck his head toward the rear window and seemed to sniff. Then he turned around again and put his head back out the open window. The Karmann Ghia rocked with the motion.

Engel stiffened. "Dog's going to trigger it. Can't you tell him to sit still?"

"Except for a couple of breaks, he's been in the car all day. We came up from the Bay Area this morning. He's pretty restless, and all this commotion is making it worse."

"Then we have to get him out of there," Engel said to Mallory.

Mallory's permanent frown grew even deeper. "How do you figure it?"

"We get a guy to hang onto the back side of the bucket on one of those tractors," Engel said. "He can reach out with a pole or something and open the door."

Mallory scowled at the closest front-end loader.

"Good idea," I said. "I'll go."

"No way," Mallory said. "You're a civilian. If you get hurt, you could sue the pants off the city. I'd get fired for malfeasance."

"You know I'm not the suing type."

"You're right. But if you got gomered, like a veggie on feeding tubes, the city would get stuck with a horrendous medical bill."

I shook my head. "I have a patron in emergencies."

Mallory looked at me. "You mean that rich girl you saved a year or so back?"

"Yes. Anyway, my dog will respond best to me. I can wear a riot helmet and suit."

"That won't help you with a bomb," Engel said.

"Better than nothing, though."

"Or we wait for the CHP chopper," Mallory said.

Spot suddenly turned around, rocking the Orange Flame more than ever. We all winced.

"Okay, let's do it," Mallory said.

They put a helmet and suit on the tractor driver and explained what he was to do.

Next, they suited me up in riot gear. The Herald janitor brought an extension pole they use for changing light bulbs. It had a lever on the handle and a rubber coated pincer at the far end. I thought I could open the car door with it from twelve feet away.

The tractor driver showed me the back of the bucket. "This mount goes up and down," he shouted through his riot helmet. "But you can sit on it. Or maybe get your feet on it, then bend down in a squatting position. I'll just cruise up to the car until you are close enough to reach out with that pole."

I was studying the position. "But I won't be able to reach around with it while I'm sitting or squatting on the bucket mount."

"Then I'll lower it to the ground once we get up there. You can step off and move to the side. The bucket is big enough that you'll have some room to move around behind it." He pointed to some hydraulic hoses. "Just stay away from here. I sprung a little leak moving snow last winter, and that stuff is slippery."

I was about to climb onto the back of the bucket when Diamond ran up. He stared at my riot gear.

"I heard about a car bomb." He glanced over at his car. "It's in the Orange Flame?"

"Yeah," I yelled from inside my helmet. "Sorry."

"To hell with the car. What about Spot?"

"That's what we're working on."

Diamond grabbed my arm. "Be careful?"

I nodded. "Hey, Diamond?"

"Yeah?"

"You'll be there for Street?"

"Stupid gringo," he said. "Go get your dog."

The tractor driver started the engine. I jumped up on the bucket mount.

I held the pole in one hand and the top edge of the bucket with the other as the tractor lurched forward.

FORTY-SEVEN

The tractor engine roared. We rolled forward. The driver turned slightly to give us more berth around the streetlight, then straightened out and headed toward the car. We slowed to a crawl, then stopped.

"You think this is close enough?" the driver yelled.

I peeked over the top of the bucket to gauge the distance to the car door. I took another look at the pole in my hand, then nodded.

The driver lowered the bucket to the pavement. I jumped off, leaned out from behind the bucket and looked around.

"Hey, Spot," I yelled through my helmet. "It's me. Time to go for a walk."

I reached out with the pole, my arm and part of my head exposed. The rubber pincer seemed to float around the door handle as I tried to maneuver it into position. Spot had his head out the window, watching me and the pole dancing near the door handle. I concentrated on holding it steady, but it seemed to move even more. It was getting dark, and they'd turned on several spotlights. The lights shining on the car reflected off its paint and chrome and made it hard to see. My muscles shook with tension. Sweat ran into my eye.

Finally, I had to stop to rest, setting the pole on the ground. I stood behind the bucket, moving my arms and rotating them. I took several steps back and forth and tried to shake the tension out of my shoulders. Behind the tractor, spread out in a semi-circle, were dozens of faces, watching from behind police cars and fire trucks. Two groups of firemen held hoses aimed at Diamond's car. I took several deep breaths, then picked up the pole again.

"Easy, boy," I called out to Spot as I once again reached out from behind the bucket and lifted the pole near the door handle. He stared at me behind my riot mask. His brow was worried, his eyes sad.

"I just need to hook this gripper on the handle and you'll be free. Here we are. Getting close. Soon as my muscles stop shaking. Okay, once again. A little up. A little to the left." The long, bendy pole floated by the door handle. "Oops, too far. Come on back. There we go. Slower. Closer. Yes."

The pole gripper hooked onto the door handle. I twisted it for some leverage, squeezed the lever and opened the door.

I didn't want Spot to leap out fast and rock the car. So I pulled the door open just a few inches.

Spot pulled his head in from the window, then stuck his nose in the crack where the door opened.

"Nice and slow, Spot," I said. "One foot at a time. No jumping." I pulled the door open a little farther.

Spot pushed his snout through the opening, then reached out one paw, then another.

"Atta boy. No sudden movements."

Spot suddenly pushed off and leaped onto the pavement.

There was a collective gasp as the Karmann Ghia rocked side-to-side, then a sigh as we all realized that Spot had made it.

I took off my riot helmet and dropped it to the ground. Spot ran up to me behind the bucket, and I kneeled down to hug him. "See, it's like filming a movie. It gets hot under the lights."

Spot wagged.

The tractor driver revved up the engine. We stepped aside as he lifted the bucket and began to back up.

Spot and I walked alongside the tractor as he backed into the streetlight.

There was a deep crunching sound. The light began to topple.

"Look out!" Someone shouted. "THE STREETLIGHT IS GOING TO HIT THE CAR!"

There was no time to look. I bent down, grabbed Spot around the chest and heaved up his 170 pounds. I took two running steps to get behind the tractor's bucket. But the bottom of the bucket was two feet off the ground. Still holding Spot in my arms, I leaped up onto the bucket mount as if I were jumping up to sit on a bar counter. My butt hit the metal just as the streetlight hit the car.

The car exploded with a thunderous boom. Fire blew over our heads and below our feet. The shockwave shook the huge bucket as if it were made of tin. The explosion blew out the windows of the tractor's cab. Hot glass shattered over the driver. His terrified face in the riot helmet was lit yellow by the fireball billowing into the sky.

In a second, the firemen hit the wreckage with a torrent from the fire hoses. The fireball was replaced by a dark cloud of steam and smoke.

I slid off the bucket mount and lowered Spot to the ground. He looked up at me, but there was no wagging.

FORTY-EIGHT

Mallory and Special Agent Ramos were talking to me inside the Herald Building. "What is it you know, Owen?" Mallory said. "You've got someone very motivated to kill you."

Agent Ramos cocked his head and leaned back just so. His air of superiority was suffocating.

"I'm not sure," I said. "I've learned of one possibility that could explain several deaths including Faith Runyon's. But it doesn't explain Glory's death which, although ruled an accident by the coroner, was a murder according to Faith and is what Faith originally called about."

"Give us a try," Mallory said.

"I think Faith learned that Camp Twenty-Five is really just a front for a golf course development."

Agent Ramos put his fist to his mouth, pretending to hide his smirk but instead making it obvious.

I said to him, "I mentioned that the paper pieces left after the boat explosion fit together to show a golf course. They match the parcel map that shows the layout of Camp Twenty-Five."

"I'd like to see these," Ramos said.

"Sorry. They were in Diamond's Karmann Ghia."

"So you think someone is planting bombs because of a golf course. But the evidence is gone," he said. "Other people have died as well? Who would these people be?"

Mallory fidgeted as Ramos spoke. He was obviously irritated by the little FBI man, but intimidated as well.

"In addition to Faith," I said, "a woman in real estate named Monica Lakeman, and a banker named Eduardo Valdez. All lived on the North Shore and all can be traced to Camp Twenty-Five. In addition, a man named Willard Kilpatrick was shot to death in Oakland about twelve years ago. He was a political consultant working for Senator Stensen's opponent at the time."

"You're not suggesting that Senator Stensen was involved."

"I don't know. But Stensen has promoted other golf courses and he is currently promoting Camp Twenty-Five. Kilpatrick was an at-large member of the T.R.P.A. board and was actively against any project that could have negative environmental consequences."

"But you said he was killed twelve years ago."

"Golf courses are like ski resorts. They take a very long time to plan," I said.

Mallory said, "Is the land for this golf course already owned by Camp Twenty-Five?"

"Much of it, yes. I spoke to Conan Reynolds a few hours ago. He's looked over some of the sales contracts. He says that when someone thought they were selling to Camp Twenty-Five, they were actually selling to two people, a man in Palo Alto and a woman in Denver. Conan has their names. Find them and we might be close to the killers."

"I'll give him a call," Ramos said. "How'd Conan get these documents?"

"Someone lent them to me. I gave them to Conan."

"Someone lent them to you?" Ramos asked.

Mallory grinned like a school boy. "Owen, let's say this golf course stuff is true," he said, changing the subject. "You've tried to fit Glory's death into this. You still think her bodyguard was involved?"

"Tyrone Handkins may have hired the man in the ski mask to come after me. Which would imply that Tyrone killed Glory, either by himself or using a hired killer. Sergeant Cardoza of Washoe County thinks Tyrone was Glory's lover and was dismayed over her rise to stardom. But if that is true, then nothing about it links Glory or Tyrone to the golf course. And it doesn't explain why Faith called me about Glory."

Ramos sat still, thinking. He was insufferable even in his silence. But I suspected he was very sharp, and I wished I thought he was working with me instead of against me. He stood up, said he'd be in touch, then left.

I went outside and found Glennie and Diamond with Spot. Glennie was pale. Diamond looked like he'd aged ten years since his suspension. Spot's left front leg was shaking. Some of the stitches on his back had opened up when I lifted him just before the bomb exploded. They oozed blood.

Glennie said, "I called Street at Caesars and told her you were okay. She'd heard about the explosion. She asked if she should come to the paper. I said I didn't know, but that it seemed like you're kind of a danger zone these days."

"Yeah, Street should stay away. I don't want these killers to think that following Street is the way to find me. I'll call her."

Mallory walked up. "Maybe you should sleep at the jail. Hard to get to you there."

"Better I keep running. You don't want these guys bombing anything else in town. I just need some transportation."

Diamond looked over at the smoking engine block, the only remaining piece of his car more than ten inches across.

"Where you going to stay?" Mallory asked.

"Here and there."

"What, you think it would be dangerous if I knew where you were staying? It's not like someone could get the info out of me." Mallory seemed affronted.

"You said yourself how motivated they are. Last thing you need is for some guy in a ski mask coming through your window tonight to try and make you talk. Better if no one knows. They could be over there in the dark as we speak." I jerked my head toward a stand of trees.

Mallory glanced over his shoulder. Glennie shivered.

"Let's go inside," Mallory said.

We sat on couches in the paper's reception area.

"They know I have to leave here," I said. "All they have to do is wait and see who I leave with. They could follow."

"Then we play a shell game," Mallory said. He turned to Glennie. "Not including women. You should leave now and drive home. Safer that way."

She looked at me.

I nodded. "They could be looking in the windows at us right now. Better if they think you don't even care what happens."

Glennie gave all of us a wide-eyed look, then stood up. She turned to me. "Call somebody tomorrow? Let us know you're okay?"

"I promise."

She left.

"Here's how it will work," Mallory said. "I'll have three officers and me each drive a squad over to, let's see, Caesars has the best parking ramp for it. You and Spot will ride with me. We get up to the fourth floor and you jump out and get into the back seat of one of the other squads. You lie down on the floor. The squads all go back down out of the ramp, get to the highway and scatter.

"They don't know which squad you're in, and they can't tell them apart, anyway. The squad you're in takes you up Ski Run to Heavenly's lodge by the Gunbarrel chairlift. Diamond is waiting in the lot. You make the transfer and leave with Diamond."

"Sounds good. Diamond?" I said as I purposefully looked at Mallory just in case we were under observation.

"I'm leaving," he said. "I can do an evasive action before I get to the base lodge. And I know a way to drive out of the lot and up to the bottom of the chairlift. When you get dropped off, come up the stairs to the lift. If anyone makes you, they'll get out of their vehicle and follow you on foot. But I'll be waiting in my pickup. Give me a sense of time."

Mallory thought a moment. "About half an hour."

"I'll be there." Diamond got up to leave. We gave him a casual goodbye, then continued our conversation in case anyone was watching. After ten minutes we walked out to Mallory's Explorer. Mallory got on the radio as he drove and soon we had three more Explorers behind us.

FORTY-NINE

We did as Mallory explained. When we got to the fourth level of the parking garage, Spot and I switched vehicles, jumping into the back door of the second one. We lay down low on the seat.

"Commander said you'd tell us your destination?" a young officer said.

"Heavenly's California base lodge, please."

Five minutes later, Spot and I jumped out in the vast empty parking lot, ran up the stairs by the lodge and found Diamond waiting in the dark by the chairlift, his pickup idling.

"Where to?" he said as he drove off, following a rutted trail that eventually intersected with a nearby road.

"I want to go home for a minute. I don't think they'll be watching my cabin after the bombing."

"You going to risk using your Jeep?"

"No. I need to borrow my neighbor's car."

Diamond nodded.

I dialed Mrs. Duchamp as we drove up the east shore. It sounded like I woke her up.

"What!" she answered in her high shriek, sounding as always like a startled drag queen.

"Mrs. Duchamp, it's Owen McKenna."

"Well, it's very late!"

"I know. Sorry to bother you. I was wondering if I could borrow one of your cars."

"What!" she shrieked again.

"I've had a little car trouble. I'll be very careful."

There was a long pause. I heard her cover up the phone and mutter something to Treasure, her toy poodle. Then she was back, louder than ever. "Well, I don't know what Mr. Duchamp would say." She was referring to a husband who, near as I could figure, had been dead for two decades.

"He would say that you know I'm as reliable as they come, and you should tell me where the keys are. I prefer the Toyota." Not only was the 4-Runner better suited to my needs, but I couldn't imagine driving around in a lavender Cadillac.

Mrs. Duchamp sputtered, then finally blurted out, "The keys are in the ignition. You know how to open the garage, don't you? Because I'm in bed."

"You sleep well, Mrs. Duchamp. Thank you."

While Diamond drove, I told him what I'd learned from Conan Reynolds and how the parcel map was shaped like a mitten, identical to the golf course puzzle.

Diamond turned off the highway, drove up the mountain, past my cabin and parked in Mrs. Duchamp's drive.

"You got a plan to bust open this golf course scam?"

"Not yet. But I'm hoping you'll join me when I do."

"I got no authority," he said.

"Me neither."

"You're not going to stay in your cabin, tonight?"

I shook my head. "Too risky. I'll keep camping."

Diamond nodded. I told him I'd call the next day.

I got Mrs. Duchamp's 4-Runner out of her garage while Treasure barked from inside the house. Diamond followed me down the mountain.

Spot and I once again found our way in the dark from the Spooner Lake Campground to the three-walled roofless cabin.

It was a colder night than before, and Spot and I shivered under Diamond's sleeping bag. The morning sun seemed to take twice as long as normal to arrive. When it did, Spot found a place where the rays came through the trees and he sprawled in the sunshine. It was hard to get him to move when I wanted to leave.

We took the 4-Runner up to Incline Village where I looked up Daniel Woods, the realtor whose sign had advertised that he could see the real estate forest for the trees. He saw me at his office.

Woods was one of the true eager beavers, all smiles and handshakes with the accompanying elbow squeeze and pats on the back and coffee proffered and total interest in me and my needs and my desires. If I didn't have trouble with toupees and bonded teeth, I might have asked him to look for a replacement for my cabin.

Instead, I said, "Dan, I'm not here to buy property, but to ask your expert opinion. I'd possibly trouble you for an hour or two and I would expect that you would charge me for your time."

His permanent smile faded a touch. "Well, we'll table that thought for now. I generally work for referrals. Why don't you tell me what you want and then I'll see if I can be of service."

"Fine. Some friends and I are looking at investing a sizable amount of money in a golf course development here on the north shore. It would be the newer design paradigm with the fairways lined with executive homes. It would be a nine-hole private course, designed by Robert Trent Jones or the equivalent. Everything first class. The project would have a clubhouse, fitness center, pool and spa, gated access. The idea is to maximize our R. O. I."

"Yes," Woods said, smiling, nodding. "Return On Investment is always paramount."

"What I'm wondering is if you could give me an assessment of value at build-out. I realize that it is hard to arrive at an accurate figure without being privy to all of the details. But we do not have your expertise. Any projections you could provide would tell us if our own projections are within shooting distance of reality. Could you do that?"

"Of course, Mr. McKenna. My next appointment isn't until this afternoon. Perhaps you could give me specifics?"

"Certainly. If I could borrow a pen and paper?"

Woods handed me a pen and a lined tablet.

I sketched from memory as I spoke. I'd spent hours putting together the golf course puzzle, so I had it memorized.

"The lake is here. The clubhouse and fitness center, there. Along this side are the first three holes with the third making a dogleg here. Holes four through seven do a zig-zag through the property, then eight and nine come back toward the lake." I pointed with the pen. "That would give these houses views of the lake. Again, everything will be oriented so that views of Lake Tahoe predominate from the greens and fairways as well as from the homes. It will be as beautiful as it is challenging. Think Edgewood on the South Shore, but interlaced with executive homes."

"Before you go further," Woods said, "you should be aware that obtaining the permits and zoning variances for a project like this is difficult at best anywhere. But in Tahoe..." Woods held his hands up, palms toward the ceiling. "I can't imagine getting approval from the T.R.P.A., never mind the myriad other authorities. I think it's possible that it simply couldn't be done."

"Yes, we're aware of that. But the developers have already acquired much of the land, and they are extremely well-connected. They might be able to pull it off. If so, wouldn't you be interested in investing in such a project?"

"Well, yes, of course. If such a development could be brought to fruition in Tahoe, it could produce a miraculous R.O.I. I would certainly be a potential investor. I have access to considerable funds myself." Woods sat a little straighter in his chair as he said it.

"I'll mention that to my friends. In the meantime, may I explain more of the project?"

"Yes, of course," Woods said, staring at my jerky sketch.

"We'll start from the lake and work in. Along here are seven contiguous lots on the lake." I made Xs on the sketch. "Then, skip over these three lots they have not acquired and we come to four more contiguous lots on the lake. You can see by the layout that all eleven of the lots will have fairways or greens behind them. Stretching back from the lake are seventy-nine other lots arranged to make the most of Tahoe views and golf course ambiance."

Woods scrawled notes across the pad as I spoke.

"From that description, is it possible for you to arrive at an estimated value of this project at completion?"

"It is really very difficult to say. Very difficult. So much depends on the details, the amenities of the development as a whole, the features in the houses, the quality of materials used and so forth. Two projects that look similar on paper can look very different on completion. And so much depends on the elusive perceived value." Woods used his fingers to draw quote marks in the air. "A prospective buyer can compare housing costs for a similar home in another executive market, membership in the local golf club, distance to recreation and cultural resources. You get the idea. But in the end, when they walk into the home's foyer, stroll up the circular staircase, wander through the master suite and imagine what their friends and family will think of the views, it comes down to their perceived value. It is an intangible. Very difficult to estimate until after the first few homes are built and marketed."

"I understand. But think of it this way. These developers will spend whatever it takes to produce the greatest return. That implies grand houses that could be in Architectural Digest. Everything from the gate house to the clubhouse restrooms will be exquisite. Therefore, I'm asking you to imagine this development as you would make it, and project its worth from that standpoint."

Daniel Woods studied me for a long moment. "They will spare no expense if it can be justified by the return?"

"Correct."

"They realize that such a development in the Tahoe Basin would be extraordinary in every degree and would indicate extraordinary attention to every detail?"

"Yes."

"In that case, let me punch in some numbers." He poked a calculator and scratched figures on the pad as he spoke. "Today, typical lakeshore housing stock in good condition is running up to one hundred thousand dollars per running foot of beachfront. New, quality construction can go even higher. From the scale of the rendering I'm thinking that each of the eleven lakeshore homes could sell in the range of ten million or more. That's one hundred ten million for the lakeshore.

"The seventy-nine other lots are harder to guestimate, but a sizable first-class home with a lake view and new construction can easily sell for three million. Add the gated community aspect and the way they are all arranged among the fairways and I'd bump that figure to four million each. If, as I assume, all of the homes will have deeded rights to a section of community beach, it could go even higher. Throw in a pier or mooring buoys, then higher still.

"I know these figures sound pricey," Woods continued, "but prices today are even higher in Glenbrook and some of the other developments around the lake."

Woods did some more calculations. "Based on what you've given me, I estimate this project at a total of somewhere over four hundred million. If I'm low by twenty-five percent, we're talking over half a billion dollars. If Tahoe real estate keeps appreciating like the last few years, then double these numbers by the time the project is completed."

Woods beamed at me. "There would be lots of motivation to figure a way through the permit process when the numbers approach a billion dollars, huh?"

"Lots of motivation," I agreed. "Now I'd like just one more thing, if you have a few minutes. I'm hoping you can print these estimates out on your letterhead so I can show my friends. Feel free to put in all the usual qualifiers and disclaimers. I just don't want them to think I pulled this stuff out of the blue. Would you be able to do that?"

Woods regarded me. "With the usual disclaimers, certainly. I have a reputation to protect." He turned to the computer and began typing. "And you'll remember to call me when they're looking for more investors?"

"Absolutely."

FIFTY

Daniel Woods refused to take payment, insisting only that I keep him on the top of my list for investors. I thanked him and left.

I found lunch for Spot and me, then stopped at Lady K.D.'s gym. She was in. She came out wearing her Spandex suit. Her arm muscles bulged. We talked in the parking lot.

"Who owns Camp Twenty-Five?" I said, wondering if she knew about Martin Elgin and Adelina Kercher.

She frowned. "It's a non-profit. Don't non-profits just belong to the public or something?"

"Who do you report to?"

"The board of directors. There's twelve of them. Well, eleven, ever since Eduardo Valdez died." Her face darkened for a moment.

"Do the board members live around here?"

"I've only met about half of them. But no, as far as I know they're from all over. The Bay Area and out of state. One is even from Virginia. Just good people looking to help special children."

"What about the bank accounts?"

She scowled at me. "That's very prying. What does that have to do with Faith dying?"

"I'll explain someday if I can figure it out. It's probably a matter of public record anyway with non-profits."

"Yes, I suppose. There's an account in South Dakota. Another is at Eduardo's bank here in Incline.

Nothing in K.D.'s manner suggested any concern about the break-in and I wondered if she even knew about it. I wanted to ask her about who has access to the safe in her office, but that would reveal that I'd made a visit there. It wouldn't take many questions before K.D. could figure out that I was the burglar. Perhaps she didn't know the documents were missing. "K.D., the names of two people have come up in my investigation and I wonder if you have ever had any dealings with them. There's a man from Palo Alto named Martin Elgin?"

She shook her head.

"What about Adelina Kercher? From Denver?"

Another shake. "Never heard of them. And I can honestly tell you that the man was never a client of Faith's."

"K.D., are you a golfer?"

She looked confused. "No, why? Oh, I remember you mentioned a golf course picture you think Faith wanted to show you."

"What about the board members? Any golfers?"

"I have no idea. I suppose some are. Lots of people golf. I can ask Suz at the Camp Twenty-Five Foundation."

I watched her face. "Thanks for your help," I said.

I left and drove Mrs. Duchamp's 4-Runner up the Mt. Rose Highway. Near the top of the pass I stopped to let Spot out in the big meadow. He tried to chase some little birds who kept flying up out of the grass and then landing behind him, forcing him to trace figure-eights. He moved better than before, but still favored his left front leg. His wound was no longer bleeding where the stitches had broken. Back in the car we headed down to Reno where I stopped at Kinkos. I had many other avenues to pursue, but I wanted to record what I'd learned while I still had the chance.

I spent the rest of the afternoon on one of their computers typing up everything I'd learned about Camp Twenty-Five and how the various victims could be connected to it:

Faith Runyon, who had overheard something about Glory's death. She'd also acquired a map of the golf course that was the real end-use for the land Camp Twenty-Five had acquired.

Monica Lakeman, who died in a questionable fall and left her estate to Camp Twenty-Five.

Eduardo Valdez, the banker on Camp Twenty-Five's board whose bank held one of Camp Twenty-Five's accounts, but who was an anti-development, obstructionist, "activist greenie" as described by Allen Lamb.

Willard Kilpatrick, the environmental consultant who played rough in politics and who was killed years ago just after Senator Stensen's opponent had hired Kilpatrick to dig up some environmental dirt on Stensen. Kilpatrick was supposedly shot by Glory's brother Luther just before Luther himself drowned.

Wheels Washburn, the mountain biker who helped me analyze tracks on the Flume and who got information from Bobby Crash on where Glory died. Bobby Crash knew Faith Runyon and maybe got the information from her.

I also noted the things I hadn't had a chance to track down:

Who and where were Martin Elgin and Adelina Kercher, the two stockholders of Camp Twenty-Five, Inc.?

Who were the other board members?

Why was Glory killed?

What was the involvement of her bodyguard Tyrone Handkins?

Where was his boss Tony Nova?

Why did the senator get involved in Diamond's suspension, and was the senator's support for Camp Twenty-Five genuine or a sham?

Did Violet Verona have any reason to make trouble for Diamond? Was she connected to Camp Twenty-Five?

Was Deputy Rockport's desire to become Sergeant ahead of Diamond just natural competition, or was it something else?

Did K.D. Scarrone know or suspect that Camp Twenty-Five wasn't what it seemed?

Who was K.D.'s ex, and was he the person who inadvertently revealed something to Faith?

Where was Bobby Crash and what else did he know?

When I finished writing my account, I made six copies, folded them and put them into envelopes.

The counter guy was kind enough to pull out phone books

for both Nevada and California and I found the addresses for the sheriff's offices in Placer County, Washoe County, and Douglas County, as well as the Tahoe Regional Planning Agency. I also addressed a set to Diamond and a set to Glennie at the Herald. Kinkos had a stamp vending machine and a scale. I stamped the envelopes, carried them outside into the parking lot and set them on the roof of Mrs. Duchamp's 4-Runner. Spot had his head out the window, trying to sniff the envelopes. It was dark and his eyes glistened in the parking lot lights.

A squeal of tires came from the side. A red Nissan SUV raced into the parking lot as if to cut through to the next street. At the other side of the lot a white limo with smoked windows was pulling in from the other direction. It looked like they were on an intersecting course. The limo honked and stopped near my vehicle, but the Nissan kept coming fast. Another honk. The Nissan rushed toward the limo, then braked at the last moment. It didn't look like it was going to stop in time. The Nissan turned toward me, just missed the limo and hit the rear corner of the 4-runner.

Spot barked and growled.

"It's okay, Spot. Just a fender bender," I said.

A man got out of the Nissan. It was too dark to see his face. He yelled an obscenity at the limo and pointed to where his car had hit mine. The Nissan had an expensive-looking winch on the front bumper, but it looked okay. Only the corners of our bumpers were munched. The driver's door of the limo opened. I tried to see through the reflections on the windshield. A chauffeur looked to be unbuckling his seatbelt.

"The damage doesn't look bad," I said to the man who'd been yelling, hoping to calm him. "Both vehicles are still drivable."

I started to turn back toward the limo when a bone-cracking blow rang off my skull above my right ear. At the same moment, the man who'd been yelling struck me in the solar plexus. It paralyzed my diaphragm. I went down.

FIFTY-ONE

I still hadn't gotten a look at either one as they grabbed my arms and jerked my hands behind my back. I felt nylon zip cuffs ratchet around my wrists.

One grabbed my hair, lifted my head off the pavement and the other pulled a dark plastic bag over my head. I was gasping for air, but I couldn't breathe. My gut was in spasm. I pushed my diaphragm out and finally sucked a little bit of air in. The air in the bag smelled like something in a hospital. My thoughts went swimmy. I heard Spot barking as my head lolled and I passed out.

I woke up in a dark place. I was lying on my side, my hands still cuffed behind my back. My gut ached from the sucker punch. My head pulsed with fire. Someone had drilled into my brain with a rusty bit. Jammed hot needles into my gray cells. Hooked up electricity. Poured on salt and alcohol.

I gritted my teeth against the pain.

At least the bag was gone.

The place I was in moved. A gentle motion of hot air hit my face and with it a nauseating, spare tire smell.

Many new car trunks have a safety release on the inside. But my hands were cuffed. Besides, the spare tire smelled old which suggested an old trunk and no release lever.

I tried moving. I was bent at the waist, but I could straighten my legs. A big trunk. I tried to spread my legs. They were shackled.

The car drove for a long time, fast at first, then slower. Then came many curves. I was pressed one way, then another. Now and then was the rush of sound from an oncoming vehicle. Mostly the soft whoosh of cars, occasionally the louder sound of a truck. Twice, an oncoming truck roared with the staccato blat-blat of the Jake brake. Which meant that the truck was going down a long hill and using the engine brake to control speed. Which also meant we were going up the long hill. The long hill with many curves that came to mind was the Mt. Rose Highway from Reno back up to Lake Tahoe.

In time, the tire-stink air washing over me became cooler. Even on hot August nights, the temperature drops in the mountains. The pass on the Mt. Rose Highway is 9000 feet, good for 20 degrees colder than Reno.

The car braked hard, then turned off to the right. There were no major roads that I knew of that went to the right off the Mt. Rose Highway. The car bounced and jerked its way over an uneven surface. We braked again and became still.

The engine went silent. I heard a door open and shut. Then another. I was considering if there might be a way I could overwhelm the men while wearing zip cuffs and shackles when I heard the sound of another vehicle. That engine turned off and two more doors opened and closed.

The trunk lid popped open and two flashlights shined in my eyes. I looked away, but not before I was night-blinded. Hands grabbed my arms and jerked me up. I knew it was stupid to kick at them, but I'm not the kind of guy to go gently into the dark night. My feet hit something soft. A man grunted. A piece of handrail flashed in from the side. There was a blinding crack on my temple and I went numb.

I had only the vaguest awareness of being dragged out of the trunk and dropped. I lay there, teeth to the ground. I heard sounds I couldn't identify. Like an electric motor under duress. In time, my eyes adjusted to the darkness. I could see nothing but the dirt in front of my face.

A man had his boot on the back of my neck. His leg weighed a hundred pounds. I managed to turn my head sideways so I could breathe without sucking dirt.

I became aware of light in my peripheral vision. I coughed and jerked and managed to turn my head and body a few degrees. The man standing on my neck didn't seem to notice.

The light was the beam of headlights. It shined on a small Lodgepole pine. There was a rope looped around the pine maybe twenty feet up and a cable that stretched back to a winch on the bumper of the vehicle. The pine was being bent back.

I remembered what Agent Ramos had said about the shape-shifter killer, the guy who liked his murders to have flair. I now understood how Eduardo Valdez had fallen from the sky. McKenna was about to do the same, attempting a space launch from a medieval catapult.

The pine was pulled back to the breaking point, then stopped. When the winch turned off, the night was silent. No one had spoken a word.

The man standing on me stepped off and shined the light in my eyes again. He bent down, grabbed my belt and picked up my 215 pounds like I was a medium-weight suitcase. He set me on my feet and waited a few seconds to see if I could balance, then pushed me in the small of my back. I made baby steps in my shackles toward the launch site.

A soft sound came from the darkness by my side. Air moving. Something rolling on the dirt. There was a thud of stick on skull. The man pushing me collapsed to the ground.

"Get on the handlebars!" A frantic whisper. "Lift your legs up so your leg chains don't catch!"

I tried to do as told. A strong arm reached around my chest and pulled me back until my butt came down on a horizontal bar. My legs came off the ground. I did my best to hold them up away from the front wheel of the mountain bike. We rolled away into the dark as the man on the ground rose up and the man working the winch ran toward us.

The bike went faster. A branch slapped at my face. We pitched down and sped up in what seemed like a free-fall into the dark forest. I started to lose my balance. The zip cuffs bit into my wrists as I reached back and down and found the center post that supported the handlebars. My fingers were vice-grips on the smooth metal.

"You made me so angry the other day," the man behind me said as we arced to the left, then right, on a dark trail he must have known by heart. "I was driving past Kinkos and recognized you by your dog. I stopped, thinking I might teach you a lesson."

The voice was familiar, but I couldn't place it. We went over another pitch and the front wheel beneath me hummed with speed. The vibration multiplied in my head. The pain was excruciating.

I could see nothing in the dark. We bounced, and I almost flew off. It was amazing that he could tell where the trail was. He was expert at handling the bike.

"Then those men grabbed you," he said. "I followed and parked in the forest a ways back. Lucky I had my bike with me."

The trail curved into a huge sweep to the left as a valley cut through the slope. We sped up to a frightening pace.

"Can't you slow down," I mumbled. My legs were straightened out before me, the chain between them dancing on the tread of the front wheel.

"Don't worry, I used to race these," the man said. "BMX, Motocross, mountain bikes, road racing. If it had two wheels, I was the man."

I finally recognized the voice.

Tyrone Handkins.

FIFTY-TWO

When we were a safe distance from my abductors, Tyrone slowed and stopped for a few seconds. I got off, and he used a pocket knife to cut the zip cuffs. I stretched and tried to relax my muscles. Then I once again balanced on the handlebars, and Tyrone took it slower than before.

"I've been riding these trails for a couple years now," he said as we swooped down and around through the forest. "I know all of the drainages below Mt. Rose. This area is crisscrossed with trails. Some are old Jeep trails, and some are single track like this one."

We descended a couple thousand feet and coasted out of the forest and onto the desert. A spectacular vista of Reno lights opened up before us. The trail smoothed out, and I concentrated on holding my legs and shackles up and away from the front wheel as Tyrone raced through the night.

Soon, we came up behind the estate of Tyrone's boss, Tony Nova. There was a gate in the fence not far from where I'd pried an opening several days before. Tyrone stopped and unlocked it. The final ride was a quick descent down to the gardens around the house.

"I've timed that ride before. You can get down the mountain faster on a bike than in a car. If we hurry," Tyrone said, "we can get up to Reno and get your dog before those men get there to wait for you to show up."

"How many men did you see?" I asked.

"Two."

I remembered three or four car doors shutting, but I was in too much pain to think clearly.

Tyrone rushed me into the huge garage where there was a black Suburban with smoked windows, the burgundy Mercedes I'd seen before, and another mountain bike. Tyrone found a hammer and chisel. He went to work on the chain between my feet, hammering the chisel against the concrete floor.

"You left a car up on the mountain," I said.

"Yeah. My old Jeep. I'll get it later."

"Now you can move," Tyrone said as he cut through the chain between my ankles. "We'll cut the ankle cuffs later."

We jumped into the Suburban, backed out into the night and headed up to Reno. "There's aspirin in the glove box. Water bottles in the center storage compartment."

I ate four aspirin, then leaned back and shut my eyes for the rest of the drive.

Spot was still in Mrs. Duchamp's 4-Runner. I got in to an eager reception. I started the car and followed Tyrone back to Tony Nova's house. The big gate automatically shut behind us as we turned into the drive.

Two garage doors opened as we approached. Tyrone pulled into one bay, and gestured me into the other. I let Spot out and he explored while Tyrone tried to figure out how to work the chisel on the ankle cuffs without cutting me. I finally lay on top of the Suburban's hood and positioned my feet against the metal post of a bike stand while Tyrone patiently swung the hammer against the chisel.

When we were done, we walked out of the garage, past the fountain to the house. Tyrone pushed alarm buttons next to the front door, then shut it behind us. He fetched beers and we sat out on the dark deck next to the covered hot tub. Spot lay at the edge of the deck, nose pointing toward the lights of Reno. I slid down on my chaise lounge so I could lean my head back and rest.

"Now do you believe that I'm not trying to kill you?" Tyrone said.

"Yes, no, maybe, all of the above." I sipped a little beer. "But thank you for giving me a ride down off the mountain."

"I couldn't figure out what I saw," he said.

"They were going to stick me up on the mast, whipsaw the boat and see if I could fly."

"What?"

I didn't answer. After a minute I said, "Tony Nova is still out of town?"

Tyrone took a deep breath. "I'm going to take a chance on you. There is no person named Tony Nova. I filed a fictitious name statement giving me the legal rights to the name Tony Nova."

"I thought it was Tony Nova who owned the company called Remake Productions."

"That's correct."

I tried to figure it out, but my head hurt too much. "Why all the names?"

Tyrone drank some more beer. "Because they are useful when you're wanted for murder."

FIFTY-THREE

I drank beer as I thought about what Tyrone said. "Only way it makes sense," I said, turning to look at him, "is that your real name is Luther Washington. You're the kid who stole motorcycles, and Glory was your little sister."

Tyrone's eyes went to the deck boards, then out to the city lights. "Yeah," he said, his voice somber.

"You've changed a lot. I never recognized you."

"Kids grow up."

"Before you supposedly drowned in the San Francisco Bay, you were alleged to have killed Willard Kilpatrick. You're going to tell me that you weren't his murderer."

"Correct. I wasn't. I've never known why I was the one they framed. Maybe it was because I ran with a gang in the area where he was killed. I'd been in trouble a lot, so it made me an easy scapegoat. Mom always kept the door locked. I think someone waited until she was taking the garbage out, then sneaked in and put the gun under my bed. Then they phoned in an anonymous tip."

"And the kid they pulled out of the water who looked like you?"

"A sad day for him, whoever he was. Even mom thought it was me. That was the hardest day of my life, having mom think I was dead. But, hard as that was, it would have been worse if I'd gone to death row on the Kilpatrick killing." He paused. "Then Glory gets killed, and everything else pales in comparison."

"I don't understand why you stayed in this area. It would have been safer to leave."

"I did leave for a few years. Glory stayed with mom. I learned something about the music business, then came back to help grow Glory's career. My plan was to find the man who framed me. Glory wanted the same thing. But first we had to earn enough money to give us options. Then we needed to figure out what happened and learn who had set me up. After I jumped bail, before they thought I drowned, I headed east and stopped in Minneapolis. I got a job at Paisley Park, Prince's recording studio. I spent a lot of time working out and getting fit. I went to community college and studied acting and even got some parts at the Penumbra Theater in St. Paul. Another thing I did was to take classes from a voice coach. I learned to enunciate and speak with correct grammar. Well, mostly correct, anyway."

"So you came back west and started Remake Productions," I said. "You and Glory made a bunch of money in the music business, and you bought this house under the name of Tony Nova?"

"No. The real estate is owned by Tyrone Handkins. Tony Nova was only for the music business. My employees believe their boss Tony Nova is a reclusive music promoter. Work instructions come by email, and occasionally through Glory's bodyguard, Tyrone Handkins."

"When did you become Tyrone?"

"Changing your name is easy in some states. A friend came to court with me and testified that I was changing my name for personal reasons and not because I was trying to evade the law."

"You lied."

"Of course. Otherwise, I was going to spend the rest of my life in prison or be executed for a crime I didn't commit. What would you do?"

"Lie."

"So the judge granted the name change," Tyrone said. "That's why I called it Remake Productions. For remaking my life. Then I remade four ghetto kids into the boy band Meen Tyme, and their concerts are overflowing with suburban girls. Hot Summerz is two unwed mothers and a recovering crack addict. I designed a look, a sound, a name, and their second CD went gold."

"What about Glory? Did she need remaking?"

Tyrone shook his head. "No. Glory was herself from the beginning. The only thing she needed was exposure. She had the voice, the style, the personality..." Tyrone stopped.

I looked at the lights of Reno.

In time, Tyrone blew his nose.

"You still think Glory's death was a mistake? That the killer was trying to kill you instead?"

"Yes," Tyrone said. "It goes back to me being set up for Willard Kilpatrick's murder. I'm alive and asking questions. Someone knows that and wants me to disappear." Tyrone looked around at the house, the grounds and gardens, the view. "When mom went into the home, Glory came here and lived with me." His voice was thick.

"You picked Nevada because it was as close as you dared get to California," I said.

"Partly. I've been in California many times since, but I don't want to live there. There are too many people in the Bay Area who knew that Luther Washington was wanted for murder. Too many people who might recognize me and decide that Luther didn't die after all."

"What is the other reason for picking Nevada?"

"Because I think that is where Willard Kilpatrick's real killer lives. Being in Nevada has enabled me to get close to him and try to obtain enough information to send a convincing case to the Attorneys General of California and Nevada."

"You know his name?"

"Yes. Senator Richard Stensen."

FIFTY-FOUR

"Why do you think Senator Stensen was Willard Kilpatrick's killer?" I said.

"After I'd been hiding in Minnesota for two years, I started to do some research. I posed as a freelance magazine writer doing a story on gang violence. I learned that Stensen had grown up poor in East Palo Alto and had some gang connections there. So it made sense that Stensen knew who to call when he wanted Kilpatrick out of the way."

"You spoke to gang members in East Palo Alto?"

"Former gang members. I hooked up with one guy who remembered Stensen very well. I met this guy in a club down by the docks. Plays mouth harp in a blues band. His name is Danny Jones. He said Stensen was an outcast kid who didn't fit in anywhere. The black and Hispanic kids ridiculed him for trying to hang out with them. And the white kids made fun of him for his efforts to fit in with kids who weren't white. His mother managed a stable at a Palo Alto riding club not far from Stanford. Stensen worked there after school. Danny Jones said the rich white kids teased Stensen. He remembered their line. 'Hey, Stensen, clean my tack, clean my horse, and when you're through, clean my shorts.'"

"Danny Jones have anything to do with Senator Stensen today?" I said.

"No. He said Stensen went off to college at Sac State and later moved to Nevada. Jones never saw him again. But he recalled that Stensen was always vowing revenge on those who wronged him."

"Willard Kilpatrick wronged Stensen by being hired by Stensen's opponent? Not much motive for murder."

"That's what I thought," Tyrone said, "until I found out that Kilpatrick was also originally from East Palo Alto. So I did some more digging and found out that he went to the same high school as Stensen. Then Kilpatrick's dad struck it rich in the computer chip business. The family moved to the other side of the tracks. They even joined the riding club, and young Willard really took to horses. A lot of coincidences, don't you think?"

"I agree. But it is a stretch to go from a coincidence to murder."

"There's more," Tyrone said. "Jump ahead about twelve years. Glory was doing a show in Vegas not long after I'd been in Oakland talking to Danny Jones. I always worked her shows from backstage, managing the band, checking her costume changes, giving her psychological support. Glory was shy and suffered from terrible stage fright. There was a little Haiku that calmed her. I always recited it to her before she went out through the curtains.

'You walk out on stage,
A flower in the winter,
Waiting for spring sun.'"

Tyrone sipped his beer and paused, seemingly unaware of his segue. Then he continued. "The last night of her gig some guys showed up outside of the stage door. Zip and Redman, our road managers, saw them and told me about it. Said they looked like TV bad guys. Black leather pants and leather vests over bare skin. Bulges under the vests like shoulder holsters.

"So Zip stayed with me. He's a big guy you don't want to mess with. Has a thing with throwing knives. Redman went out and watched them. When the concert was done, Glory and Zip and I went out the front of the casino into a cab. Redman stayed outside the stage door and watched while the leather boys got frustrated and finally left. Redman followed them out to a distant lot where they got into a white limo. He got the license number. I called a producer I know who is dialed into a computer network. He traced the license to Senator Stensen."

"You're thinking that Senator Stensen found out you were digging in his past, and he sent two guys after you?"

"Yes. Same for when Glory died. Stensen knows I'm after him. He probably suspects I'm Luther Washington. He knows that if I can make a reasonable case that he set me up for Willard Kilpatrick's death, his career could fall apart. He also knows his enemies would jump on the idea. The resulting investigation might send him to prison instead of me."

I drained the last of my beer and wondered if getting into the hot tub would ease my head pain. I decided against it. "I have a friend who is a sheriff's deputy in Douglas County. His name is Diamond Martinez. I'd like him to come over and hear your story."

"He can be trusted?"

"Completely. If you're telling the truth, he will keep your confidence. If not, we'll bring you down together."

Tyrone's eyes darted from the hot tub to the lights of Reno and up toward the dark hulk of Mt. Rose. His hesitation seemed too long.

"Yeah, sure," he said.

I still had my cell phone in my pocket. I got Diamond on the line and explained the situation.

After I hung up, I told Tyrone about Camp Twenty-Five and the golf course development. I explained my theory that Faith Runyon and Eduardo Valdez and Monica Lakeman had all been killed to help make the golf course a reality. "Golf courses are a long time in planning," I said. "It's possible that Willard Kilpatrick wasn't killed because he was working for Stensen's political opponent, but because as a member of the T.R.P.A. he was in a position to prevent the golf course from happening."

Tyrone said, "If these deaths were because of the golf course, why would they be trying to kill me?"

"Possibly because your pursuit of Kilpatrick's real killer threatens to expose the golf course scheme and the other deaths as well. They could be after me for the same reason."

A chime rang. Tyrone stood and walked to a speaker phone. It was Diamond at the gate.

We spoke in the conversation pit that wrapped around the fireplace with the huge copper hood.

"Problem is," Diamond said when Tyrone was done explaining his story, "you've got no evidence. Your scenario makes sense. So does Owen's scenario. But without hard evidence connecting the senator to either Kilpatrick or the golf course, you're both stuck. The senator's been a great promoter for Camp Twenty-Five. He's even having a fundraiser for it on Saturday night. But he might be a sucker, innocently helping out a fake cause while the real golf course developers are cheering their good fortune. What do you think, Owen?"

I was about to answer when my cell rang in my pocket.

"Hello?" I said in a cheery voice in case it was Street.

"I'll make you a deal, McKenna," the robot voice said.

FIFTY-FIVE

I pointed to the telephone and mouthed the words 'the killer.' Tyrone leaned over from my right while Diamond scooted around behind the couch and leaned in from behind me.

"I don't deal with scum," I said into the phone.

"You'll make this deal, tall boy." The synthetic voice grated. "Come to Senator Stensen's fundraiser on Saturday. You'll get to see who I kill next. Two people are on my list."

"I talked to a shrink about you," I said. "He told me you could be one of two kinds of guys. The first is a self-confident boaster, a really smart guy. So smart he'd tell me who he's planning to kill because he'd know I wouldn't be able to stop him."

"Clever, McKenna. Okay, I'll take the bait. Who's the other kind of guy?"

"The other kind is a guy who won't give me any clue about his next victim. This killer isn't as smart, and he has a sexual problem that makes him more reserved. Which guy are you?"

"Screw you, McKenna. I'll tell you who one of the victims is. You." He hung up.

Diamond came around from the back of the couch.

"Sounds like the guy has an artificial voice box," Tyrone said. "An electronic larynx."

"How do you know about that?" I said.

Tyrone's eyes flashed left, then right. "I don't know. Read about them, I guess."

I glanced at Diamond. He was staring back at me. I turned toward Tyrone. "Curious that you would read about something like that."

"I read a lot. Must have been in a magazine or something."

There was a long silence.

"You go to the fundraiser," Diamond said, "you maybe get a chance to stop this guy. But you might also get dead. Probably you are the person he most wants to kill."

"He knows I'll go," I said, "because it's my best chance of catching him."

"How you gonna get in?" Diamond asked.

"With this new threat? I'm sure I can get on the list along with a whole contingent of deputies. Either that, or they'll cancel the fundraiser."

"Don't be so sure." Diamond shook his head. "Just because this guy calls you doesn't mean he isn't working for the senator. The whole point of the fundraiser may be to get the next victim or two in a place where it will be easy to kill them. You included. The fact that the killer calls you might be part of the plan. Or maybe he's a rogue and calls you on his own. Even so, there'll be no way to trace him to the senator.

"As for getting the fundraiser canceled," Diamond continued, "don't senators and presidents have to deal with threats all the time? If they canceled speeches and appearances and fundraisers every time another wacko made a threat, we'd never see politicians at all. Instead, they just beef up security, right? Make the speech from behind bullet-proof glass."

"I'll make some calls," I said, "and warn the senator's people. If they won't cancel the fundraiser, then yes, you're probably right. If the senator is innocent, he'd stay away from the fundraiser or stay behind a shield."

"But if he's connected to the killings," Diamond said, "then he'd know he wasn't the target and would feel free to mingle with the guests."

"He might stay behind a shield anyway to create the illusion that he's innocent," I said.

Tyrone spoke up. "Owen, you notice the car those guys stuffed you into?"

"Just that it was a white limo."

"A Cadillac. I didn't see the license number, but it was just like the one the senator owns."

Diamond nodded. "All the deputies in Douglas County are alert to it. But the casino hotels in South Lake Tahoe as well as Reno also use white limos. Without a plate number, we don't know it's his."

"My guess," I said, "is that the senator is not going to have a limo he owns be used to kidnap me, even if they didn't expect me to survive to tell about it. And I imagine that he can't be directly connected to the golf course, only to Camp Twenty-Five."

Diamond nodded. Tyrone stared at the fireplace. It was the longest I'd seen him hold his eyes in one position.

"The guys up on the mountain," I said to Tyrone. "You get a look at them?"

"No, it was too dark. All I saw is two guys, although I heard four doors close. One guy was big, one small. Dark clothes."

"Not much to go on," I said, picking up my cell phone. "What do you think, Diamond? Should you give this information to your colleagues, or would it be better coming from me?"

Diamond clenched his jaw. "Truth is, my suspension would only exacerbate the situation. You tell 'em."

I got the Douglas County Sheriff's Office on the phone. "Hello, this is Owen McKenna calling. I know it's late, but I've got some information the sheriff is going to want to hear directly from me. Can you get him on the line? Wake him up if necessary."

"Hold on, Sergeant Bellamy wants to talk to you."

I waited until he came on the line.

"Waiting for your call, McKenna," he said.

"How's that?"

"Tell me why you called," he said. "Then I'll explain."

"The man who's been trying to kill me has a synthetic voice. This is the same man who shot up Diamond's house. The same man who killed Wheels Washburn, the mountain biker. He just called me to say he is planning two murders at Senator Stensen's fundraiser for Camp Twenty-Five. I wanted to alert you so that you can help in persuading the senator's people to cancel the fundraiser. I also..."

"Whoa, McKenna," the sergeant interrupted. "Slow down. Why don't you come on in and talk to us. Where are you now?"

"You don't need me in person. You only need to..." I stopped as I realized what was happening. "I'm not coming in, so you may as well tell me what you're after."

The sergeant didn't speak for a moment. "The senator's office just called. Said you'd been disturbing the senator. In fact, they even knew what your ruse would be. They said you'd call to say that the senator was in danger. That someone was going to commit murder. They also said that if the fundraiser wasn't canceled, you'd try to finagle an invitation to get in yourself so you could bother the senator more."

"And why am I bothering the senator?"

"Apparently, you don't believe that Deputy Martinez discharged his sidearm near Violet Verona and her daughter, and you're trying to discredit her and the senator, too, for taking up her case."

I took a deep breath. "I'd like to talk to the sheriff."

"No need. I just got off the phone with him. He's the one who says to bring you in."

"You think I'm making up this threat?"

"Look, McKenna. This is a United States Senator you're pestering. What don't you understand about our response?"

I said, "How do you know that the person who called wasn't impersonating someone from the senator's office?"

"Because they identified themselves by name and position." He exuded frustration.

"If something happens at the fundraiser, you'll have that on your watch."

"No, the senator's office will. They're the ones who called us. Anyway, I'm retiring. I've taken just about my last order." He hung up.

I put my phone in my pocket.

"Sounds like a problem," Diamond said. I gave him and Tyrone the gist of it, leaving out the part about Violet Verona and Diamond firing his weapon.

I slid down in my chair so I could rest my pounding head on the seat back. "Here's an idea. Diamond, you remember the search and rescue dog you met who helped me during the forest fires?"

"Yeah. Little German shepherd named Natasha. Belongs to the trainer down in Placerville."

"Ellie Ibsen," I said. "What if I could get Natasha and sneak her into the senator's estate the night of the fundraiser?"

Diamond's eyes were suddenly on fire. "Do you still have your desk lamp, the one the guy in the mask sat on?"

"Yes. I can scent Natasha on it. I also have a piece of shirttail from the night the two men attacked us. It had ripped off on your gutter. If Ellie will let me borrow Natasha, I just need to get into the Senator's estate. Natasha could find our man. I assume there is plenty of security."

"Very much so," Diamond said. "A year ago, Douglas County issued concealed weapon permits for several of the senator's security detail. Senator claimed he'd received threats. In our review we found that the senator has a complete security installation. The estate is fenced with a brick wall, and the fence is wired with sensors. There is a locked entrance gate and a guardhouse. The beachfront has video cameras and motion detectors. Just inside the fence is an asphalt path that rings the perimeter. The guards patrol on golf carts. In fact, now that I think about it, about the only thing they didn't have when we were there is guard dogs. I wonder why."

"Maybe the senator is allergic to them."

"Maybe," Diamond said.

"How big are the grounds?"

Diamond thought a moment. "Probably five acres. Most of it is wooded, but the area around the house is all lawn."

Tyrone spoke up. "Are there floodlights in the woods?"

"Don't know," Diamond said. "Probably. Why?"

"If the woods are dark, then mountain bikes are the answer."

"How do you mean?" Diamond said.

Tyrone stood up, took three steps away, about-faced and came back. "It sounds like the only way in is through the main gate. So imagine that one of the guests pulls up and flashes his invitation. The guard opens the gate. Off to the side is someone in the dark. As soon as the gate opens, he tosses something noisy over the fence to cause a distraction. The guard looks to see what it is. Maybe he even walks into the woods a bit and shines his flashlight. Meanwhile, the guest is pulling through the gate. We follow on mountain bikes, fast and silent. By the time the guard turns back around we are off in the woods. If the woods are dark, we can get this German shepherd up close to the party."

Diamond turned toward me. "This guy thinks like a crook."

"Maybe I do," Tyrone said. "But I think it's a good plan."

"I agree," I said. "But you spoke in the plural. This would be a solo operation. Just me and the dog."

Tyrone walked a few steps away, shaking his head. "No. We do it my way." He spoke in a forceful voice. "You try to leave me out and I'll blow your cover. I'm the one whose life has been on the line for a dozen years. I'm the one who is wanted for murder because of the senator. Besides, you'll need help. You needed it up on Mt. Rose."

"If they catch Luther Washington trespassing inside of the senator's estate, you'll be in prison in minutes," I said.

"Tyrone's right," Diamond said. "He should go. Me, too."

"Diamond, you of all people know the risks. Your future is tenuous at best. They catch you breaking and entering while on suspension, you'll go to prison, too."

Diamond looked at me with a blank face. "Tenuous. Fancy word for a gringo cop."

"You know I'm right, Diamond. You're letting your anger about the senator trying to influence the sheriff on the shooting incident cloud your judgment. You want revenge, that's understandable. But this is not the way. You'll throw your career away."

"And with my brown skin they'll put me in the gulag."

"Dammit, Diamond, you're not listening!"

"Yes I am, Owen! Get off your high horse. It's okay for you to pull a B and E at a United States Senator's residence, but not us? You can play the courageous knight and break the law to try to save the world, but we can't? You think that doesn't come off patronizing as hell? Sambo and Jose pick the cotton while the master goes off to war?"

I held my hands up, palms out. I was breathing hard. "Hey! I didn't mean it that way!"

Tyrone said, "The problem with white guys and brown guys is like the problem with men and women. One group holds the power. And no matter how much they think they're being good guys, it'll never work until they start seeing the world from the other point of view."

"I said I didn't mean it the way you took it!"

"Don't matter what you mean," Diamond said. "Matters how it comes across."

"Okay, I get it!" I picked up another beer, opened it and drank most of it down. I turned away and tried to take a deep breath. The silence that followed seemed to take up all the air in the room.

After a minute, Diamond spoke in a low voice. "Kant said that doing good when you're inclined to do good is no big deal. His point was that moral value is found in doing something you know you should do but is against your inclination." He paused. "I don't know what I've ever done that had moral value." His voice had a plaintive note to it. "But the killer will be at the fundraiser, and he's going to strike again. I could help stop him."

I turned and looked at him.

Finally, I said, "What time is the senator's fundraiser?"

FIFTY-SIX

I stayed the night at Tyrone's and called Ellie Ibsen the next morning.

"Hi, Ellie, it's Owen McKenna," I said when she answered.

"Owen, I'm so glad to hear your voice! At my age, you appreciate things like a familiar voice. Does that sound crazy?"

"Ellie, you could never sound crazy."

"Oh, stop. Why are you calling? I hope you are coming to visit."

"Yes, I am. And I was hoping to borrow Natasha. I have a little project for her."

There was a pause before Ellie spoke. "Would it put her in danger? It took a long time for her to heal when she helped you last year."

I winced at the worry in her voice. My hope had been that we wouldn't get to that question so fast. "Yes, Ellie, it may. But it won't be as dangerous as the forest fire. This time, I want to give Natasha a scent and send her into a group of people at a party to find a person."

"A criminal?"

"Yes."

"And this criminal could hurt her?"

"Yes. But I'll be right there. Others, too. If the person tries to hurt Natasha, I believe that we will be able to stop him."

There was a long silence. "But you can't guarantee her safety."

"No, Ellie. I can't."

Another pause. "Will Spot be there?"

"Yes. I'm hoping that Spot will also protect Natasha. But I can't promise that nothing will happen."

Ellie didn't speak.

"I'll have two men with me. All of us will try to ensure the safety of the dogs. Because Spot can hold his own in most situations, we'll concentrate on watching Natasha."

Ellie's tiny breaths were audible over the phone.

"Ellie, if this makes you too uncomfortable, I want you to say no. I will understand."

"When do you want to do this?" she said. Her voice was small.

"I'd like to come down and get Natasha tomorrow morning. The gathering is tomorrow night."

Her response was long in coming. "Well, okay," she said.

Tyrone and Diamond and I spent most of Friday making a plan and going over the details. Tyrone had an extra mountain bike and adjusted the seat and handlebars to fit Diamond. We went out for a few supplies including non-toxic, brown tempera paint. We three could wear dark clothes, and Natasha was mostly black, so we'd blend into the night. But Spot was far too visible. I planned to turn him into a Stealth Dane.

We reasoned that the fundraiser would have the senator and his men on high alert, so I didn't dare go back to my cabin to get my mountain bike. The bike I'd rented was still stashed in the forest near my campsite on the east shore. I could park Mrs. Duchamp's 4-Runner at Spooner Lake, get the bike and escape into the darkness for another night of camping. Most important, I didn't know if our invasion of the senator's estate was going to end safely or not, so I wanted to see Street before then. I said as much.

"They could be watching the hotel," Diamond said. "If she leaves, they would follow. We'd have to make it so they couldn't follow her to you."

"Or find her after we met," I said.

"I can pick her up tonight," Diamond said. "Maybe they

follow, but it won't help because I'll drive directly to a boat of some kind. They won't be prepared, so they won't be able to follow. It'll be dark. I'll bring her to you on the east shore."

I thought about it. "As long as you can move fast from your pickup into a boat."

Diamond nodded. "When we return, we'll come back to a different place on the shore. I'll borrow a car. Street will be back in her hotel room before they figure it out."

"I can arrange for you to use Jennifer Salazar's runabout."

Diamond paused. "Street will probably be safe, but seeing her still puts her at risk."

"Yeah. But it's a risk I'm willing to take. Besides, she may be able to help us get into the senator's estate."

FIFTY-SEVEN

I met Street at midnight on the east shore of Lake Tahoe. I'd come through the dark without using my flashlight. Silent. Nearly invisible. I kept Spot on a verbal leash, walking the trail just in front of me. I don't know what it was that made him obey so well and not run off exploring. Maybe he sensed something wrong, that we were on the run and in danger.

When I approached the shore, I stopped while I was still in the woods and looked out at the lake. There was a small chop and a light breeze. A crescent moon hung in the west, just over Maggie's Peaks and Emerald Bay. The moonlight shimmered on the water's surface in a silvery path that reached up to the beach. I saw the silhouette of a small boat cross over the light path. I pulled a small flashlight from my pocket, pointed it toward the boat and blinked it twice.

Diamond brought Jennifer Salazar's runabout in at a glacial pace, shifting the small outboard into forward for a moment, then back into neutral for a long coasting glide.

The tiny cove had a narrow channel that led to a small arc of sand. The water near the beach was strewn with boulders that projected three and four feet out of the water.

Diamond bumped one boulder on the port side and touched two on the starboard so gently I doubted the hull was even scratched. Diamond eased the craft up to the sandy beach.

Street was standing in the bow. When Diamond touched the bow to the sand, she jumped off. She ran up to me and hugged me as Diamond waited in the boat.

Her grip around me was strong, almost desperate. We walked a short way into the forest.

"Owen, I'm afraid."

"Me, too."

"That guy in the mask who came after you. I keep having nightmares about him. I wake up just as he's going to kill you with that handrail."

Street pushed herself a few inches away and looked up at me. I could see in the moonlight that her eyes brimmed with tears. "Owen, why does he want to kill you? And Spot, too?" Street shook. She put her head on my chest.

Spot pushed his nose between us, levering us apart.

"Spot," Street said, "can't you see I'm trying to have a talk with this guy." She attempted to put some levity in her voice.

Spot didn't move, no doubt hoping that we'd think he didn't hear and wouldn't shove him out as a result. But in the moonlight I saw the tip of his tail make a small wag at Street's protest.

Street turned her head up to me. "What if they find you at your campsite and..." She broke off.

"Don't worry. The old cabin I'm staying in is well hidden, so I can come and go unnoticed. And I've got Spot at my side when I sleep."

"How are you going to bring this to a close? You can't camp out here forever."

I told Street about the fundraiser the following night and our plan to sneak in with Natasha and Spot. "If the killer is there, the dogs will find him."

Street bent down and hugged Spot. "Can you do that, boy? Are you really that good?"

Spot wagged.

I said, "Well, Natasha will find him and Spot will help. The fundraiser will be relatively safe. There'll be lots of people around. I'll be with Diamond and Tyrone. Surprise will be on our side, too."

We were silent for a moment.

"I keep thinking about the man with the stick," Street whispered.

"Hmmm?"

"And about Billy."

"Your brother."

Street nodded against my chest. "My father used a stick on Billy."

"You mean, when Billy died?"

"Yes. Many times. Before he died was just one of them. A broomstick. The broom end broke off one of the times he hit Billy with it. My father kept the broomstick anyway. He slid it above the kitchen cabinets, up where he kept his rifle."

Street had never told me this before.

"The coroner put pneumonia as the cause of death on the certificate. Billy was coughing a lot, and maybe he did have pneumonia. But we all knew what killed him. I remember my father locking me and mom out when he called the coroner. He was shouting and stomping around and pounding on the walls. He threatened the coroner. We heard some of the words." Street raised her voice in a rough imitation of an angry man. "'It was pneumonia! You unnerstan? You put down pneumonia!'"

I held Street over Spot's bulk, wishing I had the right words, not finding any. Street shook with anger, her head and shoulders jerking against my chest. Spot turned his head to look up at her.

"I learned then not to trust anyone," she said. "Even the people closest to you. I've never had contact with any relatives since I ran away," she said. "Now I've got you, and I'm trying to teach myself that I can count on you. That you'll always be here for me." Street looked up at me again. "I don't want to lose you."

"I'll be careful."

"But you don't make hollow promises," she continued, "so you won't promise that everything will turn out all right."

I was quiet while we held each other. "You can help us," I said.

"How?" she said, a sudden hope in her voice.

"But I want you to know there's no obligation."

"Of course. How?" Maybe the idea of helping gave her a focus. Made her feel less helpless.

I explained that our major problem was getting into the fenced and heavily guarded senator's estate. I threw out some ideas, things that she could do to give us an opening.

Street looked out at the lake and up at the moon. "Let me see if I understand what you're saying," she said. "I get some fancy clothes, rent a limousine, show up at the senator's place and make some kind of distraction at the gate?"

"Right. They will require an invitation, and there's no way to get you one. I'm thinking you could keep the guard occupied long enough for us to get through the gate without him seeing. We'll be in the woods at eight o'clock. You could have your driver flash the lights as you approach so we know it's you."

"What if I can't pull this off?"

"You will, Dr. Casey. You are nothing if not excessively competent."

Street took a deep breath, then reached for my hand. We walked to the water's edge. "I better go," she said.

Diamond stayed in the back of the boat next to the idling outboard, giving us a small bit of privacy. I boosted Street up onto the bow. She stepped over the gunnel and sat down on the little bench seat in the bow. She kissed her fingertip, reached out and touched it to my lips. "Be careful. Please." Her breathing sounded as if she couldn't get enough air.

"I will. I promise."

"See you tomorrow night. Or maybe I won't see you. But you'll see me."

"Thanks. I love you."

Street held her hand up in a little wave as Diamond shifted into reverse and backed out into the dark water.

FIFTY-EIGHT

Tyrone picked me up on the highway just as dawn was throwing alpenglow on the east slopes of the mountains across the lake. He came along slowly in his black Suburban. I flicked my light on and off, and he pulled over.

We went north around the lake, turned off toward Truckee where we caught Interstate 80. The traffic was sparse at such an early hour, and we made good time from Truckee up to Donner Pass. From there it was a fast cruise down the west slope.

We turned south on Highway 49 and followed the winding road through Gold Country to Ellie's Three Bar Ranch. The sun was well into the sky when we turned off on the perfect blacktop ribbon that stretched up to the white rambler with gray trim and red front door. Before we'd come to a stop, the door opened and Ellie stepped out with Natasha at her side.

"Is that the dog lady?" Tyrone said, surprise in his voice.

"Yeah. One of the best dog trainers in the country."

"She looks awful old."

"Mid-eighties, I think. But she's got more energy than you and I put together. Let me introduce you."

We got out of the car as Ellie approached.

"Owen! I'm so glad to see you!" Ellie reached up both her hands to take one of mine. I bent down to her four and a half feet and brushed her cheeks with my lips. She smelled like lilacs.

"My pleasure, Ellie. Ellie, this is my friend Tyrone Handkins. Tyrone, Ellie Ibsen."

They shook hands. I noticed that Tyrone looked Ellie straight in the eyes. There was none of the wavering and shiftiness he had with other people.

Ellie turned to Natasha. "Natasha, please meet Tyrone."

Natasha immediately sat down and raised a paw.

Tyrone broke into a huge grin. I realized I'd never seen him smile before. He gave Natasha's paw a delicate shake.

"Didn't you bring Spot?" Ellie said, unable to see him behind the dark windows.

There was a deep woof from inside the Suburban. I opened the door and Spot leaped out.

"My God, what happened to your poor dog?" Ellie said, reaching out to caress him near the long row of stitches.

"A little scrape he got into one night," I said.

"Was it another mountain lion?" Ellie hugged him around his neck. She didn't have to bend down.

"No, nothing that exciting."

Natasha was jumping around at his face. He slapped a paw at her. She dodged and took off across the yard. Spot ran after her.

When Natasha decides to run, it is like an arrow leaving a bow. 0 to 30 in an instant. In contrast, Spot gets going like a big truck, shifting up through the gears. Eventually he gets moving at a respectable rate. But don't ask him to dodge and dart at full speed.

We watched them fly around the yard while we talked.

"Tell me again just what this gathering is and what you are going to have Natasha do," Ellie said.

"There is a man who has committed murder. He was in my office and touched some things. He's going to be at a fundraiser for Senator Stensen tonight. I think Natasha can identify him."

"Pardon me, but why not use Spot?"

"Because the man's scent is on my desk lamp. I don't think Spot is good enough to pick a scent off of metal."

"Remember, Natasha is only trained for search and rescue," Ellie said. "What if she finds this man and he tries to hurt her?"

"Tyrone and I will be there along with Diamond Martinez. He is a deputy with the Douglas County Sheriff's Department."

"I remember him. We met when you and I found that body

after the forest fire." Ellie turned to watch the dogs racing in circles around the huge yard. "You said Spot will be there, too."

"Yes. He'll take cues from Natasha. As you know, he has an instinctive desire to protect her. I can't say there is no danger, Ellie. But we'll take every precaution."

Ellie nodded. She turned and called out, "Natasha!"

The German shepherd changed directions in mid stride, ran over and sat in front of Ellie. Spot arrived a few seconds later.

Ellie said a few words to Natasha, then turned to us. "Be careful, Owen. Good to meet you, Tyrone. Good luck."

We put the dogs into the back seat and left Ellie standing there. Her eyes were moist, but no tears fell.

Tyrone took it easy on the curves as we followed Highway 50 back up into the mountains. The dogs spent some time with their heads out opposite windows, then lay down to rest.

It was the middle of the afternoon when we stopped for lunch at a diner. We were going over our plans when my cell rang.

"Hello?"

"Owen, it's Diamond. You're with Tyrone?"

"Yes," I said. There was a beep in my ear. The low-battery signal. "My battery's going, so talk fast."

"I've got some bad news. I'm going to tell you some things, and you should just answer yes or no, stuff like that."

"Sure. What's happening?"

"Early this morning, apparently right after Tyrone left, Washoe County deputies got an anonymous tip about a Remington Seven Hundred that was found near Tyrone's house. The caller said it was the rifle used in the shooting at your cabin. Are you with me?"

"You bet," I said. Tyrone was eating a pastrami sandwich and watching me as he chewed. His eyes darted from me to the table to the door and back. My phone beeped again.

"They rushed the tests. The round they dug out of your cabin wall? Rockport gave it to them. It matched the rifle. And the rifle is registered to Tyrone."

"Really," I said, keeping my voice as casual as possible.

"Sergeant Ralph Cardoza called to ask me what kind of vehicle you are driving so they can intercept you. I didn't know which wheels you two are in."

My phone beeped again. "Okay, great," I said. The phone beeped one more time and shut itself off. I put it back in my pocket.

"Who was that?" Tyrone said.

"A friend who met Natasha last time I brought her to Tahoe. I guess Diamond told him we were bringing Natasha up again. He wants to see her. He keeps talking about getting a shepherd, but can't make up his mind."

"She certainly seems like a good dog." He sounded upbeat and cheery. A change from the usual demeanor.

My brain was in a spin, re-evaluating everything in terms of this new information. I tried to reorganize my thoughts. If Tyrone had been trying to kill me all along, then why the charade? Why hadn't he shot me earlier? There had been several opportunities. Why did he save me from the killer up on Mt. Rose?

After a quarter hour, we were back in the Suburban, riding in silence. My best thought was that maybe there were two killers with a contract for my head. Perhaps Tyrone thought that killing me at an event like the fundraiser tonight held the best chance for obscuring the real culprit. Tyrone, the masked man, Senator Stensen and any others involved could escape in the commotion.

The only other possibility was that Tyrone had somehow been set up. It is rare for a lab to make mistakes in identifying which gun a bullet came from. So the way to frame Tyrone would be to steal his gun and use it on me. Diamond said it was Rockport who gave the bullet to the lab.

Everything was falling apart. But I had no other plan.

FIFTY-NINE

We stopped at my office on Kingsbury Grade to fetch the lamp for scenting purposes.

"I'll just be a minute," I said as I got out.

"I'll come with," Tyrone said. "Stretch my legs. I've never seen what a detective's office looks like."

"We'll let the dogs out, too," I said, thinking that I wasn't going to let Spot leave my side.

Spot and Natasha came with us as we walked across the lot and up the stairs. The office was empty and unchanged except for a huge pile of mail under the door slot. I kept the dogs away from the broken desk lamp as I found a plastic garbage bag and used it to pick up the lamp from where it still lay on the floor. I pulled the bag down over it and twisted the plastic shut, sealing off whatever smells the lamp still had on it.

We had a couple of hours to kill, so we took the dogs up to a hiking trail and let them run. Before we left to meet Diamond, I got out the brown tempera paint and brush.

"Spot, c'mere." He sniffed the paint and brush. "Hold still," I said as I began to paint his back, careful to stay away from his stitches.

Spot turned circles and looked around at his side as I painted. He tried to lick the paint off, but didn't like the taste. He worked his tongue against the roof of his mouth in that strange manner dogs use when they're trying to eject something from their mouth. Eventually, he became resigned to my project and stood there with his ears back and a sulking look on his face as I turned him from a Harlequin Dane into a mud-brown, camouflaged one.

When the paint was dry, we loaded the dogs into the Suburban and headed toward the senator's compound on the lake. A half mile away, we turned off onto a dirt road, pulled into the forest and parked. We got the mountain bikes out of the back and let the dogs out. I held the lamp in the plastic bag. The baggie with the torn shirttail was still in my pocket. I told Spot to heel. I asked Tyrone to do the same for Natasha.

"Natasha, heel," Tyrone said. She trotted around to his left side and stood with her head next to his knee. He took two steps forward. She stayed next to him. Tyrone broke into another grin, and for a moment he seemed like the man I'd been talking to before Diamond gave me the news about his rifle.

We walked through the twilight toward the senator's spread.

"Up here," Diamond whispered from a rise in the darkness. We climbed up a short slope to an area surrounded by boulders and manzanita bushes. Jeffrey pines were scattered across the landscape. We had a filtered view of the highway 100 yards away. Diamond glanced at Tyrone. Tyrone didn't notice. Diamond turned to Spot, touched him, then looked at the palm of his hand to see if it had been contaminated by the paint.

Diamond pointed down to where the asphalt drive made a graceful curve up to the huge gatehouse. The gatehouse was a stone and timber-frame affair with a heavy roof and a hint of Asian architectural accents. Thirty feet inside of the gatehouse was the guardhouse, a smaller structure of similar design. Through the guardhouse window we could see two large men in blue uniforms. One spoke on a phone. Just visible to his side, the other worked on a computer.

The first vehicle to arrive was a catering truck. The wrought-iron gate slid sideways. The truck pulled through and stopped. The gate shut behind it. A guard came out, stepped up on the running board and shined his flashlight in the window. From our distance, his sidearm looked large and heavy. After a minute the truck moved on.

Soon, a limousine pulled up and stopped. It was a stretch Mercedes. It looked impressive, but the guard put it through the same inspection as the catering truck. He leaned over to converse at the driver's window, then did the same at one of the rear windows. Someone held out a card and the guard studied it before letting them continue on to the senator's mansion.

For the next half hour a steady stream of polished luxury vehicles turned in off the highway. A line formed as guests arrived faster than the guards could process them. Eventually, all the vehicles got through the gate. The driveway was empty once again.

Diamond whispered, "Maybe she isn't coming."

"She'll be here," I said.

"The shooter could be getting ready to make his move."

"Maybe," I said as I raised my eyebrows in question and flicked my eyes toward Tyrone. "But he might wait until everybody is half drunk. More confusion that way. More escape routes."

I continued, "Street's going to try and distract the guards. We'll bike through the gate while it's still open. We'll have to go under the lights, but if we're fast and silent, we should be able to make it."

Tyrone spoke up. "After we get through the entrance, Owen and I go through the woods around to the north side of the house. Diamond goes to the south, right?"

"Yes," I said. "We can assume that the party will mostly be outside on the lake side, correct?"

"I think so," Diamond said. "I was there once. There is a large patio area between the house and lake. To the north side of the patio, the ground rises up to a forested area. The patio will probably be well lit. You two should have a good view from up on the rise. You can wait until we see any men we think are candidates for the man with the ski mask. Then you can send the dogs."

"You'll be on the other side?" I said.

"Yeah. There's a broad lawn with several trees, most of it dark. I'll be out in the trees. I'll make my move as soon as I see the dogs alerting. How do you think Natasha will behave?"

"When Natasha alerts on someone, she will jump up on the person."

Diamond nodded. "While I was watching earlier, two different golf carts cruised up and down the drive. One turned off on the path that follows the perimeter fencing. Two security guys in each one. Big guys. There must be more at the house, too. They all have guns. We have none."

"Good to know," I said.

Diamond looked at me, then at Tyrone.

"You both ready?" I said.

"Ready as we'll ever be," Tyrone said.

Diamond nodded. There was something in his eyes I'd never seen before. Hesitation. Or fear.

"You can still back out," I said to them. "You're both taking a bigger risk than I am."

"The biggest risk you're taking is getting yourself killed," Diamond said. "I don't think I can take a bigger risk than that."

"Roger that," Tyrone said.

A vehicle on the highway slowed, then turned into the driveway. Its headlights flashed.

"Show time," Tyrone said.

The limo was a black, double-stretched Lincoln. It waited while the gate opened, then it glided silently under the gatehouse. When the guard walked out, the limo stopped prematurely. Its tail end remained close enough to the gate that sensors prevented the gate from closing. The guard walked over and spoke to the driver. Then he moved back and leaned down at a rear window. He stayed there for a long time. The guard went back to the driver's window and gestured, his arms directing the driver to turn around. The limo didn't move. The guard reached for his radio and said something. The second guard walked out of the gatehouse.

Diamond whispered, "Here comes the second guard. No way can we get by both of them."

"Gotta try," I said. "Now or never."

We jogged out of our hiding place, staying next to the brick fence. Diamond was in the lead. Tyrone was next. He rolled his mountain bike on his right while Natasha heeled at his left. I was last. With my left hand I held Spot's collar to prevent him from running in case he got too excited to heel. My right hand gripped the plastic bag that contained the desk lamp and balanced it on the handlebars of my bike. We stopped in the dark just outside of the gate. We peeked around at the limo.

Both guards were at the driver's door. We could see nothing through the blackened windows. The left rear door opened and Street got out. "I swear it was in my purse," she said in a loud voice. "Let me move into the bright light and I'll find it."

She sashayed past the guards into the light that shone down from floods.

The guards turned and stared.

Street wore a tight black dress so small that it could have been made from two silk handkerchiefs. It was held up by spaghetti straps. The neckline was well below her shoulders. The hem line was just below her crotch. She wore dark nylons and very tall spiked heels. Her feet were slightly pigeon-toed in that awkward girl-posture that often accompanies high-heeled shoes. She stopped under one of the floodlights and dug in a small black purse, then lifted one knee up and set her purse on her thigh. The guards were motionless, eyes fixed on her. A single perfect ankle flexed just a bit as she balanced in her spiked heel. Street angled her purse to let the floodlight shine in. Turning away so the guards couldn't see, she reached in and got something dark in her hand. "Oh, damn," she called out. "Now I ran my stockings." She bent over, ran her hands down her leg and, still facing away from the guards, casually let go of several objects onto the drive. I saw the objects move.

I whispered, "Get ready!

Street suddenly started screaming. "OH, MY GOD! OH, MY GOD! HELP!" She began a frantic, high-stepping dance.

Spot strained on his collar.

"HELP!" Street turned circles and jumped up and down as several huge cockroaches scurried about under her feet.

The two guards ran toward her.

The three of us jumped on our bikes. We pedaled through

the gate, past the limo. The dogs trotted alongside.

Street jumped up on one of the guards as they approached. She clutched her arms around his neck. Her legs wrapped around his waist like a vice. She screamed.

"Christ, we got roaches!" the other guard shouted. "Giant suckers!" He stomped his foot on the asphalt.

Street kept screaming. The guard holding her yelled into his radio.

"I got one!" the other shouted. "Got another!" He turned and pounded his shoe on the ground.

Diamond, Tyrone and I rode into the area illuminated by the floodlights. We were in full view.

"There! Got 'em all!" The guard shouted.

"NO!" Street screamed. She pointed away from us. "THERE'S ANOTHER ONE! HURRY! GET IT!"

The guard ran the direction she pointed.

The floodlights were so bright the drive felt like a stage set. Spot's nails clicked on the asphalt. I was certain the guards could hear. We hit the soft dirt on the other side and raced into the dark forest.

When we were well away from the guards we stopped. Our collective breathing sounded like bellows.

"Here's where I split," Diamond whispered. He pedaled off through the woods in a big curving arc.

Tyrone and I pedaled into the dark woods. Our tires went over branches. They broke with loud snapping sounds.

Soon, we heard the sounds of a party. A murmur of voices and laughter floated in the forest. A jazz band played a Miles Davis tune. The laughter grew and turned into a mix of raucous bellows and soft giggles. We came even with the mansion down below. It was a timber-frame lodge with huge wooden beams, walls of rough-cut granite and lots of glass. We got off our bikes and walked the rest of the way to a point in the woods overlooking the patio. We put the bikes on the ground and lay down on our bellies. I told the dogs to lie down next to us. We were close to the party, but no one was looking up our way.

The band was on the corner of the patio. A wall of rock and a burbling waterfall made a sort of band shell behind them.

In front of the band mingled a group of 30 or 40 well-dressed people. The women wore floor-length gowns. The men had on suits and tuxedos. I heard glasses clinking and saw a waiter with a silver tray of champagne glasses handing them out to the crowd. Another waiter passed out hors d'oeuvres.

At the back of the house were large French doors standing open. The party flowed in and out of the house.

One woman stood out speaking to a threesome of men. It was Violet Verona, the woman whose daughter's doll was hit by Diamond's ricochet. Her platinum hair went high above her head and her diamond earrings threw light beams like a disco mirror. She wore a shimmering, snug blue dress that showed just how well she'd maintained herself through her half-century.

Off to one side was a bar. The bartender wore a tux. To his side were two men in suits. Bulges under their arms. No smiles on their faces. Security.

They spoke without any animation. A third man appeared. They had the size and heft and posture of athletes. Any of them could have been the man in the mask. I kept scanning the crowd.

Red Hues Suz, the woman from the Camp Twenty-Five office, wore a flowing red dress. Red bracelets covered much of her arms, and a large red pendant sparkled below a gold necklace. The red of her hair looked as natural as Spot's new brown tone. She flirted with an elegant older man who looked as if he could afford to give away yachts as party favors.

A huge man came into view out on the patio. I recognized him by his thick neck and the gauze wrap on his arm. Allen Lamb, the ex-football player from the bank in Incline Village. He faced away from me. A thin woman in a purple pantsuit was by his side. His bulk obscured the other person he was conversing with. In time, he shifted and the third person came into view. The movie-star smile and thick blond thatch were unmistakable. Bobby Crash grinned and nodded at the woman. He threw his head back in laughter and smacked Allen Lamb on the shoulder.

In another minute, two more security men appeared. One of them was Deputy Rockport. They talked to each other, then walked to the edge of the patio. One of them spoke into a walkie-talkie. Rockport pointed up to the trees where we were hiding. The other started hiking up the hill toward us.

"Shit," Tyrone whispered. "We've been made."

I pulled the lamp out of the plastic bag. "Natasha!" I said. "Smell this! Do you have the scent? Do you?" I held the lamp out and she stuck her nose on it. I pointed down the hill at the crowd on the patio. "Find the suspect, Natasha! Find him!" I knew Natasha was a search dog and wasn't trained as a police dog, but I said the words anyway. "Find the suspect!"

Natasha took off running. Spot jumped up to follow, but I grabbed him. I wanted him to have a scent as well and not just follow her.

I watched Natasha as I fumbled the Ziplock bag out of my pocket. She shot down the hill to the side of the security guard. He had his hand under his jacket, on a gun. He pulled it out, spinning to follow Natasha, but didn't shoot.

I got the shirttail out and stuck it onto Spot's nose. "Smell it, Spot! Smell it!" I wrapped it around his snout so that he couldn't mistake the scent. "Find the suspect, Spot! Take him down!"

Spot jumped up and ran down the slope after Natasha. I stood up and grabbed my mountain bike. Tyrone did the same. We watched Natasha run straight into the crowd. A woman shrieked. People scrambled as Natasha raced through them."

"Look out!" a man yelled. "There's a police dog!"

Natasha threaded her way through the crowd as if she'd run the same obstacle course a hundred times. There was no hesitation, no slowing. She headed toward a group of people that included Violet Verona. Natasha leaped up onto a large man in a blue suit, a man I'd met several times.

"Who's that?" Tyrone said.

"Sergeant Cardoza," I said as I jumped on my bike. "From Washoe County." Tyrone followed and we pedaled down the hill.

I watched Cardoza bat Natasha off of him. She leaped back up. She was jumping on him in the joy of discovery like search dogs do when they find a lost victim.

"POLICE!" I yelled. "FREEZE!"

Cardoza bent down and pulled a small gun out of an ankle holster.

Women screamed. A glass shattered on the patio. The bass player bolted, knocking over his music stand and letting his bass tumble over.

Tyrone and I moved fast, but Spot was faster. He blasted through the crowd. He didn't thread his way like Natasha, but bowled people aside.

"POLICE!" I shouted again as I raced down the hill on my bike. "DROP YOUR WEAPON!"

Then came another shout from the lawn behind Cardoza. Diamond. "POLICE! DROP THE GUN!" he yelled.

Cardoza swatted Natasha away again. Spot ran in. Just as I expected him to attack, he veered to the left, ran past Cardoza and Natasha and shot into the house.

"Follow Spot!" I yelled to Tyrone. I pedaled toward Cardoza. He was looking out toward the dark lawn from where Diamond had shouted.

I dropped my bike on the fly and ran for cover where the rock wall rose up behind the band.

"CARDOZA! DROP IT! YOU'RE SURROUNDED, SERGEANT!"

A voice nearby said, "That's not Cardoza."

I turned. It was one of the security guards hiding behind the piano. "I know Sergeant Cardoza," the man said, his eyes wide with fright. "That's not him." Another security guard was nearby, equally afraid. Rockport seemed to have disappeared.

The man who'd claimed to be Sergeant Cardoza spun around. He pointed his gun into the air and fired a round. A sharp crack. People gasped. Natasha pulled away at the blast of the gun.

"You stupid cops won't take me!" he shouted. His eyes showed white in the patio lights. He ran several steps toward the crowd and grabbed Violet Verona. She screamed and dropped her champagne glass. He jerked her to his front, locked his big arm around her neck and put the gun to her temple.

Diamond appeared behind the gunman, moving up slowly. I came up in front of the gunman, distracting him. The man turned and saw Diamond.

"Don't move one more step!! I swear I'll blow her brains into mush!"

Diamond stepped back. Behind him cowered two security guards.

The gunman jerked Violet backward out onto the lawn. The gun barrel was jammed to her head. She whimpered. Blood ran from where the barrel had pierced the skin at her temple.

Bobby Crash ran out from the crowd. He sprinted toward Violet and the gunman. The gunman swung his gun around and fired. The bullet hit Crash in the face and snapped his head back. I knew he was dead before his legs collapsed. Violet screamed.

"Stay away!" the gunman yelled. "I'm not playing games!" He put the gun back to Violet's temple. "One step closer and she dies."

The gunman made his way toward the dock, half a football field away. Violet's cries rose out of the dark. Someone flipped on the dock light. The gunman and his victim became a silhouette, the thick man dragging the slender woman. The crowd pressed in behind us. People yelled into their cell phones. A siren rose in the distance.

I gestured at Diamond for him to circle around down by the dock. I grabbed my bike and ran the other direction, back up the steep slope. When I got to the top, I jumped on the bike and pedaled along the ridge, through the dark trees toward the lake.

Behind the gunman I could see five or six boats at the pier. They were tied up in a temporary fashion, which meant they belonged to party guests. Any number of them would have keys in the ignition. I couldn't let him out onto that dock or he would escape, and Violet would die for certain.

When I'd pedaled even with the gunman and Violet, I stopped.

They were directly below me, 30 yards down the slope. I moved into the darkness behind a massive tree trunk. I whistled, then cupped my hands around my mouth and yelled down toward the house.

"SPOT!" I shouted. "SPOT, COME!"

I got on my bike and raced down the hill toward the gunman.

Spot appeared in the crowd back on the patio. He ran out onto the huge lawn. Tyrone followed. I raised my arm as I pedaled down the slope and pointed at the gunman. "SPOT! TAKE HIM DOWN!" I yelled.

I've seen it happen before where some combination of command mixes with Spot's instincts. A dog can pick a threatening person out of a group. Spot had that look. His eyes were narrowed. His jowls lifted with each galloping leap showing glints of saliva-wet fang. His nose was pointed directly at the gunman. I knew the gunman could shoot my dog. His accuracy with Bobby Crash was perfect. But I could distract him.

"Give it up! Drop your weapon and I'll call off the attack!"

The man looked hesitant. He glanced up at me racing down from above. He turned and looked up the long lawn at Spot. Some atavistic paralysis stopped the man for a moment.

Violet sensed it. She jerked in his grip and jammed a thumbnail into the hollow of his throat. He let go for a moment. She broke away, running toward Diamond.

The man raised his gun.

Diamond shouted, "Violet, drop to the ground!"

Diamond cranked his arm back like a pitcher winding up. He let fly with a handful of good-sized stones.

Violet dove to the grass.

One of the stones hit the gunman above the eye. He reached up, touched a growing drop of blood, then looked at his fingertip.

Diamond dove on top of Violet.

The gunman aimed at Diamond and Violet and fired his gun.

I shifted up a gear and pedaled faster.

The gunman fired at Diamond again. And again. And again, in rapid sequence. He saw me, turned and pointed the gun at me.

I leaped off my bike and hit him with a hard tackle to his middle. The gun flew through the air. He hit the ground. Rolled. Jumped to his feet. He had a small knife in his hand. I moved in. He tried to slash me. Movement came in the corner of my vision. Spot leaped into the air. His growl was ferocious.

The man tried to slash Spot. Spot caught the hand with the knife. The man screamed. I heard the bones of his hand breaking like twigs.

I ran to where Diamond lay on top of Violet. I dropped to the ground. Diamond and Violet lay motionless. Diamond was face down. Violet was underneath him. Dark circles of blood were growing on Diamond's back.

"Get an ambulance!" I yelled to the crowd.

I bent over Diamond and Violet. I tried to plug up the sucking wounds with my fingers. But they were too far apart, and I couldn't reach them all.

SIXTY

Two days later Doc Lee tracked me down at Street's condo. I spoke to him for a minute and hung up.

"Well?" Street said. Her face had dark smudges under her eyes and new wrinkles across her forehead. The little acne scars were more pronounced than normal. Her eyes had grown larger in the last few days.

"Diamond's going to make it," I said. "He'll be several more days in the ICU, but they expect he'll make a pretty good recovery."

"What about the collapsed lungs and the possible brain damage from going so long without oxygen?"

"Doc says his lungs will be fine. But we won't know about any brain damage for another week or so."

Street forced a small smile. "I want to be very happy about it, but..." she stopped. "You should let Violet know."

I found her number. Street pet Spot while I dialed. The tempera paint had washed out, but it left his white fur stained beige. With the black spots he looked vaguely like a leopard.

"Hello, Violet," I said when she answered.

"Owen, how is he?"

"That's why I'm calling. I just spoke to Doc Lee. He says Diamond's going to make it."

There was a big sigh. "Thank God. What about... you know. Will he be all there?"

"We don't know, yet, Violet. Doc says maybe in a week."

"He saved my life."

"I know," I said.

There was a long silence.

"I called Senator Stensen," she said. "He called the sheriff. I don't know how, but it turns out they misunderstood me. I was so upset when it happened. Maybe I explained it wrong."

"What do you mean, Violet?"

"The doll my daughter lost by the casino door. We came back for it later and saw it from way down the block. Then that man ran out and Diamond fired at him. I saw the doll get hit by the ricochet. I was so upset. But it's not like we were close..."

I hung up on her.

Street looked at me. I told her what Violet said.

"Jesus," Street said, shaking her head.

After a long moment, she brightened. "Isn't Diamond's birthday next Thursday? Maybe we should put together a little party for him."

"Good idea."

We were making calls when the phone rang. It was K.D. Scarrone.

"Lady K.D.," I said.

"Yes, only please drop the lady part. I'm no longer in the madam business. Losing Faith has almost destroyed me. I never realized how much of a friend she was to me until she was gone." K.D. paused. When she resumed talking her voice was thick. "Friend, hell, what am I saying. She was like my daughter. Anyway, I just called to thank you, Owen. I heard how you caught the guy who killed her."

"Yeah," I said.

"I wondered about the cop who got shot. I understand he was your friend. But I'm afraid to ask."

"He's going to be okay," I said. I didn't see any reason to express my doubts.

"I wish I could do something for him. To show my appreciation."

"We're having a birthday party for him. Maybe you'd like to come along. I'm sure he'd like that."

"That is so kind of you to ask. I'd love to join you."

EPILOGUE

The hospital administrators didn't squawk about a cake and party favors, but they had a problem about bringing in the dogs. I solved that by saying we wouldn't.

It was early evening when we all tiptoed into Diamond's room. Yellow-orange sun rays came through his window like horizontal fire. Natasha heeled at Ellie's side. Tyrone had a bundle of balloons and a bag of party favors. Street carried a big white cake with the candles afire. Spot and I stayed back with Rockport.

K.D. stood to my side. She wore a white blouse, navy skirt and navy pumps on bare legs. She clutched a small present wrapped in white paper and white ribbon. There was a card on it with a red heart on the front. She looked like the new girl at school, privileged to be invited to someone's birthday party.

Behind me, in the hallway, two nurses and a woman in a suit were fussing about the dogs. Rockport glanced down the hallway toward the elevators. He turned and looked the other direction toward the stairwell with the Exit sign above it.

Diamond lay partly elevated. A soft snore rose from his lips. The flesh where the ventilator tube had been inserted in the base of his throat was raw and pink. Plastic tubes and colored wires connected him to machinery and monitors.

"Surprise," Street said quietly. Diamond slept. Ellie shook his leg. Tyrone blew gently on a noisemaker.

Diamond opened his eyes at the commotion. He looked at us. After a long time he said, "I could've cleaned up." His words were slow and slurred. "If I knew you were coming."

"You are the palest Mex I've seen in a long time," I said, "but otherwise you don't look half bad."

With noticeable effort, Diamond touched a button on a remote control next to his hand. A motor whirred, and his bed rose until he was sitting part way up. Realizing he was in no shape to blow out candles, Street blew them out while we all sang Happy Birthday. Then she cut him a piece of cake and held it to his mouth. Diamond took a bite and got crumbs all over his bed. I couldn't tell if any got in his mouth. Then he looked at Spot.

"Where did you go, dog?" he said. His speech sounded like he had rocks in his mouth.

Spot looked at Diamond, then at the cake.

"I scented him on the shirttail and he ran into the house. But the person he was looking for must have left. Or else Spot was confused. He doesn't have Natasha's skill by any stretch." I glanced at Rockport who was staying back by the doorway next to K.D.

"Oh," Diamond said, giving me a blank look. "What about the senator." Diamond's speech was so thick he was hard to understand. "We broke a lotta laws busting into his place. And me on suspension."

"I think the senator forgave us. Catching the killer was worth our transgressions."

After a moment Diamond mumbled, "He talk?"

"The shooter? He won't for awhile. After Spot munched his knife hand, the shooter got the knife in his other hand. Spot got hold of that wrist and crushed it. But the guy was a real fighter. He tried to give Spot a head butt."

Diamond looked at me, then turned to Spot. I wasn't sure if Diamond was processing or not.

"So Spot took hold of his face. Broke his jaw and some other stuff. The killer can't talk. Not even with the electrolarynx. He's under twenty-four hour guard down the hallway."

"Keep him from running," Diamond said.

"Protection, too. There was a substitution in his medication late one night. An alert nurse discovered it and prevented him from getting a deadly overdose."

"So we have to wait," Diamond drawled, "until we find out who his accomplice was."

"Maybe not," I said. I pulled the Ziplock bag with the shirt-tail out of my pocket. "Spot, c'mere. Let's try this again."

Spot came over. I took out the torn shirttail and held it to his nose. "Take a whiff, Spot. Do you have the scent? Do you?"

Spot sniffed the shirt, then looked up at me, excitement on his face. Natasha watched from over by Ellie. The little shepherd quivered. A deep frown creased Tyrone's forehead. His eyes flicked around the room. He glared at the window, then at the doorway. Rockport moved over to the door and put his hand on the doorjamb. The move was meant to be casual, but he shook with nerves.

"Do you have the scent, Spot?" I said again. "Okay, find the suspect!"

Spot stared at me, his eyes intense, not sure if I meant it.

"Go on, Spot, find the suspect!"

Spot turned and trotted toward the door. Rockport cowered.

Spot went to Rockport, then past him. He turned his head sideways and gently put his jaws half way around K.D.'s waist.

She shrieked. "God! What is he doing? Stop him! He'll kill me! This is a terrible mistake!" She stood rigid, like a vibrating board. She dropped the present and jerked her arms to her chest. She stared down at Spot's jaws wrapping around her body.

"It's no mistake, K.D. You were the creator of the Camp Twenty-Five land scam. Your boyfriend Baker Camden was the muscle. It was Baker who masqueraded as Sergeant Cardoza."

"No, it's not true!"

"K.D., you know how animals have a sixth sense. Like your cat. You even said how he can tell who is safe and who isn't. Dogs have that sense, too. If my dog thinks you're dangerous, he might bite down a little too hard. He could cause serious damage. The courts wouldn't give much sympathy to a murderer."

"You can't threaten me. I'm innocent!"

"Spot, is K.D. telling the truth?"

He didn't know my words, but he knew my tone and what I wanted. He growled, deep and loud. His jaws tightened their grip on K.D.'s waist.

K.D. lifted up on her toes and screamed. "OKAY, OKAY! But it was Baker who did the killings! I came up with the golf course plan, but he was the one who said people had to die to make it work. I just did the paperwork!"

I saw Mallory just outside of the door, out of K.D.'s sight. He held up a tape recorder. "K.D.," I said, "Spot just demonstrated that it was you who tore your shirt up on Diamond's roof. You had a gun. That's not paperwork."

"Yes, I was there, but Baker made me! He said I'd die like the others if I wasn't in all the way! I never hurt anyone!"

"And you drove the getaway car when Camden set the bomb in Diamond's Karmann Ghia. When Camden is able to talk, he'll confirm that it was you with him."

"Yes... But he forced me!"

"Okay, Spot. Mallory's here. You can let her go."

Mallory came through the door with three other officers. K.D. saw his tape recorder and looked furious. Mallory took hold of K.D.'s wrist and Spot released her. Mallory took her away.

After a moment, Diamond said, "So the senator wasn't behind the scam."

"No. Stensen was an unwitting dupe just like you suggested. His ex-wife K.D. used him all along to promote the Camp Twenty-Five concept that she planned to turn into the golf development."

Diamond looked at me with dull eyes.

"From the time they divorced twelve years ago, the senator had been doing as K.D. requested. She was his first campaign manager and got him elected. She also collected dirt on him like having eyewitnesses to the senator's liaisons with Faith Runyon. She used him for his connections and his support of Camp Twenty-Five. She even borrowed his limo to kidnap me. But now that the golf course scam is exposed, I think he is glad to be free of her."

Diamond's eyes appeared to go in and out of focus. He looked at Spot. "Good boy," he said.

Spot looked at Diamond, then at the cake.

Diamond stared past my head. "This guy who pretended he was Cardoza..." he said.

Rockport spoke up, "K.D.'s partner is an ex-military guy named Baker Camden. Used to work with K.D.'s father. He found out Cardoza was on vacation and passed himself off as Cardoza."

Maybe Diamond was processing. Maybe not. His face was blank.

I said, "We think Baker Camden was one of K.D.'s johns before she even met the senator. It looks like she and Camden schemed to have her marry the senator, then divorce him."

"They own the land for the golf course?" Diamond mumbled.

"Yeah. K.D. and Camden have been buying lots and old cabins for years under the Camp Twenty-Five moniker. Tyrone figured out that they had used fictitious name statements to use the names Baker Camden and K.D. Scarrone. Their real names are Martin Elgin and Adelina Kercher. If anybody did try to learn the details of Camp Twenty-Five, Inc., they wouldn't think K.D. and Camden were involved. Camden served as Chairman of the board. The board members were fooled. What board member ever reads the fine print? The board actually had no authority at all. But they gave Camp Twenty-Five an aura of legitimacy and helped convince Tahoe landowners to sell.

"The plan all along was to have the Camp Twenty-Five project fall apart and be replaced by the golf course on which they stood to make hundreds of millions. K.D.'s genius was to identify the major opponents to the development and kill them in advance. There was almost no way to trace the murders because there appeared to be no motive. They weren't going to bring the project to anybody's attention until they owned all the property and all the slow-growth and no-growth advocates were eliminated."

"Tight pair," Diamond said.

"Not tight enough," I said. "According to K.D.'s neighbor, they would argue often and loudly. Just after Camden tried to kill Tyrone on the Flume and accidentally killed Glory instead, he and K.D. came home yelling at each other. A minute later, the neighbor saw Faith Runyon sneaking out the downstairs door as if K.D. and Camden were unaware she'd been there. It may have been then that Faith overheard something about Glory's death."

"And Faith told it to Bobby Crash who told Wheels Washburn?" Street said.

"Could be," I said. "We'll never know."

Diamond raised his eyebrows a bit, the first expressive facial move since we arrived in his hospital room.

"Camden was stationed once at the army base in Herlong," I said. "He knew where to steal the mist bomb. He was good at planning murders that looked like accidents. Or murders where all the evidence was destroyed. When he was unsuccessful at killing Tyrone, he broke into Tyrone's house and took one of Tyrone's rifles to shoot me with. It almost worked. I would have been dead and Tyrone would have gone to prison for murders he didn't commit."

Diamond's face was a gray wall.

"I think we should open presents," Street said.

Spot was still looking at the cake.

Diamond saw and reached for the cake. "A present for Spot," he mumbled.

It was a bad idea, but I didn't think I should intervene.

Diamond held it out. "World's largest Danish."

Spot looked at Diamond, then at the cake, then took the world's largest bite. Frosting went everywhere. He looked like he was in a shaving cream commercial.

"Okay, Spot, that's enough," I finally said.

"Diamond, can you sit up enough to look out the window?" Ellie said.

Diamond frowned. We helped boost him up, careful not to pull out the tubes.

"In the parking lot," Ellie said, pointing. "Violet Verona bought you a new used Karmann Ghia to replace the one that got ruined."

Diamond squinted out at the parking lot which burned under a Turner sunset. "The Green Flame," he finally said.

"And there's another thing," Rockport said. "Sheriff wanted to be here, but couldn't. Spot, are you ready?"

Spot was still licking frosting off his chops as he looked up at Rockport. Rockport pulled a badge out of his pocket. The sheriff had altered Diamond's badge to show his new sergeant status. Rockport handed it to Spot. Spot took it in his teeth. "Take it to Diamond," Rockport said.

Spot chewed on it, the metal clicking on his teeth.

"No, Spot." I pointed toward Diamond. "Take it to him."

Spot went over, gave the badge another chomp, then reluctantly dumped the badge on Diamond's lap.

Diamond picked up the wet badge. "Got dog slobber on it," he said.

"Best way to polish it," I said.

Diamond's fingers were slow, but he managed to pin it on his hospital gown.

"Hey Diamond," I said. "They said you would recover physically. But we were wondering if your brain felt okay? You know, do you feel like you can think clearly? Or are you going to be slow like the rest of us, now?"

Diamond looked at me. His eyes were empty ponds. When he spoke, he slurred again. "In his essay on liberty, John Stuart Mill more or less said that the principal right of any man is the right to be left alone." Diamond reached a finger up and wiped some frosting off his lips. "Either we stick to cake and Karmann Ghias or I'm going to exercise my right and kick your asses outta here."

About The Author

Todd Borg and his wife live in Lake Tahoe, where they write and paint. To contact Todd or learn more about the Owen McKenna mysteries, please visit toddborg.com.